HEROES A

BOOK NINE OF THE KELSEY'S BURDEN SERIES

CRIME THRILLER SERIES
KAYLIE HUNTER

This book is a work of fiction. All names, characters, places, businesses, incidents, etc., are the imagination of the author, and any resemblance to actual persons or otherwise is coincidental.

Copyright 2021 by Kaylie Hunter
All rights reserved.

Book cover design by Evocative at 99designs.com

BOOKS BY KAYLIE

KELSEY'S BURDEN SERIES
LAYERED LIES
PAST HAUNTS
FRIENDS AND FOES
BLOOD AND TEARS
LOVE AND RAGE
DAY AND NIGHT
HEARTS AND ACES
HUNT AND PREY
HEROES AND HELLFIRE

STANDALONE NOVELS
SLIGHTLY OFF-BALANCE
DIAMOND'S EDGE

For an up-to-date book list, visit
www.BooksByKaylie.com

Chapter One

CHARLIE
Tuesday, 8:35 p.m.

Catcalls from the men of Aces greeted me as I descended the mansion stairs into the living room. I looked down at my low-cut blouse, paired with my short skirt and kitten heels. Admittedly, the outfit was a little—*uhm*—adult. But after spending three days playing Slapjack and Marco Polo with the kids, I craved feeling like a grown-ass woman again.

From across the room, perched on Whiskey's lap, Sara giggled. "You look pretty, Aunt Charlie."

"Thank you, Sara." I threw Sara a wink before walking around the corner into the combo kitchen-dining area.

"So that's what all the clamoring was about," Kelsey said from the other side of the kitchen island. She eyed me from head to toe.

Ryan sat on the other side of the dining room table, reading from his tablet. The corner of his mouth curved upward as he used his finger to swipe the screen.

I looked back at Kelsey as I grabbed my purse from the far countertop. "Too much?"

"For a stakeout at a seedy no-tell motel?" She focused on the fry pan she was drying as she smiled. "Nah. Just right I'd say." She turned, reaching on her tiptoes for the pan shelf.

Wild Card walked into the kitchen, grabbed the pan from her, and placed it on the shelf which was just beyond her reach, then turned to me and scowled.

Bones walked in but stopped at the doorway, eyeing me sideways.

"What?" I asked.

Wild Card snorted. "We're just waiting for you to try to ditch us again."

"Sorry, boys. But neither of you were invited."

Kelsey pointed to them but pinned her eyes on me. "They go where you go." She picked up another pan and started drying it.

"I'll be with Spence."

Bones crossed his arms over his puffed-out chest. "It's not up for discussion. Besides, I thought you said tonight *wasn't* a date." He lifted an eyebrow.

"It's not a date. It's a stakeout in Spence's truck. I offered to bring food and keep him company while he waits for his money shot of the cheating husband."

"And after the stakeout?" Kelsey asked.

I grabbed the edge of my blouse, just above my boobs, tugging it upward half an inch. "Anything's possible. We'll just have to wait to see."

Aunt Suzanne laughed as she entered the kitchen carrying an array of dirty drinking glasses. "What happened to your '*no cops or anyone associated with cops*' rule?"

I couldn't hide my smile. "Rules were meant to be broken."

Kelsey handed the now dry pan to Wild Card before placing both her hands on the island counter and narrowing her eyes at me. "You're still taking security. I don't care if Bones and Wild Card look like perverts sitting with binoculars outside Spence's house all night. Until Mr. Tricky is caught, you need to stick close to your security team."

"Especially now that we know Mr. Tricky is unhinged," Bones said.

"What makes you think he's unhinged?" I asked.

"Stuart Grenway?" Bones asked, shaking his head at me. "Are you so accustomed to murder scenes you've already forgotten the assassin-for-hire who had his throat slashed?"

"Not to mention he was wrapped in a red bow with a Merry Christmas sign taped to his chest," Wild Card said, chuckling. "You don't see that every day."

I waved a dismissing hand at them. "That was so last week. Besides, we don't know Mr. Tricky killed Grenway."

"Who else would've done it?" Kelsey asked.

I shrugged. "Benny the Barber."

They all looked at each other with puzzled expressions, then pivoted their attention back to me, waiting for an explanation.

"Benny likes to play games. Like hanging a *Gone Fishing* sign on the barbershop door." I glanced up at the clock, checking to make sure I had time to explain. Seeing I did, I pulled out a chair and sat across the table from Ryan. "Benny also had some type of personal connection with Pauly which means Benny had his own reasons for wanting Grenway dead." I dug out my favorite lipstick from my purse, applying a layer. "I also think Benny was behind the drive-by shooting in front of his barbershop."

"Why would he shoot out his own windows?" Ryan asked.

"My guess would be he was trying to get me into trouble with internal affairs. Maybe even get me suspended. Benny needs the heat to die down so everything returns to business as usual. But my investigation of Pauly and Roseline's murders kept circling back to question Benny."

Everyone was quiet as they considered my theory.

"The internal affairs angle doesn't ring true," Ryan said as he set his tablet aside. "But if Benny was the shooter, there's another angle to consider."

"What angle?" I asked.

"He was trying to kill you."

"Agreed," Bones said, leaning against the wall. "If you're dead, Mr. Tricky wouldn't have a reason to stick around town. Benny would get rid of both problems with one bullet."

"Or would've," Wild Card said, grinning. "If he could still see well enough to actually hit his target. I mean, hell, how old does a hitman have to be before he can retire? Benny's gotta be in his late seventies at least."

Kelsey sat next to me at the table. "If it *was* Benny—and I'm not agreeing it was—he would never kill Charlie. He's too afraid of me."

I rolled my eyes at her. "Benny's a sociopath. He's not afraid of you. Maybe cautious of crossing you, yeah, but even that's an exaggeration of your powers over him."

"Say you're right," Wild Card said. "If Benny killed Grenway, why the Merry Christmas note?"

"That's Benny playing games. Making it more entertaining. On the flip side, Mr. Tricky is in mission mode. He's planning and executing attacks with one sole focus—*me*. Killing Grenway didn't further his agenda."

Kelsey worried her lower lip between her teeth before asking, "Weren't you the one who thought Mr. Tricky killed Grenway?"

"At first, yes. But during my three days of poolside lounging, my brain kept circling back to the scene. The more I thought about it, the more I leaned toward Benny."

"Which means Benny's also a threat," Bones said.

"Not really. I mean, Benny's always been a threat. He's a hitman. I'm a cop. We don't mix. But his agenda is different. He wanted me to stop trying to question him about hitman contracts. He accomplished that when Grenway was killed." I dropped my lipstick into my purse and snapped the closure shut. "I was hoping we'd get some DNA on the recliner at Grenway's house. It looked like the killer had moved the chair to watch Grenway as he died. But the forensic team didn't find a speck of anything. Which is another reason to suspect Benny. He never leaves trace evidence."

"All of this is very interesting, but bottom line, it's just another reason you need a security team," Kelsey said.

I sighed. "I'll take Beast."

"You'll take Beast, Bones, and Cooper." She stood and walked back toward the sink. "End of story."

"I'm not a teenager, Kelsey."

"Good. Then behave like an adult. Make responsible decisions to protect yourself and those around you."

I hated it when she was right. I glared before stomping in the direction of the door. Wild Card whistled for Beast and the three of them followed me outside.

~*~*~

We stopped at the club to pick up takeout from Chef Edwin. Bones and Wild Card had already eaten, but since I knew they had bottomless stomachs, I ordered enough food for everyone, including Beast.

After Wild Card parked curbside behind Spence's truck, I passed them their bag of food before climbing out of the back with Beast.

Spence's truck had a crew cab, so I opened the door to the back for Beast, then pulled out Beast's dinner—a small pot roast and boiled potatoes—opening the container and setting it on the floor for him.

Spence shook his head as I slid into the front passenger seat. "You are corrupting my dog. What happened to no table food?"

"I don't see a table. Besides, that dry food you feed him smells gross. Beast deserves better."

Spence glanced past me at the motel as he accepted the offered takeout container. He'd parked across from the motel on the opposite side of the one-way street. From where we sat, he could face me while watching the motel through my side window.

I opened the container of garlic bread and wedged it between the gear shift and the center console to share with Spence.

Spence glanced back at me. "When Beast wakes you at three in the morning for a bathroom break, just remember I warned you."

I opened my own container which was loaded with what Chef Edwin calls his Italian sampler: lasagna, spaghetti buried under meatballs, and alfredo smothered noodles. "Whatever. I'm a night owl anyway." I dropped the containers filled with salads back inside the bag before tossing it to the floor beside my purse.

"This is good," Spence said with a mouthful of food, pointing with his fork at his meal container.

I nodded as I chewed and swallowed, glancing at the motel. "Has the loser husband shown his slimy face yet?"

"Not yet. Should be here soon, though. According to his wife, he dropped the line of having to return to the office tonight to finish a pile of paperwork."

"Why do they always use the working late excuse? It's a dead giveaway."

Spence's eyes scanned my outfit, pausing on my low-cut top. "Beats me. Personally, I'm a one-woman kind of guy."

I rolled my eyes. "Monogamy is overrated. It's too... domestic."

"Have you ever tried?"

"Not marriage. But I just escaped a committed relationship. We tried living together, but it was an absolute nightmare. Totally crashed and burned."

"What happened?"

"We just kept fighting. About *everything*: toothpaste, coffee creamer, wearing pajamas to bed."

"Please tell me you weren't the one wearing pajamas. Especially not flannel. It would completely ruin my fantasies."

"I don't even own pajamas. I either sleep nude or fall asleep fully dressed. Sometimes with my shoes still on."

"I can see that." Spence grinned to himself as he forked another mouthful of food, waiting to reply until he chewed and swallowed. "So... Your *ex* was the one who wore pajamas?"

"No, but he hated it when I slept in my clothes. He said he'd rather I wore nightgowns than sleep fully dressed so he bought me nightgowns. What the hell is that about?"

"He must be one of those tightly wound guys. Instead of buying you nightgowns, he should've just taken off your shoes and thrown a blanket over you."

"Yeah, well, it wasn't our only fight. Not by a longshot."

"Your apartment's kind of small for two people. How did that work?"

I swallowed my food before answering. "Our experiment was at his condo in Atlanta. He's a Fed. Travels a lot for work."

Spence laughed. "Wait... You moved to a city where you have no friends, no job, and into someone else's home without any of your own belongings? And what did you plan on doing all day? Sitting and waiting for him to return from work with dinner ready and on the table?"

I scrunched my nose as I thought about it. "Yeah. Something like that."

"And you actually thought the arrangement had a chance?" Spence paused to use the napkin to wipe his mouth. "You are a fast-paced kind of girl. You need to keep your mind and body moving forward at high velocity. A *housewife—*" Spence shook his head as he smiled, "—you are not."

"Thank you, Dr. Ruth," I said somewhat snarkily. I closed my half-empty container and tucked it inside the bag on the floor. "What about you? Any serious relationships?"

"The normal. High school sweetheart. Then a few relationships here and there, but nothing serious. The last few years I spent taking care of my sister, then rebuilding my business after she died. Haven't dated in a while. Haven't even met anyone interesting." He glanced over at me and winked. "Until now."

"Slow down, cowboy. Have you already forgotten I'm the girl who doesn't believe in monogamy?"

"You seem to fully support relationships like your aunt and uncle's. You just haven't been in a relationship with a man who lets you run wild."

"And let me guess, you're that man?"

A slow grin appeared as Spence leaned toward me and stared at my lips. "Not sure. Probably depends on how wild you run."

I leaned a few inches closer, purring back a teasing reply. "And how wild does a girl have to get before it becomes too much?"

He tossed his empty container into the back for Beast to lick. "I definitely like a little wild." He was still watching my lips as his upper body moved across the center console.

I watched his lips part as he leaned in, closing the distance between us. "Garlic bread?" I raised the chunk of bread between us, blocking his lips from mine.

A challenging expression flashed across his face before he snapped his teeth onto the bread. He leaned back into his seat as he chewed, but the subtle smile he wore while watching the motel told me I wasn't the only one who liked to play games.

CHAPTER TWO

KELSEY
Tuesday, 9:30 p.m.

"Please? Just a little longer?" Nicholas whined.

"No," I answered as I tucked a blanket around him. "We agreed, remember? Three chapters, then lights out without complaining." I glanced over at Sara who was already sound asleep.

Nicholas pouted, rolling onto his side. "But I'm not tired."

"Sure, you aren't," I whispered, leaning over to kiss his forehead. "Goodnight, my sweet boy."

"Night," Nicholas snapped, punching his pillow into a ball.

I knew he'd be asleep in seconds of closing his eyes. I shook my head as I walked out of the room, pulling the door behind me but leaving a sliver of light to shine through. After all the years of missing him, I was thankful to have him back in my life—even when he was being a whiny brat.

I stood outside the door and listened. I could hear him shift positions, rolling around, then he sighed a deep, long sigh.

Anne walked into the small sitting area and smiled at me. "Is Sara asleep?"

I nodded, but motioned for her to follow me, not speaking until we were around the corner and heading toward the stairs. "Sara was out as soon as her massive curls hit the pillow. They played hard today."

"You know they're never going to want to go home again, right?"

"Oh, I'm not worried about that," I said as we walked down the stairs. "We just need to tell them all their Christmas presents are in Michigan. They'll book the plane themselves."

"Very tactical thinking. I like it."

"Speaking of tactical thinking, did I hear Sara convince you today to let her wear makeup?"

Anne pointed a finger at me and scowled a fake smile. "Don't even start. I wasn't manipulated. Whiskey already gave me an earful."

"Sara's too young for makeup."

"I only agreed she could wear makeup for her dress-up parties, and even then, only lip gloss and blush."

I raised an eyebrow at Anne as we turned the corner on the stairway landing.

"Yeah," Anne said on a sigh. "She worked me over. I thought I was doing well by putting my foot down on the eye shadow and mascara. I didn't realize she set the bar high to negotiate down."

"You have to give her credit. She's good. She could be a politician by the time she's a teenager."

"She gets it from you, you know. She watches you negotiate and strategize."

"Well then it's a good thing she has your kind heart." I threw an arm over Anne's shoulders as we reached the bottom of the stairs. "She'll put her manipulative powers to good use, eventually."

We turned as we heard someone walking toward us.

Jackson crossed the room and stopped in front of us, staring down at me. "Grady's outside. He's packing. I thought you'd want to know."

"Thanks. Everything still quiet on the security feeds for the dentist office?" I'd spent two days surveilling—and *nothing. Zip. Nada.*

"All's quiet according to Tech. I told him I'd watch the cameras tonight so he can crash. He's been burning the candle at both ends."

"What about Tyler?"

"He's doing another patrol, then he's going to call it a night, too. He's worse than Tech."

I nodded before making my way toward the door. I wasn't surprised to hear Grady was leaving. Not after the big reveal a few days prior that Cooper and I were still married. As shocked as I'd been, Grady had been devasted. I'd watched the last bit of hope evaporate from his eyes. It was heartbreaking. Since then, he'd mainly stayed to himself.

Outside, four guards manned the driveway entrance. Wayne tipped his head to the far right where Grady was loading one of the SUV rentals.

"Going somewhere?" I asked Grady as I walked over.

"We're good together," Grady said without looking at me. He picked up the duffle bag lying by his feet and tossed it into the cargo space in the back of the SUV.

"In many ways, yes."

"*In every way!*" He turned to face me. The sad expression he'd been wearing the last few days was replaced with anger. "We work well together. We think alike when it comes to getting a job done. Our shooting and fighting are compatible. And the sex—*is phenomenal*. So, *why*, Kelsey—" he leaned forward, "—*why him?*"

"This isn't about Cooper."

"*The hell it's not*! It has everything to do with him. If he wasn't in the picture, we'd have worked this out. You'd have forgiven me."

I took a deep breath as I stepped closer to Grady. "Maybe. But it would've been a mistake."

Grady placed his hands on my shoulders. "Give me another chance. I'll make things right between us."

I watched him as I lowered my voice to barely above a whisper. "Grady, do you remember what you said after your mission to Mexico? When you called me to break up?"

"You know I didn't mean anything I said. I was trying to keep Sebrina away."

"But when you called, you said that Nicholas wasn't your kid. You said I was never going to marry you. That I was stringing you along. That I never would have kids with you." I placed a hand on his chest. "You were right, Grady." My heart was breaking as I watched his anger turn into hurt from my words, but he needed to understand. "Nicholas is *my son. Mine.* No matter how close I get with anyone, he'll always be the most important person in my life."

"I respect that, but plenty of single mothers get married and have more kids."

"I'm not sure I want more kids. After everything that happened with Nicholas, the thought of having even one more child to protect scares the hell out of me. And as for marriage, even before everything imploded between us, you knew I was struggling to commit."

Grady shook his head. "You were wearing my engagement ring."

"Yes—but why? *Why* was I wearing it, Grady?" I took a step back, wiping the river of tears from my cheeks. "Was I wearing the ring because I wanted to marry you? Or was I wearing it because everyone expected me to?" I shook my head. "Did you see me rushing around planning a wedding? Shopping for a dress?"

"You needed more time to adjust. I understood that. You'd been through a lot."

"No, Grady. I didn't need more time. I knew in my gut that we shouldn't marry. I didn't know why I felt that way, but I knew it would be a mistake."

"I don't believe that. We're good together."

He wasn't hearing me, and I desperately needed him to. "Remember when I told you that after we split up Pops made me promise to think about who I saw myself growing old with? He wanted me to envision my life forty or fifty years from now. And for the first time, I allowed myself to think long term. I hadn't done that before. Not really. Especially after Nicholas was taken. Living day to day was struggle enough. But when I stepped back, really stepped back, and looked at my future from Pops' perspective, all the confusion I'd been feeling faded away. *I saw it.* I saw what my future looked like."

"And I wasn't in it." Grady's eyes closed as he tilted his head skyward.

"You *were* there—But not by my side."

"Friends? Is that where all this is heading? The friends speech?"

"Please, just listen. I need you to understand." I stepped closer to him again, hoping with all my heart that I found the right words. "I envisioned myself sitting in a rocking chair on a front porch. And on that porch with me was *everyone*. All my friends. My family. Men of Aces." I waved my hands to the imaginary space around us. "The yard was filled with kids, running around playing tag. There was food on the grill, and laughter... So much laughter you could hear it from a mile away." I closed my eyes and smiled at the vision. When I opened them, I stared up at Grady. "My future was *full*. It was lively. I was surrounded by people who loved me and people I loved. It was busy, noisy, crowded even, and I felt at home."

He raised a gentle hand to wipe my tears. "And there's no room for me?"

"You don't have the same dream. In your future, you see yourself raising children and having a family of your own. Your *own* home. Your *own* property. And when you're old, you and your wife will rock on your own porch while holding hands and watching the sunset."

He leaned his forehead against mine, whispering, "What's wrong with that dream, Kelsey? It sounds perfect."

"It is perfect," I whispered back. "*For you*. But please don't try to force me to be that woman. I don't want to sit quietly and watch the sun fade. I want to shout and laugh. I want noise so loud it's hard to think straight. I want—" I turned, waving a hand at the mansion "—I want an enormous house that despite how many bedrooms it has, there's still not enough beds for all the people who visit. I want my family to keep building houses along our street in Michigan so I know we'll always be close. I want to vacation in Texas, ranch hopping to find a bed to sleep in, but knowing everyone will be at Pops' house for breakfast in the morning. I want *that* life, Grady. I need it. I grew up alone, trying to raise a girl only two years younger than me." I placed my palm on his cheek. "I don't want to settle down into a quiet family. I don't want fewer people around me. I want more. I want my life and my son's to be bigger."

"You love me," Grady whispered. "We can figure this out. We can build a future that works for both of us."

"I do love you. That's why this is so hard. You are my friend. You're the best partner I've ever worked with. And I'm so grateful to you for pulling me out of that dark place I was in after being abducted. But as husband and wife?" I shook my head. "We're too much alike. We're both too serious." I took a step back and wiped the fresh round of tears. "I realized the reason I could never commit to you was because something was missing. Until now, though, I could never figure out what that something was."

"And you've figured it out?"

I nodded as I glanced back at the mansion. "It was me, Grady. I realized the part that was missing was the *real me*. The woman who gets in food fights and plays tag on the beach with her kid. The woman who isn't always fighting the monsters, but who used to enjoy life."

"Wild Card."

"No, Grady. You're not listening. *Me*! I'm choosing to have a life where work is work and playtime is about family and friends. And when I grow old, I'll be sitting in that rocking chair with the porch brimming with everyone I love."

Grady was quiet as he looked away, staring off at nothing. "So that's it?"

"I hope not." I reached down and clasped his hand in both of mine. "I know you need time, but I do love you. I want you to be a part of my life. To visit us on my porch and laugh with us. I want to keep working with you at Aces. I want you to remain part of the family."

Grady shook his head. "I can't watch you be with someone else, especially Wild Card. I won't."

"I know you're jealous and angry with him, but you're not being fair. Cooper is your friend. And every time we've needed him, he's been there—no matter the emotional cost to himself. We both counted on him."

"Then he's a better man than me," Grady said before pulling his hand from mine and storming toward the mansion.

I wasn't sure how long I'd stood there crying before I felt arms wrap around me.

"It's going to be okay," Pops said in my ear. "Whatever you had to say, he needed to hear it."

I pulled back just far enough to wipe my tears with the wad of tissues Pops handed me. "Will he ever forgive me?"

"I don't know," Pops said, using his thumb to tilt my head upward. "But if you were honest with him, and yourself, that's all you can do. Only Grady can decide what to do with the information."

"It hurts," I said as I wiped my nose. "Why does it have to hurt?"

"Because, baby girl, you love deeply. It's the only way you know how to live. You live life with a passion that few people understand, and even fewer ever experience. But the hurt will fade. And with any luck, you and Grady will find a way to stay connected."

"I can't imagine him not being a part of my life—of Nick's life."

"Let's go help Hattie in the kitchen," Pops said, steering me toward the mansion. "You always feel better when your hands are busy."

I nodded, but as we walked toward the doors I heard surround sound text message alerts. I felt around my pockets for my phone as I watched all the guards pull theirs to read the text. I didn't know where my phone was. "Wayne? What is it?"

"*Code red!*" Wayne yelled before he started ordering the guards to pull one of the SUVs over to block the driveway.

I ran the other direction. Toward the mansion doors.

Chapter Three

CHARLIE
Tuesday, 9:08 p.m.

With the empty takeout containers cleared, Beast snoring in the back seat, and Spence leaning over the center console of the truck to be closer to me, I'd decided stakeouts weren't so bad. We'd spent the last twenty minutes talking, teasing, and laughing.

"Have I told you how amazing you look in that outfit?" Spence asked as he tucked a lock of my hair behind my ear before trailing his finger down my neck.

"A girl never gets tired of hearing compliments."

"I no longer care that Bones and Wild Card are watching us."

We were close enough that I felt his warm breath on my face. "Who?" I asked just before his lips captured mine.

The kiss was hot, wet, and had me pressing my nipples against his chest. But just as suddenly as the flame ignited—it was snuffed out when Spence suddenly pulled away and reached into the back seat. His hand returned into view, holding his camera.

I watched, stunned, as he transformed into his P.I. persona, snapping rapid pictures of the motel parking lot through the partially steamed window.

"Were you watching the motel while you were kissing me?" I asked as I lowered the window.

"If I say no, will you forgive me faster?" Spence answered without looking at me. He was trying not to smirk.

I rolled my eyes and looked toward the motel where a john was exchanging cash with a hooker. I then looked down at my blouse which was doing its job by exposing an abundance of flesh. "I don't think this has ever happened to me before. I feel used." I shifted my blouse upward, back to *peek-a-boo* mode.

"I'll make it up to you," Spence said, clicking picture after picture. "And me being distracted has more to do with being broke than your sexual appeal." He adjusted the camera's manual lens, then started snapping pictures again.

I thought back to the days when Kelsey and I were young; we could barely scrape enough cash together to pay rent. The memory made me feel somewhat mollified. Being broke sucked. Big time.

Turning to watch the motel, I saw the hooker walk with the husband to room six. She hesitated before entering. The cheating husband grabbed her forearm and tugged her inside.

"Is that it? Was that the money shot?" I asked.

"I wish." Spence fiddled with his camera, reviewing the pictures. "Damn. He paid her sixty bucks."

"And that's bad, why?"

"He bought an hour. I need to take pictures after the deed is done. I was hoping he'd buy a quickie."

"Sixty bucks? That's all she makes sleeping with that asshole?"

"Some make a lot less, but fifty to sixty is the going rate for this motel. It includes the room. The hookers rent the rooms for a half day, then rotate the johns in and out."

I was about to reply when a scream sounded from the motel. My years of training had me bailing from the truck, kicking off my kitten heels, and grabbing my purse which held my gun. I ran barefoot across the street, pausing in the motel's parking lot to listen for which room the distress signal had come. Spence ran past me to room six, kicking in the door and charging inside.

By the time I caught up, Spence had the shirtless man on the floor and was beating the ever-living shit out of him. I stepped back to let Bones and Wild Card pass me. They were built for this sort of thing, not to mention dressed for it.

Bones smirked, pausing to look over his shoulder at me with a raised eyebrow.

"*Break that shit up!*" I ordered them, pointing at Spence who continued to whale on the perp.

Both Bones and Wild Card peeled Spence off the john.

I walked into the bathroom, returning with two towels. I tossed the dry towel at the adulterer scumbag on my way past. I held the other towel, the one I'd soaked with cold water, gingerly to the prostitute's face. With her back pressed to the headboard and her knees tucked to her chest, her body trembled as she raised her hand to place it over mine. I slipped my hand out from under hers before tugging the sides of her ripped shirt closed.

I looked back at Bones who was stationed between Spence, who paced back and forth like a caged animal, and the john, who'd shifted to a sitting position and leaned against the wall.

"What's the damage?" I asked Bones.

"The asshole got what he deserved," Bones said, shrugging. "The woman is worse. Shouldn't be a problem if you want to call it in."

I looked at the prostitute. She had a broken nose, an eye already swelling shut, and her neck was bright red where the john had wrapped his hands around it. I dug my phone from my purse and called dispatch.

When I ended the call, I looked over at Spence, waiting for him to make eye contact. "You need some fresh air," I told him. "Don't leave, but go cool down before you have to give an official statement."

Spence snapped his head in a partial nod before turning out the door. He was still breathing heavy and looked barely in control.

Bones followed Spence. Wild Card shuffled closer to the john and leaned against the wall.

~*~*~

It took ten minutes for the cops to show and another twenty minutes to convince the prostitute, now known to us as Roxy, to press charges. Another forty minutes was wasted while everyone gave their individual statements.

I sighed out of exasperation as we watched the last police cruiser pull away from the curb.

"Was *all that—*" Wild Card waved a hand toward the departing police car, "—really worth it?"

"Depends how you look at it," I answered, glancing back at Roxy who'd moved to sit on the motel's stairway that led to the second-floor level. I looked back at Wild Card. "If we get lucky, the D.A.'s office will plea the case and Roxy won't have to testify. It's unlikely she'd show up in court if it went to trial anyway. With a criminal record, the hope is he'll be appropriately discouraged from beating on the next prostitute. But if the jackass isn't that smart, he'll be in a hell of a lot more trouble as a repeat offender."

"My way is more effective," Spence said as he used his thumbnail to scrape dried blood from his other hand.

Bones smiled as he scanned the area for unforeseen threats. It was obvious he agreed with Spence's methods over mine.

I glanced again at Roxy. She was holding the wet towel, now filled with ice, to her swollen eye. Her nose had stopped bleeding but needed to be reset. She'd refused our offer for a ride to the hospital. I walked over and stood in front of her.

Roxy looked at me with her good eye. "I thought I was a goner. Can't tell ya the relief I felt when you all busted through that door. That asshole was gonna kill me for sure."

"I don't doubt it felt that way. I'm glad you pressed charges. I know that wasn't easy."

"Well, not much in life is easy. If it were, I sure as hell wouldn't be here living the dream."

"You sure you don't want a ride to the E.R.?"

"Not the first time I've been knocked around. I'll be fine."

"If you promise not to sue me, I'll reset your nose. It'll hurt like a bitch, though."

She lowered the towel and leaned her head back. "Do it."

I squatted in front of her, placed one hand on her jaw to hold her steady, grabbed the bridge of her nose, pulling up and out, and then setting it back in place.

"Son of a—" Roxy muttered.

I lifted her hand, the one with the makeshift ice pack, back toward her face. "Hurts like a bitch, I know, but it should die down to a dull throb soon. But your eyes will keep watering for at least ten minutes."

She used a finger to trace the bridge of her nose. "How did you learn to do that?"

"A hooker named Margo taught me."

"I know Margo. She's one tough bitch. Heard she's living the good life now. Works as a bouncer or something."

"She did. For a year or so. Then she moved to North Carolina to be closer to her sister."

"How is it you know Margo? And why'd she teach you how to reset a broken nose?"

"We met while joining forces in a street brawl. The result of the brawl was both of us having broken noses. Margo reset mine, then had me reset hers."

"You reset Margo's nose? I would've peed myself. Margo's no joke," Roxy said. "What was the brawl about?"

"Turns out, Margo intervened when she saw a pimp beating on one of his girls. Then the pimp's crew jumped in to give Margo a beatdown. By the time I showed up, Margo was on the ground. I was off duty so I decided to teach the boys a lesson. And—*oh man*—that woman can *fight*. As soon as she managed to get upright again, those men didn't stand a chance against us."

"Sounds about right. Margo always watched out for the weaker girls. Protecting them when she could."

I thought about Kelsey's dentist office case and the missing prostitutes. "Speaking of other prostitutes, you heard anything about girls disappearing lately?"

Roxy nodded. "Sheila. Goes by Cinnamon on the street. She disappeared about two weeks ago. Don't know much. Her pimp threw her shit out the window before snatching a street kid—barely fifteen—to replace her." She frowned, then winced. I knew from experience that the bruising that was visible was nothing compared to the nerve endings under the bruises that were going haywire. "The girl is just a kid. Margo would've handled shit like that, too."

I fisted my hands. "Who's the pimp?"

"Harlan. Don't know his last name."

"You know where he lives?"

She narrowed her good eye at me. "You going to tell him who told you?"

"No. Are you going to tell I was asking about him?"

"Not if you can get that girl out." Roxy looked around to ensure we were alone. All the hookers had retreated to their rented rooms, knowing the johns would be scarce for an hour or two. "Harlan has a place on the corner of Center and Oak. Three-story apartment building. His place is the top left unit on the street side."

"How many guys hang with him?"

"His one and only boy stays near the corners with the working girls while Harlan gets high and watches TV. Should just be Harlan and maybe one or two of his girls in the apartment."

I pulled a business card from my purse and handed it to her. "If you need anything, call me. Day or night."

"And you'll do what? Arrest my john?"

"I have resources. You'll find it's handy to have my number."

"Yeah?" Roxy said, snorting. "Do you have a magical wand you can wave to pay for my room tonight?"

I walked into the motel office and rented a room for Roxy for the next five days. When I returned, I handed her the room key and a twenty-dollar bill. "Here. Get yourself a few groceries. I'd give you more, but—"

"Yeah, yeah, I get it. I'm a junkie. Can't be trusted."

"You have an addiction." I pointed to the track marks on her arm. "That doesn't mean you can't get clean and turn things around."

"I was clean once. But whoring is a helluva lot easier when you're high."

"If you get clean again, give me a call. I'll help you find a job that doesn't involve this shit."

Her one good eye narrowed at me again but she didn't say anything. She didn't trust me. She probably didn't trust anyone. I could relate.

I walked over to where the boys were standing a few car lengths away.

"Ready?" Wild Card asked.

I looked at Spence. "Did arresting the cheating husband mess up your case?"

"Nope. I have a clause in the contract that if I witness illegal activity, it's at my discretion to call law enforcement. Between the pictures I took of the husband before he entered the motel room and the mug shots you're going to get me, I'll get paid."

"You calling it a night then?" I asked him.

"I wish. I've got five more cases I haven't touched yet," Spence said.

"You know you can turn down cases, right? You don't have to take all of them."

"Sure, but I need to build my client list. And turning away customers is the opposite business plan."

"Hire some help, man," Bones said.

"Can't pay much. Not yet. Hard to find reputable people with my budget."

"What's next then?" I asked

My phone, Bones', and Wild Card's started beeping.

We all read the displays: *Red Alert. Headquarters.*

"That's not good," Bones said. He was already pushing buttons to call in.

Chapter Four

KELSEY
Tuesday, 10:05 p.m.

Running up the three flights of stairs, I turned down the hall and ran into the sitting area just outside the kids' room. There I found Tyler, Whiskey, Anne, Katie, Tech, Trigger, Haley, Alex, Jackson, and Ryan already in position to protect the kids. How everyone had beaten me to the kids' door, I didn't know.

"Kids are sound asleep," Anne said, walking over to rub a hand on my arms. "Take a breath."

I leaned over, my hands on my knees, and exhaled. My heart raced, pulsing against my skin all the way to my skull. "You're sure, Anne? You saw them?"

"Saw them with my own eyes," Anne answered, rubbing my back.

I inhaled again as I straightened. "Then let's not wake them. I don't want them to worry." I tilted my head toward my bedroom, leading them through my room and onto the upper balcony which stretched from one side of the house to the other on the third floor.

Anne followed behind me. "Nice. I wish our room had a balcony."

Haley looked around, then back at my room. She looked over her shoulder at Alex and whacked him in the stomach, her scowl communicating some unspoken displeasure. Alex laughed but didn't explain as he shifted out of hitting range.

"Don't complain," Ryan said to Anne. "I've been sleeping on a couch in the game room."

"There's an extra bed in the bunkroom with Carl and the kids," Trigger said. "You're welcome to it."

"And listen to Carl snore? Nope," Ryan answered. He looked back at me. "You calling Donovan?"

"I have no idea where my phone is."

Tech tossed me my phone. "You left it in the lounge."

I called Donovan and he answered on the first ring.

"Let me put you on video," Donovan said. "Hang on, Bones is calling in, too. Isn't he with you?"

"He's with Cooper, bodyguarding Charlie."

"Yo," Bones said as his face appeared in a box next to Donovan's on the screen. "What the hell is going on, man?"

I looked at Bones' video feed, turning my phone sideways so both their squares enlarged. "Bones, why is the motel door behind you kicked in? Everything okay?"

Bones glanced behind him and smirked. "Small skirmish. Spence's surveillance gig took a bad turn. We're fine. What about Headquarters? What happened?"

"I assigned Arty to man the security feeds tonight," Donovan said.

"Who?" Bones and I asked at the same time.

"Arthur Kemp, otherwise known as Arty," Donovan said with a raised eyebrow. "The guy Kelsey hired to run backgrounds and research?"

"Shit. Yeah, I know who you're talking about now," I said, giggling. "We just call him Kemp." I looked over at Tech and Bridget. They were both grinning back at me and shaking their heads. I sort of thought of Kemp as this invisible person who sometimes emailed me information. I couldn't remember the last time I'd spoken to him face to face.

"Anyway," Donovan continued. "*Kemp* spotted a man breaching our perimeter. I've looked at the video, but I don't recognize the guy." Donovan looked away, then nodded to someone off screen. His screen image changed to a video of a man lurking in the dark near the apartments at Headquarters.

I tapped the image to switch it to full display as Ryan, Trigger, and Tech crowded close to watch. When the video ended, I exited full screen to see both Donovan and Bones again.

"What do you guys think? Recognize him?" Donovan asked.

"Looks like Mr. Tricky," Charlie said, her face appearing smushed next to Bones'. "What's he doing in Michigan?"

"That's a good question," I said. "But whatever he's doing, I don't like it. Charlie, Bones, get back to the mansion. Donovan, how are you on security?"

"We're stretched pretty thin here between the crew who went with you to Florida and the security jobs we had already booked. I called James and Nightcrawler to see if the clubs could donate manpower to tighten the perimeter. But, Kel, I don't like this. Lisa and Abigail were in the apartments. This guy got too close."

"You have a right to be worried," Charlie said. "He's trained. And I'm talking Green Berets or Navy Seals trained. He's taken me down twice already. The bikers won't be able to stop him unless they go into *shoot first and ask questions later* mode, which is a whole different kind of danger to your family."

"We'll send some guys back," I said. "Give us an hour to sort staffing. I'll have a team fly back tonight, though."

"You sure?" Donovan asked. "I can close Headquarters and move Lisa and Abigail to Florida."

"We'd love to see you, but no. We need to protect home base. The case I'm working isn't going anywhere, so I'll give it another week, then fly the rest home. We've got more bodies here than beds anyway."

"That'll work then. I'm moving everyone into the gym for the night until reinforcements get here. Lisa won't like it, but tough."

"Listen to you," Bones said on a chuckle. "Finely growing some balls in your relationship."

"Is that what you think?" Bridget called out toward my phone. "That men should be in charge in a relationship?"

"Shit," Bones said before disconnecting.

I watched the tension ease from Donovan's face as he grinned and disconnected. I tucked my phone in my back pocket. "I want to check on the kids, then we'll regroup in the dining room."

Everyone started moving back through my bedroom. Alex and Haley were in front of me and I watched Haley whack Alex again.

"You two going to share with the group?" I asked.

"No," Alex said, wrapping an arm around Haley's waist and hurrying her away.

Anne giggled. "They're acting so strange."

"If you think that's strange," I glanced over to look at her, "you should've been in my room last night listening to Alex play Tarzan to Haley's Jane in the room beneath me."

"Ewe," Anne said, turning toward the stairs. "Now I'm glad I don't have your room."

I laughed as I walked over to Tyler who was standing guard outside the kids' room. "Mr. Tricky was spotted on video in Michigan. We're going to divide security and send some guys back."

"I don't like it," Tyler said, crossing his arms over his chest as he looked back at the kids' door. "Something's off. Why would Mr. Tricky be in Michigan? So far, he's only gone after Charlie."

"I don't know. But I'm not leaving a huge part of my family unprotected."

"I get that. We have too many guys anyway. I'll go back on patrol."

"No, you won't," I said, stopping him with a hand on his forearm. "I need you to get some sleep. Bones and Cooper are on their way back. We'll make sure the mansion has coverage."

"Fine. But you need to greenlight the security cameras and alarms. We need to wire this place if we're going to stay here."

"Deal. Now find somewhere to bunk down and get some sleep."

Tyler glanced behind him at an empty couch. He grabbed the far end, swiveling it toward the center of the room. The couch was now positioned parallel to the walkway to the kids' bedroom.

Throwing himself down with his head closest to the door, he looked up at me as he folded his hands behind his head. "Done." He closed his eyes.

I shook my head as I turned off the light to the sitting area and snuck into the kids' room. Carl, Nicholas, and Sara were sound asleep. On another bunkbed, Trigger was lying on the bottom bunk, saluting me before closing his eyes. Bridget was settling in on the top bunk.

"What's Bones going to say?" I whispered to her.

"Please," Bridget whispered back with enough snark that I could hear her eyes roll in the darkness. "He'll be on patrol all night doing his protector shit. He won't even notice I'm gone."

I quietly laughed as I walked over to kiss Nicholas and then Sara, before slipping out of the room.

I took my time as I relocated to the first floor, but when I walked into the dining room I was greeted by a room of worried faces. I looked around and spotted Grady leaning against the kitchen island.

"Grady, I know you want to leave, but—"

"You were right," Grady said, interrupting me. "We work well together. I'll stick around until we catch Mr. Tricky. But then..."

I nodded. *But then he'd disappear.*

I walked over and took the cup of coffee Hattie offered me. "Tech, how far out are Bones and Cooper?"

Tech tapped on his keyboard and a few seconds later, grinned at his screen. "Just pulled into the driveway."

We all turned to face the door, watching them as they entered.

"What's the plan?" Bones asked.

Cooper walked into the kitchen, stole my cup of coffee, then walked to the other side of the island and sat on a barstool.

Hattie smirked as she handed me another cup.

"Where's Charlie?" I asked Cooper.

"She had an errand. Spence and Beast are with her."

I didn't like it, but Charlie was a big girl. Besides, Mr. Tricky was in Michigan. She should be relatively safe. For now, at least.

I looked around the room. "How many men do we have here?"

"About thirty," Grady answered. "Tyler's had three ten-man teams on rotation."

"Can we cut that in half? Go down to five-man teams?"

"This place is big," Bones said, looking toward the veranda. "Lots of doors and windows. It's a lot of ground to cover."

"I promised Tyler we'd install security cameras. Does that help?"

Cooper, Bones, and Grady looked at each other, mentally communicating and evaluating the situation. After a few minutes, first Grady gave a nod, then Cooper.

Bones turned back to me. "We can make it work. We'll use thermal cameras on the perimeter fencing, then we can focus bodies on the front drive."

"I ordered all the equipment last week. It's stacked in the garage," Tech said. "I doubled the quantity from the list Tyler gave me then added a few bells and whistles of my own. We even have a sensor that can alert our phones when someone pulls into the driveway and will show us the camera feed."

I looked at Hattie. Her frown mirrored mine. Neither of us cared for all the security monitoring.

Bones, on the other hand, smiled ear to ear as he bumped fists with Tech.

"Whatever," I said. "Just keep the cameras *outside*. And don't you dare link that driveway sensor to my phone. I'd never sleep."

"You can turn the app on and off, you know," Tech said.

"But would she?" Grady asked. "Or would she leave it on and jump for her phone every time the alert activated?"

"Good point," Tech agreed. "I'll just link the alert to the security teams' phones. I'm going to start now, though. I won't be able to sleep anyway."

"I'll give you a hand," Whiskey said.

"Me too," Cooper said, sliding his cup toward the center of the island before following them out.

"Well," Anne said, watching where they'd left the room. "I better go find some flashlights. I'm not sure they've noticed, but it's dark outside."

"There's flashlights in Charlie's trunk," Uncle Hank told Anne. "The keys should be above the visor."

Anne nodded before walking toward the door.

"Who stays and who goes?" Grady asked me.

"I'll leave that up to you and Bones to figure out. Just remember, this is Lisa and Abigail we're talking about. They need *real* protection."

"I'm staying here," Ryan said. "At least until the end of the week. Then I need to fly home for a few weeks."

"I'll go to Michigan," Jackson said, standing as he looked over at Reggie. "Reggie can go with me. I'm sure Wayne will fly back, too."

"But I don't want to go," Reggie whined. "I like it here. And it's cold in Michigan." Reggie continued to complain as he followed Jackson out of the room.

"We'll split the rest of the guys," Bones said. "Then Grady and I can rotate security shifts with the remaining men. Tyler and Whiskey can stay close to the kids. That leaves Cooper assigned to Charlie, and Ryan and Trigger helping you with the dentist case."

"I have Trigger and Bridget. We'll be fine."

"I took another week off work," Uncle Hank said. "I started this case. It's only right I help you finish it. Charlie can help, too."

"I can help," Alex offered.

I threw a hand over my mouth, covering my laugh at the thought of Alex helping on a case. Several muffled chuckles were heard. We all looked at Alex. He was wearing the white silk robe I'd bought him last year for Christmas, kitten heeled slippers, and his face was smothered with the green goo he'd told me shaves years off your skin.

"Uh, thanks, Alex," Grady said, trying to keep a straight face. "We'll keep that in mind."

"I get no respect around here," Alex huffed, before stomping his heels out of the room.

I looked at Haley who was dressed in a fluffy pink robe but sporting the same green facial goo.

"What can I say?" Haley said, shrugging. "He's a complicated man." She winked at me before following Alex's exit path.

"I don't get it," Bones said, shaking his head.

"Nor do we need to," I said before looking across the room. "Katie, can you arrange flights?"

"Already on it," Katie said from behind her laptop. "There's an eleven-thirty flight out tonight, heading to Detroit. I just booked the last ten seats. They'll have to fly commercial, though. And then their connecting flight to Kalamazoo won't be until six o'clock."

"We'll put the rest of the guys in the rentals and have them drive back," Bones said. "We'll make it work."

Bones walked away, toward the front of the house, with a trail of security guards following him. Grady walked out the back veranda door with more guards. Together, Grady and Bones would divvy up the security teams.

"Katie," Hattie said. "Are there any direct flights to Michigan in the morning?"

Katie looked at Hattie, then Pops, then back at her computer. "There's a nine o'clock direct flight to Kalamazoo. Arrives midday."

Hattie looked at Pops who shrugged, before she looked back at Katie. "Book two seats, please. I'd like to go home. I don't want Lisa and the baby to be alone for all of this."

"They have Donovan," I said, putting a hand on top of hers. "Are you sure?"

"We both know Lisa will put on a brave face for Donovan and pretend she's fine. I want to be there for her. You have enough family here to lean on. And you have your aunt to make sure you eat occasionally." Hattie looked at Aunt Suzanne.

"I'll make sure she eats, even if I have to wrestle her to the ground and force feed her," Aunt Suzanne said.

"Now that," Uncle Hank said, "is something I'd like to see."

"That would definitely rank high in the *Kelsey's Finer Moments* video collection I started," Katie agreed.

Chapter Five

CHARLIE
Tuesday, 11:15 p.m.

With Spence's help, I'd managed to convince Bones and Wild Card to return to the mansion without me. Spence practically had to swear a blood oath to Bones that he'd guard me until I was home. And as much as I wanted to go with them, I couldn't get the image of the teenage girl Roxy had told me about out of my head.

"So..." Spence said as we watched them drive away. "Does this *errand* you need to take care of have anything to do with a pimp named Harlan?"

"You heard that, huh?" I asked as I looked around the motel parking lot.

"Yup."

"Any chance you'll forget you heard it? Let me sneak off on my own?"

"Nope. You're stuck with me, like it or not."

"I'm not going there as a cop. What's about to happen is miles away from legal."

"Sounds like my kind of fun," Spence said, throwing an arm over my shoulder and leading me back to his truck.

~*~*~

It only took twenty minutes to cross town to Harlan's apartment. We sat in the truck, staring up at the third floor of the apartment building.

"You should stay in the truck. It's better for me if there are no witnesses," I told Spence.

"You need backup. Besides, there's a reason I became a PI instead of a cop. I'm not so good with following orders." He got out of the truck.

I opened my door and stepped out, scanning all four street corners. No one was paying any attention to us.

From the sidewalk, Spence nodded toward the entrance. "Come on. Let's go see Harlan the pimp and save the teenage girl."

As we started for the building, a town car pulled up and parked. An identical car pulled up behind the first one and Mickey, flanked by his guards, got out and walked toward us. "You both should leave," Mickey said as he walked past us.

Spence and I glanced at each other, pausing in surprise, before hustling to follow Mickey into the building and up the stairs to the third floor. Standing on the other side of the pimp's door, Mickey looked at Spence, then me. We both remained stubbornly in place. Mickey gave one of his goons *the nod*, and the goon threw his shoulder into the particleboard door. The door shredded under the pressure, blowing apart in three pieces—with a chunk between the door handle and the deadbolt remaining attached to the doorframe.

Mickey entered first, stepping sideways around the other two pieces of the door, with his shoulders back and head high as if he was walking into a business meeting.

Spence, Mickey's goons and I pulled our guns before following him inside.

Harlan stood frozen in front of his couch, staring at us with his jaw dropped to his chest and his eyes round with fear. What happened next took mere seconds, but I captured every action as if it played in slow motion. Harlan looked at Mickey, then at me, then back at Mickey. Then he grabbed a tacky palm tree shaped lamp that was sitting on top of the end table and launched it across the room at the window. The glass shattered as the lamp exited the building. Then Harlan jumped over a hooker who was lying on the floor and leapt—hands together in front of him like he was diving into a pool—out the gaping hole in the glass.

Harlan's scream could be heard by all as he descended but was silenced with the final and grotesque *thud-splat* which followed.

We stared at the window, not moving.

"Well... I've never seen that before," I said.

Spence pointed at the window. "How does that make any sense?"

"Fucker loses his mind when he's high," the hooker from the floor said. She lifted her body from the floor, crawling to the couch and grabbing the remote. "At least I finally get to watch whatever I want." She used the remote to start flipping through the TV channels.

Mickey looked at us and started laughing. He was laughing so hard he had to put his hands on his knees. There was something quite disturbing about seeing a crime boss laugh like a normal human being.

"We need to get the girl, then get the hell out of here," Spence said before advancing down the hallway.

I followed Spence.

The first bedroom was filthy, but based on the men's clothes scattered across the floor and the mirror above the bed, I was guessing it was Harlan's. The bedroom on the other side of the hallway had a half-dozen twin mattresses lying on the floor with a stack of clothes placed at the end of each. On the corner mattress, a teenage girl was balled into a fetal position, watching us.

Spence nodded for me to go to her.

Walking on top of the other mattresses, I squatted a few feet from her. "Ready to get out of here?"

She didn't speak. She just continued watching us. Spence remained near the door, not entering the room.

"We're here to take you somewhere safe." I leaned forward and tugged on the back of her knee to get her moving. "It's okay. Let's go."

Her eyes welled with tears as she slowly stood. "What about Harlan? He said he'd kill me if I tried to leave."

"Harlan's dead. He can't hurt you. He jumped out a window. And not the one near the fire escape."

"I can leave? It's over?"

"Yes. We're here to get you out."

I watched her fear slip away as it was replaced by another emotion just as powerful—panic.

"I need to go. I've been away too long. I have to go." She rushed across the mattresses.

I grabbed her arm, trying to stop her. She turned and kicked my knee, the one I'd injured two weeks prior during an alley scuffle with Mr. Tricky. The rush of pain caused me to drop to the filthy mattresses as the girl launched toward the door.

Spence latched his arms around her as she tried to slip past him. He leaned back, lifting her feet high above the floor.

The second he touched her, the girl started shrieking blood curdling screams.

I winced at the decibels as I climbed up and started limping toward them. Spence, with his arms still pinned around her small body, carried the girl down the hall and into the living room. As soon as she saw Mickey standing in the room, she went dead silent.

Spence continued past Mickey, exiting the apartment. I followed them, hearing Mickey and his goons behind me as we walked down the stairs.

"Please," the girl cried, trying to look over Spence's shoulder at me as I limped down each stair. "You have to let me go."

"There's no reason to be afraid. I'm taking you to a safehouse for runaway teenagers. They'll help you."

"You don't understand. You have to let me go," she whimpered as we walked outside.

Finally, recognition sunk in. She wasn't afraid of Spence, or even Mickey. There was someone else she was scared for. Someone she loved. And whoever it was, they were in danger.

"Something's wrong," I told Spence as I grabbed his arm to prevent him from shoving her inside his truck. I captured the girl's face in my hands. "Tell me. I can help."

"I can't. Please, just let me go."

"Sweetie, I've been in your shoes. I know what a shitty hand life can throw at you. Whatever it is, I'll help you."

A river of tears streaked her face as she looked back at me. She glanced around, but between Spence holding her, me standing in front of her, Mickey beside me, and his goons guarding his back, she had no escape route.

She looked back at me. "My brother. He's been alone too long. I left him to go find us food, and then..." She shook her head, clearing her thoughts. "I need to get to him."

I didn't know how long she'd been held by Harlan in the apartment, but I was guessing based on the faded bruise along her jaw that it had been a good portion of a week.

"Where is he?" Spence asked her as he loosened his grip on her.

It was all the window she needed. Rearing a foot back, she kicked her heel into his balls. As she broke away, she shoulder-slammed into me, knocking me off balance. I could've stopped her. I could've reached out and grabbed her arm. But in a split second I decided it would be faster to follow her than the time it would take to convince her she could trust us.

Opening the truck door, I let Beast out and pointed. "Follow the girl."

Beast launched past us, chasing after the girl as Spence and I ran to follow.

I ignored the jolts of pain in my knee, knowing there were lives at stake if I lost the girl. When Spence ran past me, I slowed, confident he could keep up with the kid.

Two blocks away, my knee buckled and I stumbled forward, landing face first on the sidewalk. I looked up to see the girl, Beast, and Spence turn the corner at the end of the block as I tried to peel myself up from the concrete.

Mickey's town car pulled alongside the curb. The back door opened and Mickey sat staring at me. "Hurry up, or I'll leave you."

I limped to the car, sliding in beside him. The car jetted forward and turned the corner. We drove five more blocks before we saw the three of them, one at a time, slip inside a condemned building.

In the time it took us to pull the car alongside the curb, stop, and for me to open the back door, Spence had already returned, rushing out of the building with a small limp boy in his arms. Spence transferred the boy to me then pushed us both to the center of the seat. He stepped back, letting both Beast and the girl inside before he squeezed into the last narrow remaining space. Beast sat on the floor in front of Mickey, his tongue hanging out as sweat dripped on to Mickey's pant leg.

I ignored Mickey's disgusted look and glanced at the boy in my arms. "Go!" I yelled to the driver.

The girl, partially sitting on Spence's knee, hovered over her brother's lifeless body as she cried.

"Fast!" I yelled.

The car launched forward as a car somewhere behind us slammed on its brakes.

I looked down at the boy's ghostly face as I took his pulse. He was alive, but unconscious. "Go to the mansion!"

"We need to go to the hospital," Spence said, placing a hand on my shoulder.

I looked at the girl, her face strained by fear. I looked at Mickey. "Call Kelsey. Let her know we're coming in fast and need medical assistance."

Mickey pulled his phone while instructing his driver where to go.

I held the boy tight to my chest, rubbing his bare arms, trying to warm his chilled body while I hoped

Haley had enough training under her belt to save him.

Chapter Six

KELSEY
Wednesday, 12:05 a.m.

I had just nodded off when my phone rang. Groaning, I looked at the display, surprised to see Mickey's name. "This better be good," I answered.

"I'm with Detective Harrison and we're heading your way. There's a young boy who needs medical attention. We should be there in less than five minutes."

"Why is she bringing him here instead of taking him to the hospital?"

"We don't know if the boy and his sister are safe at the hospital. They're street kids. From what I can tell, the boy's malnourished, dehydrated, and ice cold." Mickey paused for a long moment. "Kelsey, the boy's young. Maybe five or six. Shit's gotta be pretty bad at home if his sister has him with her, living on the streets."

"*Shit!*" I started scrambling off the bed. "We'll be ready."

I grabbed a sweatshirt before rushing out of the room. Tyler, Bridget, and Trigger were standing in the sitting room. They must've heard my phone ring.

"Bridget and Trigger, grab a mattress off one of the bunks and bring it downstairs. Tyler, go wake Haley and have her meet me with her medical supplies in the kitchen."

I ran over and knocked on the door to Anne and Whiskey's bedroom. The door flew open. "The kids?" Anne asked.

"Not ours. But Charlie's on her way with a kid who's in bad shape. I could use your help." I didn't wait for a reply as I ran toward the stairs and down to the main level. By the time I reached the living room, Bones, Cooper, and Grady were standing ready to be pointed toward a threat.

"Uncle Hank, wake Hattie, Pops, and Aunt Suzanne. Bones, let security know to let Mickey's car through when he arrives. Cooper, blankets. Grady, more blankets."

"What do you want us to do?" Anne asked from behind me. Whiskey stood beside her, holding her hand.

"Clear the dining room table and call Doc. Haley might need his help."

Within minutes half the house was awake and rushing to do whatever they could think of to help. Hattie and Aunt Suzanne were in the kitchen cooking various soups. A twin mattress was placed on top of the dining room table with a pile of blankets stacked at one end. Trigger rigged a hook and chain from the chandelier to hold an I.V. bag. Haley laid out medical supplies on the breakfast bar.

When Mickey's town car pulled into the driveway, I watched from the doorway as Cooper grabbed the lifeless boy from Charlie's arms and ran past me into the house. I gasped, feeling the acute emotional pain from seeing the boy's ghoulish skin tone.

Charlie and a teenage girl rushed behind Cooper. Mickey and Spence were next through the door before I closed it behind them.

In the kitchen, they laid the boy on the mattress. Anne whimpered but helped Whiskey start wrapping blankets around his body. I ran to help from the other side of the table. I looked over to see Haley staring down at the child while the hand that held the I.V. needle shook violently inches away from the boy's arm.

Grady grabbed Haley's wrist with one hand and with the other, turned her face to look at him. "Take a beat. Focus on one task, then the next."

Cooper wrapped a rubber tube around the boy's arm, just above the elbow.

"You ready, Haley?" Grady asked. "Just think of one task at a time. Find his vein," Grady coached.

I watched her focus on the boy's arm, her eyes narrowing to the spot, and then with skilled practice she set the needle into the vein and taped it in place. After that first action, Haley started moving on auto-pilot: setting the I.V. drip, listening to his heart, taking his blood pressure. With each step, she called out her findings to Doc who was on speaker on the cellphone beside her.

"Now what?" Haley asked Doc, looking down at the phone.

"Now the hard part," Doc answered. "We wait and pray."

I couldn't stand there and do nothing. I lifted the boy's arm that was closest to me and started rubbing his cold skin, hoping the friction would improve blood flow, help warm him, if nothing else. Cooper, Anne, and Whiskey each took a limb and did the same.

The next twenty minutes felt like hours, but every five minutes Haley rattled off the boy's vitals and each interval increased our hopes as his results improved. We were eventually rewarded with the boy's eyes fluttering open.

"Mackenzie..." he whispered on a raspy voice.

"I'm here, Liam. I'm right here," his sister whispered from beside him as she stroked his hair. "Sleep. It's okay. We're safe. Go to sleep."

"Don't let him find me," Liam said before his eyes drifted closed again.

"Never," Mackenzie whispered back, leaning into his shoulder to cry.

I felt a hand clasp mine, and looked over to see Cooper staring at the boy. He glanced up at me, fury in his eyes. "I feel the need to hurt someone."

"You are not alone, brother," Whiskey said.

I glanced back at Mackenzie. She'd had more than any teenage girl could handle in one day. "Not now, boys. Not now." I stroked the girl's hair, offering her a small amount of comfort. "Anne, why don't you take Mackenzie upstairs to shower and put on some clean clothes. Alex, can you find some clothes for both the kids to wear?"

"Sure thing, luv," Alex said.

Anne led the despondent girl up the stairs with Alex quietly following them. As they disappeared from our view, I nodded to Aunt Suzanne and Hattie. They carried large bowls of warm water to the table. Bridget grabbed some wash cloths. Together, we cleaned the dirt off the boy's body and applied disinfectant to the bites on his arms and legs, likely from roaches, before redressing him in a pair of sweatpants and a t-shirt of Sara's. The clothes were too big, but they were clean.

"I'm going shopping to buy them some clothes," Alex said. "Anyone want to come with me?"

"Now?" I asked, looking up at the clock. "It's almost one in the morning."

"So?" Alex said, raising an eyebrow.

"Whatever," I said, waving him off. "Just take security with you."

"I'll go," Trigger said.

"Me too," Bridget said.

Bones sighed. "I have no idea where they plan to shop at this hour, but I'm going with them to make sure they don't break in anywhere."

"Who? Us?" Bridget said, placing her hands on her hips, trying to pretend to be insulted.

"I've seen what you can do with a lockpick set, remember?" Bones said, tweaking her nose before shoving her toward the door.

"Where's Charlie?" Spence asked, looking around.

I looked toward the French doors. "She's outside on the veranda. I'll check on her."

"I'll go," Spence said, walking out.

"Why's Charlie outside?" Grady asked. "She's the one who brought the kids here."

"Charlie saves them," Aunt Suzanne said from the kitchen. "But unlike Kelsey, she's careful not to get attached. It's just too painful for her."

"That's why she works homicide," Uncle Hank said. "It's easier for her to deal with the dead than the lost."

"Smart," Mickey said, looking toward the glass doors.

"It's not about being smart," I told him. "It's about surviving the shit life's thrown at her. She protects the innocent the best she can, then gets them to people who can nurture them back from the edge."

"And she doesn't have a problem with getting her hands bloody, if necessary, either," Cooper said, nudging me with his elbow.

"What are you talking about?" I asked him.

"She didn't tell you about the finger chopping thing she did?"

"What finger chopping thing?"

"I heard about that," Mickey said with a slight curve upward to his lips. "Effective."

I looked between them then narrowed my eyes at Cooper. "Talk."

"Can't. Charlie kept my secret when I told her you and I were still hitched. It's only fair I keep hers."

I saw Grady wince when Cooper mentioned the marriage thing, but I ignored it and looked at Mickey.

He stared back, appearing amused. "I'll tell you, but only because it's funny. Not because I feel threatened by you in the least."

"Uh huh," I mumbled.

"Charlie chopped the end of some wife beater's fingers off and ordered him pack his shit and leave his wife alone. Warned him she'd chop the rest off if he showed his face again. I really hope the asshole slips up so I can find out if she'll follow through with the threat."

"Let's hope he doesn't," I said, rubbing the tension from my forehead.

"Why? Would she do it?" Mickey asked.

"Hell, yes," Charlie answered from the doorway. "Kelsey raised me to never make a threat I wasn't willing to follow through with."

"Kid, you're going to be the death of me," I said before turning and walking away.

Chapter Seven

CHARLIE
Wednesday, 4:32 a.m.

Two hours into my nap on the couch in the main living room, a piercing scream from the kitchen had me tossing the blanket off, pulling my gun from my holster, and running barefoot into the kitchen. There, I found Alex standing on top of the kitchen island and wearing a towel on his head, a gorgeous white silk robe with lace edges, and foam toe separators keeping his toes apart enough for the blood red polish to dry. I looked around the kitchen, but other than Bones and Wild Card who'd rushed in behind me, no one else was around.

"What the hell, man?" Wild Card yelled at Alex.

Alex pointed. We looked over where a gecko was crawling across the tile floor.

"You are such a girl," I said. I retrieved the gecko and carried it outside, leaving it in a rock bed around the corner. Returning to the kitchen, I spotted Mackenzie and her brother by the living room entrance.

"I'm going back to bed," Bones said, stumbling toward the stairs.

"Everything okay?" Mackenzie asked as her brother tried to make himself small beside her.

"Alex is afraid of geckos. Can you believe that?"

"Geckos won't hurt you," Liam told Alex, peeking his head out from behind Mackenzie's hip.

Mackenzie looked at me, then at Alex. "I like your robe."

"Isn't it divine?" Alex said, climbing down from the island. "Check out this hand stitching. It's perfection. Each stitch is so small and perfectly aligned." He walked over and held out the robe's cuff for Mackenzie to inspect. She nodded, feigning interest, before raising an eyebrow at me.

I glanced between her and Liam. They were both pale and their skeletal structure too prominent behind their thin skin. "You two want to sleep for a few more hours? Or are you hungry?"

"Is there any more soup?" Liam whispered from the safety of Mackenzie's hip.

"Do you want soup or do you want scrambled eggs with cheese?" Aunt Suzanne asked, walking into the kitchen. Uncle Hank dragged his feet as he stumbled in behind her.

Kelsey charged into the room with one eye still closed as she tried to focus.

"Everything's fine," Wild Card told her before he turned to start a pot of coffee. "Go back to bed."

Kelsey left the way she'd arrived.

It appeared my day was starting early—whether I was ready for it or not. I looked over at Mackenzie. "Will you be okay if I run upstairs for a quick shower?"

Mackenzie looked at Uncle Hank, Wild Card, and Aunt Suzanne. She seemed unsure, suddenly nervous.

"Mackenzie," Aunt Suzanne said, gaining her attention. "There's not a single person in this house who would ever hurt you or your brother. But if it makes you feel safer, then I swear I won't leave the room until Charlie returns." Aunt Suzanne held up a hand as if she was being sworn in to testify.

Mackenzie didn't say anything, but nodded at me before she led her brother over to the table. She chose the chairs closest to the open French doors. *Smart kid*, I thought as I walked down the hallway. *Always know your exit strategy.*

~*~*~

Thirty minutes later, I returned to the kitchen. Mackenzie bolted upright from her chair. Her eyes were locked on the badge clipped to my jeans. She grabbed Liam's hand, jerking him out of his chair and causing him to knock over his juice glass in the process. She was oblivious to the juice running off the table as her eyes remained fixated on me.

"Yup," I said, answering her unasked question. "I'm a cop, A detective, actually." I walked into the kitchen and filled a cup of coffee. "But when I was thirteen, I ran away with my cousin Kelsey. Remind you of anyone?"

"So?" Mackenzie asked. "You're a cop now."

Uncle Hank looked at Mackenzie over his cup of coffee. "I'm a cop, too. Doesn't mean we'd turn you over to social services."

Mackenzie's eyes danced between us. Liam, sensing her fear rise, tucked his small body behind his sister.

"Before you decide to bolt," Aunt Suzanne held up a plastic food container, "mind waiting for me to fill some containers of food for you?"

I pointed toward a bag in the living room. "And you should take that bag of clothes Alex bought for you." I set my coffee down before retrieving the bag and setting it on top of the table. The duffle was huge. Liam could easily sleep inside if it weren't overflowing with clothes and shoes. I pulled out clean clothes for them. "And you should get dressed first. Running around in your PJ's is bound to look suspicious in this neighborhood. Someone might call the police."

"You'll need money," Uncle Hank said, pulling his wallet.

"Good call," Wild Card said as he stood and pulled his wallet. "I'll grab a couple prepaid phones too."

I grabbed the antibacterial ointment and some bandages before walking over to my purse and pulling an envelope of cash.

We piled up the loot and miscellaneous supplies as the kids watched.

"Let's program our numbers into a phone before they leave," I said.

Aunt Suzanne set two plastic grocery sacks filled with containers of food next to the duffle as we passed a prepaid phone around the table, adding our numbers. After the phone circulated, I tossed it on top of the overflowing duffle.

"Is that everything?" Uncle Hank asked.

"I think so," I answered. "We'll just have to trust Mackenzie to call us the next time she's nabbed off the street and can't get back to her brother. Nothing else we can do."

Mackenzie looked at the bag, then back at me. "You'd let us leave?"

I nodded. "I've been in your shoes. I won't keep you here against your will."

"But you're a cop."

"Obviously not a very good one," I said, laughing as I picked my coffee.

Uncle Hank chuckled. "She's a great cop. She just follows her own set of rules which gets her in a lot of trouble."

"What about you?" Mackenzie asked Uncle Hank with narrowed eyes. "Are you a bad cop too?"

"I usually follow the rules, but Charlie's the one who brought you here," Uncle Hank answered. "The way I see it, it's her decision, not mine. If Charlie says we're not calling social services, then we're not calling. Her house, her rules."

"You live here?" Liam asked me with big eyes.

"No," I answered. "I live in a one-bedroom apartment downtown. But I recently bought this place."

"Are you rich?" Mackenzie asked.

"Rich enough that I don't have to worry about getting fired. But I'll also never forget all the years we were poor either. Which is why that orange juice dripping off the table is bugging the crawdads out of me."

"Sorry," Mackenzie said, grabbing a napkin and wiping up the juice.

"No reason to be sorry," Aunt Suzanne said, walking behind her and wiping the table clean. "You have plenty of reason to be jumpy. But if you choose to stick around for a day or two, you'll realize you're both safe here."

"He'll find us," Liam whispered to his sister. "They're all rich. Like *him*."

He emphasized *him* with such contempt I was sure he was referring to whoever they were hiding from. Whoever he was, I was determined to find him and make him pay—with or without proof of any wrong doing.

"She's rich," Wild Card said, pointing to me. "We're normal." He pointed to Uncle Hank and himself. "And Charlie doesn't judge people by how much money they have or don't have. She judges them based on if they're good people. If you ever want to tell us who hurt you, we'll handle it."

"No. We can't tell you," Mackenzie said, moving her arm back to snag her brother to her hip again.

"You can," I said as I sat, "but there's no hurry. You can stay here for a few days whether you tell us or not. After that, I can help you find a place where you'll both be together and safe. But for now, I'd like you to stay. I want to make sure your brother is getting the food and rest he needs."

Mackenzie looked down at her brother. Though he looked worlds better than he had the night before, he was still bone thin and pale. "And when we leave," Mackenzie eyed the bag of clothes and money, "we can take all that?"

"That bag is yours," I promised. "No one will stop you from taking it and leaving."

~*~*~

Aunt Suzanne and Uncle Hank agreed to watch the kids while I snuck out to go to work. I took Beast with me, but told Wild Card to stay at the mansion since I'd be at the precinct all day. Surprisingly, he didn't argue.

On the drive in I stopped to purchase six dozen donuts, dropping four boxes off at the first-floor breakroom and carrying the remaining two to the detectives' room on the second floor.

Beast whined as we left the boxes on the entranceway table. I wasn't about to feed him a donut, but guilt had me digging him out a peanut butter treat from my bag. He seemed happy, his backside swaying to and fro as he crunched his snack.

Turning to the right, I walked away from the homicide department, down the hall, and entered the next suite which handled special victim crimes.

In this room, they investigated cases a lot worse than murder. They worked sexual assaults, missing persons, and sex crimes such as trafficking and prostitution.

On many occasions, homicide cases crossed over to missing persons, which is why I was familiar with the room, the detectives, and the researchers who worked this unit. More than once, I'd found myself walking down the hallway to identify a Jane or John Doe from the corkboard that took up nearly an entire wall of missing person flyers. The same photos were in our database, but somehow seeing the papers pinned, one on top of another, made the people pictured more real. More desperate to be found.

As I crossed the room to the corkboard, a detective sitting on the other side of the room glanced up and nodded before focusing back on his computer. I started at one end of the board, scanning the hundreds of flyers, both adults and kids, as I moved to the other end. I was three quarters down the wall when I found Mackenzie and Liam's pictures.

I moved another foot away, sensing eyes on me, as I read the kids' flyer with my peripheral vision. I had just finished when I heard footsteps approaching.

"Going to close a case for us?" Warren asked, leaning his back against the corkboard to look at me. "Lord knows we could use a few less flyers up there."

"Just browsing. Trying to stay on top of things." I spotted a flyer underneath another, and pulled the top sheet back. "On second thought," I said, pulling the flyer from the underside off the board. I guess *I am* going to solve a case for you." I handed the flyer to Warren. "Carl was found a few years ago. My cousin has guardianship over him. It went through the court system and everything."

"Geesh," Warren said, shaking his head. "I'm not surprised. We're too busy to circle back on cases after they've gone cold. I wonder how many others are up there that are no longer missing. It's a shame really. Guys like this," he held up Carl's flyer, "they're so low on our radar because brass pushes us toward media cases. Like this one," Warren pointed to Mackenzie's picture. "Smart teenage girl. Straight A's. Then there's a car accident. Her mother dies, and two months later, the girl runs away, taking her little brother with her."

Since he pointed out her flyer, I made a point to study it. "Why would she do that? Grief?"

"No idea, but something doesn't add up. And their stepfather is a country club asshole. He doesn't seem too worried about the girl, but he's hounding us daily about getting the boy back. If'n you ask me, something smells rotten about the case, but I can't put my finger on what it is."

"You think he's guilty of something?"

Warren shrugged. "The boy's teacher said Liam would burst into tears at the slightest onset. She was worried about abuse, but Liam wouldn't confide in her."

"What about the girl?"

"This girl," Warren said, pointing to Mackenzie's photo, "is one smart kid. She's avoided the shelters and hasn't been spotted in any of the homeless camps. And I questioned each of her friends—went at them hard with questions—but nada. It was obvious they had no idea she was planning to bolt. My sergeant thinks the girl ran when she found out she was being shipped off to boarding school."

"Away from her brother," I mumbled aloud on accident.

Warren's eyes narrowed. "Is that important?"

I didn't know him well, but Ford always said Warren was a standup cop. Not a showboat like some of the other cops, but committed to the job for all the right reasons. I decided to answer his question with just enough detail to see how he'd react. "It's important if she thought her brother wasn't safe."

Warren looked around the room before lowering his voice to say, "I wouldn't say much more on this side of the detectives' floor. There's been a hell of a lot of handshaking between top brass and daddy dearest." Warren looked around again. "I also wouldn't mind being pulled to homicide to help on a case for a few days. Maybe I just happen to track down dirt on the stepdad in the process."

"Sorry, Warren," I said, patting him on the shoulder. "I don't have the juice right now to get you reassigned. I've got my name stamped on at least three open and active I.A. cases. That's a new record—even for me. I usually like to space them out."

Warren nodded, holding back a grin as he watched the door. "I get it. I'll do what I can from here. I'll let you know if I find anything."

"Sure." I started for the door, projecting my voice to be heard as I walked away. "By the way, there's donuts in Homicide."

Warren, the detective from the far corner desk, and two admins who appeared out of nowhere from back offices, all rushed past me.

I should've bought more donuts, I thought.

As I walked back toward Homicide, the elevator dinged and the doors opened. Quille and Ford stepped off the elevator, then retreated as the herd rushed past them toward the smell of sugary pastries. I saw Ford's head pop back out, look both ways, then he stepped out, followed by Quille.

"Donuts?" Ford asked me as he handed me a cup of coffee from the four-cup tray he was carrying.

"Yup, and thanks," I said, inhaling deeply to smell the rich Cuban coffee.

A few years back, I'd learned that one of my favorite coffee shops was halfway between Ford's house and the precinct. I got him a VIP card that allowed him to pick up coffee free of charge and I paid the bill monthly.

I inhaled another deep breath before taking a drink.

"Did you just moan?" Quille asked.

I winked at him. "It doesn't take much to get me excited these days."

"No, no, no," Quille said, holding up his hands. "I don't want to hear it. You're young enough to be my daughter." He stomped down the hall, shaking his head.

Ford and I remained near the elevator, grinning at each other.

"I forgot to give him his coffee," Ford said.

"You can take it to him in a minute." I pushed the button to call the elevator to open. "First, take an elevator ride with me?"

Ford raised an eyebrow, but when the doors opened, he followed me inside. I pushed the up button.

Ford's eyes flickered to the elevator panel, then back at me. "The roof, huh? This early in the morning?"

"I need to bounce something off you without anyone hearing me admit to committing a crime."

"Are you going to get me fired? If you are, just tell me now. I need to prepare myself for the thought of working mall security."

"I promise, I won't get you fired."

"You and I both know you can't make that promise."

"Okay, I promise that if I get you fired, I'll find you a job that pays better."

Ford sighed. "Will I like the job?"

"If you don't, I'll keep finding you jobs until you find one you like."

"Deal," Ford said, stepping off the elevator into the cool morning air. He set the tray of coffee cups by the door and then walked with me to the other side of the roof. "All right. What did you walk into this time?"

"I can't tell you everything. But between us, there's a case in missing persons that Warren is assigned to. I sort of hinted he should look closer at the stepdad, but I'm already regretting it."

"Why are you regretting it?"

I half shrugged. "I'd rather not say."

Ford took a drink of his coffee. "So... If it's a stepdad we're talking about, that means the missing persons case involves a kid. And if you're pointing the case toward the stepdad, that means he was abusive in some way. And then there's you *being you...*"

I grinned at him over my coffee. "What's that mean?"

"It means you regret talking to Warren because you don't know how he'll react if you do something crazy."

"I'm just trying to figure out the best way to protect—" I was about to say *them*, when I stopped myself, "—the kid. That's all."

Ford didn't miss my near slip, but he continued to play along. "What happened to the kids' mom?"

"Car accident."

"Died?"

"I think so."

"I'd start there. Tasha could share the file without raising any red flags."

"Good idea. But what about Warren? What can you tell me?"

"Warren's a by-the-book cop most of the time, but on occasion he'll let things slide. If the stepdad gets a beat down, Warren would probably look the other way." Ford had been looking toward the horizon, but turned to narrow his eyes at me. "But if the stepdad shows up *dead*, I have no doubt Warren will go to internal affairs."

I sighed. "I shouldn't be allowed to speak to anyone before having at least four cups of coffee."

Ford looked down at my cup. "That's not your first?"

"No. It's only my third."

"And I thought my day started off too early," Ford said as he strolled back toward the elevator.

Chapter Eight

CHARLIE
Wednesday, 9:56 a.m.

We regrouped in Quille's office to catch Quille up on the cases. Today was his first day back from a long overdue vacation which started as a three-day weekend and had extended into five days. I didn't blame Quille for taking the extra days off. He'd earned it. When I started working for him years ago, he had a full head of hair. Now he only had a few wispy strands that he refused to shave.

"Where's the mountain of paperwork that usually greets me when I return from vacation?" Quille asked, looking at his clean desk. "I got up with the roosters to make a dent in the pile, but I can't find the pile."

"Don't get too excited, boss," Ford said, pulling out a guest chair and sitting. "Kid piled the mess in a box then tossed it under your desk."

Quille leaned over and picked up the overflowing box, setting it on top of his desk. I walked past Ford and sat on top of the credenza.

"Think anyone would notice if I threw it all in the trash?" Quille asked.

"Everyone except Kid would notice," Ford said. "Next year's vacation requests are in there somewhere."

I pointed toward the box. "I put those in the yellow file folder. They should be easy to find."

Quille pulled the yellow file folder from somewhere near the bottom. He dropped the file on his desk, moved the box to the side, then dropped into his chair with a sigh. "All right. Catch me up. What did I miss?"

"Chambers' official transfer came through," I said. "The paperwork is somewhere in the pile. Chambers also agreed to take Gibson off our hands and train him to be a *real* detective. They're working a robbery-gone-wrong case. Sounds like they have a good suspect, but they're still putting the pieces together. We also had two suspicious deaths come in, but my money is on natural causes. The autopsy reports should be in later today. Then there's Ford's case..."

Quille turned to Ford.

"I picked up a jumper. But I don't think he jumped."

Quille motioned for Ford to continue, rolling with his hand in a circular wave.

"The victim was a traveling salesman for a manufacturing firm. The guy sounds solid, no red flags popping up. And his belongings were packed for his flight out the next morning. Nothing points to him planning to take a nose dive off the Royal Finn's balcony."

My ears perked with interest. "The Royal Finn Beachside resort? That place is nice. Have you ever seen the penthouse suite? Absolutely *spa-abulous*. It has a heated bathtub that's the size of a small pool."

Quille pointed between him and Ford. "Do we look like the kind of guys who'd be able to access a penthouse?"

Ford lifted his feet to prop them on the other guest chair. "Speak for yourself. I saw the penthouse suite at the Sunset Beach Towers. Of course, there was a dead body inside the room, but, hey, at least I got to see how the one-percenters live."

I refrained from telling him that the Sunset's penthouse paled in comparison to the Royal Finn's, and the one-percenters would never stay there. "Could your salesman have fallen? Tripped and tumbled over the railing?"

Ford shook his head. "Not unless he was beyond hammered. And his blood alcohol came back clean."

"Was there anything shady in his background check?" Quille asked.

"The guy was squeaky clean. Happy wife, two kids, and a dog. House was paid off and the 529 education accounts for his kids were fully funded. No debts whatsoever. Not even a credit card. Zero arrests or traffic violations. The only dirt Abe found was that the victim had a weird ritual, like a baseball player or something. The night before a big sales pitch he'd check into his hotel and watch a porn."

"Maybe his wife found out?" I asked.

"She already knew and didn't care. His weird habit was the reason they could afford to buy a new car and go on tropical vacations twice a year."

Quille leaned back in his chair, rocking it back and forth. "Where does that leave you? Do you have any theories? Sales meeting gone bad? Competition snuffed him out?"

Ford raised his hands in an I-don't-know gesture. "Beats the hell out of me why someone would whack him."

"Robbery?" I asked.

"Nope. Wallet, watch, and laptop were all in the room still."

"What did this guy sell?" Quille asked.

Ford looked between us with a grin on his face. "Lightbulbs."

"That's it? Just lightbulbs?" Quille asked.

"Yup. Just lightbulbs. But a shitload of lightbulbs. The guy was earning a mid-six-figure salary."

"Selling lightbulbs? Are you shittin me?" Quille said.

"I don't get it," I said. "You can go to any store and buy lightbulbs. Were these magic lightbulbs?"

"Nope, just energy efficient. He sold mass packages to firms with older and outdated buildings. He'd go in and assess their electrical usage, then pitch them how much a year they could save if he had their bulbs upgraded to newer ones. The bigger the building, the more money he could save them, and the more commission he made when they handed him a check."

"We're in the wrong business," Quille said.

"You're just now figuring that out?" Ford asked as he stood and turned toward the door. "If either of you come up with any fresh ideas, let me know."

I slid off the credenza and started to follow Ford out but stopped to look back at Quille. "I forgot to ask, how was the cruise?"

"The cruise was great. The time alone with Miranda was great. But I have a feeling when Miranda realizes the vacation is over, she's going to get cranky again. I decided to sneak out while she was still sleeping to avoid another retirement argument."

"You can't avoid the subject forever."

"I love Miranda, but she married a cop. End of story."

"And that's why I'm single," I said, starting out the door.

"*That's not the only reason you're single!*" Quille hollered behind me.

I raised a finger over my shoulder. *The naughty one.*

~*~*~

I still didn't have the suspicious death autopsy reports I needed and Tasha's shift at the morgue didn't start until noon on Wednesday. Rather than waste my energy chained to my desk writing boring reports, I told Ford I'd check out his crime scene at the Royal Finn. I was doubtful I'd find anything. Ford was a thorough detective. But a second set of eyes never hurt. And if nothing else, it was a good excuse to procrastinate tackling the paperwork that had piled up on my desk.

Arriving at the hotel, I signed out a keycard from the manager who'd informed me that Beast couldn't be in the hotel. I then explained to the manager that I had PTSD and Beast was my companion dog. The manager didn't have a choice but to allow it, but he wasn't happy, which was evident when he walked back to his office and slammed the door shut.

As we rode the elevator to the sixth floor, I looked at Beast. "It wasn't completely a lie."

Beast turned his head sideways as if saying *yeah, right.*

"My shrink says my nightmares are probably PTSD linked. And you're my bodyguard, so that makes you my companion, right? So, see? Not really a lie."

Beast snuffed loudly, something between a sneeze and cough.

The elevator doors opened and Beast padded ahead of me into the hallway. I followed him out, down the hallway, and around the corner, stopping in front of the victim's room. After motioning for Beast to lie down, I strapped on a pair of latex gloves before swiping the keycard and entering.

Forensics had already swept the room, collecting prints and DNA, but letting Beast inside to track doggy hair everywhere wasn't an option since the scene hadn't officially been released yet. Besides, I was almost certain, well, *sort of* certain, that Beast wouldn't bite anyone if I left him unsupervised in the hallway.

Signing an entry log on the back of the door, I documented my presence in the room. Ford had logged some of the victim's personal items as evidence, but at this point in the investigation there wasn't a need to bag everything.

I read Ford's report from my tablet. The victim's wallet, room keycard, and phone were found on top of the dresser. His laptop had been lying on the bed, and his toothbrush in the bathroom was logged as evidence too. After a big sales pitch downtown on Friday, the victim wasn't seen again until his death early Sunday morning. The tech unit had searched his phone and found a confirmation of a return flight home for early-morning Sunday. And other than a call to his wife around dinnertime, no other calls in or out.

"Why did you stay another day? Why not leave Saturday?" I asked myself aloud.

I searched the main room first. The victim's open suitcase sat on the pop-out luggage stand with his clothes packed inside. A single set of clothes, including underwear and socks, were stacked on the dresser. I opened the dresser drawers, then looked in the trashcan that sat next to the dresser. He'd tossed the local sales flyers and scent packs from drawers into the trash. That meant he'd used the dresser but then at some point, probably Saturday night, he had repacked for his flight, leaving out only the clothes he'd need to change into the next morning.

"Ford was right. This guy hadn't planned on dying."

I looked at the bed. It was still made, including the decorative pillows and the bedcover folded with its triangle wedges in the bottom corners. He hadn't gone to bed yet. I checked the report and confirmed his time of death was around three in the morning.

"All the good stuff happens at three in the morning. What were you up to?" I realized I didn't know the victim's name, so I scrolled to the top of the page on the tablet. "*Bernard Bacon*? Really? With a name like that, you couldn't have been doing anything too exciting. Unless maybe you were with a hooker?" I looked back at the still-made bed. "Nope, not a hooker. Unless..."

I turned to face the balcony.

"What if you were having sex on the balcony and things got wild enough for you to fall?"

I opened the door and took a half step into the piercing sunlight. I imagined a man and woman getting a little crazy, exhibition style, in multiple positions. But unless Bernard was a weightlifter, he would've pinned the woman's back to the railing. And let's face it—why bother exercising when he was stuck with a name like Bernard Bacon? It wouldn't be worth the energy. Which meant if there *had been* a sexual mishap, the woman would've been more likely to go over the rail.

Another theory knocked down, I stepped closer to the railing and looked below. Six very long stories down, someone from janitorial service was using a broom and soapy water to scrub the bloodstain off the concrete. They were supposed to leave it, along with the crime tape which was wadded into the nearby trash can, but I couldn't blame them for cleaning the area. Blood and brain splatter weren't the best marketing tools.

I straightened, looking around at the general view. The Royal Finn was shaped in a large C, with the inner curve on the oceanside, and the outer curve toward downtown Miami's nightlife. But this room was on the end of the outer C, and its view was less than spectacular. Directly in front of the balcony, a good thirty yards away, was the neighboring building's tar-patched rooftop with rattling air and water units. Between the buildings there was nothing but concrete.

Across the side street, I could see a souvenir plaza—common real estate near any decent sized hotel in Florida. Also common was a burger or pizza restaurant at the end of a plaza, which this one also sported based on the neon pizza-slice sign mounted to the side of the building.

"Bernard, why did you have a room with such a bad view? Did you get a discount?" Turning to walk back inside, I stopped when I saw something out of the corner of my eye. Looking back, I realized it was only a woman exiting one of the plaza stores, hurrying to her car which was parked on the street. I was about to turn again when I noticed the car parked in front of hers. Something about the car was familiar, but I didn't know why.

Shaking off the feeling, I reentered the hotel room just as someone knocked on the door. Knowing Beast was guarding the hallway, I felt confident the person on the other side was a good guy. I crossed the room, opened the door, and discovered an annoyed Wild Card staring back at me.

"You're supposed to be at the precinct surrounded by cops," Wild Card said as he strolled past me into the room.

"Don't touch anything. This is still an active crime scene." I dug out another set of gloves and handed them to him. "How did you find me?" I asked before stepping into the bathroom.

"I got tired of losing you, so I put a tracking app on your phone."

"That's cheating."

"Hey, you're the one who keeps breaking all the rules. And you should be thanking me. I didn't rat you out to Kelsey."

"Thanks. I mean it. I've had my fill of her ordering me around the last few days."

"Did you ever stop to think that if you applied an ounce of concern for your own safety, she wouldn't have to boss you around?"

I mumbled a few choice words under my breath as I looked around the bathroom. Dirty towels were lying on the floor. In the trash were two mini one-use bottles of shampoo. I looked back at the towels. There were *two* towels lying on the floor. "Housekeeping didn't clean his room Saturday."

Stepping back into the main room, I inspected the bed again. "He didn't sleep."

I walked back into the bathroom for a second time and picked up the trash can. Grateful for the gloves, I shifted a dirty tissue out of my way and found a small cardboard and plastic package. I flipped it over. The packaging was for a memory card.

I carried the package out and dropped it into an evidence bag, documenting where I'd found it and recording the time and date.

Wild Card walked over and looked over my shoulder at the package. "Where's the camera?"

"What camera?"

Wild Card pointed to the evidence bag. "That memory card is Pro-rated. Only professionals spend the big bucks for a terabyte memory card with one-hundred-seventy megabyte read speed."

"Say that again?"

Wild Card sighed and then re-explained in exaggerated slow speech, "You can take a lot of pictures, very fast, and the memory card will keep up." His eyes narrowed as he paused to think. "That type of memory card also works great for video recording. Maybe he had a video recorder, not a digital camera."

"Either way, you're saying the memory card is a little over the top for a lightbulb salesman?"

"You don't need that much juice to store a PowerPoint presentation."

I flipped through the screens on my tablet, searching the evidence log report, but I didn't see a camera or recorder listed. Circling the room again, I rechecked each drawer, the singular closet, under the bed, under the bathroom sink, and flipped through Bernard's suitcase. No camera or video recorder.

I stood in the center of the room for a long moment, puzzling over the scene before I turned to the balcony. Following a new hunch, I leaned over and inspected the balcony floor, sweeping my eyes in a grid pattern from one end of the balcony to the other. And then I saw it. Three small black marks—scuff marks—evenly spaced apart to form a triangle. My guess? They were from a tripod stand.

I straightened and looked at the view again from that end of the balcony. The souvenir plaza.

"What are we looking at?" Wild Card asked from behind me.

"Why would someone take pictures of that strip mall?"

"Don't know. Maybe a better question is why would a car outside a strip mall have so many parking tickets?"

I looked at the car parked on the street in front of the strip mall, and sure enough, it appeared to have several parking tickets tucked under the windshield wiper. I pulled my phone and took a picture of the car, zooming in on the plate. Returning to the room, I took a picture of the memory card package. I sent both pictures to Abe and Ford with a message to find the owner of the car and ask someone if the victim owned a camera or recorder.

Before I tucked my phone away, it rang. I hit the green icon.

"You think it was a homicide then?" Ford asked.

"I think there's enough pieces not fitting that something shady went down. I just don't know what the pieces mean."

"Abe's running the car. I never saw a camera at the scene."

"I have to meet Tasha at the morgue. If you find anything out on that camera, let me know."

"Will do." Ford disconnected.

I sighed as I took one more glance around the room. "Let's head out," I said to Wild Card. "There's nothing else to see here."

CHAPTER NINE

CHARLIE
Wednesday, 11:35 a.m.

By the time we walked from the victim's room down to the hotel's parking garage, Wild Card had searched his phone and found a local camera shop only a few blocks away. With almost half an hour to spare before Tasha would be at the morgue, I agreed we could visit the camera shop. Wild Card followed me there in his rental.

The store owner recognized Bernard Bacon's photo and even located the receipt for the memory card he'd bought Friday night. More interesting, the owner remembered Bernard's portfolio and the conversation they'd shared. The camera shop was small enough that, not surprisingly, they didn't get a lot of walk-in customers.

The shop owner told us Bernard was a people watcher—and an insomniac. Most of Bernard's photographs were described as night scenes, photos of people outside nightclubs or of homeless camps. Bernard entertained himself when he couldn't sleep by taking pictures. The insomnia explained both why Bernard's bed was still made and why there were tripod marks on his balcony. But there couldn't have been much people watching activity at three in the morning, especially in that area with Bernard's crappy hotel view.

Wild Card shadowing me came in handy when he asked questions about Bernard's camera equipment. I took notes while they chatted about special lenses and accessories, detailing equipment beyond my comprehension. What I did absorb was that Wild Card was impressed with Bernard's camera enough to buy the same model for himself. By the time we left, Wild Card had a shopping bag overflowing with two thousand dollars' worth of electronics.

I pointed at his shopping bag. "Do you even know how to use all that?"

"Yup. I used to take pictures all the time. Even sold a few." He set the bag on the floor behind the driver's seat of his SUV before shutting the door. "But my old camera has been acting up. And I haven't had a lot of shopping time to buy a new one."

"But two thousand dollars? Seems a bit much."

"This model has built-in Wi-Fi, so I can upload pictures from anywhere. Might come in handy with all the traveling lately."

"Wait—didn't you buy the same model as Bernard's?"

"Yeah. So?"

"If the killer took the victim's camera, maybe it was because Bernard took pictures the killer didn't want anyone to see."

Wild Card nodded, latching on to my theory. "But the camera was Wi-Fi equipped, so Bernard could've uploaded the photos to a cloud drive already."

I called Ford and gave him the information. I had no idea if it would lead anywhere, but it was one more string we could tug on. After hanging up, I looked at Wild Card. "I'm heading to the morgue next. You're not one of those *puke at the sight of an autopsy* types, are you?"

"Don't know. Never saw one. I've seen my share of dead bodies, though, so doubtful."

"A lot of people make that assumption. That's not exactly how it works, though."

I slid into my car and turned over the engine, but waited for Wild Card to climb into his SUV. When he was ready, I pulled away from the curb with him following close behind.

~*~*~

Somehow Wild Card managed to stay behind me through the lunch-hour traffic. He parked beside me in the city's parking garage and we followed Beast across the garage, into the elevator, then off the elevator, down a hallway, and into the morgue reception area. Beast made a sharp turn, padding over to the far wall and throwing himself down on the cool tile floor.

"I take it he's been here before?" Wild Card asked while grinning at Beast.

"I was hoping you'd visit, big guy," Huey, the morgue's receptionist said to Beast as he maneuvered around the counter and squatted to give

Beast an enthusiastic ear scratching. "I've got a present for you."

Based on Beast's snuffling at Huey's other hand, Beast had already smelled the present. Huey handed Beast a brownish-colored bone. Beast looked happy as he slobbered and chomped on one end.

"That's not..." I started to say, pointing at the bone.

"Human?" Huey asked with a wicked grin. Huey was a hell of a morgue receptionist, but he looked more like a bouncer in a biker bar. When Huey smiled, I sometimes itched to pull my gun.

My tummy rolled, and I held my breath and looked up at the ceiling, away from the bone, trying to keep myself from puking.

"No, it's not human," Huey said, laughing as he walked behind the counter. "It's a rawhide soaked in beef stock."

Wild Card looked at me, smirking. "It does feel a little gruesome watching Beast chew on a bone in a morgue."

I shook off the icky feeling and looked back at Huey. "Is Tasha here?"

"Yeah. She's working the autopsy for Ford's jumper. Bernard Bacon." Huey laughed. "Poor guy. What a name."

I glanced at Wild Card, then back at Huey. "How long ago did Tasha start the autopsy?"

"She got here early." Huey glanced at Wild Card, then back at me. "She should be at your favorite part."

I didn't say anything as I walked through the next set of doors, down the hall to room three, and grabbed plastic cover gowns for myself and Wild Card. A few minutes later we were wrapped and ready, and I led us into the autopsy room.

I heard Wild Card choke, then gag, then the doors swing open again as he ran out. At the table in the middle of the room, Tasha was cranking the rib cage open. It took me a good year to be able to stomach watching a full autopsy. Some cops like Ford didn't even try. They just waited for the results to be emailed over.

"Anything in the external physical exam I should know about?" I asked as I walked over.

"I thought this was Ford's case?" Tasha said, tipping her head back to make eye contact through the splatter face shield.

"It is Ford's case. I told him I'd check in with you."

Tasha shrugged, focusing her attention back on Bernard. "Nothing overly interesting, except a bruise on his back."

"Can I see?"

"Now's not a good time to roll the body, but I took pictures." Tasha inclined her head toward her computer along the far wall. "Feel free to scroll through them."

Walking across the room, I started clicking through the pictures, pausing to view one of Bernard's back, which showed the bruise Tasha had mentioned. It was a long reddish-purple marking on his lower back, just above his buttocks.

Bernard was average height and the hotel railing was high. The mark on his back would be too low to be caused by the balcony railing if he'd hit it while flipping backward over its edge.

Another scenario flashed through my brain.

I left the autopsy room and retrieved Wild Card and Huey, leading them into one of the lab rooms. The room was empty of people but had a high island-styled workstation on the far side. The workstation was close to the same height as the balcony railing.

I looked at Huey and pointed to the spot in front of the workstation, turning him so his back was toward the countertop. "Wild Card, pretend this countertop is the balcony railing and try to throw Huey over it."

Both Huey and Wild Card grinned at each other, happy to play demonstration dummies. Wild Card grabbed Huey and shoved—but Huey didn't budge.

"Huey, you have to play along," Tasha said from the doorway as she stripped her bloody gloves and tucked them in the biohazard bin. "Let Wild Card move you."

Wild Card tried again, but when Huey bumped against the countertop it hit him at mid back, too high to replicate the bruise on Bernard.

"Switch roles," Tasha said, moving them into position. Tasha moved Wild Card a few feet in front of the counter. Next, she guided Huey a good fifteen feet away. When she had them positioned, she tipped her head back to look up at Huey. "Okay, charge Wild Card."

Huey bolted forward.

Wild Card's face morphed from his usual goofy grin to *oh-shit* as he held his position.

Huey slammed into Wild Card, grabbing him by the front of his shirt and launched him up, then over, the workstation. On the other side of the island, Wild Card bounced off the far wall of cabinets before he dropped out of sight to the floor between the cabinets and the workstation.

"Oops," Huey said as Tasha and I gaped at the counter.

I waited, but when I didn't hear or see Wild Card, I called out in my sweetest and most guilt-laced voice, "*Cooper*?" I walked around the workstation. "Are you okay?"

"I don't want to play with Huey no more," Wild Card said as he stretched a hand up to grab the countertop and pull himself upright. His other hand massaged his lower back as he stood.

Tasha, brimming with excitement, ran over. "It worked! Look, it's a match!" Without asking for permission, she pulled the back of Wild Card's t-shirt up to his armpits. She used one hand to hold the shirt as she ran her other hand across the skin on his lower back just above his jeans.

"Uh, Charlie? What's happening?" Wild Card asked as he squirmed away from Tasha.

"The big bruise you're going to have on your back matches the bruise Tasha found on Bernard."

"Meaning what? That Huey killed Bernard?" Wild Card asked as he pulled his shirt down.

"I have an alibi!" Huey said.

"Do you even know the time of death?" Tasha asked Huey.

"Doesn't matter. I'm sure I have an alibi."

Huey was looking a little pale so I decided to let him off the hook. "Relax. I know you're not the killer." I turned back to Tasha. "Any defensive wounds?"

"Hard to say. When Bernard hit the concrete, he landed on his stomach. Parts of him sort-of... *popped*. A six-story fall destroys a lot of evidence." In normal Tasha fashion, she talked with her hands flailing around, representing the plunge then splaying her fingers apart when he hit the ground. "Now, if he would've bounced," she demonstrated with her hands again, him hitting the concrete, bouncing off the ground and flipping over like a pancake, "even the bruise on his back would've been destroyed. Lucky for us, he didn't bounce." Tasha smiled at me as she pushed her glasses up the bridge of her nose.

"How'd the killer get into the hotel room?" Wild Card asked as he took another step away from Tasha.

"The hallway camera on the sixth floor went out of service five minutes before Bernard died," I answered. "The killer likely used a laser light. Then he either stole a keycard or convinced Bernard to open the door."

"Room service," Huey said, nodding. "That's how they get inside the room in the movies."

"Okay, maybe I do need to get your alibi," I said to Huey, crossing my arms over my chest.

Huey pointed toward the doors. "Hear that? The phone is ringing. I better get that." He hurried out.

"Huey's not really a suspect, is he?" Tasha asked.

"No! Of course not." I turned back to Tasha. "I'm just messing with him."

"Oh, good. You had me worried for a minute." She fisted a hand and punched me in the arm. "You're so funny."

"Okay." I glanced at Wild Card then back at Tasha. "Thank you. That's very kind of you."

"You're welcome. But I better get back to room three."

"Before you go, I need a favor."

Tasha studied my face, blinking rapidly as she often did when she was thinking. "Why do you have that look on your face?"

"What look?"

"The look that says I'm not going to like doing this favor, but you're not giving me a choice."

"Remember when I cleared your friend Terrance of a murder rap and got him out of prison?"

Her eyes narrowed, knowing something was coming. "Yeah..."

"Well, I need the details on a car accident victim, but you can't let anyone know I was asking about it."

"Did I do the autopsy?"

"I have no idea."

"When was the car accident?"

"I have no idea."

"Do you know who the victim was?"

"No, but I know her husband's name. I'm guessing since they were married, they shared the same last name. Barrett. That's the name."

Tasha's eyes bugged out. "You want *Councilmember Barrett's wife's file*?"

"Is that a problem?"

"*If I get caught, it is*!" Tasha pushed her glasses up her nose again.

"Why? You can look at any file you want, can't you?"

"The state medical examiner himself signed off on Mrs. Barrett's death certificate. I'm not even sure an autopsy was performed."

"How can that be? As the driver in a fatal accident, she should've at least had a partial autopsy."

"She wasn't the driver. Her husband was."

"Oh." I tilted my head, thinking, then realized I was starting to mimic Beast and straightened. "And the husband wasn't injured in the accident?"

"No. But I saw pictures on the news of the accident. The passenger side of the car was demolished from hitting the concrete pylon under an overpass. Based on the damage to that side of the vehicle I suspect Mrs. Barrett died instantly."

"Did the media say what caused the accident?"

"Councilmember Barrett spoke to the media himself. He said they were having a pleasant conversation on their way to dinner when his wife suddenly grabbed the steering wheel and jerked it toward her. Barrett was unsure why she turned the car toward the pylon, but speculated she must've seen an animal or something in the road."

"And let me guess, the state police were in charge of the scene?"

"Yes. Why is that important?"

"No reason." I patted her shoulder on my way past, heading to the door. "Never mind pulling the report. I doubt there's much there. I have another way to get the information."

"Oh, goodness, I'm glad to hear that. I like my job. It's so relaxing."

Wild Card and I stopped to look back at Tasha. Though she'd stripped her bloody gown, face shield and gloves, she was still wearing the plastic booties over her shoes which were splattered with blood. Not to mention that ten minutes ago, she was cracking a cadaver's chest open.

Wild Card shoved me through the doors before I could comment.

When we got to the parking ramp, I stopped to make a phone call. "Andrew, it's Kid. I need a favor."

Andrew laughed on the other line. "What else is new. Hit me."

"I need everything you can pull on Councilmember Barrett's car accident."

"The one that killed his wife?"

"Do you know of another accident he was in?"

"Be nice. You're the one calling *me* for a favor, remember?"

"Right. Sorry. Can you get me the info?"

"Sure. Where do you want me to send it?"

"I don't want you to send it. I need it loaded on a flash drive and hand delivered. Call me when it's ready and we can arrange a meet."

"Very cloak and dagger. I like it." Andrew disconnected without salutations.

"What's this Councilmember stuff about, anyway?" Wild Card asked.

I was about to answer when I felt someone watching us. "Get in my car. *Now*." I opened the door for Beast who jumped into the driver's seat, then into the back as Wild Card rushed to the other side and slid into the passenger seat. In less than thirty seconds we were all inside the car, and I squealed the tires as I sped down the two garage levels and out the exit. Two blocks away, I pulled the car to the curb and parked.

"I don't know what just happened but I didn't see anyone tailing us," Wild Card said.

I pulled my phone and called Huey.

"Miami-Dade Medical Center."

I rechecked my phone's display, then moved it back to my ear. "You realize you just answered your cellphone with the morgue's greeting, right?"

"It's easier to answer all the phones the same. My friends and family don't mind. Did you forget something?"

"I think someone was in the parking ramp when I left. Do me a favor? Keep an eye on Tasha and don't let her leave without a security escort?"

"You got it. I'll handle it myself."

"Thanks." I disconnected and called Ford, putting him on speaker after he answered. "Change of plans. I'm not coming back to the precinct this afternoon. Can you check on the suspicious death cases for me? I completely forgot to ask Tasha about them when I was at the morgue."

"Already done. Quille and I reviewed the reports about thirty minutes ago. And I've got Abe and Natalie tracking down whether Bernard uploaded any photos to a cloud drive."

"Great. What about the car with all the parking tickets across the street from the hotel?"

"I left a message for the car's owner. Haven't heard back yet. Owen Flint. He's a real estate developer. Abe couldn't find a connection between Owen Flint and Bernard Bacon."

I glanced over at Wild Card. He was staring at my phone.

"Kid? You still there?" Ford asked.

"Yeah, I'm still here. Did you send the forensic team back to the hotel?"

"After I convinced Quille to sign off, yeah. He wasn't happy about it, though."

"Quille's about to be less happy. Have the team do a sweep on and around Flint's car. I need any trace, no matter how small, logged into evidence."

"You're joking, right? You don't seriously expect to run forensics on a public sidewalk, do you? Quille's never going to sign off on that."

"Tell Quille that Owen Flint is the guy behind the dentist office case my cousin is investigating. He'll sign off."

"What dentist office case?"

"I'll explain later. But can you oversee the scene and have the car impounded?"

"You think the car's owner killed Bernard?"

"I don't know. Owen Flint fell off my cousin's radar. We've been looking for him, but..." My phone beeped, indicating another call. "Gotta go." I hit the button on the steering column to end the call, then pushed the green button to answer the next one. "You got what I need, Andrew?"

"You know I do."

"Meet me at the club. I'll buy you a drink."

"I'll be there in ten."

"I feel as lost as Ford sounded," Wild Card said from the passenger seat.

"Call Kelsey. Let her know to call off the search for Owen Flint and tell her about the abandoned car."

I pulled into traffic and drove toward the club.

CHAPTER TEN

KELSEY
Wednesday, 12:30 p.m.

I returned to the outdoor lounge, handing Tech the lemonade he'd asked for. "Cooper called. Owen Flint's car was abandoned near a hotel where Charlie's investigating a homicide."

Tech watched me as I sat in the chair next to him. "Are they connected? Owen Flint and Charlie's homicide?"

"Not sure yet. The victim was an insomniac photographer. Her running theory is the victim took a picture *on accident*—which resulted in him being thrown off his sixth-floor balcony *on purpose*."

"Ouch," Tyler said from his sentry position just inside the shade of the lounge's canopy.

The sun was inching toward Tyler as it moved westward. He'd likely have to shift to a new spot soon. Bones and Tech had ditched their sleeveless leather club jackets as soon as we hit Miami weather, but thus far, Tyler had remained in jeans, biker boots, and a t-shirt under his leather cut.

"You know, Tyler, if you lost the jacket, the jeans, and the boots, you might actually enjoy the sunshine."

"I worked my ass off to earn this cut. I'm not taking it off just because it's a little hot outside."

"Suit yourself." I turned back to Tech who was grinning. "Is there anything I can do besides watch this boring video of patients coming and going in the dentist office?"

"Not really. You said you weren't taking on any new cases, and I already have people assigned to everything else."

"There's got to be something."

Tech raised an eyebrow at me. "How bored are you?"

"Bored enough that I spent the last hour shopping online for a new coffee pot."

"Do we need a new coffee pot?"

"No. That's how bored I am."

"You could shop for a swimsuit coverup for Katie," Tech said, throwing dagger eyes toward the pool.

After Pops and Hattie left the mansion this morning, the swimwear shifted from conservative to barely there. Alex wore a string bikini top with a sarong around his waist. Though he wore the most fabric, the same top on one of the girls would've crossed the line. Katie and Bridget wore bikini tops that covered enough of their top half, but their bottoms were mere strips of fabric.

Anne was the only one who remained conservatively dressed, wearing a one-piece swimsuit. Luckily all the kids except Mackenzie were too young to really notice. But Nicholas was only a year or two away from noticing girls in a different way, so best to address the issue now.

I picked up my phone from the coffee table and focused its camera on the pool area, zooming in on Bridget as she bent over. I snapped a picture.

Tyler heard my phone and chuckled as he glanced back at me.

I attached the picture to a text and hit send. A few minutes later, I got a thumbs up reply from Charlie. "Okay, now what?" I asked Tech, setting the phone down.

"Go play poker with the boys," Tech said. "Take a break."

I looked over to where Uncle Hank sat with his poker buddies playing cards. It was their standing Wednesday game. The regular meetup had started long before Jack, Pimples, and Juan had retired from the police force. Pimples, otherwise known as Brody, had been Uncle Hank's partner for twenty years. I used to enjoy watching them work together.

When Pimples retired, Uncle Hank took a position as a training officer. He said he wanted to teach the new generation the right way of doing things before he retired. Personally, I think it was an excuse to hold off retiring. Aunt Suzanne was a handful to deal with and the thought of spending every day together likely had Uncle Hank clutching at his chest.

I looked back at Tech. "They won't let me play poker with them."

Bones walked over and sat in the chair next to me. "It's just a friendly game. They're not even playing for money."

I cupped my hands around my mouth. "Hey, boys Can I play cards?"

"*No!*" Pimples, Uncle Hank, Juan, and Jack yelled in unison.

Joe Jr., another one of the players and a former cop from several generations before everyone else, had fallen asleep and startled awake. Throwing himself forward in his chair, he dropped his cards and yelled, "*Bingo!*"

I laughed before turning back to Tech and Bones. "See? They won't let me play."

"What did you do?" Tyler asked over his shoulder. "Cheat?"

"Of course not. They just don't appreciate the fact Lady Luck shines her light on me more than others."

"So... You didn't cheat, but they think you did?" Tech asked.

"Uncle Hank knows I didn't cheat. But the rest of them, yeah, they think I cheated."

"I'm going to walk the perimeter," Tyler said. "You two," he pointed between Bones and me, "watch the kids until I get back."

"Don't we have three men already patrolling?" I asked.

"And Katie, Whiskey, and Anne are with the kids," Bones said. "How many more guards do they need?"

"Just watch them," Tyler snapped before stomping through the decorative grass to take a shortcut around the house.

"I think the heat's getting to him," I whispered to Bones as I glanced over at the kids.

Mackenzie sat alone on a far chaise lounge, ready to bolt any minute. Liam, on the other hand, was in the shallow end of the pool with Sara, tossing a beach ball back and forth. Whiskey tossed a weighted ring into the pool and Nicholas disappeared under the water, racing to retrieve it before it sank to the bottom.

Bones shifted in his chair and propped his sandaled feet onto the coffee table. "Any luck tracking Miguel or Santiago Remirez?"

I nodded toward Tech, letting him explain.

"We found Miguel," Tech said. "He's with his wife and two sons in their California cliffside mansion. When I tracked Miguel's condo in Atlanta, I found a shell company that led back to the California property, and another condo in Vegas. Miguel appears to be spending most of his time with the family, but he did take a private jet to Texas yesterday to check in on the textile plant. It was only a day trip, though."

"What about Santiago and Sebrina?" Bones asked.

I shook my head. "They're still in the wind."

"Jackson reached out to a contact in Mexico," Bones said. "His buddy is digging around to see if Santiago or Sebrina are at the family compound."

"Smart, but doubtful," I said. "Charlie was right when she said I'd underestimated the Remirez cartel.

I have a feeling when we see them again, it won't be a pleasant reunion."

"What about Shipwreck?" Tech asked. "Think we'll see him again?"

I couldn't help but smile. "I think Shipwreck is either hiding or dead. Neither the Remirez cartel nor Sebrina had any further use for him. He was expendable."

"What's the plan then?" Bones asked.

"I don't have one yet."

"Bullshit," Tech said, swiveling in his chair to face me. "You've had nothing but thinking time this week. I can practically see your brain tossing around strategies. You're just not sure which one you'll need."

"Maybe," I said with a shrug. "But it doesn't matter. Our immediate priority is to shut down the trafficking ring and to find Mr. Tricky. Any new sightings of him in Michigan?"

"Nothing," Bones said. "I talked to Donovan this morning. He was up all night, guarding headquarters. He said nothing happened the rest of the night."

"It doesn't make sense," I said more to myself than anyone. "Why? Why did Mr. Tricky go to Michigan?"

"I don't like it," Tyler said, returning from his patrol. "We're missing something."

"Where are we with installing the new security equipment?" Tech asked.

"Some of the exterior cameras are mounted, but not wired yet. They should have the rest of it installed over the next few days. I'm hoping at least two of the cameras will be live by tonight."

"Why is it taking so long?" Tech asked.

Tyler waved a hand at the massive house. "This place wasn't exactly designed to retro fit security cameras. There are too many balconies and privacy walls on the mansion. Then there's the perimeter fencing embedded with thick patches of tall grass and bushes. It's been a challenge finding locations where a camera will even capture enough space to make installing it worth it."

I glanced at the kids again, but other than Mackenzie they were still playing.

"Wait—" Tyler said, looking around. "Didn't Carl come back from the bathroom yet?"

"I don't know," I answered. "I didn't see him, but I was watching the kids."

"When I say 'watch the kids'—*that includes Carl! That always includes Carl.*"

"Relax," Bones said, leaning back. "I'm sure he's inside with Aunt Suzanne."

Tyler pointed to the small building behind the tiki lounge. "He used the pool bathroom!"

Unfortunately, I knew Carl well enough to know he took his daily poop at precisely nine every morning. If Carl went into the bathroom before Tyler started his perimeter walk, then he would've had plenty of time to pee by now. And if he'd gone inside the mansion, he would've walked right past us.

I turned toward the pool bathrooms but heard a boat engine start. My head snapped back to Tyler. We stared at each other, silently communicating for a split second before he ran toward the pool. I ran in the opposite direction, toward the private dock on the side of the property.

I pulled my gun just prior to rounding the corner on the stone pathway, nearly crashing into two security guards who were running from the front of the house toward the docks. We all turned, running along the narrow landscape path, with me on the guards' heels.

When the path opened I heard the guards groan before they stepped aside to let me pass. I ran down the dock and leapt onto the boat, grabbing the steering wheel to stop myself from launching off the other side. In my leap and land, I'd slammed into Carl, knocking him to the floor of the boat.

I lowered the throttle to the idle position, then turned off the engine. The engine puttered, then died. If Carl had remembered to untie the boat from the dock, he would've been long gone before I'd gotten to him.

I looked down at a pouting Carl. "Do you know how dangerous taking a boat out on the ocean is? What if you'd gotten lost?"

"You'd find me, remember? You have the tracker," Carl said, holding up his beaded necklace which had a built-in tracker.

"That only works if you stay near cell towers, Carl," Tech said from the dock. "How many towers do you think are in the middle of the Atlantic Ocean?"

Carl stared out across the water, then looked back at Tech. "We should change my tracker to run on satellite."

"Or maybe, *you should stay on land*!" I yelled as I climbed off the boat, taking the keys with me.

At the end of the dock, Bones grinned at me. "Can we take the boat out for a spin?"

"Knock yourself out." I tossed him the keys. "And consider yourself Carl's official babysitter for the rest of the day."

"Now wait a minute," Bones said.

I didn't stop to let him argue. I followed the trail back to the lounge, confirming that the pool area was now empty. I grabbed my phone and laptop before walking into the house. Once inside, I called out the all clear and Uncle Hank stepped around the corner, holstering his weapon. Seconds later, the house went from silent to noisy as everyone re-emerged.

Chapter Eleven

CHARLIE
Wednesday, 1:04 p.m.

Arriving at The Outer Layer, Wild Card and I rode the elevator up to the third floor.

"So, who's this Andrew guy we're meeting?" Wild Card asked.

"He's a reporter. Works for the Daily Sun Miami Newsbeat. He's helped me with a few cases in the past in exchange for tidbits of news here and there. Don't tell Quille. He's been hunting for the department leak for years."

"Isn't that a big no-no?" Wild Card asked as we stepped off the elevator.

"Sure. But I only give Andrew details when they'll eventually be public knowledge. Besides, he usually has the answers already, he just needs me to confirm the facts." I spotted Andrew at the bar and started his way, talking to Wild Card over my shoulder. "Not to mention it's super fun to hear Quille screaming about the anonymous source when he reads the paper."

"You ever going to tell Quille it's you?"

"Maybe when he retires, but not while he's in a position to assign me a stack of paperwork as punishment." I pulled out the barstool next to Andrew. "Andrew, this is Wild Card. We can speak freely in front of him."

"Sounds good. What are we drinking?" Andrew said, sliding a flash drive in front of me.

I pocketed the flash drive and held up three fingers to the bartender.

"Hey, Kid," Bruce said, tossing the bar rag over his shoulder. "The usual?"

"Yup. Thanks, Bruce."

"What's your usual?" Wild Card asked, sitting on my other side.

"I have a few, but they're all based on the time of day. Since it's midday, my usual is a Screwdriver. Vodka is harder to smell on someone's breath, the orange juice gives my system a sugar kick. It also isn't strong enough to knock me on my ass and send me to bed early."

"I've seen you pound back more drinks than someone four times your size," Bruce said as he set the drinks in front of us. "I don't think there's a drink strong enough to knock you on your ass."

"Well, seeing as she's wearing a gun," Andrew said looking over at me and winking, "let's not test that theory, aye?"

Bruce laughed before asking me, "You need anything else, Kid?"

"No, the drinks will do. Where's Garth? He usually greets me at the elevator when I'm in the building."

"He's been upstairs most of the day. Mr. Baker is in a supremely cantankerous mood. You might want to stay clear."

Wild Card snorted. "Kid? Stay clear? That's not her MO. She's more likely to run upstairs and start poking the bear."

The thought did have a certain appeal. Winding Baker up when he was in one of his moods was entertaining.

"So, what's the flash drive all about?" Andrew asked, pulling me from my thoughts of torturing Baker.

"Before I answer that, what's your impression of Councilmember Barrett?" I asked Andrew.

"Randall Barrett is a total dickhead."

Wild Card laughed, pointing a thumb toward Andrew. "I like him."

I ignored Wild Card and focused on Andrew. "Any dirt on Barrett?"

"Nothing. Not a damn speck. And I've been trying to get something on the guy for years."

"What's your interest in Barrett?"

Andrew took his time before answering, taking a long drink first. "Cops work on hunches. They follow their gut instincts. Follow the evidence. But for reporters, we usually follow the story from one interview to the next. Building the story until we have enough information to publish."

"But that's not the case with Barrett?" I asked as I picked up my glass.

"Nope." He downed the rest of his drink and motioned to Bruce for another. "A few years back, I pissed off my boss and he assigned me to interview guests as they came and went from some fancy-schmancy fundraiser as punishment. It was boring as hell."

"I bet."

"But as I was packing up for the night, I saw Barrett and his wife exit through the alley. They were hurrying down the sidewalk toward the parking garage. At first, Mrs. Barrett's ass was the only thing I noticed. I mean, *wow*, the dress she wore was backless right to the tops of her round—"

I held up my hand to cut him off. "I get it."

"Sorry," Andrew said, grinning. "Anyway. Once I pulled my eyes from her ass, alarm bells started going off. I grabbed my camera and rushed to follow them."

"Why?" Wild Card asked.

"Something was off, man. The way she walked, leaning away from her husband like she was cowering. Barrett, stiff shouldered and holding her in a firm grip by her upper arm, hurrying her away." Andrew reached over and grabbed my bicep, tightening his fingers around my arm in demonstration.

Though he wasn't hurting me, I removed his hand from my arm. "Then what?"

"I started taking pictures even though there was really nothing to see. Barrett must've heard my camera because he slowed. He let go of her and wrapped his arm around his wife's waist. Then he whispered something to her before he turned so they both faced me. He waved, like it was photo op and

Mrs. Barrett stood there with this perfect smile on her face, but..."

I looked down at the bar top and whispered, "Her eyes told a different story."

"I kept the picture." Andrew dug in his attaché and pulled out a photo. "It's haunted me. I followed the Barretts for weeks after I took it. I even tried to talk to Mrs. Barrett once, but her bodyguard got between us."

"Why would a councilmember's wife need a bodyguard?" Wild Card asked.

"She wouldn't," I said as I studied the photo of the couple. Mrs. Barret had the face and body of a movie star, but her eyes were absent of any real feeling. Like hope had been beaten out of her years ago. "She wouldn't need a bodyguard for protection, but a man like Barrett might hire someone to keep tabs on her."

"Yeah," Andrew said, nodding. "You're getting what I'm saying. Something was off."

Wild Card took the photo from me. "Any pictures of her bodyguard?"

Andrew dug in his bag until he found another photo, handing it to Wild Card.

"Yeah, he's not a bodyguard," Wild Card said, snorting. "He's a thug. Look how he's squared off, spoiling for a fight. More like a bouncer than a bodyguard." He handed me the photo.

The man in the photo was all muscle from his thick neck to his wide thighs. While he was dressed in nice clothes, he was facing off with the photographer rather than escorting Mrs. Barrett, who stood off to the side in the background of the photo, to somewhere safe.

"After the accident, did you investigate? Find anything new?" I asked, setting the photo down.

"Tried, but nothing to dig up. One of the freelance photographers called me about five minutes after the accident happened. I went straight to the scene, but there was nothing to see. The state police closed ranks around Barrett. His wife was shipped off to the hospital. The only time Barrett spoke to the press was the next morning, when he staged the kids beside him to," Andrew paused to air quote, "*grieve his wife.*"

"Wait," I said. "Why the air quotes?"

"No reason," Andrew snapped, reaching for his drink.

"Don't stop now," Wild Card said. "Spit it out."

Andrew shook his head as he set his drink down. "You'll think I'm nuts, just like my boss."

"I already know you're crazy," I said, elbowing him. "But you're the good kind of crazy. Tell us anyway."

Andrew looked around, then leaned closer. "I'm not sure she's dead."

I had no idea what Andrew had been about to say, but stating Mrs. Barrett might not be dead was nowhere in the vicinity of possibilities. "Come again?"

"Told you! You think I'm nuts."

"I don't think you're nuts, but I thought the state medical examiner signed off on her death. That's not true?"

"That's what Barrett told the press. But death certificates are a matter of public record, and when I went to pull a copy, no one could find it."

"Maybe the ME's office was behind on their paperwork."

"Went back weeks later, they said they must've misplaced it."

"Then they ordered a new record, right? They reached out to the ME's office?"

"I tried everyone I could think of and couldn't get a copy."

"Okay, wait a sec," Wild Card said, leaning on the bar to look over at Andrew. "If Mrs. Barrett is alive, where would Barrett hide her?"

"With the money he now controls? He could have her stashed anywhere. But that car was totaled. If she's alive, she might not be whole. Hell, she could be breathing through a machine for all I know."

"How wealthy is he?" I asked.

Andrew shook his head. "It was Mrs. Barrett who was rich. Family money. Old money. Her maiden name was Sophia Catrella. She inherited her father's money a few years back. I haven't been able to find out if Barrett inherited after her death announcement or if the money was put into a trust for the kids. Guess it doesn't matter since he's now their legal guardian."

At the mention of kids, Wild Card's head snapped in my direction. "What kids?"

Andrew slid another photo down the bar toward Wild Card. "Mackenzie and Liam Barrett."

"Interesting," Wild Card said after looking at the photo.

I was hoping Andrew wouldn't notice Wild Card's hands fisting or his shoulders tensing.

"Mrs. Barrett was a widower before she married Barrett. The kids are from her first marriage."

"Do you have anything on the first husband or his family?"

"No. Never occurred to me to look into it. Should I?"

"Might be a dead end, but doesn't hurt to dig around."

Andrew glanced at me with narrowed eyes. "You ready to share why you're so interested in Barrett?"

I looked around the bar, but no one was paying any attention. Bruce was drying glasses at the far end while chatting with a couple. None of the other tables were close enough to hear. "If I share, I need your word you won't talk to anyone."

"You know me, Kid. I won't go to print until you give me the all clear."

"That's the thing, I can't promise I'll *ever* give you the all clear."

Andrew leaned back, studying me. "Okay."

"That's it? Just, okay? No big deal?" I asked.

Andrew chuckled. "Over the years, I've squashed multiple stories of a female vigilante in Miami. The supposed victim was always some asshole who deserved it. Usually suspected of domestic abuse or pimping women out, sometimes even child abuse. The way I figure, the woman was doing Miami a favor. Taking out the trash. I've got a kid sister who went through some shit, and let's just say the legal way didn't exactly work in her favor."

I kept my face unresponsive.

"I'm not stupid, Kid. If you do something to protect the wife—if she's even alive—or something to get the kids away from that asshole, I'm not going to print a story that works against you or them. You have my word."

I looked over my shoulder at Wild Card. He shrugged.

I looked back at Andrew. "The kids ran away. Barrett is working with brass to keep it quiet, but keeping it quiet is also working in the kids' favor. That's why I don't want the story to go to print. It will make it harder for them to hide."

"Shit," Andrew said, physically jolting back in his seat. "How the hell hasn't that leaked yet?"

"That's what has me worried. Barrett seems determined to get the boy back, but he was planning on shipping the girl off to boarding school. He might want to keep it quiet because the kids could incriminate him in something."

Andrew nodded. "And if you're advocating for the kids, but running blind, then the kids aren't talking."

"Would you?" Wild Card asked. "If you were in their shoes?"

"Hell no. But I'm also not a teenage girl towing my baby brother through the streets. Her options are limited."

"Not anymore," I said, downing my drink before setting the glass on the bar. "I need to bounce. I'll check in with a few sources on the possibility of the wife still being alive. But remember, mum's the word until I say otherwise. If I dig up anything new, I'll reach out."

"You know how to find me," Andrew said, turning to raise a hand for another drink.

"Bruce," I called out. "Put the drinks on my tab and give yourself a generous tip."

"Sure thing. Be safe out there."

"I'll do my best," I said as I gathered my purse and started toward the elevators.

Wild Card hurried to walk beside me. "Andrew seems like one of the good guys, but..."

"Yeah, I know. Even though he's been trustworthy in the past, telling him was a risk. We'll just have to hope he keeps his mouth shut."

"Fuck that," Wild Card said, pulling his phone. "I'll let Bones know the kids might be in danger and to plan an escape route if needed."

~*~*~

While Wild Card stayed in the fifth-floor hallway talking to Bones and Uncle Hank, I walked down the hall toward Baker's office. Halfway there I heard Baker yelling, and before I reached the door it opened.

Garth walked out carrying two duffle bags and towing a suitcase on wheels. He looked at me and grinned, but continued down the hall. Evie stomped her heels behind Garth, tossing a glare in my direction as she lifted her nose in the air to snub me as she passed.

Baker stepped out into the hall, throwing his hands in the air. "This is ridiculous! You know that, right?"

"Oh, look," Evie said, pivoting to point a finger at me. "Your girlfriend is here."

"Whoa!" I said, taking a step back in shock. "What the hell?"

"Ignore her," Baker snapped. "She's lost her *damn mind*!"

Evie stomped onward, catching up with Garth as he turned the corner toward the private rooms.

I pointed down the hall where they'd disappeared. "She's not seriously going to stay in one of the sex rooms, is she?" I asked Baker.

Baker glared at me but didn't say anything.

"How exactly did she hear about you and me?"

"She asked if we'd ever been a thing. I should've lied." Baker walked back into his office and slammed the door shut.

"What did I miss?" Wild Card asked as he walked toward me, pocketing his phone.

"Baker and I used to keep each other company. Evie found out, and she's not happy."

Wild Card smiled, but didn't say anything.

"Let's leave."

Wild Card placed his hands on his hips, looking down at me with a scowl. "You're kidding."

"What? This isn't my problem."

"They're your friends."

"So? They need to sort this out on their own."

Wild Card pressed his lips together.

"Look, I can't really deal with that," I said, pointing down the hallway toward the sex rooms. "Whatever that is, it doesn't even make sense to me. Who cares if Baker and I used to have sex? Why does it matter?"

"Because she thought the two of you were friends."

"One thing has nothing to do with the other."

"You sure about that? Then why didn't you tell her about your past with Baker?"

I scrunched my nose in annoyance. Wild Card was right. I didn't tell Evie because I figured she'd get upset. I wasn't the jealous type by nature, but I'd experienced the cruel emotion before. It left a nasty aftertaste, "Okay, fine. I'll talk to Evie. But you need to go talk to Baker."

"Baker and I aren't exactly friends."

"Baker doesn't have friends. He has business associates." I followed the hallway, down and around the corner to the next door which separated the sex rooms from the offices. Using my security badge, I swiped the card through the reader, before pushing the door open.

On the other side of the door I saw Garth leaning against the wall, still wearing a grin.

Evie came out of the second door on the left and shuddered. "Are they all that horrible?"

"Some are worse than others," I answered for Garth. "You don't want to see the last two rooms."

"I'm not talking to you," Evie said, using her keycard to unlock the third door, disappearing inside the room.

I looked over at Garth. "Any suggestions here? I'm a little out of my element."

Garth shrugged. "A little honesty might help."

"Isn't that what got us into this mess? Baker deciding to be honest with her?"

"*What the hell is that supposed to mean*?" Evie said, storming out of the room and charging toward me. "Are you saying this is my fault?"

"Is that an option?" I asked.

Garth placed a hand over his face, shaking his head.

"*You knew I liked Baker*!" Evie shouted while pointing at me.

I watched her finger, only inches away from my chest, but maintained my cool.

"You knew I liked him, and yet, you didn't tell me!"

"*Tell you what*? That for years Baker and I would occasionally hook up? Why do you care? It never meant anything."

"You say that now, but—"

"*No, Evie*! There is nothing between Baker and me, not like that at least. There was no cuddling. No talking until the wee hours of the morning sharing our *feelings*. No dinners out or flowers on special occasions. It was one-hundred-percent booty calls. And if one of us was already with someone else when we got the call, no big deal."

"That's such bullshit." Evie started to point at me again, but Garth grabbed her shoulder, shaking his head at her. She took a step back, not willing to test how far I'd allow her to jab that finger in my direction. "A woman doesn't just have a casual fling with a guy like Baker. She'd get attached."

"To be honest, Evie, a lot of women have had casual relationships with Baker. But they knew upfront that for him it was just sex. And if they got clingy, they were gone. Cut from his sex roster." I walked over to her and grabbed her arm to get her to stop pacing. "Until you."

"We haven't even had sex," Evie said, knocking my hand away.

"And that right there proves you are different. Did you ever stop to wonder why he hasn't maneuvered you into his bed?" I asked her, stepping in front of her so she couldn't walk away. "Why would the king of one-night-stands spend time with you?"

"Maybe he's not interested in having sex with me," Evie said, her shoulders slumping.

"Or maybe he's scared to death that he's going to screw up whatever's between you two. Maybe he doesn't know how to handle having feelings for someone."

Her eyes snapped to mine, but she looked skeptical.

I glanced at Garth over my shoulder. "Garth, have you ever known Baker to go this long without sex?"

"Nope," Garth said from behind me. "Man runs a sex club. He could sell his little black book and make a fortune."

"And have you ever seen Baker, or me for that matter, behave in a way that made you think either of us had intimate feelings for the other?"

"Nope."

Evie was looking at the floor, no longer pacing like a caged animal.

"Evie, you have nothing to worry about. When I realized you liked Baker, I told him to stop being an idiot and go for it. I'm guessing he's still acting a bit like an idiot, but mainly because I don't think he's ever had feelings for someone until now. Not anything beyond Baker's version of friendship, that is. I've known him a long time, and before you, I never saw him track a woman's movements or make up excuses to be near her. To him, women came and went from his life. There was always another on standby. I also think him telling you the truth about his history with me is his weird way of trying to deepen a relationship with you."

"He's such an idiot," Evie said, shaking her head. "Why would he think telling me about his sex life—*before we've even had a physical relationship*—was a good idea?"

"You're right. I'm an idiot," Baker said, walking toward us. "I have no idea what I'm doing when it comes to you. Kid is also right, though. For some reason, you are different. I don't know why, but you make my head spin. It's both infuriating and exciting."

"Yeah, well, I'm still mad," Evie said.

"Fine. Be mad. But you're not sleeping in one of the sex rooms. I'll sleep down here and you can have my suite."

I couldn't help but smirk. Garth coughed a laugh behind me.

"Both of you," Baker said, pointing to us, "shut it."

"These rooms are icky," Evie said, looking over her shoulder.

"Yes, they are," I said, then looked back at Baker. "Didn't you say we needed to shut down the rooms?"

Baker nodded. "Legal says when the new ordinance goes into effect mid-January, the rooms would be considered a house of prostitution. They're still sorting out whether the fourth floor needs to be closed."

"Then let Evie work on redesigning the rooms up here. We can turn them into high caliber suites that would appeal to the business district."

"Might work," Baker said. "Being private as they are could appeal to a lot of corporate execs. Let me put some numbers together."

"Kid," Garth said.

I turned to look at Garth but he was watching his phone. "What is it?" I asked, stepping next to him to look at his display.

"You recognize this guy?" Garth turned his phone screen towards me and sure enough, Mr. Tricky was sneaking up the back stairway.

I watched the display as Mr. Tricky spotted the hidden camera, staring right at us. He turned, bolting down the stairs.

"Garth, get Evie and Baker somewhere safe!" I yelled as I ran toward the door separating the two sections.

Swiping my badge, I pushed the door open and ran down the hall, passing Wild Card.

"Where's the fire?" Wild Card yelled, running behind me.

"Mr. Tricky's here!"

I swiped open Baker's office and ran across the room, entering the private stairway. Halfway down the stairs, Wild Card passed me. He was using the railings to swing and leap over each set of stairs, his feet only touching the ground at the stairway landings.

When I reached the bottom, I threw open the door and stopped to stand next to Wild Card. "Any sign of him?"

"Nothing. He must've had a car waiting."

I leaned over, hands on knees, to catch my breath. "I'll ask Garth to check the security cameras." Before I could pull my phone from my back pocket, it pinged that I had a message. Garth had texted me the make, model, and license plate of Mr. Tricky's car. I called dispatch and put out a BOLO.

Ten minutes later, my phone rang. It was Quille.

"Please tell me they found him?" I asked.

"Sorry, no such luck. He ditched the car. It wasn't hard to find, either. He set it on fire."

"Shit! Where?"

"Near Shaker's night club on 116th."

"I'm on my way."

Chapter Twelve

KELSEY
Wednesday, 6:11 p.m.

On the outside patio, most of us had just finished eating dinner when Charlie strolled outside with a tote bag looped over her forearm and carrying a plate piled high with grilled chicken, macaroni salad, and wedges of melon. Cooper followed her out, carrying two plates of food and a beer tucked under his arm. He moved to the other side of the table and sat in the chair next to me.

Charlie set her plate down before opening the tote bag. "I stopped for presents." She pulled out a wad of olive-green fabric, tossing it to Katie. Then another for Bridget, Alex, and Haley.

They unfolded the knee-length army-green coverups, their faces puckering in response.

"I was asked to go shopping," Charlie told them. "New rule for the four of you is as follows. Unless you're in the pool—*swimming*—then I expect you to be wearing either a full set of clothes or these coverups. Also, anyone found altering the coverups or taking them off after I leave, will find themselves on a plane back to Michigan. Got it?"

They looked at me, hoping for support. When I met their gazes with a stern look, they started pulling on the coverups.

Anne beamed a smile, seeming happy to be excluded from the humiliation.

As the sulking foursome ventured inside, Aunt Suzanne enlisted the kids to help her clear the table of empty plates and glasses. Little Liam was the first to dash around the table, gathering dirty silverware. The other kids were less enthusiastic but knew better than to argue. As they carried the first wave of dishes inside, Spence walked out, chewing on a drumstick.

"We have plates, you know," Charlie said before taking a bite of her own chicken using a fork.

"No time. I have six cases to work tonight. And this is the first thing I've eaten today."

"You can't keep going like this, man," Bones said. "You need to hire help."

"Can't. I can barely afford the neighbor lady who's answering the phone." Spence stopped chewing and leaned toward Charlie, sniffing her. "Why do you smell like burnt tires?"

"I was at the scene of a fire. Mr. Tricky torched another car."

Spence snorted but turned back to Bones. "I need time to pay off bills and replenish my bank account before I can hire more investigators."

"Would you consider IOUs?" Uncle Hank asked.

Spence sat next to Charlie as he answered Uncle Hank. "As in someone works cases now, but I don't pay them until someday in the unknown future? You know anyone dumb enough to take that gig?"

"There's a big difference between dumb and trusting," Pimples said, leaning back in his chair as he glared at Spence. "The question is, are you trustworthy? A man of your word?"

Spence studied Pimples for a long moment before answering. "I'm a man of my word, but I can't promise when you'd get paid. It could take me a month to get caught up." Spence shrugged. "But it could just as easily take me *six* months."

Pimples looked at Uncle Hank who gave him the nod. Then Pimples looked down the table at Juan and Jack, who both remained unresponsive. Pimples turned back to Spence. "We can take three cases off your hands. We're in no rush to get paid, but we'll track our time. Down the road, you can start paying us back in small installments."

Spence looked at Pimples first, then Juan, then Jack. "You're kidding, right?"

Charlie leaned toward Spence and whispered loud enough for everyone to hear, "Don't be a fool. They might be old, but they can handle the work."

Spence glanced at the men again before looking back at Charlie. "You'll vouch for them?"

"Hell, yes, I'd vouch for them," Charlie said. She glanced across the patio where Joe Jr. had fallen asleep at the now deserted poker table, still holding his cards. "Well, maybe not Joe Jr." She looked back at Spence. "I mean, I love the guy, but he's a handful. Best if you leave him out of this arrangement."

Spence looked back at Pimples. "You're serious then? You'll take some cases knowing I can't pay you right now?"

"No sweat. We don't need the money."

Juan cleared his throat. "Don't misunderstand him. We aren't looking for fulltime gigs. But taking a few cheating husband and missing cat cases off your hands might be a nice break between poker games."

"I turned down the missing cat case, but I've got plenty of cheating spouses. I'll grab some files," Spence said, stealing a chunk of melon from Charlie's plate as he stood.

"We'll go with you," Jack said, standing to follow. "It'll be safer for everyone if we take off before Joe Jr. wakes and wants to ride along."

Juan and Pimples dragged themselves out of their chairs.

I looked at Charlie, watching her as she watched Spence leave. When she turned back, she caught me staring.

"What?" she asked.

"Nothing. Nothing at all." I didn't even try to hide my smile.

Charlie picked up a blueberry from her plate and threw it at me. "Shut up."

Cooper caught the berry, popping it into his mouth.

I leaned back in my chair. "You really do smell like charred tires. Any chance you'll shower after you eat?"

"That's the plan," Charlie said between bites.

"Are you sure the torched car was Mr. Tricky's?" Ryan asked.

Cooper uncapped his beer. "It was his. We were at The Outer Layer when Garth spotted Mr. Tricky on the security feed, sneaking up a back stairway. We made a mad dash to catch him, but he had too much of a lead on us. He ditched the car a few blocks away."

"And it's not just charred tires you're smelling," Charlie said, reaching across the table to take Cooper's beer. "There was a body in the trunk."

"A body? Whose?" I asked.

"Well, luckily, they got the fire out before the trunk was fully engulfed, so I can answer that. The body belonged to the one and only Owen Flint."

Everyone at the table stopped eating, drinking, and talking as their heads swiveled to Charlie.

"Yeah, you heard me right," Charlie said. "Owen Flint was in the trunk of Mr. Tricky's getaway car."

"Dead?" I asked.

"Oh, yeah. At least a few days dead. Which is odd because the temps have been in the high eighties, which means Mr. Tricky must've moved Owen to the trunk today."

"Or back to the trunk," Cooper said. "My guess, the body started in the trunk Sunday morning, then was stored somewhere, then put back in the trunk today."

"So far, your theory lines up with Tasha's. She said the lack of decomp suggests he was stored in a cooler or freezer. But even though the fire didn't reach the trunk, the body's internal temp was skewed by the massive heat surge. Determining how the body was stored would be impossible at this point."

Bones grinned across the table at Charlie. "So that's not the chicken I'm smelling?"

"Gross," I said, leaning away from the table.

Charlie returned Bones' smile, flashing her teeth. "Probably not. More like a mix of smoked tires and slow roasted Owen Flint."

"Charlie Harrison, your table manners are slipping," Aunt Suzanne said, skewing her face from where she stood behind Charlie.

Nicholas, Sara, and Mackenzie were standing next to Aunt Suzanne. Mackenzie paled, but Sara and Nicholas just giggled.

"It's okay," Nicholas told Mackenzie. "The dude was a bad guy. We don't care when the bad guys die."

Cooper and I looked at each other, sharing a frown. The kids were going to need a lot of therapy when they were old enough to understand how messed up their childhoods were.

"Can we swim now?" Sara asked.

"No," Anne said as she walked over to the patio hammock and threw herself into it, setting it off in a wide sway. "I'm all done playing lifeguard. I can't take any more sun."

"Same," Whiskey said, walking over and stopping the hammock long enough to join her.

"I'll watch them," Haley said, coming out of the kitchen with Alex and Katie. "Alex can help."

I was happy to see they were all dressed in one-piece swimsuits and shorts. "Thanks, Haley."

The kids squealed as they raced toward the pool.

"No sweat," Haley said as she started toward the pool. "It's the least we can do for having such a spectacular room. Right, Alex?"

"Of course, luv," Alex said, smiling mischievously as he threw his arm over her shoulder and hurried her away.

"What was that about?" Katie asked as she sat.

"No idea." I looked around the table. "So, Mr. Tricky killed Owen Flint. Is that making sense to anyone? Because honestly, my brain is exploding."

"It makes sense if you erase all the bad assumptions we've made about Mr. Tricky," Cooper said. "He was never after Charlie because of one of her homicide cases."

"Damn. You're right," Ryan said. "This is about the cartel."

Charlie pointed at Ryan. "Bingo. Mr. Tricky is working for either Miguel or Santiago Remirez. And Owen Flint worked for one of them, too. But Owen screwed up, so either Miguel or Santiago ordered Mr. Tricky to get rid of him."

Trigger folded his arms over his chest. "That might be our fault. Between the fire at the dentist office and me mugging Owen, we might've spooked the cartel."

"That's if our theory is even right that the cartel is behind the sex trafficking," I said. "We haven't proved a connection yet."

Charlie waved her fork as she shook her head. "Too many coincidences to *not* be true. Why else would Santiago, Sebrina, and Owen rendezvous at the club to have private meetings? I doubt they were there for a threesome."

Bones chuckled. "With Sebrina, you never know."

Grady flinched from his position near the patio door. Bones noticed and stopped laughing.

Bones had previously shared some of their past with me. From the sound of it, Sebrina enjoyed a spicy sex life. Based on what he'd told me, The Outer Layer would be somewhere she'd feel comfortable.

Bridget pulled out a chair next to Bones and sat. "The part I don't get is, why would the cartel go after Charlie? She wasn't part of the trickery that went down in Michigan."

I looked at Bridget, puzzling her question through my mind until the answer suddenly materialized. "Because they can't get to Nick," I said as the world around me started to spin.

"*Kel*!" Grady yelled, rushing to my side. "Breathe, babe."

Cooper grabbed my hand. "You heard Grady. Breathe."

I nodded, but couldn't get my lungs to work. They felt like they were full of water.

"The kids are safe," Grady said, rubbing my back. "You said it yourself, the cartel can't get to them."

The fact that I could hear them—that I hadn't passed out—had me focusing harder on trying to breathe. I was struggling, though. Gasping and wheezing.

Next thing I knew, I was hit in the face with ice cold water and half-melted ice cubes. Air whooshed into my lungs as I jumped upright and backward, pushing my chair away from the table with the back of my legs. The chilled water rolled off me, some of it down my blouse, as I shook the front of my blouse away from my skin.

I looked over at Charlie who tossed a pile of napkins my way before sitting down again.

"What the fuck, Charlie?" I yelled.

"Their way," Charlie pointed between Grady and Cooper, "wasn't working." She grinned at me as she popped a chunk of pineapple in her mouth.

"Nice," Cooper said with a goofy grin.

I glared at Cooper.

"What?" he said, his grin widening. "You look sexy when you're soaking wet."

Grady chuckled. "It's a better look than grayish-blue while gasping for air from a panic attack."

I picked up the napkins and wiped my face and neck. Now that the initial shock was wearing off, I had to admit, at least to myself, the ice water bath had helped cool me off.

"Any change in the Remirez family?" Charlie asked, distracting everyone.

"No change. Miguel is still in Cali and we're still searching for Sebrina and Santiago," Tech said, tucked behind his laptop at the other end of the table.

"You seem pretty unfazed about the cartel targeting you," I said to Charlie as I knocked a few ice cubes out of my chair before sitting again.

"Better me than someone else in the family, don't you think? Besides, I don't plan on letting him succeed."

"What does he want, though?" Bridget asked. "To kill you?"

"Payback," Bones said. "Kelsey made all three of them look like idiots. Powerful people don't take kindly to humiliation."

"Maybe," Ryan said. "Or it could be about leverage. If the cartel can get their hands on Charlie, they can make Kelsey back off the dentist office."

"It could be for a lot of reasons. Doesn't matter," Charlie said. "How's the case going?"

"Boring as hell," Trigger said. "Ryan and I ran surveillance all day, but there was only a slow trickle of patients. I don't think the word is out they've reopened."

"In a way, that could be good," Charlie said before taking a drink of her beer.

"How so?" I asked.

"They were closed for what? Three weeks? A month? They'll have clients getting anxious for new women." She took a bite of a strawberry. "They'll be desperate. Maybe even reckless. They'll grab the next age-appropriate woman who walks through the door."

"And that's good, how?" Katie asked.

"She means it will be easier to set a trap," I answered for Charlie. "I like it, but we don't have the manpower."

"We could get the manpower," Uncle Hank said. "Might have to tap into the blue line, but we could get the bodies to cover a sting."

"No," Charlie said. "I don't trust the blue line on this one. Bunch of gossips. Word will spread."

Cooper shook his head at Charlie. "You can't send someone inside, undercover, and risk them getting abducted, either."

"I'm not talking about *just anyone* going undercover."

Knowing how Charlie's mind worked, I shook my head. "No, Kid. This isn't a game."

"I didn't say it was. But if it's me, we can plan the sting with fewer bodies."

"I said no!" I stood, rage filling me. Before I said something I'd regret, I stormed toward the patio doors and into the house. I shouldn't be surprised by Kid's reckless behavior at this point, but nevertheless, it pissed me off.

I sensed Grady enter the mansion before he spoke. "At some point, you're going to have to come to terms with Kid being a grown-up."

"I'm aware she's an adult. What I take issue with is her general lack of self-preservation."

"You mean her willingness to risk her life to protect the innocent? Just like the rest of us?"

"She wants to play *bait* in a human trafficking case!"

"Then you do it," Grady said.

"I can't. You know I can't. My priority is to stay close to the kids. We've already cut the security staff in half. I'm not putting them at risk."

"But if you didn't have to be at the mansion, you'd do it?" Grady asked.

"Of course I would," I answered as I filled a glass from the premade pitcher of margaritas. "It's a smart plan. We could use a GPS tracker and wire a mic for sound. We'd need four, maybe five people working the perimeter. We could run the rest remotely."

When Grady didn't reply, I turned to face him. He stood near the door with his arms crossed over his chest and a grin spread across his face.

I pointed at him. "You tricked me!"

"No. I just needed you to look at the op objectively. It's doable. We can keep Charlie safe."

I glared as I stormed past him out the patio door. "Fine!" I announced to the table full of people. "Charlie can go undercover!"

Charlie grinned. "Glad you approve. But we'd already decided I was doing it anyway."

At the far end of the table Katie stood. She picked up her chair, moving it away from the table so she could step around it. Her devilish smile instantly put me on alert as she stepped behind Charlie, tapping her on the shoulder. Charlie turned and looked up at Katie.

Before I had time to react, Katie lifted a fist and punched Charlie.

Charlie was thrown sideways, knocking her and her chair to the ground. She raised her arms to protect her face from another hit.

I stood frozen, looking between Charlie on the ground and Katie, who was laughing.

Charlie sat up, spit a wad of blood, and then playfully swatted Katie in the leg. "Nice right hook, slugger."

Cooper, Bones, and Ryan laughed. Uncle Hank looked skyward, sighing.

"What the hell is going on?" I asked as I helped Charlie stand.

"Charlie said she needed a legit reason to go to the dentist," Katie said with a shrug. "Problem solved."

"And what was wrong with her going in for a cleaning?" I asked.

"Like her perfectly-straight white teeth wouldn't have been suspicious," Katie said, rolling her eyes.

"She's right," Charlie slurred out one side of her mouth. She used her fingers scooped an ice cube out of Bridget's glass and held it against her jaw. "The bruise and loose tooth are a better sell. It also fits with your theory the patients are drugged. No reason to give me drugs for a routine cleaning."

"Katie could've broken your jaw!" I yelled at Charlie.

"She didn't," Charlie said, moving her jaw gingerly in a small circle. "But I'm not sure the tooth will survive. Damn. That smarts."

Uncle Hank knitted his fingers behind his head as he chuckled. "Between the faded bruises and gash on your chin from last week and now a swollen jaw, you look worse than most of the women at the domestic abuse shelter."

Charlie tried to smile but winced. "If you think that's funny, then you should know I promised Aunt Suzanne I'd go with her to a wedding this weekend. Guess who's taking her now?"

Uncle Hank's face transformed into a stormy expression as everyone laughed at him.

Charlie tossed the half-melted cube into the landscaped bed. I could see her trying to keep her expression clear, but she was obviously in pain.

"Do you need an ice pack?" I asked her.

"No. We both know the swelling and bruising will sell the op tomorrow. We'll do the sting late morning. With a bit of luck, I'll be able to get an appointment with my regular dentist for the afternoon."

"Did she break a tooth?" I asked.

"I don't think so." Charlie moved her tongue around inside her mouth. "It's definitely loose now, though." Charlie opened her mouth to show me her lower molar, but her gums were bleeding too much to tell if the tooth was cracked.

I grinned at her as I sat in the chair next to her. "Maybe you should stop trying so hard to make your undercover stories so authentic."

"What fun would that be?"

The clicking of a camera had us both turning our heads. Cooper was snapping pictures of us.

"New camera?" I asked him.

"Yeah. Pretty sweet, huh?" Cooper said, holding the camera up to show me.

"We went to a camera store today to backtrack Bernard Bacon's pre-murder whereabouts," Charlie said. "Wild Card and the shop owner talked a bunch of mumbo jumbo, half of which I didn't understand, but hopefully the details help with the case."

"How is a camera shop owner going to help with a case?" I asked

"Turns out, this model of camera has wireless upload to the cloud," Charlie answered.

"Meaning what?"

"Watch," Cooper said, walking around the table. "I'll show you." He walked me through several steps then a loading bar appeared on the screen, flashing until it reached a hundred percent.

"And what was that?" I asked.

Cooper looked disappointed that I hadn't understood. He always overestimated my technological abilities. "I just used the mansion's wireless internet to upload the pictures to a cloud folder."

I looked at Charlie. "You think Bernard might've uploaded photos?"

"I have no idea, but with his camera missing, I've got my fingers crossed he did. It's probably the only way we'll prove Mr. Tricky killed him."

"How exactly does this Bernard Bacon guy connect to Owen Flint and Mr. Tricky?" Bones asked.

"Yeah," Tech said. "One plus one is not equaling two here, ladies."

"Why would Owen Flint be on a deserted street at three in the morning?" Charlie asked them.

"Beats me," Bones said.

"Okay, let me rephrase," Charlie said. "Is there any version of your imagination where Owen is on a deserted street in the middle of the night and he's there for honorable reasons?"

"No," Ryan said. "That's the point, right? He was being shady."

"Exactly," Charlie said.

"And whoever he met," I said, nodding as I followed her logic, "forced Owen to leave with them. That explains why Owen's car was abandoned."

"Exactly," Charlie said. "And it was probably Mr. Tricky who met with Owen."

"And Bernard Bacon took pictures of whatever happened," Cooper said.

"That's my theory," Charlie said. "But Abe and Natalie haven't found anything yet."

"Hey," Cooper said, showing me his camera again. "You have to see this photo I took of Nick and Sara earlier." He flipped through the slideshow until he found the one, then held the camera out for me.

In the picture, the kids were in the pool and Nicholas had Sara on his shoulders. Sara was gripping his hair to hold on. They both were laughing as Sara was captured falling to the side.

"Can you print copies?"

"I can do better than that. I'll send the photo to your phone. Hey, Grady, you should come see this." Cooper held the camera out.

Grady had been keeping to himself, leaned against the side of the house. Rather than responding to Cooper, he turned and went back inside.

"Damn. He's still pissed we're married," Cooper said.

I narrowed my eyes at Cooper. "He's not the only one."

"It's your fault," Cooper said. "You're the one who took off to Michigan without leaving me a forwarding address." Cooper turned his back to me as he snapped some pics of Anne and Whiskey cuddled together in the hammock.

I fisted my hands as I glared at the back of his head.

Charlie giggled.

Chapter Thirteen

CHARLIE
Thursday, 5:03 a.m.

I stared back at the long list of unanswered questions on my notepad. Pulling an all-nighter researching had proved to be a waste of time. I'd been unable to locate a death certificate on Mrs. Barrett. I'd been unable to find dirt on Councilmember Barrett. I'd reviewed every document and picture on the flash drive Andrew had given me and found nothing that helped. I'd then switched my focus between Bernard Bacon, Mr. Tricky, and Owen Flint, but until either Bernard's photos were found or the sting op occurred, I was stuck treading water.

I heard sounds in the front room and looked up. Pimples, Juan, and Spence walked through the living room and into the kitchen. Juan went straight for the coffee pot, starting a fresh pot. Spence walked over and tipped my chin up, looking at my jaw. He shook his head but didn't ask how it happened. Pimples kicked a chair toward Spence before sitting beside me.

"What's shaking, sweetheart," Pimples asked.

"Nothing. I'm stuck," I said, pointing to my list of questions.

"Which case?" Pimples asked, picking up the pad of paper and reading through the list.

"All of them."

"Who's Sophia Catrella Barrett?" Pimples asked before handing the list to Spence.

"My mother," Mackenzie answered. She stood at the entrance to the back hallway, looking at me with panic in her eyes.

"Relax," I told her. "I'm not turning you over to your stepfather."

"He'll find us. We have to go."

"Don't be silly," Juan said from the kitchen, guarding the coffee pot as it slowly dripped to fill. "You're safe here. If anyone comes looking for you, Uncle Hank will take you and your brother by boat to a private marina. From there, the plan is to get you to Charlie's safe house. And from what I hear, it's actually a fancy condo."

"But you all could go to prison," Mackenzie said.

"Nah," Pimples said. "We're good at playing stupid. Trust us. We've been neck deep in worse than this."

Mackenzie still seemed uncertain. I figured there was a fifty-fifty chance she'd bolt.

"Mackenzie, I have a question," I said. "Were you at the hospital when your mother died?"

"I was at the hospital, but I wasn't allowed to see her. My stepfather came out and told us she'd died. Then he made us go with him to talk to the news people."

Pimples cursed under his breath.

"Do you remember anything strange? Anything or anyone at the hospital that didn't make sense?"

"Like what?" Mackenzie asked, coming over to sit at the table.

"I don't know, anything that felt odd."

"Kid," Pimples scolded. "Give the girl a break. You're talking about her mother's death."

"It's okay," Mackenzie said, not taking her eyes off me. "My stepfather had someone give me a shot. It made me drowsy. I don't remember much after that."

I felt everyone's eyes on me, but I continued watching Mackenzie. I reached across the table, placing my hand on top of hers. "I know it's hard to trust people. To put faith in people you barely know. But I promise you, Mackenzie, I'm going to take your stepfather down. I'll make sure he never hurts you or Liam again. Okay?"

She nodded, but didn't say anything when she stood and left the room. I knew she didn't believe me, but maybe she'd at least wait around long enough to see if I was telling the truth.

"Damn," Juan whispered, leaning over to look down the hall to make sure Mackenzie had left before walking over with a fresh cup of coffee for me. "Bring us up to speed. What do we know?"

I spent the next twenty minutes giving them the details about Councilmember Barrett, his wife, the kids, the accident, the suspicion of abuse, and ended with the possibility that Sophia might still be alive. We kept our voices low in case Mackenzie snuck back down the hall to listen.

When I was done, Spence pulled out his laptop. "I'll see if I can access the medical records through their insurance company. You can fool the public, but not Blue Cross."

Juan set his cup of coffee down and started for the door.

"Where are you going?" I asked.

"You all have your ways of getting information. I have mine," Juan said as he continued toward the front door without looking back.

I listened to the front door open and close, followed by the sound of a car engine starting.

Wild Card walked into the kitchen, rubbing his eyes. He'd been working security patrol with Bones. "What's got Juan riled?"

"Councilmember Barrett," I answered.

"Well," Wild Card said, looking over his shoulder back toward the front of the house, "glad Bones jumped in the car with him then."

"Did Juan say where he was going?" Pimples asked.

"He about bit my head off when I asked. Told me the fewer people who knew, the better. That's when Bones jumped in the car with him."

I looked over at Spence. "I'm sort of jealous."

"Not me. I've had enough action for one night."

"Why? What happened?"

"Joe Jr. happened," Pimples said, chuckling. "He tracked us down outside a motel. About twenty minutes into the stakeout, he announces he's gotta pee. Leaves before we can argue."

Spence shook his head, listening, but kept his focus on his laptop.

"Next thing we know," Pimples said, "flames start shooting out of one of the motel windows. We start taking pictures as the cheating wife runs out of one of the rooms, making a dash for her car. We take her picture, her boy toy's picture, and everyone else's as they ran for their lives."

"Joe Jr. set the motel on fire?" I asked, trying not to laugh.

"You got it. Decided it was time to take action, he says. No reason to sit around with our thumbs up our arses, he says."

"Where is he now?"

"Napping in the back seat of my truck," Spence said. "It seems it only takes a little bit of excitement to tucker Joe Jr. out."

"Well, at least you got the money shot," I said.

"Actually," Pimples said. "It was a two-for-one deal. A guy from another case was in one of the other rooms with his mistress."

"Bonus. But did anyone get hurt?"

"Naw," Pimples said, walking to the refrigerator and pulling a carton of eggs. "We stuck around until the fire department arrived, then got the hell out of there. The fire looked scary, but everyone was safe enough."

"Safe?" Spence said, turning to look at Pimples. "*It was a fire!*"

"Yeah," Pimples said, nodding. "But at least it wasn't a rocket launcher."

I snorted, remembering Joe Jr. setting off a rocket in Jack's apartment.

Spence scowled at me.

"What? I warned you Joe Jr. was a handful." I looked back at Pimples. "Where's Jack?"

"Sitting on the last case for the night. We pulled random files. He got the good one. Got himself a diamond theft case."

"I wouldn't classify a mugger as a diamond thief," Spence said.

"The mugger stole the woman's diamond necklace, didn't he?" When Spence didn't answer, Pimples jerked his head in affirmation. "Then I guess we got ourselves a diamond thief."

"So where exactly is Jack sitting?" I asked.

"Outside an all-night pawn shop. He's got a description of the guy."

"It's a waste of time," Spence said.

"Oh yeah?" Jack said, walking in and slapping a file folder on the table. "Case closed. Your mugger is in lock-up."

Spence sat back in his chair. "No way."

"Yes, way. And I got the pawn shop owner to pull the diamond necklace from the safe in exchange for not turning him in to the cops." Jack dropped the necklace on the table.

"Holy shit," Spence said, laughing. "You guys closed three cases tonight."

"Not bad for old farts," Jake said, fist bumping Pimples on his way to the coffee pot.

"We still got it," Pimples said, doing a little box step dance.

Chapter Fourteen

KELSEY
Thursday, 7:02 a.m.

I wasn't surprised to find half the household awake and scattered around the kitchen when I walked downstairs. I was surprised to see Gardy and Cooper sitting next to each other, looking through pictures on Cooper's camera. I smiled to myself as I went to the coffee pot and filled a cup.

"Where's Charlie?" I asked to anyone who'd answer.

"Here," Charlie answered, staggering into the room. Her makeup from the day before was smeared, she had bedhead, and while she was wearing different clothes, they were ripped in so many places, a swimsuit would've covered more.

"Well don't you look special," I said, grinning over my cup at her.

"Too much?" Charlie asked.

"No," Aunt Suzanne answered for me. "Everyone will believe you're a hooker." She rolled her eyes as she carried empty glasses to the sink.

Charlie grinned as she looked down at her outfit.

"Aunt Charlie, why do you look like that?" Sara asked, scrunching up her little nose.

"I'm going undercover at the dentist office."

"What happened to your face?" Nicholas asked.

"Your Aunt Katie punched me."

The kids turned to look at Katie.

Katie smirked back at them. "She wanted me to hit her."

"Sure, she did," Sara said, giggling.

They're going to need so much therapy, I thought again, shaking my head.

As if reading my mind, Aunt Suzanne snorted and said, "Don't overthink it. There are worse parents in the world. At least these kids will go into their adult lives with no illusions."

"We ready for the sting?" Charlie asked.

Grady stood and turned toward us. "Tech has a mic and tracker for you. You'll have Trigger, Wild Card, Ryan, and myself on perimeter. Bridget will be with Trigger. Kelsey will run the op from here. She needs to stay close to the kids."

"Works for me. Bones isn't back yet?" Charlie asked.

"He texted and said he wasn't going to make it," Uncle Hank said. "He's still with Juan."

The vagueness of the statement followed by the looks exchanged between Uncle Hank and Charlie piqued my curiosity. "What are they up to?"

"Knowing the two of them, probably nothing legal," Uncle Hank said, chuckling to himself.

Mackenzie walked over and stood by Charlie. "When will you be back?"

"Not until later today. But don't worry. Uncle Hank's staying here."

"I got your back, Mackenzie," Uncle Hank said. "The boat is fueled and ready to go if we need to split. And the guards out front will stall anyone who shows up looking for you."

Charlie flashed me a look, letting me know now was not the time to ask questions.

"Hey, Bridget," Charlie said. "How's my apartment remodel coming?"

"It's almost done, but honestly, why would you want to live there when you can live here?"

"This place is too big. Too noisy. I've barely slept in days. I want my own bed and my own walls back."

"Too bad," I said, walking past her to the table. "Until Mr. Tricky is either dead or behind bars, it's not safe for you to be alone."

"Says you."

"Says everyone," Uncle Hank snapped.

I looked back to catch Charlie's eye roll, but she didn't argue.

"You have an appointment at two o'clock with your regular dentist," Aunt Suzanne told Charlie. "Hopefully, he'll be able to fix whatever happens at the clinic during this stupid undercover sting."

"It's not stupid," Charlie argued.

"You're right. The sting isn't stupid," Aunt Suzanne said, placing a fist on her hip. "But having Katie knock your tooth loose, then going undercover to have dental work performed at a free clinic... That is beyond stupid."

"Hear, hear," I agreed, holding up my coffee cup.

Charlie stuck her tongue out at me, but then winced. Grady chuckled as he filled a plate with eggs and toast. The kids chattered excitedly about something before Liam, Nicholas, and Sara raced out the patio door. I started to follow, but Grady raised a hand to stop me before following them outside with his plate of food. Whiskey kissed the top of Anne's head and exited too.

"Did the kids eat?" I asked.

"They ate at about six this morning," Charlie answered. "It was just before I went to bed."

"You're walking into a sting operation with only an hour of sleep?" I asked with a raised eyebrow.

"More like thirty minutes," Uncle Hank said. "But you know Kid. That's her norm. She'll be fine."

"Do you guys need an extra set of eyes on the U.C. operation?" Spence asked. "I've got time thanks to my new investigative team."

"Sure," Cooper said. "You can ride with me."

"Take my car," Uncle Hank said, tossing Cooper the keys to his caddy. "Your rental has been in the area too many times."

"But I need the Caddy today," Aunt Suzanne said. "Haley agreed to go to the Kinnley baby shower with me."

"Not happening," I said. "Security is already too thin. You'll have to skip this one."

"We'll be fine," Aunt Suzanne said. "It's a baby shower. We don't need security."

"Not happening. And that's my final answer."

Haley giggled. "Told you."

"I'll figure something out," Aunt Suzanne muttered.

I looked at Charlie but she shrugged. We both knew Aunt Suzanne was impossible to control.

I took my coffee and walked outside. The kids were in the tiki lounge, running around while Tech pretended to chase them, roaring with his arms outstretched like a bear and tickling them when they were within reach. Grady and Whiskey sat at the far end as they talked and laughed at the kids. Tyler was leaned against a post, smiling with his eyes closed as he relaxed. Sensing me, he opened them, dipped his head in a nod, then reclosed them.

I followed the patio past the lounge, past the pool, and to the far railing overlooking the ocean. The morning sun was well above the horizon, reflecting off the water as the waves lapped over each other, fighting to reach the shore first.

I tipped my head back, closing my eyes to feel the sun on my face and the cool breeze lift my hair into a wild spin.

"Are you okay?" Anne asked, walking up beside me.

"I like it here," I answered her, without opening my eyes.

"You want to stay, don't you?"

I heard a sadness in her voice, causing me to open my eyes and look at her. "Years ago, when I first came to Miami, it was like I'd found my home. I loved it here. I loved the hot weather, the nearness of the ocean, and the fast pace. I loved everything about this city." I looked away, toward the horizon. "By the time I left, all I felt was anger and pain. This city nearly destroyed me. And Nicholas. Ever since, I've been afraid to return. Afraid history would repeat itself. But now..."

"You see home again," Anne whispered.

I reached over and wrapped an arm over her shoulders. "Yes. But's it's not my only home, Anne. I feel the same way when I'm in Michigan or when I'm on the ranches in Texas." I tugged her closer to me. "It's not about which city or state I'm in. Close your eyes and listen. Do you hear it?"

I waited for her to close her eyes, then closed mine again. The kids giggled in the background. The dogs barked. Whiskey and Grady chuckled. Aunt Suzanne yelled playfully at Uncle Hank. Katie called out to Tech.

"That's home, Anne. The noise. The feeling of family. It's not constrained to a zip code."

"So... You're not moving," Anne said on a sigh.

"I'm not moving, but I'm no longer standing still either. I need all of you in my life, and that includes spending a few weeks each year here with Charlie. It includes spending time in the winter in Texas. And it includes you, Katie, Lisa, and Alex in Michigan."

"What does that look like? We'll see you, what? A few weeks a year?"

I leaned my head against hers. "You're all stronger now. You pulled yourselves out of your dark pasts. You've thrived. You've found love and laughter. And you'll still have me. You'll still have

Nicholas. We're family. And no matter where Nicholas and I are, we'll be on the first flight back to Michigan if you need us."

Anne pulled away and turned toward the house with her head bent to the ground.

I knew she was crying, but I didn't stop her. Of all of us, she was the most sensitive. The one who felt everything the deepest.

I looked back across the ocean and sighed.

Chapter Fifteen

CHARLIE
Thursday, 9:35 a.m.

I walked into the dental office with an ice cube held against my jaw, dripping water off my hand. "I need someone to look at my tooth," I told the receptionist.

"Did you break it, hon?" she asked.

"Don't know," I said with a half shrug, tossing the melted cube into a nearby trashcan. "Hurts like a mother, though."

"Well, have a seat and fill out this form," the receptionist said as she handed me a clipboard. "I'll see if we can squeeze you in to see the dentist."

I looked around the nearly empty waiting room and barely contained the eyeroll as I picked a chair facing the wall-mounted television. For the next thirty minutes, I distracted myself by watching a network television show about renovating a house for a young couple in Arizona. And of course, just before the big reveal, my name was called by a petite woman with big teeth.

Annoyed but ready to focus on the sting, I followed the woman down the hall where she nudged me into a small room and then pointed for me to sit. I lowered myself into the dental chair and closely watched her dart from one side of my chair to the other, then back again, as she jabbed pieces of plastic-coated cardboard into my mouth and took bite wing x-rays. So far, the only thing unusual about her behavior was the skill at which she could conduct a one-sided and nonstop conversation about her day, only requiring an occasional grunt or nod from me to ensure I was still listening.

Ten minutes later, the dentist came in, glanced at the x-rays, then plunged a metal tool and two gloved fingers into my mouth. He shoved at the loose tooth.

My nails dug into the chair arms. "*Ahh!*"

"Sorry. I'm sure that doesn't feel good. That tooth needs to come out," the dentist announced before abruptly leaving.

I looked toward the doorway to see which direction he went, but the petite woman was already guiding me out of the chair. I followed her into the hall, taking a moment to look around, but no one was in the hallway. The petite woman nudged me into the next room and the next chair.

I had barely sat when she flipped the chair to the horizontal position, causing my head to spin. Before my brain settled, a tall skinny man with a bushy unibrow strapped a mask over my nose.

I tried to say something, but the pain from the tooth made me wince, causing me to inhale a lung full of laughing gas. *Whoa*, I thought as my brain wandered. *I wonder why they called it laughing gas? It had never made me laugh. It was more of tingle. A buzzzz. Like the time I went for acupuncture and they connected the needles to little wires and the other end of the wires to 9-volt batteries. That kind of tingling.*

"Are we all set here?" the dentist asked, appearing out of nowhere next to me.

I nodded, not completely sure what I was agreeing to. My brain was still focused on the memory of the electrified acupuncture treatment from years ago, comparing it to the current buzzing feeling in my toes.

"Let's get on with it then," the dentist said, hooking my mouth with his finger and pulling my cheek out. Pulling a big needle out of thin air, he jabbed it into my gums.

"Ahhh!" I screeched as I felt the sting of the needle.

I was about to shove him away, when he retreated, rolling his chair away as he spun the chair, turning his back to me.

I closed my eyes, trying to take my mind off the pain as my mouth rapidly numbed. *This was crazy. Was I really going to do this? Let him pull my tooth? No. I needed to stop this.*

I went to say something but realized my tongue and mouth weren't cooperating. I swallowed, moved my jaw in a circle, then tried to speak again while the dentist was rolling his chair back my way.

"I—" I started to say. My words froze as I saw the tool in his hands that looked suspiciously like pliers. I cringed backward, scooching my body up the chair away from him.

"That's it," the dentist said as he forced my mouth open with his thumb, shoving the plier-like tool inside. "A little resistance helps it pop out sometimes. You must've done this before."

I felt mounting pressure in my mouth as I tried to move away from him, then the pressure was gone. I took a breath, forgetting the laughing gas was still attached to my nose causing me to inhale another lung full of the tingles.

My body felt like it was floating while my brain scrambled to keep up with my surroundings. The dentist held the medieval pliers in front of me, the other end clamped down on my now extracted tooth.

"*Uckk*," I said to myself, trying to swear.

"I suppose to someone outside the dental world, it would look gross," the dentist said, misunderstanding the word I was trying to communicate.

The dentist rolled away, his face disappearing and being replaced by the man with the unibrow. Mr. Unibrow lifted the mask from my nose and held a plastic dish in front of me. "Spit, please."

I did, bloody saliva dropping into the dish.

"That was a good spit."

I glared up at him. If he patted me on the head, I was going to break his fingers.

"Don't smoke or chew gum for the next few days," the dentist said as he left the room.

I stared in the direction that the dentist had disappeared.

"This is Cuddles," Mr. Unibrow said, placing what appeared to be a cross between a poodle and string mop in my lap. "She'll keep you company while the nitrous oxide wears off. I'll be back in a minute." He left the room, leaving Cuddles on my stomach, staring up at me.

"*Yurr ugh-ee*," I told Cuddles.

She barked twice, then jumped off my lap and ran away.

I leaned my head back, staring at the ceiling. *Fuck*, I thought before I started laughing.

The petite woman's head appeared, looming inches from my face. "All set?" she asked as she grabbed me by the arm and pulled me upward, then off the chair.

She half dragged me down a hall as she rattled off a list of aftercare instructions, then put a piece of paper explaining everything she'd told me into my hand. She turned me in the other direction, and with a little shove, nudged me out the side door.

Now outside, I looked around. I was in the alley.

I stood there confused, waiting for something to happen. I patted my thighs, then my hips, and moved upward toward my shoulders. Nope, only my mouth was numb. I hadn't received anything stronger than the nitrous, which was already wearing off. I looked around, wondering what the next move was.

Deciding to walk north in the direction of my fake residence, I kept my eyes peeled for someone suspicious. I turned out of the alley and kept going. But nothing happened.

Eventually someone would pick me up—either the good guys or the bad guys, right?

Kelsey's voice sounded in my ear. "You weren't followed, Kid. Walk to the end of the block and turn left. Cooper will pick you up."

"Naw one 'ollowed meeh?" I felt something on my chin and wiped the drool off with my shirt. "Shaat. Need a dwen-ist." I followed the two white lines on the pedestrian walkway to cross the intersection.

Kelsey laughed in my ear. "I'm so glad we're recording this. Cooper is taking you to your regular dentist. Hopefully they can fix whatever was done to you. If not, just remember—I told you this was a bad idea."

I sat down on the curb and wiped the drool from my chin again.

A car pulled up and Spence got out of the passenger front seat. He walked over and pulled me up from the curb. Using the bottom of his t-shirt, he stretched his shirt toward me to wipe my chin. Then he threw an arm over my shoulder and guided me to the car as he laughed.

As I slide into the back seat, Wild Card looked between the seats at me. "We explained the situation to your dentist office, and they agreed to get you in for an appointment ASAP instead of waiting for your two o'clock appointment."

I sighed, leaning my head back and closing my eyes.

Twenty minutes later, I checked in with another receptionist and was directed to take a seat in the waiting area. The tv mounted to the wall was showing another house renovation episode.

I walked over, grabbed the cord to the tv, and yanked it from the outlet.

Several patients and the receptionist gasped, leaning away from me as I crossed the room and sat with my back against the wall. The receptionist kept her eyes locked on me as she appeared to have one hand resting on her phone behind her desk, ready to call in backup if needed.

I leaned my head against the wall and closed my eyes. *Shit.*

Chapter Sixteen

CHARLIE
Thursday, 2:00 p.m.

Thankful that Wild Card and Spencer had relocated my Mustang to the dental office, I drove one handed, holding an icepack to my cheek with the other. The icepack wasn't for the pain. No, I'd had enough Lidocaine injections to numb my mouth for a month. I'd be lucky if I didn't chew my tongue or lip in half before the shots wore off.

The icepack was for the swelling which my regular dentist said would likely get worse. He had to dig out part of the gum and root system of the now missing tooth and install a base post or something like that. He fitted me for a temporary crown and in ten days, my permanent crown would be set. A fake tooth. All because of an undercover sting which had netted zero results.

I parked on the street in front of the precinct, got out, and waved a hand at Spence and Wild Card who'd been following me. I entered through the glass doors as Quille was leaving.

He stopped when he saw me. "Whatever happened, don't tell me. Just fill out an incident report and leave it on my desk." He shook his head and exited.

The desk officer grinned as he buzzed me into the inner lair.

On the second floor, I found Ford leaned back in his chair tapping a pencil against his lower lip. As I walked toward him, he looked up at me and stood. "What the hell happened?"

"Tooth pulled." I pointed to the photos of Bernard on Ford's desk. "Where we at?"

"Nowhere. Abe and Natalie were ordered to work a missing person case. Something about some missing kids."

"Which kids?"

"I don't know. It's one of Warren's cases, though." Ford looked around the room, ensuring no one was listening. "During the investigation of a dead pimp, someone reported a teenage girl who matches the description of a missing person. I guess the girl had been staying with a pimp. The brass is in a frenzy for answers."

"Fuck the brass." I dug through the pile of papers on Ford's desk, grabbing the specs for Bernard's camera.

Walking across the room with Ford following, I entered the tech lab where the researchers for the precinct worked. Researchers were shared with the other units, as needed, but Abe and Natalie were officially assigned to the homicide unit.

Six sets of eyes swiveled my way.

One of the researchers stopped his repetitious tossing of a foam ball against the wall. "Please tell us you have something fun to do."

"I've got two tickets to this Saturday's Miami Dolphins game," I said, using a push pin to put the tickets on the corkboard. "Whoever gets me the photos that Bernard Bacon took the night he died, wins. We suspect he loaded the photos to a cloud drive, somewhere in the big bad internet world."

"What kind of camera?" Abe asked.

I looked down at the spec sheet in my hand and read the make and model. "Cannon Rebel."

"EOS?" John asked.

"I have no idea." I pinned the specs of the camera to the corkboard.

Seven researchers rushed the board to get the camera specs. Natalie stayed at her computer, typing like a madwoman with a sly grin on her face.

I waved Ford toward the door.

"Aren't you worried you'll get in trouble for distracting them?" Ford asked once we returned to the main room.

"At this point, what's one more disciplinary action in my file?"

"Yeah, that makes sense. What if they come up empty?"

"Those tickets are primo and the researchers know it. They won't come up empty."

"Was it worth the tickets? They must be expensive."

"I don't even like football. I buy the tickets to bribe people with. The last set weren't even used. I forgot about them."

"I'll have to remember that," Ford said, chuckling as he sat back in his chair. "Walk me through your theory again while we wait."

"Bacon gets back to the hotel after a late business meeting Friday. Saturday is a mystery, but then Saturday night, he works on his laptop for a few hours, talks to his wife before she goes to bed, and then knowing he won't be able to sleep, he sets up his camera on the balcony to take pictures."

"We never found the camera. I double checked with the crime lab, and it wasn't in the room or his rental car."

"That fits my theory, too. Just keep following me here. It's late. He can't sleep. He's taking pictures on the balcony when Owen Flint shows up, parking on the street down below the hotel."

"Wait, Owen Flint is the dead guy in Mr. Tricky's trunk, right?"

"Right. But whoever Flint was meeting, likely Mr. Tricky, spots Bernard. The perp goes to Bernard's room, gains access, and launches Bernard over the rail. Then the perp snags the camera and tripod and hightails it out of there."

"There was no forced entry. How did the killer get inside?"

"Maybe the killer lifted a keycard off a hotel employee. Or picked the lock, though that type of lock isn't easy to pick. Huey thinks the bad guy pretended to be room service."

Ford laughed. "Does Huey have an alibi?"

I sat down on the edge of the desk. "I asked, and he said yes. It might be fun to run a background on Huey, though."

Ford grinned at me, shaking his head. "I already cleared the hotel staff's keycards. They were all accounted for. And Bacon's door didn't show anyone else enter the room electronically, so Huey's theory might be right."

A round of *boos* erupted from the research lab and Natalie strutted through the door, heading our way. She waved the Dolphin tickets in the air, then nodded toward the conference room. "I emailed the photos, but I can show them to you on the big screen."

We followed her into the conference room. Ford dimmed the lights as I turned on the conference room TV.

Natalie sat at the end of the table, working her keyboard until the display on the wall came alive. "I'm showing over 200 pictures for the night Bacon died. I turned on the timestamp display and set to flip through the pictures every three seconds so holler when you want me to stop."

Per the timestamp, Bernard had started taking pictures around nine that night. And he took pictures of everything, from streetlights to a closely zoomed photo of a paper bag drifting on the breeze along the sidewalk. It wasn't until the timestamps crossed over the two o'clock hour before anything of interest caught my attention.

"Stop," Ford and I said in unison.

"Is that—" Ford started to say.

"Hot damn," I answered, walking over to look closer at the wall monitor. "Mr. Tricky."

"What's he doing?" Natalie asked.

Mr. Tricky had Owen Flint pressed up against a car with his hand wrapped tight to the front of Owen's shirt as if both holding him from running and holding him upright. The other hand was out of sight, but based on the pained expression on Owen's face, Mr. Tricky had either punched Owen or stabbed him.

"Next picture," I said.

The next image flashed, then the next. Mr. Tricky kept Owen's body pinned against the car, holding him in place, until he had the passenger door open. Then he dropped Owen's body into the seat before lifting and shoving his legs inside the car.

"Stop again," Ford said, pointing at the monitor. "Owen is either dead at this point or unconscious."

"Appears so."

"What do we know about the victim?"

"Owen Flint was wanted for questioning in an off-book case. He was a real estate developer working with a Mexican cartel involved in sex trafficking here in Miami."

"Off book? As in? CIA?" Natalie asked.

"No," I said, laughing. "Off book, as in, the team who's investigating is not part of law enforcement. But they've got mad skills. If anyone can shut down the trafficking, it'll be them."

"What does that mean for my homicide?" Ford asked.

"It means we continue to follow the evidence but stop short of interviewing anyone. I don't want either of you to end up on Mr. Tricky's radar. Capiche?"

"What about running this guy through facial? Last I knew, the only picture we had was pretty grainy."

"I acquired another photo of him yesterday and sent it to the Feds to run. Best to let them handle this one."

"I got no problem forgetting I saw this," Natalie said, closing her laptop. "Let me know if you need anything else, though."

"Actually," I said.

Natalie stopped and looked at me. When I didn't answer, she shut the door and leaned against the wall, waiting.

"About that missing kid case..."

Natalie's eyes narrowed as she studied me. "Yeah?"

"I think the girl might be better off if nobody found her."

Natalie's eyebrows rose. She waited, but I didn't say anything. She looked out the conference room window, then looked back at me. "Just tell me one thing," she said, holding up her index finger. "Are those kids safe?"

I held her gaze as I answered, "Yes."

Natalie set her laptop on the conference room table and pulled her phone out of her pocket. After a minute, she spoke to whoever she called. "I need a favor. Find a way to shut down the precincts network servers for the rest of the day." She paused a long moment, listening. "Yes. I'll give you the other Dolphin's ticket." She disconnected, then grabbed her laptop and exited the room.

As Ford and I followed her out, everyone around the detectives' unit started grumbling as their computers crashed. Ford and I looked at each other, before splitting off in opposite directions.

As I pulled out my desk chair to sit, my phone rang. I glanced at the display, seeing it was Kelsey.

"What's up?"

"Stay at the precinct until Cooper comes back. I had to send him on an errand."

"What kind of errand?"

"To a baby shower. Aunt Suzanne and Haley snuck past security."

"Who's in more trouble? Them or security?"

"I'll let Uncle Hank deal with Aunt Suzanne, and I'll deal with Haley. As for security, well, let's just say that Aunt Suzanne duping them won't be forgotten anytime soon."

"Oh, no. What did she do?"

"She told them there was a man breaking into the pool house."

"And they believed her?"

"I think they believed Haley, who was nodding and pointing in that direction."

"Have the boys bring Aunt Suzanne and Haley to the precinct. I'll keep them with me until things cool down there."

"You sure? Will you have time to watch them?"

"Won't have to. I'm planning on handcuffing them and leaving them in an interrogation room until I'm ready to leave."

"Nice. Just remember that Haley normally wouldn't do something like this."

"Oh, I know perfectly well who the instigator was."

Chapter Seventeen

KELSEY
Thursday, 7:57 p.m.

"What are you thinking so hard on?" Ryan asked as he uncapped a beer before handing it to me. He sat across from me on one of the other lounge chairs.

Several others turned their attention to us. Between the tiki lounge, the patio off the backside of the kitchen, and the pool area, everyone had scattered in small clusters, chatting as they enjoyed the cool air coming off the ocean.

"Everything. Nothing." I took a drink of the beer. "I'm missing something. Something important."

"You?" Ryan asked, smirking. "You don't miss anything."

"Owen Flint's dead. Mr. Tricky killed him. We think Mr. Tricky was hired by the cartel."

Ryan set his beer on the coffee table. "I'm with you so far. Keep going."

Others started gravitating toward the tiki lounge to listen. Charlie nudged Spence who was busy working on his laptop and when he looked up, she motioned for him to follow. Cooper, Uncle Hank, and Grady also moved closer. Bridget and Trigger were sitting nearby but stopped talking to look back at me. Tech was the only one still focused on something else, as he watched the three monitors in front of him at his makeshift tiki lounge office, which consisted of an eight-foot folding table and a rolling chair.

After sitting in the chair next to me, Charlie propped her bare feet on the coffee table. "The cartel hired Mr. Tricky to kidnap me. Then what?"

"Exactly," I said, setting my beer down.

"Exactly, what?" Ryan asked.

"Mr. Tricky was hired to kidnap Charlie. So why go to Michigan? What was that all about? And how did he make it back to Florida so fast? He had to have flown, but Tech can't find a flight anywhere."

"Being we don't know his name I'm not surprised Tech couldn't find a flight," Charlie said. "Mr. Tricky could've flown back to any city in Florida, then rented a car back to Miami."

"But why?" I asked. "We know he was in Miami Sunday around three in the morning, then Tuesday night he's spotted in Michigan."

Cooper pointed to Charlie. "Then he's back in Florida, stalking Charlie by mid-afternoon Wednesday. About twelve hours later."

"He couldn't have driven," Uncle Hank said. "It's a twenty-hour trip. And that's without stopping for gas or bathroom breaks."

Everyone looked at Tech, but Tech shrugged. "I called Genie to help. But she can't find him either."

"What about the pictures?" Charlie asked. "Did she get a hit on facial recognition with the pictures I sent her of Mr. Tricky?"

"Nothing, nada, zip," Tech answered, shaking his head. "Nothing popped in the system."

I raised a hand, getting them to look back. "It's not really about his method of transportation or even his name, though that would be a nice have. The real question is why did Mr. Tricky go to Michigan at all? Why take the time to travel all the way there just to turn around and come back?"

Ryan narrowed his eyes at me. "I thought we already agreed he couldn't get to the family here, so he was trying to get to them there."

"Then why not stay for a few days? Try again?" Charlie asked. "Kelsey's right. We're missing something. There has to be another reason Mr. Tricky went to Michigan."

"Is Miguel still in California?" I asked Tech.

Tech nodded. "Donovan put a team on him. We'll know if he moves."

"What's his residence like in Cali?" Bridget asked.

"Cliffside suburb," Tech said, pulling pictures up onto one of the now mounted screens.

Bridget looked at Trigger.

Trigger shrugged. "With a distraction, maybe."

"You two are insane," Ryan said. "You think you're going to just mosey into his house and plant bugs?"

Bridget looked at me.

We stared at each other, communicating in silence for a good minute before I answered. "Fine, but I want Jackson, Reggie, and Bones to go with you. Take the jet to Vegas and drive from there. I don't want Miguel to know you're coming."

"Where am I going?" Bones asked as he walked across the patio toward us. Juan followed behind him.

"Recon mission in Cali," Ryan answered. "Bridget and Trigger need protection because they're going to do something stupid again."

Bridget stuck her tongue out at Ryan.

"When?" Bones asked.

"I'd like to leave in the morning," Bridget said.

Bones looked at Grady. "Can you take my place if I have to tag out?"

"Yeah, sure," Grady said, looking at Bridget, then me.

I shrugged, just as puzzled as Grady. It was unlike Bones to assign someone else to protect Bridget.

"Appreciate it," Bones said. "We walked into something today. I'd like to see it through."

"No sweat, but," Grady looked at me, "taking Reggie anywhere near Vegas is problematic." Grady was referring to the time Reggie left our getaway car unattended so he could play slot machines. Reggie wasn't the most focused security guard. "Can I take one of the other guys instead?"

"I'm thinking you'll need a four- or five-person team. Someone to create a distraction for Miguel's security team and then two guards monitoring the situation as Bridget and Trigger plant the bugs."

"Yeah, you need an oddball for the distraction part," Charlie said, patting Grady's chest. "You muscular men will only make the Remirez guards twitchier."

"Or," Bridget said, looking back at me, "Trigger can put on a show for the guards and I can take Grady or Jackson inside with me to plant the bugs."

"I'll leave it up to you to decide," I said, nodding to Bridget. "At the moment, I'm more interested in whatever Bones is working on."

"Basically, I've been following my man Juan here all day," Bones said, clapping a hand on Juan's shoulder.

Juan looked around, then back at the mansion. "Where are the kids?"

"They're inside watching a movie," Cooper said.

"It wouldn't be good if Mackenzie or Liam overheard us," Juan said to Charlie.

"I take it you found something," Charlie said, rubbing her hands together.

"What's this all about?" I asked.

"Mackenzie and Liam," Charlie answered. "I've been doing a little digging but not getting anywhere. Juan ran with it."

I looked at Tyler.

Tyler nodded, understanding my request. "I'll make sure the kids don't come out here." He pivoted, moving toward the house.

The rest of us moved closer, tightening our circle so we could lower our voices.

"What did you find?" Charlie asked Juan.

"The theory about their mother being still alive is a real possibility," Juan said.

"Wait," Tech said, sneaking into our circle. "Whose mother? What is everyone talking about?"

"Charlie met with a reporter yesterday," Cooper said. "She was looking for dirt on Mackenzie and Liam's stepfather, but instead she was told there was a possibility Sophia, their mother, wasn't dead."

"The theory seemed too farfetched," Charlie said. "But I checked the records and couldn't find a death certificate either. I couldn't pull the files at work without tripping an alarm." She looked at Tech, pointing toward him. "And I knew you were busy helping Kelsey. So I asked Spence to run background checks for me, and Juan went to do whatever Juan does to also find answers."

Spence, standing behind Charlie, placed a hand on her shoulder. "I'm still digging, but it's obvious someone was hired to scrub the internet. I found very little information on Sophia. Barrett, on the other hand, is a political machine. I wouldn't be surprised if he runs for a higher office soon with all the interviews he's been doing."

"What about Sophia's family?" Charlie asked Spence over her shoulder. "Did you find out anything about her family or her first husband?"

"Other than Sophia and her first husband lived in New Jersey, no. Even before she married Barrett, she kept a low profile. Her first husband worked for his family, handling their accounting. Nothing noteworthy popped so far."

"I could use a break from the dentist case," Tech said. "I can help you dig."

"Before the two of you venture into the internet world," Bones said, placing his hands on his hips. "We have something to discuss."

Bones looked back at Juan, but Juan merely waved for him to continue.

"Juan asked around at the hospital first, and no one witnessed Sophia Barrett's death," Bones said.

"That fits with what I heard as well," Charlie said. "Most of my contacts work in the E.R. but they said when Sophia came in, she was in bad shape and shipped off to surgery. Next thing they knew, Barrett was announcing to the press she'd died."

"I'm friendly with a nurse in the I.C.U.," Juan said with a slight blush. "She said Sophia was taken to their VIP section after surgery, but staff was limited to her neurosurgeon and one nurse."

"Do you have the nurse's name? I might be able to run her down," Charlie asked.

"That's the kicker," Bones said. "The nurse who took care of Sophia died three days later."

"Shit," Ryan said. "That's not good."

"No, not good at all," Charlie said. "How'd she die?"

Juan crossed his arms over his chest, peering down at Charlie. "Got caught in a corner store robbery a block from her house. Shot three times."

"That sounds awfully convenient for Barrett if he really did fake his wife's death," Charlie said.

"I thought so too," Juan said.

"The neurosurgeon?" I asked, trying to keep up with their conversation.

"Can't find him," Bones answered. "He was a no show for work the day after the nurse was killed. Hasn't reappeared since. But Juan tracked down another nurse who, on the day of Sophia's supposed death, witnessed two men moving a sheet-covered body from the VIP room to the elevator. The nurse didn't recognize the men, which is why she remembered it. She's worked there for two decades and knows almost everyone."

I tapped my chin, thinking. "So... Either Sophia died. Or those men were hired by Barrett to move her somewhere."

"We took a peek in Barrett's home office," Juan said.

"I didn't hear that," Uncle Hank said.

It had been years since I spent much time with Juan, but the mischievous look on his face reminded me of the man I used to know. The man who was encouraged to retire because he wasn't all that good at following the law.

Juan smirked at Uncle Hank. "And I found something, too."

"What kind of something?" Charlie asked, beaming an eager smile.

"Billing statements," Bones said. "Monthly billing statements from a medical facility on the other side of town."

"What kind of medical facility?" Bridget asked.

"According to their website, the kind that takes care of long-term patients."

"Please tell me there was a patient name on the statement?" Charlie asked putting her hands together as if she was about to pray.

"Nope," Juan said. "But there was a room number. Number 206."

"Give me the name of the facility," Tech said as he stepped out of our circle and moved toward his computers. "Let me see if I can hack their system."

Spence grabbed his laptop, moving to sit next to Tech at the table. Bones texted them a photo of the billing statement. We all waited quietly as they worked.

"Admission date for that room is in our timeline," Spence said.

"But the name on the room is listed as Jane Doe," Tech said.

"At least it's a female," Spence said. "And damn, the drugs they're pumping into her are a little extreme. In what world is that normal?"

Several of us looked over Spence's shoulder at the medical chart, but to me it was just a bunch of mumbo jumbo.

"Where's Haley?" I asked.

"I'll text her," Katie said.

"Haley's hiding from you in her room," Charlie said. "She thinks you're still mad at her for sneaking off earlier with Aunt Suzanne to the baby shower."

"I think Haley has suffered enough. Did you really need to put her in a holding cell?"

"They were safe," Charlie said, giggling. "The other women in there were undercover cops. They were just messing with Aunt Suzanne and Haley. They weren't in any danger."

"Which Haley never figured out, but my wife did," Uncle Hank said. "I swear, nothing scares that woman."

"They were cops? Are you kidding me?" Haley asked, pushing her way into the circle. She looked at Charlie. "The one with the tattoos scared the shit out of me. She told me she was going to make me her bitch as soon as the shift change was over."

"That was Crunch. She's the bomb," Charlie said. "By the way, she wanted me to give you her digits. She thought you were hot." She pulled the note out of her pocket and passed it to Haley.

Haley shuddered, crumpled up the piece of paper, and dropped it on top of the coffee table. "Why were you guys looking for me?"

"Look at this," Tech said, pointing to his screen. "Patient was in a car accident a little over six months ago. Does this look right?"

Haley leaned over to read the screen. "Pentobarbital... Let's see..." Haley murmured a few other words from the screen. "That's odd?"

"What's odd?" I asked.

"I'm only a med student, but it appears they have the patient in a medically induced coma."

"And that's odd?"

"No. Not based on the injuries the patient suffered. But what's odd is that if she was still critical enough to need to remain in the coma then I'd expect her to be at a hospital. Not in an aftercare facility. I'm not even sure they're allowed to administer those types of drugs."

"What would happen if we broke in and stole her from the facility?" Juan asked.

"You can't," Haley said. "She's on a ventilator."

"Can't isn't an option," Charlie said. "This could be Mackenzie and Liam's mother."

Haley looked back at the computer screen. "Well, in that case... I'll need an ambulance, some uniforms, Bridget, Trigger, and some fake transfer papers."

"I can get the ambulance and a driver," Charlie said, pulling her phone and stepping away.

"Spence and I will work on the transfer forms," Tech said.

"I'll find some uniforms," Bridget said, walking away.

"She's going to need round the clock care," Haley said. "And until we wean her off the drugs, there's no telling what her mental state will be."

"We can't bring her here," Juan said. "The kids can't see her like that."

"Charlie's safe house," Cooper said. "It has controlled access into the building and it's under the radar."

"We can't get the ambulance until early morning," Charlie called out.

"Before eight will work best," Haley answered her. "Before too many administrators start their day."

"About 6:30?" Charlie asked.

"Perfect," Haley answered. "I think." Haley worried her lower lip between her teeth. "If I do this," she said looking over at me, "then I'm no longer in trouble for sneaking off with Aunt Suzanne, right?"

"I'm not holding that over your head, Haley," I said. "If you're not comfortable doing this, then just tell us what has to happen. We'll take care of it."

"Working a con with Bridget will feel like the old days. I'm in either way." Haley straightened and faced me. The corners of her mouth turned up. "To be clear, I just wanted to make sure you'd hire a lawyer for me if we got caught. One afternoon was enough. I've been rehabilitated."

"You're covered. I alerted Cameron, our Miami lawyer, when we came to Florida," Katie said. "He's been waiting for one of us to get arrested ever since."

"I have a better idea," I said to Haley.

"Don't get caught," Cooper finished for me as he rejoined the circle and exchanged my beer with a fruity looking cocktail.

"Why thank you," I said before taking a drink. "Ahh, that's good." I turned to face him. "Now, what is it you want?"

Cooper laughed. "Can't a man do a nice thing for his wife without her becoming suspicious?"

I narrowed my eyes at him. "That's not funny."

"It's a little funny," Bones said, chuckling. "Sorry, Grady."

"It's fine. I thought it was kind of funny, too," Grady said, smirking at me. "But I'm with Kelsey. What are you up to?" he asked Cooper.

"I have a job I need to take care of out-of-state. I arranged a jet to get me there, though. If all goes well, I'll be back by mid-morning."

"We're running really short on security," Bones said, looking around. "Can it wait?"

"Wish it could, man, but it's time sensitive."

"Go, then," I said. "We'll figure it out."

Cooper leaned in, slapped a kiss on my cheek, then jogged away. We all watched him leave.

"He's off to do something stupid, isn't he?" I asked.

Bones and Grady just smiled.

I took a long drink of my cocktail.

Chapter Eighteen

CHARLIE
Thursday, 8:47 p.m.

"You sure about this?" Uncle Hank asked me. "If you're wrong, it's game over. They'll take your badge and never give it back."

"He's right," Juan said, leaning his arms over the patio table as he watched me. "You've asked too many questions already. As soon as Sophia goes missing, someone's gonna come knocking on your door."

"Let's face it, I.A. eventually is going to strip me of my badge. I'm not exactly the departments most upstanding cop."

"Are they still scratching their heads about that shooting at Benny's barbershop?" Spence asked.

I laughed. "That one works in my favor. They assigned a car to sit on the barbershop. The patrol officers in the neighborhood drop off coffee for the I.A. officers every morning. Then they pass me an update. Benny hasn't been seen all week."

"What happens when he does pop his head up?" Juan asked.

"Mickey happens," Spence said, holding his coffee cup out for Aunt Suzanne to fill as she made her way around the table. "Nobody shoots in the vicinity of Mickey and lives."

Jack walked through the patio doors. He crossed the patio and dropped a flash drive in front of Spence. "Two more cases closed. I'm calling it a night."

"Good," Juan said. "You can give me a ride home."

"Where's Pimples?" Spence asked.

"He already went home," Jack said. "Wanted me to tell you he's got a lead on the missing person case he's working, but he'll have to drive to Tampa in the morning."

"Juan, you should go with Pimples tomorrow," I said. "I'm not the only one who asked too many questions about Sophia. It would make sense if you had an alibi tomorrow morning."

"Yeah, I can do that," Juan said, knocking his knuckles on the table as he stood. "Play it safe tomorrow."

Jack and Juan left through the patio doors.

"You sure about this?" Aunt Suzanne asked. "Awful lot on the line for a woman you don't even know."

"I don't need to know her," I answered, looking over my shoulder at Aunt Suzanne. "I know that look in Mackenzie and Liam's eyes. The one they share with each other when they're trying to decide whether to stand still or rabbit. Councilmember Barrett is a bad guy. And if he's hiding his wife in a medical facility under an alias, it's for nefarious reasons."

"His rich wife," Spence said, turning his laptop. "Your friend Andrew was right. Sophia's attached to old Italian money. Her first husband was also connected. Mafia connected. He died in a sailing accident."

I glanced at Uncle Hank before leaning toward Spence's laptop. "Connected to who?"

"Italian mafia in New Jersey," Spence answered.

"No freakin' way," I said, standing to pull my phone from my back pocket.

~*~*~

Twenty minutes later, we all stood around the table grinning. I had my phone on speaker with the volume turned up as we listened to several voices arguing in Italian, one shouting over the next. The first person I'd called was Lisa, being the mafia princess that she was. She wasn't positive, but she thought she had a distant cousin by the name of Sophia Catrella. Lisa then patched Phillip into the call, who conferenced their mother into the call, who put her phone on speaker with their father. Next, they patched in a whole lot more Italian speaking people, and all out chaos erupted.

Lisa yelled something in Italian that silenced everyone, then she started barking orders. Then she started speaking to individuals based on the names, but I had no idea what she was saying. If I had to guess, she was issuing orders to certain people. I tried to follow the best I could but then suddenly everyone disconnected.

A minute later my phone rang. It was Lisa.

"Yeah," I answered, keeping the phone on speaker.

"Can you get Sophia out of the facility?" Lisa asked.

"We have a plan," Bridget called out.

"Good. The Family is on their way, but it's best if Sophia is somewhere safe before they get there."

"When you say the Family..."

"I mean the whole damn mafia Family," Lisa said. "My father, brother, two uncles, three aunts, and a pile of cousins. Miami is about to be invaded by some very pissed off Italians."

"So... Sophia is a relative?" I asked.

"Yes. She's my second cousin on my Uncle Rollo's side, but she's more than that. She's also a Tannelli widow. Her husband was a high-ranking member of the Family. When Sophia remarried, the family lost touch with her, but they're not happy to hear that she and the kids were mistreated. Whether the woman in the facility is Sophia or not, those kids will be protected from their stepfather. That you can be sure of. Their grandmother will be coming straight to the mansion along with a few cousins. She hasn't seen them in years, but Mackenzie should recognize her."

"Then what?" I asked a little worried. "No offense, Lisa, but if they come to Miami guns blazing, I might have to arrest them."

Lisa laughed. "You watch too many movies. Three of my cousins are lawyers. They'll file for legal guardianship of Sophia and the kids. Another relative is a doctor. She'll need access to Sophia when she gets there. She's concerned with Sophia being in a medically induced coma this long."

"We're not positive it's her. No way to know until we get the woman out of the facility."

"They know that. The plan is to help the woman, no matter who she is, and find out what's going on."

"When will they get here?" Kelsey asked.

"Early tomorrow morning. But if you don't want guns being waved around like in the movies Charlie watches, best if Sophia is already somewhere safe before they get there."

"We'll make it happen," Haley said.

"I need to go. All the yelling woke Abigail," Lisa said. "So much for the new bedtime schedule."

"Stay safe," I said before hanging up.

"Wow!" Spence said, throwing himself in his chair. "That was intense."

"If you think that was intense..." Bridget said, grinning. "You should've been at Lisa's wedding reception."

"Why? What happened?" Spence asked.

"We had a minor issue with a bomb," Grady said, shrugging. "Let's just say Lisa's family," Grady air quoted the word family, "wasn't thrilled."

I winked at Kelsey. "Good times."

Chapter Nineteen

KELSEY
Friday, 2:05 a.m.

I was lying in bed, wide awake, trying to decide whether to continue tossing and turning or get up and start my security shift two hours early. If I didn't sleep now, I wouldn't get another chance until midday. From three floors away I could hear Uncle Hank and some of the guards playing poker in the kitchen. They weren't being loud, but with the doors and windows open, sound traveled.

I rolled over, closing my eyes, but reopened them a few seconds later.

I wasn't sure why I couldn't sleep. My body was tired, but my mind kept reaching out to try to solve some mysterious question. The problem was, I couldn't figure out what the question was, so there was no way I could solve it.

I heard my phone chirp, indicating a text message. Rolling in the other direction, I picked up the phone, reading the display.

Tyler: *You awake?*
Me: *Yeah.*
Tyler: *Something feels off.*
Me: *I'll check on the kids.*

I pulled on yoga pants and tossed a t-shirt over my head before padding in bare feet out of my room.

Stopping in the doorway, I waited for my eyes to adjust to the dark sitting area. As the pitch black started shifting into recognizable objects such as the couch, a lamp, and the walls, I realized there was a shadow of what appeared to be a person standing at the end of the couch. Then the shadow moved toward the kids' room.

I couldn't see who it was. The silhouette was too big to be Anne, but too small to be Whiskey. It could be any of the security guys, though, most likely based on size, it was Trigger.

"Hey," I called out.

The person stopped, turning toward me. I still couldn't make out any features, but I didn't need to. Jager started barking from within the bunkroom, clawing at the door hard enough to make it shake in the frame.

The shadowy figure jumped back and I caught the glimpse of a knife in his hand. This wasn't Trigger or any of the other guards. No one on our security team would be reaching for a weapon when they heard my voice in the dark.

I knew there was enough moonlight behind me for the man to see my silhouette. I took a small step back, hoping he'd take the bait. I needed to draw him toward me. I needed him away from the kids' room.

Without uttering a noise, the man barreled toward me, his knife raised in the air. I ran backward into my bedroom, drawing him further away from the kids.

He slashed the knife downward and I raised my forearm to block it as I turned inward, shifting my back against his chest. I pulled on his wrist with my other hand as I turned, dragging his wrist with me, intending to flip him over me. It was a move I'd practiced a thousand times but before I had full control, he punched me in the ribs with the other hand then shoved me away, knocking me into the tall dresser.

I ducked as he turned toward me, slashing the knife where my head had been. I needed space to fight him. Using my foot against the dresser, I pushed off, slamming into him to force us into the center of the room.

I felt the knife pierce my skin as we stumbled. I ignored the pain, stepping back to gain my balance. Just as I was about to kick him in the knee, another figure charged into the room. One minute, my attacker was in front of me. The next, he appeared to be flying backward, out onto the balcony.

Time slowed to milliseconds. I realized as the two figures started falling backward over the railing that the second person was Tyler. I dove toward the balcony, reaching out and grasping an ankle as it disappeared over the edge.

I screamed as the weight of his body jerked at my arms, nearly pulling them out of their sockets as I was dragged upward, about to be pulled over with him. As my body was pulled upward, I bent my knees, locking them under the top rail.

I heard Tyler yell from below. My grip on his ankle held, but I couldn't move to reposition myself. I didn't know how long I could hold him.

"*Help*!" I yelled as I heard people running throughout the house and grounds.

Anne ran onto the balcony and looked over the rail.

"Anne, help me hold him," I begged.

"Don't let go!" Anne said before turning and running back toward my room.

Grady ran out, leaning over me to grab hold of Tyler's ankle. I felt some of the weight lessen from my strained arms and shoulders, but I didn't let go.

"Kelsey!" Tyler yelled from below us.

"We've got you!" I called back.

"If I don't make it—"

"Almost ready!" Anne yelled from the veranda below. "Hang on!"

The sweat on my hands was causing my grip on Tyler to slide, but Grady's grip held firm.

I heard chaos below me and focused on the noise, praying they were able to reach Tyler from the second floor. He wouldn't survive a head dive onto the stone patio. Even if he managed to flip his body upright, he'd easily break a good number of bones.

I listened to Anne, Alex, Haley, and Ryan below us.

"Are you sure—" Ryan started to say.

"*It will work*!" Anne yelled back. "*Tyler*! *Grab our hands*. Come on. Swing yourself toward us."

"I can't," Tyler answered. "They'll drop me."

Grady and I didn't say anything to reassure him. Tyler was right. We barely had a hold on him.

"*Do it!*" Anne yelled.

Tyler's weight shifted, causing my grip to slide from his ankle to his boot. Grady's grip slid too. Tyler's foot slipped out of the boot, and I screamed as his weight disappeared.

Everything seemed to happen all at once. I landed on my ass on the balcony floor with Tyler's boot still in my hands. Beside me, Grady stumbled to catch his balance. Tyler, Anne, and Alex screamed from below. I closed my eyes, squeezing them shut.

"*We've got him!*" Ryan called out from below. "He's okay."

I tried to inhale, but my breath was trapped in my lungs. Grady pulled me up, dragging me with him into my bedroom, through the sitting room, and toward the stairs. Before I knew it, I was dropping to my knees on the second-floor balcony where Tyler was stretched out on a king size mattress.

One end of the mattress was propped up just beyond the balcony railing, the other was on the balcony floor. Tyler was lying in the middle, feet still pointing upward and his head closest to the floor, while he panted, holding a hand over his chest. His right foot was bare except for the sock dangling off his toes.

"Fuck," Ryan said. "I thought you were a goner, man."

"You're not the only one," Tyler said, chuckling as he panted.

A solid breath of air filled my lungs as I lunged at Tyler with my fists. I swung out, punching him in the ribs and rearing back for another blow when I was dragged backward. My second punch met nothing but air as I screamed at Tyler. "*You're an idiot! What the hell were you thinking!*"

Solid arms wrapped around my waist, carrying me into the second-floor bedroom.

"*Let me go!*"

"Whoa, girl," Grady said in my ear.

"*I'm not a fucking startled horse!*" I yelled back, thrashing in his arms.

"More like a wild stallion," Ryan said, laughing as he stood in front of me. He looked behind me at Grady. "You got her?"

"Yup," Grady answered him, his voice chuckling in my ear. "Just adrenaline."

Just adrenaline, repeated like an echo in my mind. *Fuck*, I thought, trying to reel in my anger. He was right. I was reacting to the adrenaline.

I forced myself to stop thrashing as Ryan returned to the balcony. After taking a few deep breaths, I felt my feet return to the floor, but Grady's arm remained pinned around my center.

"I'm okay," I said more to myself than to Grady. "I'm okay."

His grip lessened. I unclenched my hands, shaking them in the air before dragging them through my hair.

"You still feel like killing me?" Tyler asked from the balcony doors.

"No," I said. "Sorry, but you scared the hell out of me. Don't do that again!"

"You were scared? You weren't the one dangling upside down." He started past me toward the door. "I'm going to check on the kids." And then he was gone. Back on duty. As if nothing had happened. I'm not sure he even asked about his boot.

I looked around at everyone, but no one was looking at me. They were focused on the room itself. I looked about, seeing what they were seeing.

A jacuzzi large enough for four grown men sat in the corner of the room. On the other side was a sitting area with large screen TV. Beyond the sitting area was a short hall with what appeared to be a walk-in closet on one side and an enormous bathroom on the other. I looked behind me at the massive wood post king size bed draped behind a canopy of chiffon curtains. The bed, stripped of its mattress, still looked luxurious as it sat between oversized nightstands which were covered with various candles.

Looking back, I turned slowly in a full circle. The room was huge. It was about the size of the kitchen and dining room on the first floor and even had a small kitchenette near the sitting area.

"What the hell?" Katie said, perching her fists onto her hips as she narrowed her eyes at Alex.

Haley ducked her head, looking embarrassed as she stepped away from him.

"I can explain," Alex said, holding his hands up. He was wearing a colorful head wrap and his silk white robe with his massive manly feet sticking out the bottom.

"Explain?" Katie snapped. "Tech and I are sharing a room with two other security guards. Kelsey is in a room the size of a closet. When Hattie and Pops were here, *you had them share a room with Wild Card!*"

"It's not like Wild Card ever sleeps in his assigned room," Alex said, backing away from Katie.

I looked over at Grady. "You got this?" I tilted my head toward Katie.

Grady smirked as he dipped his head in a clipped nod.

I turned out the door and followed the hall to the stairs, returning to the third floor. I found Tyler sitting on the couch outside the kids' room. His missing boot sat on the floor beside him.

He didn't look up when he heard me. He remained sitting, leaned forward with his elbows on his knees and his hands webbed into his hair. "The kids are fine. Trigger was inside the room with them, and as soon as all hell broke loose, Whiskey was out here guarding the door. They're already half asleep."

I sat on the couch beside him, placing a hand on his knee. "Tyler, I..."

"Yeah, I know. You were just scared when you hit me."

"No, Tyler," I said, staring at the floor. "I wasn't scared. I was *terrified*. Losing you..." I sighed, trying to find the words. "You're not just one of security guards who comes and goes from our lives. You're *family*."

Tyler shifted to wrap an arm around my shoulder.

I leaned my head on his shoulder. "You should've stayed with the kids."

"The kids were safe. Whiskey was guarding the door by the time I got upstairs."

"I could've handled it. I could've handled..." My thoughts skipped to the man who'd been in the house. "Who the hell was that?"

I felt Tyler shrug. "No clue. But whoever he was—he's no longer a threat. He landed face first."

I looked toward my bedroom, remembering the fight. Once we were in the moonlight, I was too focused on the knife to look at his face.

I stood, wincing when I felt a sharp pain. I lifted my t-shirt, inspecting where the knife had cut me.

"Need stitches?" Tyler asked, leaning forward to inspect the cut.

"No, it's not deep. I'm going to throw a bandage on it, then head downstairs."

I went to my room, slapped a gauze pad on with bandage tape, then hurried to the first floor. My mind was now solely focused on whoever had breached our security. How did he get in? How did he know which room they were sleeping in? How did he get past security?

On the first-floor patio, I stopped to stand next to Charlie. "Who is he?"

She squatted, but looked up at me. "Santiago Remirez."

I glanced at the body, watching the pool of blood splinter off in the stone crevices in multiple directions. "Shit."

"Yeah," Charlie said, turning back to inspect the body. "Oops." She giggled.

Unlike her, I didn't think the situation was funny. When Miguel found out his baby brother was dead, he'd raise a hell storm. It wouldn't matter that it was self-defense. This was a cartel family. Santiago's death would result in a full out war.

"I need to get Liam and Mackenzie out of here before the cops show up," Uncle Hank said from beside me. "I'll take them to Charlie's safe house."

"No. We need the safe house for Sophia," I said. "Move the kids to the apartment above the garage. Keep them out of sight."

Uncle Hank nodded before rushing inside.

"Charlie, take Haley, Trigger, and Bridget to the condo until you're ready to grab Sophia. There's not enough time on the schedule for I.A. to spend a half day questioning you."

"You sure? Might help to have a witness who wears a badge."

"I called Cameron," Katie said. "We'll be fine with a lawyer here."

"Sounds good to me," Charlie said, standing. "I'll call Quille before I leave. With any luck, he'll assign Ford or Chambers to the case."

"See if you can get Tasha, too. Tell her we need to clear the body before the kids see it."

Charlie nodded as she hurried inside.

I looked down at Santiago's body and kicked him in the ribs. "Bastard."

Chapter Twenty

CHARLIE
Friday, 6:35 a.m.

"Wait—" Ralph Stoggs, the paramedic I'd enlisted the ambulance from, said from the driver's seat. "We are kidnapping her? You didn't tell me we were committing a crime."

"I told you not to come," I said from the passenger seat of the ambulance as I scouted the near-empty parking lot. "I needed the ambulance, not you in it."

"Besides, it's not an abduction; it's a rescue mission," Bridget said from the back of the ambulance.

"At least we think it's a rescue mission," Trigger said, laughing. "If we find out otherwise, we'll bring her back."

"*Bring her back*? You can't just return a comatose patient! What do you think the police will say? *Oh, thanks. We were looking for her*."

"Chill," I said. "I'm certain Sophia's being held against her will. We just need to get her out and sober her up to confirm it."

Haley snorted from the back seat. "That's all? You realize I've never actually worked with a coma patient, right?"

Ralph's head swiveled to the back of the ambo. "Are you saying that not only are we kidnapping this woman, but there's a chance you could accidentally kill her?"

"Our plan is to keep her meds flowing until her family doctor gets to Miami. The doctor will know what to do."

"A family doctor? That's not going to work either," Ralph said.

"Not that kind of family," Trigger said from the back. "Mafia Family, dude. The woman we're snatching is related to the top tiers in New Jersey. We just have to keep her alive until the mafia gets here."

"*Mafia*?!" Ralph leaned his forehead against the steering wheel as he mumbled curses.

"We doing this or what?" Bridget asked, unfazed by Ralph's meltdown.

"The building has cameras at the entrance doors," I said, peering through binoculars.

"No worries," Bridget said. "Our disguises will hold."

Bridget and Trigger were both dressed in white orderly uniforms. Bridget's hair was tucked under a sleek blond wig and she had thick-rimmed glasses that made her eyes appear larger. She also wore theatrical putty on her face to alter her nose and cheekbones. If her image was caught on camera, facial recognition software wouldn't identify her. I was also wearing a wig and facial putty, but instead of glasses I had colored contacts. Trigger had bleached hair and a fake mustache, but since he refused the facial putty, he'd have to keep his face turned away from the cameras.

"What if Sophia has a bodyguard?" Haley asked.

"She won't," I answered as I turned back to face them. "Barrett is too arrogant at this point. He wouldn't bother paying a guard for this many months, especially with Sophia drugged the way she is."

"Crap," Bridget said, standing in a half-bent over position as she walked up and reached a hand out to my face. "Your face is drooping. You need to stop sweating."

"You layered my face in an inch of goo," I said, trying to scowl at her. "And I'm wearing a long-sleeve pant suit. Even this early in the morning, it's too hot in Miami for a suit."

"You're playing the lawyer, remember?" Bridget said. "You can't walk in wearing shorts and flip flops."

"I never wear flip flops. I'd rather be barefoot."

"That's not an option either," Bridget said, leaning back to look at my face again. "There. I think I got it. We should be good, but let's get on with it."

I handed Stoggs a hat. "Drive up to the entrance and park, but stay in the ambo and keep your head down. We swapped the plates and put magnetic signs over the ambulance numbers. The only way you—or the ambulance—will be identified is if you look up."

"Got it," Stoggs said as he put the hat on and pulled it low on his forehead.

I jumped out of the ambulance and moved to my Mustang. When I flashed my lights, the ambulance pulled away from the curb and I followed it down the drive to pull beside the main entrance of the medical facility.

Here we go, I thought as I parked my car behind the ambulance and slid out, carrying a leather attaché.

Trigger and Bridget made quick work of moving the gurney out of the ambulance. Haley carried a medical bag, one strap thrown over her shoulder.

I entered the building first, pulling out a stack of papers. "I'm here to oversee the transfer of a patient," I told the guard, flashing my stack of papers at him.

"It's a little early for a transfer," the guard said, looking at the papers. "Administration doesn't get her for another twenty minutes or so."

"The patient is a VIP client. Room 206. Second floor in the east wing. We need to do this early so there are fewer eyes. Wouldn't want the media getting ahold of this or heads will roll—yours included."

"Oh," the guard said, scurrying to a clipboard. "I'll need everyone to sign in. Take these papers to the second floor and show the floor nurse. She'll know what to do."

We signed in and then he buzzed us through the secure doors. The elevators were midway down the hall in an alcove. There were two elevators, one on the right and the other on the left. I pushed the panel to call the elevator on the right. It was already on the first floor, so the doors whooshed open.

I stepped back to let Trigger and Bridget inside with the gurney first. Haley and I then stepped inside and she pushed the button for the second floor, followed by wiping off her print.

When the doors opened again, I tucked my shoulders back and raised my head as I walked out and down the hall toward the nurse's station.

I motioned toward the door to 206 as I cut off the charge nurse, handing her the stack of papers. "These are the transfer orders for the patient in room 206. We need to expedite her transfer to another facility."

"I'm not authorized to approve transfers," the nurse said, looking at the stack of papers.

"The forms have already been signed and approved." I took the stack back, making a show of flipping through the pages and dramatically pointing to the signature page. "See, Michael Amman signed off as well as the patient's legal guardian." I flipped through additional pages, coming to another signature page. "And here's Dr. Presh's signature, approving the patient transfer."

"But I wasn't made aware Jane was being moved," the nurse said. "Usually, they tell us so we can be ready."

"My client didn't want the time and date to be announced. Fewer eyes that way. We fear the media learned of her whereabouts, and for her privacy we wanted her transferred at the most discreet time."

"Her privacy? I wasn't aware she was famous," the nurse said, seeming to get excited. "I don't recognize her. Is she famous?"

"She is." I made a show of looking around, ensuring we were alone as I leaned closer to the nurse. "Her name isn't Jane, either."

The nurse whispered back. "I knew someone with money was paying the bills, but her entire file is under the name Jane Suther. Is it even legal to use a different name for medical files?"

I heard the doors to room 206 open behind me. I rested a hand on the nurse's forearm, continuing to whisper, "You wouldn't believe the paperwork involved with faking someone's name. What a mess. And then—" I rolled my eyes, "—we got wind that someone's figured out it's her! Can you believe that? So frustrating."

"So..." The nurse leaned in as she took a quick glance around. "Who is she? Can you tell me now that she's leaving? Is she an actress? Or a model?"

"Afraid I can't share those details. Sorry." I watched my team push the gurney into the elevator alcove. "I *can* say, she's rich. And her husband is a politician. But don't tell anyone." I held a finger to my lips. "It needs to be our little secret."

"I won't say a word." She made the zip-the-lips motion. I knew by her excited smile that she'd be talking to anyone who'd listen within less than five minutes. But I was okay with that.

"Well, thanks for the assistance," I said, shoving the papers into my bag. "I'll be sure to tell my client you were most helpful."

She was about to say something, when the look on her face went from excited to confused. "Are you okay?" she asked, taking a small step back.

"Uh, yes. Why?"

"Your nose is falling off," she said, taking another step back. "What the—"

I took off running down the hall toward the elevators. "*Emergency!*" I called out to the extraction team. As I turned the corner into the elevator alcove, I felt my fake nose drop off my face. I tried to catch it but missed.

Trigger jumped out of the elevator, grabbed the nose from the floor, and tossed it to me. "Go! I'll take the stairs and clear the exit!" He ran the other way as the elevator doors closed.

"Oh, shit," Haley said, staring at my face. "You're melting. It's like something from a horror film."

Bridget uncapped a small plastic bottle from her pocket, dripped some of its contents on the underside of the nose, then stuck it to my face. Then she dabbed a little goo under the cheek and slapped the falling piece back up.

"Will it hold until we're past all the security cameras?" I asked Bridget.

"Uh-huh," she answered, looking away.

I glanced at Haley, not being able to read Bridget. Haley shrugged, also noting Bridget's odd behavior.

"We need to book," Bridget said as the doors opened.

I exited first, on the lookout for the guard. Not seeing him in the first hallway, I used my elbow to push the door panel for the automatic door. After walking through, I stopped to look around the lobby. The guard's feet were disappearing into a room off to the side. I watched Trigger step over the guard's body, then out of the room, shutting the door behind him.

I pointed to the room. "You didn't, yeah know, kill the guard, did you?"

"No, of course not," Trigger said, keeping his head tucked down. "I stun gunned him, then injected him with a sedative."

"What sedative?" Haley asked as they maneuvered the gurney across the room and out the main doors.

"One from your bag," Trigger answered as he jogged past us to open the back of the ambulance. "I pocketed one earlier, just in case."

Haley let go of the gurney and swiveled to face Trigger. "You gave him Propofol? Are you insane?"

Bridget swung the gurney in a half circle, lining it up with the back of the ambulance and pushed forward with enough force to launch it into the back of the ambo. "Argue later, kids. The nurse would've called someone, probably the police."

Trigger and Bridget jumped into the back, but Haley hesitated, looking back at the building.

"What is it? What's wrong?" I asked.

"He could have a reaction. He could stop breathing or have a cardiac event. Someone needs to monitor him."

"Okay," I said, steering her to the back of the ambulance. "I'll get him medical attention."

I pushed her forward, forcing her into the back of the ambulance before I slammed the door closed. I then ran to the Mustang and slid behind the steering wheel.

As I pulled away from the curb, I pushed the button on my steering column for hands free calling. "Call Pimples."

"Calling Pimples," the phone repeated back to me over the stereo speakers.

"You get pinched?" Pimples asked when he answered.

"No, but Trigger injected the guard with Propofol. The guard will need medical attention in case he has a reaction."

"I'll take care of it," Pimples said before disconnecting.

Pimples had more burner phones than a gangster. He'd get word to 911 to send an ambulance—one without a kidnapped victim in the back.

CHAPTER TWENTY-ONE

KELSEY
Friday, 7:04 a.m.

As each hour passed, more cops and crime techs appeared. Half of them were just standing around socializing. One even brought a box of donuts. Tasha had already bagged and transported the body back to the medical examiner's office. Two of her technicians remained to collect the smaller remnants with a specialized vacuum.

I shuddered, looking away from the kitchen window.

"Mrs. Harrison, will you please answer the question?" the female I.A. investigator ordered.

"Again, it's Miss Harrison," I said, narrowing my eyes at her. "And I've answered your question three times."

"You can understand my confusion," the woman said. "First you say Detective Harrison is your cousin, then you say she's your sister."

"I can see how that would confuse someone at your IQ level," Ryan said.

She pivoted toward Ryan, pointing her pen at him. "I'm not going to tell you again to remain silent."

Cameron rubbed his hand across his mouth, trying to wipe the smile away before he answered the woman. "It's simple, really. Biologically they are half-sisters. Legally, they are cousins. It's all a matter of public record if you wish to spend more time researching their family tree, but it has nothing to do with the man who died."

"I'll decide what's relevant," she said, writing something in her notebook. "Explain why the security cameras weren't recording."

"For the tenth time," Tech said from the dining room table. "We just bought the equipment. It's not fully installed yet."

"Sounds pretty convenient to me," she said.

"If the system had been live, there wouldn't have been a body on the back patio," Ryan said with a mischievous grin. "The guy would've never made it into the house. The body would've been near the gate or at the fence line."

"Then you're admitting you would've shot him?" she asked.

"We might've warned him before we shot him, but yeah. It's our job to protect the family," Tyler said, crossing his arms over his chest. "We would've done whatever had to be done."

"Including killing him. Not just wounding him."

"Oh, for fucks sake," I said, throwing my hands in the air. "This is a witch hunt. It has more to do with your obsession with busting Charlie than the facts, and I'm done with it. Get the fuck out of my house!"

"That's not up to you. You can't tell me to leave. This is an active investigation."

I pulled my cellphone from my back pocket, calling the one person with enough clout to put this woman in her place.

"What did you do now?" the police commander asked when he answered.

"I'm in Miami. A man broke in with the intent to harm. During a struggle he was knocked off a third-floor balcony. But I.A. is here trying to dig up unrelated dirt on my cousin, and frankly, the bitch is pissing me off."

"What's her name?"

"Detective Brenda Willer."

"Give me a few minutes."

I hung up, pressing my lips together as I glared at the detective. "Before your phone rings, you should know that you *suck* as a detective. That's probably why you hate Charlie—because she's a hundred times better detective than you. Pisses you off, doesn't it?"

She was about to respond when her phone rang. She looked at the display, then back at me with saucer-sized eyes. She stepped outside to take the call.

"Who did you call?" Cameron asked.

"The head of the Miami PD."

"Nice," Ryan said, grinning.

I leaned to the side to glance out the kitchen window. The detective pocketed her phone and looked over her shoulder in my direction. I wiggled my fingers in a wave and smiled. I was rather enjoying being on her shit list.

She turned away, ordering the other officers to pack up before she returned inside, stomped past us, and ordered other officers in the living room to leave. She continued onward to the front door. The front door slamming shut alerted us of her ultimate departure.

"Well, that was fun," Tyler said, relaxing into a bar stool and sliding his coffee cup toward me.

"I'll hire a crew to finish installing the security equipment," Tech said.

"Actually," I said, turning to face everyone. "We need to leave. Splitting the staff has exposed us. It's not safe for the kids here."

"Wait," Ryan said. "Was that the plan?"

"Was what the plan?" Bones asked.

"Mr. Tricky's trip to Michigan," Ryan said.

"Damn," I said, leaning against the counter. "You could be right, Ryan. Mr. Tricky was in and out of Michigan so quickly that I couldn't put my finger on what he was up to. But he could've predicted that making an appearance in Michigan would cause us to send half our guards north."

"Then why was it Santiago and not Mr. Tricky who came at us tonight?" Bones asked.

"Could be lots of reasons," I said, shrugging. "If Mr. Tricky is working for the Remirez family, then he might've shared the plan with Santiago. Maybe Mr. Tricky only wanted to decrease the staff but told Santiago the mansion was still too guarded to infiltrate. Maybe Mr. Tricky planned on sneaking inside, but Santiago had other plans or ordered him to stay back."

"Any of those would make sense," Bones said. "Add in the fact that Santiago was a crazy bastard, and it's even more likely. He wanted revenge. He wasn't about to let you win a second time."

"Since the rest of his body is being sucked into a forensic vacuum, I'd say Kelsey won again," Ryan said.

Tech stood, stuffing his hands into his pockets. "So, back to Michigan? And do you want me to still hire an installation crew for the security equipment?"

"Yes, and yes. I'll ask Lisa's family to oversee the installation. They can move in as we move out."

"Is it safe for them here?" Ryan asked.

"The cartel will know we left Florida. We don't have any other enemies here, so as soon as we leave they'll be safe."

Spence cleared his throat. I'd almost forgotten that he and Uncle Hank's cronies were huddled near the entrance to the living room. "What about Charlie? She's not likely to leave willingly to hide in Michigan."

"We can protect her," Pimples said. "Take shifts."

"I've got a handle on my cases, thanks to Jack, Juan, and Pimples." Spence slapped Jack on the shoulder, nodding to Pimples and Juan. "I have time to shadow Charlie if she decides to stay."

"What about me?" Joe Jr. complained. "I helped, too. Where's my praise?"

"*You set a motel on fire!*" Spence said.

"Got you the money shot of the boyfriend running out naked, didn't I?" Joe Jr. said. "And didn't have to wait all day to get it either. You should appreciate that."

"*Someone could've been killed!*" Uncle Hank yelled at Joe Jr.

"Back in my day, a man did what he had to do to get the job done," Joe Jr. said, nodding indignantly.

"And when was that?" Pimples asked. "Back when grudges were resolved with dueling pistols in the middle of town square?"

Joe Jr. muttered under his breath.

"I'll handle Charlie," I said. "She doesn't have a choice but to relocate. Mr. Tricky is too big of a threat. She'll need to come with us."

Cooper entered, walking past Spence but stopping short when he saw the forensic team with their vacuum on the patio. He glanced at me with a raised eyebrow. "What did you do now?"

"If I have to repeat what happened one more time, I'm likely to shoot someone."

"In that case," Cooper looked around then back at me, "just tell me who died. No one's bawling or punching walls, so I'm assuming it was someone we didn't like." He walked over next to me to get a cup of coffee.

"Santiago," Bones answered.

Cooper stopped filling his cup, looking over at Bones, then around the room. "Damn. Didn't see that one coming."

"Unfortunately, neither did we," Bones said. "Thought you weren't due back until mid-day?"

"My appointment went quicker than expected," Cooper said, topping off his cup before turning around and leaning against the counter. "I was able to drive back early." He looked over at me as he took a drink.

I knew the look he was giving me. It was the reason he'd been nicknamed Cooper. He was unpredictable. He took risks. And at all costs, he protected those around him.

"How did your mysterious appointment go?" I asked.

"Successful. I have a package in the trunk. Mind helping me?" Cooper pointed to Uncle Hank, Bones, and Grady. "It's heavy. I could use some help lifting it."

"What kind of package?" I asked.

"It's a surprise. Actually, like a present."

"What kind of present?" I asked, unsure I wanted to know.

"I'm guessing it's not flowers," Katie said, giggling.

"Nope, not flowers," Cooper said, smiling.

"This ought to be good," Grady said, folding his arms over his chest.

Cooper carried his coffee through the dining room toward the front door. Bones, Uncle Hank,

Grady, and I followed him out and to a sedan I didn't recognize. I thought it was one of the forensic employee's cars until Cooper hit the unlock button on the trunk. The trunk popped up about two inches, and Cooper raised the lid another two feet to show me what was inside.

A man. Dried blood coating the side of his face. A swollen eye, starting to turn black.

I slammed the trunk closed, turning to look around. Two of the forensic techs were packing their belongings into the back of their van, not paying attention to us. Only one police car remained in our drive, but the officer was nowhere in sight.

"Who is that?" I asked as I leaned against the back of the car, watching the parking area.

"Colby Brown," Cooper answered as he casually leaned against the car and took another sip of his coffee. "Miguel's right hand man in Atlanta."

I stepped closer to Cooper, lowering my voice. "And why is he in your trunk?"

Uncle Hank, Bones and Grady moved in closer to hear.

Cooper grinned at me. "I sort of beat the snot out of him until he told me everything he knows about Miguel." He shrugged. "The plan was I'd turn him in to the police for his outstanding warrant, but I got a little carried away. Now I'm thinking he needs to be stored somewhere until some of the bruising heals."

"And where did you plan on keeping him until then?" I asked.

Cooper looked around. "Well, I was thinking here, but wasn't aware the mansion was a crime scene."

I groaned, rubbing a hand against my forehead.

"Take him to the club," Uncle Hank said. "Garth will handle it."

"Nice," Cooper said.

I raised an eyebrow at Uncle Hank. "Does Garth handle a lot of things like this for you?"

"For me, no," Uncle Hank said with a mischievous smile. "For Charlie, yes."

I groaned again.

"What?" Uncle Hank said as he chuckled. "You have two motorcycle clubs and a security company full of men who handle these things for you. Charlie has Garth. He's a one-stop problem solver."

Chapter Twenty-Two

CHARLIE
Friday, 7:42 a.m.

It wasn't until we arrived at the condominium and unloaded the gurney from the ambulance that I got a good look at the patient. I exhaled, relieved to see it was indeed Sophia Barrett we'd just kidnapped.

Hearing someone walking across the parking lot, I turned, hand on gun.

"Ms. Harrison," a woman, flanked by two men, said as she walked toward me. "I'm Dr. Saventi. I believe your patient is my cousin, Sophia."

"I didn't expect you this early," I said, holding a hand out to shake hers.

"I was on the first flight out. I was told I'd be needed as soon as possible. One of your men, *uhh*... Baker? He sent a car to pick us up at the airport and brought us here."

"Were you followed?" I asked.

"No," one of the men who was flanking the doctor said. "Garth said to tell you all is well."

I relaxed, knowing that Garth would've ensured no one had followed. "We need to get her inside."

The two men took control of the gurney. I led the way through the back entrance and into the elevator, selecting the button for the top floor. On the way, Haley and the doctor discussed Sophia's medical status while the doctor took Sophia's vitals. I only understood the basics of their conversation. Apparently, Tech had already forwarded the medical file to the doctor after hacking the medical facility's servers last night.

The doors opened and I led everyone to the condo, unlocking the door and then holding it open. I pointed toward the back bedroom, and almost everyone moved in that direction.

My face, my real face, was irritated under the fake face, so I turned toward the bathroom as they settled Sophia. In the bathroom, I pulled off the wig, tossing it on the floor before slipping the colored contacts out. Then I started pulling on the putty mask to remove it.

Most of it popped off easily enough. I jerked on the nose, feeling it resist. Whatever adhesive Bridget had used was doing its job. I pulled harder, and the putty gave. I jerked on the chunk on my cheek, just as hard, and it gave as well. I looked in the mirror. A section on the bridge of my nose and left cheek remained. I scraped at it, but it didn't come off. It was cemented to my face. "Bridget!!!"

Bridget stepped into the bathroom, looked at me, then backpedaled into the living room.

I stalked her step for step. "Why isn't this coming off?"

"Well... You see... I had limited options. The security cameras..."

"Bridget?" I asked, continuing forward. "What did you do?"

"There really was only one way," Bridget said, shrugging as she reached into her pocket and pulled out the adhesive from earlier.

"*Super glue!? You super glued this shit to my face?!*"

"It was either that or the cameras would've captured your real face. What's worse? A little stuck putty or prison?"

"But now what? I can't exactly walk into the precinct with the evidence glued to my face!"

"No," Trigger said, studying me. "I think you'll need to lie low for a few days."

"We can try nail polish remover," Bridget said. "Maybe that will help."

"Not likely," Trigger said. "You secured the putty to her skin. She'd have to soak her entire face in a tub of nail polish remover long enough for it to work its way under the putty."

"Lovely," I said as I stomped into the kitchen. I opened the cupboard and pulled out a package of Chips Ahoy cookies.

Trigger walked over and stole a handful. "I'm going to go with Stoggs to move the ambulance. We'll strip the magnetic side panels and swap the plates back."

"Sounds good," I said before stuffing two cookies in my mouth.

I pulled my phone, texting Kelsey that we made it to the condo. She texted back that when everything was secure, to send the team back to the mansion to pack. They were fleeing to Michigan, and I was ordered to go with them. *Typical Kelsey*, I thought to myself. The woman would never stop bossing me around.

I typed back, asking about Mackenzie and Liam.

Kelsey responded that a security team would stay until the Family took over the kids' protection. They were expecting our guests at the mansion soon, and the last of the cops and forensic team was packing up so they'd bring the kids out of hiding soon.

I relayed the information to Bridget and Haley, who were waiting in the living room. They pouted when they heard they were relocating back to Michigan. I told them to wait for Trigger, then drive back to the mansion.

I left the apartment and made my way to the first floor and to my car. After swapping the plates back and removing the peel-away plastic that covered the bottom portion of the car making it look two-tone, I slid into my Mustang and drove east, heading toward the mansion.

Half way there, I realized my apartment was a mere block away. I had a bottle of nail polish remover in the bathroom cabinet. With any luck, I could get at least part of the putty off my face.

I turned left, not yet knowing the bad decision I'd made.

CHAPTER TWENTY-THREE

KELSEY
Friday, 10:03 a.m.

From the kitchen, I watched the flow of bags and boxes being carried outside and sighed. Somehow, without leaving the mansion, Alex, Haley, Bridget, and even Anne, had managed to shop while in Florida. They'd arrived in Florida with one bag each and were returning to Michigan with at least double if not triple the luggage. Katie and Bones offered to sort everything in the driveway, splitting the belongings into four piles. One pile was being shipped via FedEx back home. Another was given a green light to fly back with the family and guards. A third would be driven back to Michigan in our personal SUVs. And the last pile was being carried back inside to store until our next visit—which they were already planning.

"Can't we stay here?" Nicholas whined. "There's nothing to do at home."

"There's plenty to do at home," I said, using my fingers to comb his bangs out of his face. "Besides, Christmas is coming. You kids can help Hattie decorate."

"We still have shopping to do, too," Anne told him. "Remember? We have to find that gift you wanted to buy." She winked at him, and he ducked his head, peeking at me to see if I noticed.

Whiskey picked up the kids' duffle bags. "Cheer up, bud. Since your Aunt Charlie bought this place, we can come back and visit soon."

"Yeah, right," Nicholas pouted. "I'll be all grown up by the time we come back."

"Not true," I said, nudging him. "Now, make yourself useful and help carry everything outside."

"And lose the pouty face," Anne said. "Or we'll have to pack you in a box and ship you back via FedEx."

Sara giggled, racing over to help lift a bag twice her size. I shoved Nicholas in that direction. He took the hint and walked over to take one of the straps. Together, they lugged the bag through the living room.

"You know that's Bones' bag, right?" Cooper said, grinning over at me.

"Shit," I said, laughing. Knowing Bones, he filled it with weapons covered under a thin layer of t-shirts.

"I got it," Anne said, jogging after the kids.

I spotted Mackenzie sitting beside her brother on the couch in the living room. They were both huddled together at one end, Mackenzie splitting her attention between the front door and the back patio. Their own duffle bag sat near her feet.

"Quit looking like you're ready to run," I said, walking toward her. I sat in the middle of the couch next to Liam.

"Everyone's leaving," Mackenzie said, looking down at her bag.

"Yes and no," I said. "We located your grandmother. She's on her way." I looked at the time on my phone. "Actually, she should be here any minute."

"Our grandmother?! No. She'll turn us over to our stepfather..."

I held up my hand to stop her. "Not Barrett's mother. Your grandmother on your real father's side."

"Grandma Tannelli? I barely remember her."

"But you *do* remember her?" I asked.

"A little. She used to let me cook with her."

"So that's how you got to be so good at cooking," Aunt Suzanne said as she walked over. "I knew it."

"But it's not safe," Mackenzie said to me. "If..." she looked at me and then Liam, then back at me. "If our stepfather finds us, she could get hurt."

"Your stepfather is no match for your grandmother. I'm not sure if you know this, but your mother was born into an old Italian family. From what I hear, your father was also part of the family."

"Ewe," Mackenzie said. "Like cousins?"

I laughed. "No. I'm not saying your parents were related. I'm saying they both were from old Italian families who were allies in business."

Mackenzie studied me as I watched her process this new bit of knowledge. Her face shifted into big eyes and her mouth dropped open when the pieces shifted into place. "*The MOB? My grandparents are in the mob?*"

"Hush, *il mio bambino!*" an older woman barked from the front door. "We do not speak of business with outsiders. Now, come over here. I must see with my own eyes you are healthy."

Mackenzie instantly recognized the woman, bursting into tears as she fled the couch and launched into the woman's arms. "Nonna!"

"There, there, *nipotina*. You're safe now," the woman said, transforming from a warrior barking orders to a loving grandmother.

Liam looked over at me, seeming unsure.

"It's okay, Liam," I said. "I wouldn't leave you guys unless I knew you'd both be protected. Your grandmother is a lot more powerful than your stepdad. She'll squash him like a bug."

"Really?" Liam asked.

"Really, kid," Phillip said, rolling two leather suitcases inside the house. "Never cross your grandmother. She's old Italian. They hold grudges." Phillip had a teasing grin on his face as he held a hand out to Liam. "I'm your cousin, Phillip. I'm here to take care of your stepfather if he kicks up a fuss about your guardianship transfer."

Liam shook Phillip's hands, but still looked leery. "What's a guardianship?"

"It's the legal paperwork that says who gets to make decisions for you and your sister until you're older," Phillip said, leaning over with his hands on his knees. "After the judge signs it, we can take you back to New Jersey with us and keep you safe."

Liam looked at me, then back at Phillip. "My stepfather will stop you. He won't let me leave."

"You don't need to worry about your stepfather," Phillip said, ruffling Liam's hair. "We have a team of lawyers who will put him in his place. And if that doesn't work, I'll make sure he's educated on who's in charge."

Liam looked at me again. I nodded. He looked back at Phillip as another group of Italian men and women entered, invading the house. A big man with more silver covering his thick hair than the original black, ordered others around in Italian. Grandma Tannelli took issue with something he said and started arguing back.

Next thing I knew, there were Italians everywhere, all yelling at each other, and carrying bags in various directions. With the chaos of yelling still in full swing, Grandma Tannelli smiled at me before guiding Mackenzie into the kitchen with an arm slung over her shoulders.

I looked back at Liam. He was smiling as he listened to everyone.

"Do you know what they're saying?"

He nodded. "My mom taught us. She wanted us to know Italian. Whenever my stepfather wasn't around, we switched to Italian to practice. She said it would make him mad if he heard."

"Well, you can speak all the Italian you want now," a woman said, walking over and nudging Phillip aside. "I'm your Aunt Vianna. Your father's sister. Do you remember me? You were just a little guy when I saw you last."

"I don't remember," Liam said, leaning closer to me, but not seeming really scared.

"Well, good thing I brought pictures then," Vianna said, sitting next to him.

Within minutes, Liam had her phone in his hands and was scrolling through the photos. He leaned against her as she pointed out photo after photo of his mother and father, along with other family members. I discreetly stood, walking outside with Phillip.

Once we were far enough away from the house, Phillip turned to face me. "Are you sure it's okay for us to use this house?"

"I'm sure. We need to get back to Michigan. We have a cartel gunning for us and we're too exposed here. The cartel got too close last night."

"Tyler told me," Phillip said nodding. "I'll make sure the security equipment gets installed. We brought a small army of guards, though. If you change your mind and decide to stay, we'll have the manpower to protect everyone."

"No," I said, looking around at everyone. Half the people were carrying stuff outside, loading it into vehicles. The other half of the people were unloading vehicles, carrying things inside.

"Haley—" I called out as she was passing. "Any word on," I looked back at the mansion, then lowered my voice, "the patient?"

Haley shook her head. "Dr. Saventi said it could be days or months before she wakes, if she wakes at all. And with the type of injuries she has, there's also a chance of brain damage."

"But it was definitely her?" Phillip asked.

"Oh, it's her. Dr. Saventi agreed."

"Where's everyone else? Bridget, Trigger, and Charlie?" I asked.

Haley raised an eyebrow, looking around. "Bridget and Trigger are upstairs packing. Now that you mention it, though, I haven't seen Charlie."

"She didn't ride back with you guys?"

"No. She left before us."

Charlie wasn't the type to check in with me remotely, but if she was at the mansion, she would've sought me out.

I called Charlie's phone, but she didn't answer. "Grady!" I called out. "Has anyone seen Charlie?"

Grady looked around the parking lot. "Her Mustang isn't here."

Tech walked over. "I haven't seen her either."

"Hang on," Cooper said, jogging over. "I got this." He was grinning as he pulled out his phone, selecting an app. A red dot flashed on a map. "She's at her apartment."

"Nice," Tech said, looking over Cooper's shoulder at his phone.

"That's one way to keep track of her," Spence said, chuckling. Beast trotted over and sat next to Spence.

"Beast is here. You're here," I said, pointing to Cooper. "Bones is here." I pointed to Bones who was loading one of the SUVs that was being driven back to Michigan. "So, Charlie must be alone? Again?"

"And that surprises you, why exactly?" Cooper asked.

I scowled at him.

"Right," he said, handing me his duffle bag. "I'll head over there and grab her. We're about done here anyway."

"We need to get to the airport," Katie said. "I told them we'd be there by eleven."

"Everyone take off," I ordered. "Make sure Bones and Bridget stay close to the kids. If I don't make it back to the airport in time, leave. Don't wait for us."

"You got it, boss," Katie said, jogging over to update Grady and Bones.

"Charlie's probably napping," Aunt Suzanne said. "She hasn't slept more than an hour at a time since being moved to the mansion."

"Whatever she's doing, she's once again on my shitlist. She knows better."

"She's been on her own a long time now," Aunt Suzanne said. "You left, remember? Charlie had to learn to adjust. Instead of the dynamic duo, she became a lone wolf, relying on herself for protection. You can't expect her to change her habits just because you're in Florida."

I was quiet a long moment, thinking of what she was saying. It was true. I had to flee Florida, leaving

Charlie here on her own. She was unprotected. She was alone. For the first time in our lives, we were several states apart. And while I found a new family first in Texas, then in Michigan, Charlie continued to live alone, only touching base with Uncle Hank, Aunt Suzanne, Baker and Garth.

"Are you and Uncle Hank packed?" I asked her, changing the subject.

"We're staying here. I already cleared it with Mrs. Tannelli."

"It's not safe."

"We ain't running," Uncle Hank said. "And I doubt Charlie will leave either, but I hope she does. Spence offered to help me keep an eye on the dentist office and be on the lookout for Mr. Tricky."

"We'll help too," Juan said, standing behind Uncle Hank with Jack and Pimples.

I was about to argue when Phillip put an arm over my shoulder. "I brought an army, remember? We'll keep them safe."

"Listen up," Tyler called from the other side of the drive. "The kids will be with me in the second vehicle, along with Bridget and Bones. Ryan and Katie, you're in the first vehicle with Carl, Alex, and Haley. The rest of the family and guards will divide between the third and fourth vehicle. That leaves Spence." He turned to look at Spence. "Are you still good to follow behind and protect our backs to the airport?"

"Locked and loaded," Spence said, walking away with Uncle Hank following.

"We'll go with Kelsey," Grady said, nodding at Cooper.

"Really?" Ryan asked as the others fell silent.

Grady looked at Ryan. "You got something to say?"

"Shit," Ryan said, looking around. "Didn't actually mean to say that out loud."

Several people laughed.

"Anyone know which room Charlie was staying in?" I asked. "I'll pack her stuff."

"She had the room next to mine," Grady said. "On the second floor." He started for the house.

As I turned to follow, Cooper jogged over to walk beside me. "Did you take care of that package?" I asked him.

"Yup. Garth had no problem storing it for me. He seemed almost happy about it."

"Good." I followed Grady up the stairs. "Maybe on the ride over to Charlie's apartment you can share any information Colby Brown bestowed upon you."

On the second floor, Grady pointed to the closed door to the left before he walked into the next room. I opened the door and sighed. Charlie's a slob. Clothes were scattered everywhere. I had to walk over piles of both clean and dirty clothes to reach a trash bag on the other side of the room that was being used as a suitcase. You'd never know Charlie was a multi-millionaire. I picked up the first trash bag, with only a few shirts in the bottom and started scooping clothes from the floor. Cooper grabbed a wad of clothes from the bed and dropped them into the bag.

CHAPTER TWENTY-FOUR

KELSEY
Friday, 10:38 a.m.

Cooper took two garbage bags, leaving me with just one oversized trash bag to carry. As soon as we stepped outside, oversized men with guns strapped to their hips took the bags from us and loaded them into my SUV. Cooper grabbed his duffle and my small suitcase that were sitting by the front door and tossed both on top of the garbage bags.

I looked around to see if there were any more bags sitting around and noticed instead that three ladders had been erected along the front side of the mansion. At the top of each was a man installing a camera. Another half dozen contractors were roaming around with wire or sticking their heads out windows, working with the men on the ladders.

Phillip walked over, stopping to stand beside me. He looked toward the ladders. "Should be done by tonight."

"Good. I'll feel better knowing your family has the security system operating."

"Umm," Phillip said, looking to the side of the house. "You're aware that some of your men are still here, right?"

"Who?"

"I believe you call the one guy Tech. And I don't know who the other guy is."

"Where are they?"

"The tiki lounge."

"What's Tech doing?" I asked as I followed the path around the mansion.

"He wanted to stay until the equipment was installed. He said he needed to ensure it was looped over to his secure server. He also said something about not abandoning a case you were working on."

"Tech!" I called out as I rounded the corner of the house and spotted him.

"Don't start yelling at me!" Tech said, not looking up from his laptop. "I already heard an earful from Katie."

"Why didn't you leave with everyone else?"

"He cleared it with me," Grady said, walking over from the back patio. "After I take you, Wild Card, and Charlie to the airport, I'll come back and stay with Tech and Trigger. It makes sense to keep an eye on the dentist office and the mansion for a few days."

"Trigger's still here too? I thought he was going with Bridget and Bones to Vegas?"

"Bones was issuing orders before they even left the driveway," Grady answered. "Trigger bailed from the operation. I called Jackson and he said he'd find a fourth."

I ran a frustrated hand through my hair. "Mr. Tricky is still at large. What if Phillip's family becomes a target because a group of us stayed behind?"

"Mr. Tricky doesn't give a shit about me," Tech said. "I'm not even on his radar."

"I might be on his radar," Trigger said, walking over in his swimming trunks, water dripping off his skin. "But I'm willing to risk it for a few more days of sunshine."

"And I'd love it if Mr. Tricky breached the line," Grady said, punching a fist into his other palm.

"I don't know who this Mr. Tricky is, but it sounds like fun," Phillip said, grinning. Phillip was still wearing his three-piece Armani suit and not sporting even a hint of sweat under the Miami sun.

"Your family is here," I warned Phillip. "Mr. Tricky is dangerous."

"My family, much like yours, is in a constant ebb and flow of danger. We'll handle it. And as a repayment for saving Sophia and her children, it would be our pleasure to handle the cartel problem for you as well."

"Thanks, but no. The cartel problem will follow us to Michigan and we'll handle them on our own turf like we did last time. That I have no doubt. But if you do see Mr. Tricky, feel free to capture him and turn him over to the police. They have a few questions for him."

Phillip sighed, bored by my instructions. "Predictable."

Grady chuckled. "No worries, Phillip. Once Kelsey flies north, we're in charge and can do as we please."

I ignored them, turning my attention back to Tech and Trigger. "How long are you two staying then?"

"Maybe a day or two. Longer if anything starts jumping off at the dentist office. Ryan was coming back too after he helped escort the family to the airport. He said there was no point relocating because he promised Tweedle he'd be home by the end of the weekend."

"Fine. I'm not going to argue with all of you but stay at the mansion until it's time to fly back to Michigan. Don't make yourselves targets."

"I got no problem with that," Tech said. "I'm the brains; Grady's the brawn. And well... Trigger's the..." Tech raised an eyebrow, thinking.

"The beauty?" Trigger asked, wiggling his eyebrows.

Grady shook his head at Trigger before looking back to me. "You've already missed your jet, but Katie booked you guys on a commercial flight. We better get moving or you'll miss that too."

I looked over at Phillip. "You sure you have it handled here? What about Sophia and the kids?"

"I'm a Bianchi," Phillip said with his shoulders back and head held high. "We protect our own. They'll be safe. And the lawyers have an emergency hearing scheduled at the court for one o'clock today."

"Any news on the kidnapping? Are the police still searching for Sophia?"

"We contacted the police after we confirmed it was Sophia. We've informed them that she's being kept at a safehouse under family protection until the matter is cleared through the court system."

"Did we get out clean then? On the kidnapping?" I asked, looking between Phillip and Grady.

"There was a minor mishap with Charlie's disguise," Grady said. "But Bridget handled it. She super glued it to Charlie's face."

I stared at Grady, but he wasn't joking. I looked back at Tech, hearing him laugh. He turned a monitor, showing me a still image of Charlie as she left the condominium building. A chunk of putty remained stuck to her cheek and another on the bridge of her nose.

"It's not permanent, is it?" I asked.

Grady shrugged. "It will wear off eventually."

"*Are we leaving or what?*" Cooper yelled from the side of the mansion.

"Yeah!" I called back, turning to walk that way. "We're going."

~*~*~

The ride to Charlie's apartment was awkwardly quiet. Cooper sat in the back seat. Grady drove. I rode shotgun, trying to think of a safe conversation starter. The three of us hadn't been alone together since—well, since maybe never. I couldn't think of a time the three of us were alone together. There was usually either a group of people around or I was alone with only one of them.

I looked over my shoulder at Cooper to see if he was just as uncomfortable.

"So..." Cooper said, smirking as he inspected his nails. "Want to hear about Colby Brown?"

"Hell, yes," Grady said, sighing. "Anything to ease the tension."

I turned sideways in my seat to look back at Cooper without needing to crank my neck. "First, tell me why you decided to go off on your own to pick up Colby without backup. I could've sent Bones or Ryan with you."

Cooper smirked as he pointed at me. "And that was why I didn't tell you."

"He didn't want to further reduce security at the mansion," Grady explained. "We were already running on a skeleton crew for a place that large."

"We could've made it work."

"If I'd needed backup, I would've said something," Cooper said. "But I didn't. And I made sure Bones and Ryan knew where I was going in case I ran into trouble. Now, do you want to hear about my little chitchat with Colby?"

"In a minute," Grady said. "But before we get to Charlie's, I wanted to say something." Grady looked at Cooper in the rearview mirror. "I'm sorry, Cooper. I've been a dick to you. I'm not happy you kept the marriage a secret, but—"

"Actually, I didn't keep the marriage a secret," Cooper said, interrupting. "More like I kept the non-existent divorce a secret. Because you know, everyone knew we'd been married. Get it? The big secret was I never filed for the divorce?"

"We get it!" I said as I watched Grady's grip on the steering wheel tighten.

"You really need to stop pushing my buttons, man," Grady snapped.

"You two are so serious..." Cooper said as he looked up at the ceiling of the SUV, an expression of exasperation on his face. "Look, it's not like it changes anything. You two obviously are getting back together. Between Grady starting to speak to me again, and you," Cooper waved a hand toward me, "starting to speak to Grady again, it's only a matter of time before you two lovebirds work it out. Not sure why you both have to be so cranky about it."

I turned in my seat, facing forward. We all stopped speaking again. I felt Grady making sideways glances my direction but I didn't look his way.

"Give me Charlie's keys," Cooper said, leaning up between the seats with his hand out. "I'll warn her you're coming to collect her."

I handed him the keys as Grady pulled into the parking lot behind her apartment building. The SUV had barely stopped before Cooper bailed from the vehicle.

Grady shut off the engine and looked over at me. "Why didn't you tell him we weren't getting back together?"

His eyes held a mixture of hope and sadness. "It wasn't the right time. I keep telling you, Grady, our break up isn't about Cooper. When the time is right, I'll explain everything to him. But it's not a discussion I'm willing to have in front of you or anyone else."

"So," Grady said, looking away. "You haven't changed your mind." It wasn't a question. He sounded more like he was telling himself, than me.

"I'm sorry. I've made my decision."

Grady dipped his head in a clipped nod before climbing out of the SUV. I followed suit, sliding out the passenger side and heading toward the building's back entrance where Cooper had left a rock propping the door open. Grady opened the door wider, kicking the rock to the side before stepping back for me to enter first.

"You're mad," I said as I started up the stairs.

"No," Grady answered. "Just thinking."

"About?"

"The whole porch thing—you know, where you saw yourself surrounded by everyone. It's been stuck in my head."

We turned on the stairway landing to walk up the next flight.

"You were right. I can envision you sitting on the porch you described. The one where you are surrounded by everyone. You're happy there. You're laughing. It's noisy and crowded, and you love every bit of it. And..." His words hang in the air as we climb the last few stairs.

"And?" I asked as we paused at the end of the hallway.

"And, I see myself standing in the background, leaned against the side of the house, annoyed. Wanting time alone with you. Wanting our own porch. Wanting our children and grandchildren playing in the yard, not everyone else's."

"I'm sorry," I said, placing a hand on his arm. "I know this is hard. If I could make it easier, I would."

Grady nodded, but looked away. "I need time. Time before you start a relationship with Wild Card or anyone else. I need time to adjust before I see you move on. I'm not sure I can handle seeing you with someone else right now."

"I feel the same," I admitted. "I don't think I could handle seeing you with someone else either. I love you, Grady. Us not wanting the same things out of life doesn't change how I feel about you. I just know I can't keep trying to be the person you want me to be. I can't keep trying to change."

He wrapped an arm around me, pulling me into his body, holding me close. It felt good to be held by Grady. Familiar. Loved.

I felt him kiss the top of my head, before he moved away, clearing his throat as he walked down the hallway. "We're going to miss our plane if we don't get moving."

He didn't look back and I didn't say anything as I followed him to Charlie's door. The apartment door was wide open. We both walked through the threshold then stopped to look around.

"Oh, shit," I said.

"This is Charlie's place?" Grady asked, looking around.

"It used to be. Charlie's going to kill Bridget. It's bad enough Bridget superglued theatrical putty to her face, but this..."

"It's nice, but Charlie will hate it."

The apartment was beautiful. The appliances were sleek. The furniture looked luxurious and in tasteful creams and browns. The problem was the layout.

Bridget had somehow acquired the apartment next door and reconstructed the two apartments into one singular apartment. The kitchen was in the center, with three angled walls behind it and an arched breakfast island closest to the door—which presented both problem number one and two. Anyone sitting at the island would do so with their back facing the door, which Charlie would never do. And the walls behind the kitchen prevented a clear view of the apartment to ensure no one lurked somewhere else in the apartment.

To the left and to the right, the main areas presented additional safety concerns. To the left, her former living room was easily viewable and much improved aesthetically, but the oversized armoire was placed in the center of the room on the same wall as the door. Someone could easily hide on the other side. Grady must've agreed because he walked over to ensure no one was there.

To the right where the neighboring apartment used to be, an archway led into another area. From the apartment entrance, there was no way to know if someone was in that room. Cooper stood in the archway with his back turned to us and his large frame blocking me from seeing more than part of a desk and a landscape painting on the wall.

The problem with the remodeling was that Charlie had lived in the same apartment all these years because the layout made her feel safe. She liked opening the door and being able to see the living room, kitchen and dining room was clear before she closed and locked the door. Then she'd only need to search the bedroom and the bathroom. This layout would require her to expose herself as she cleared each room and hoped someone didn't sneak up behind her. And even then, she'd be unlikely to be able to sleep more than an hour or two. It was the same reason she'd barely slept the last week except for occasionally napping on the couch closest to the kitchen during the day when everyone was coming and going.

"Maybe Whiskey can think of a way to fix it," Grady said, taking out his phone and snapping pictures.

"Shit, what a mess," I said, shaking my head.

Cooper had remained quiet and was still standing in the center of the archway to the other room with his back turned toward me. I started toward him, but he turned to face me as I approached. My feet froze to the floor as I saw his expression. The blood in my body felt like it dropped from my head to my toes. "No…" I said, shaking my head and moving toward the other room to pass him.

"She's not here," Cooper said as he rushed to stop me. He reached out, cupping my face, and staring down at me with his tear-filled eyes.

My body started to tremble. "What is it?" I felt myself sway. I knew whatever was in there had to be bad by the way Cooper watched me. "What's in there?"

"I need you to go with Grady," Cooper whispered. "I need you to go with Grady to the airport. Go home, Kelsey."

I clutched the front of his shirt as a tear slid down my cheek. "Tell me."

Cooper leaned his forehead against mine, keeping one hand on my face as he wrapped the other arm around me to hold me close.

"Cooper," I whimpered. "Please."

"They took her. They took Charlie."

My legs gave out, but he held me upright. I gasped for air, my vision blurring behind a wall of tears.

"It's going to be okay, Kel," Cooper said, rubbing my back. "I'll get her back. I'll bring her home."

I gripped his shirt tighter in my fists, pulling myself closer. "No, no, no… She's not gone. She's here. Or, maybe she's on her way back to the mansion."

He tightened his hold on me.

"Please, Cooper. Tell me you were wrong."

"Her phone is here. And a note. The note is pinned to a... well, it's pinned to a... Kelsey, they have her. I'm sorry. Somehow they knew..."

I pushed away from Cooper, wiping my cheeks with the back of my hand. "Pinned to a what?" I asked as I took a deep breath and looked past him at the archway entrance before looking back at him. "What's in that room, Coop?"

Cooper looked away, unshed tears threatening to spill.

Taking a deep breath, I walked toward the room, dreading what was on the other side.

Cooper reached around and grabbed my arm. "Kel—"

"I need to see," I said, jerking free and walking forward.

Propped upright in the center of the room, facing the doorway, was the stuffed animal Nicholas had had as a young child. A puppy with a smiling, lopsided grin.

I glanced around the room, then back at the stuffed animal. I spotted a note pinned to the puppy. The message, clearly written in black marker, said: *Leave Miami or Charlie dies*.

"Not again," I whispered as my knees buckled, dropping me to the floor.

I picked up the phone sitting next to the stuffed toy and turned it over. It was Charlie's. Unlike me, she always carried her phone.

The phone was proof she'd been here. That they really had her.

"Not again. No. Not again."

Chapter Twenty-Five

KELSEY
Friday, Noonish

I watched, listening to everyone around me. Cataloging every move, every word, filing the information in my brain. They thought I was mentally checked out. They even had a paramedic, some friend of Charlie's, take my vitals. But I wasn't. I was fully aware of everything happening around me. I was aware that I still sat on the floor, knees folded beneath me, still facing the stuffed animal in front of me.

It wasn't just any stuffed animal. It also wasn't a replica of the stuffed toy left behind when my son was kidnapped. It was *the same one*. Stained on one paw by chocolate syrup and a slight tear on another paw from where Nicholas used to suck on it when he was outgrowing his pacifier. I stared at the lopsided smiling stuffed dog, maintaining an emotionless expression. I wanted to scream in anger, but I refused to give in to the emotional release.

Because I knew that whoever took Charlie, whoever was behind this, was watching me.

I knew every inch of that stuffed animal, which I'd stored in my basement in Michigan. And the last time I'd looked at it, the left button eye had been hanging by a mere few threads. Now the eye was tightly sewn on, but the button had been replaced with a video lens.

Tech walked past me to the other side of the room. I'd sent him a text message about the recorder. He squatted behind the dog so he wouldn't be seen on the camera. From his bag, he took out his laptop, then a scanner. I sat helplessly frozen, staring at the dog while Tech worked.

Time slipped away again, until suddenly, Tech jumped up and moved to stand in front of the window.

Cooper walked past me and the two of them whispered while Tech pointed out in the direction of the back parking lot. I couldn't hear their words, but I didn't need to. They were hunting the other end of the recorder's signal.

Cooper nodded then crossed the room toward the apartment door as he called for Grady to follow.

I stayed. I did my part. I stared at the stuffed dog.

At least twenty minutes passed before Tech walked over and kicked the stuffed dog over, face first onto the carpet. He took out his pocket knife and cut the back of the toy's head open before pulling the camera and microphone. He pulled the battery, tossing it to the floor.

"You did good," Tech told me.

"Did it work?" I asked. I rotated my head on my shoulders, trying to loosen my stiff neck muscles.

Tech shook his head. "No. I'll check nearby security footage, but the car we think he was in took off before we could get to it."

Uncle Hank stormed into the room from the kitchen area. *"That bastard was watching?"* He stomped to the window and looked around the street below. "First, he takes my girl, then he watches us like a stalker?"

"It wasn't about you," I said, reaching up to take Tech's offered hand to help me up from the floor. "He was watching me." I stopped talking, looking back at the camera unit.

Tech read my mind. "It can't transmit without the battery."

"Maybe we'll get lucky and get a print or serial number off that thing," Quille said, looking down at recording unit and motioning for an officer to bag it.

"You won't get anything, but knock yourself out," I said before walking out of the room and then out of the apartment.

I walked away from the noise, the crowded rooms of cops and investigators, down the hall, down the stairs, out of the building and into the parking lot. I tipped my head back, feeling the heat of the sun on my face. Inhaling deeply, I caught the scent of cigarette smoke. I looked over to see Grady smoking as he spoke in hushed tones with Cooper.

"Do you guys have any leads?" I asked as I walked toward them.

"Not yet. We were just talking about next moves," Grady said.

"I think you should go back to Michigan," Cooper said. "Be with Nick."

I reached into Grady's shirt pocket and pulled his cigarettes, lighting up. Grady seldom smoked, usually only when he was stressed. It had been months since I'd smoked, but I couldn't resist the smell as I lit up. After inhaling deeply, I answered Cooper. "I'm staying. I'll talk to Nick later and explain the best I can. Until then, we need to circle the wagons."

I pulled my phone and selected everyone in my contact list. I typed the text message: *Charlie kidnapped. Meeting at 2:00 at her apartment building. Michigan to remain in lockdown until further notice.*

There was a lot more I wanted to say. A lot more I was feeling. But the message was a good start. Allies would head to Miami. The family would close ranks to keep everyone else safe. When the jet landed in Michigan, the security team traveling with the kids would be alerted before they ever stepped onto the tarmac.

And more importantly, everyone would understand my meaning. The cartel had crossed the line, triggering what could only be interpreted as an act of war against us.

I hit the send button, then inhaled another deep breath of cigarette smoke as the cellphones around me chirped that my message was received.

I pulled Charlie's phone from my other back pocket and sent a similar message to all her contacts.

It was time to rally the troops.

CHAPTER TWENTY-SIX

KELSEY
Friday, 1:55 p.m.

The parking lot of Charlie's apartment building was a madhouse.

On one side of the lot was Quille, Ford, Chambers, the young detective Gibson, along with likely every cop in Miami. Standing firmly on their side of the lot was Tasha from the medical examiner's office, some huge guy with tattoos standing next to her, Uncle Hank and his poker buddies, and Aunt Suzanne. At the end closest to the building, but still on the law enforcement side, were our friends from the FBI: Maggie, Kierson, and Genie.

On the other side of the lot were those firmly on the not-so-law-abiding side. Mickey McNabe stood strong and defiant talking to Spence while six of Mickey's goons guarded his back. Chills, a local gang leader, stood a few feet away with at least twelve of his gang members. Phillip and his father stood with several members of their family. Baker, Garth, and Evie were grouped together next to Ryan and Cooper.

There were more people. Lots more. Everyone from hookers to lawyers and from the homeless to millionaires. As every minute passed, more people arrived. My phone also held over fifty responses from those who couldn't make the two o'clock deadline but who were ready to contribute in any way they could. The response received was overwhelming.

Tech walked over and handed me a megaphone he'd borrowed from Quille, then braced my arm as I climbed onto the hood of my SUV and stood.

"Thank you all for coming on such short notice," I called out over the megaphone. "As most of you know, my son was kidnapped when he was only five years old. It took me *years* to find him. Each day over those long years was pure torture. Worrying if he was alive. Worrying if he was hurt. Worrying that if he *was* alive, my next move could get him killed.

"My sister Charlie shared that burden with me. Grieving the same loss. It's an experience we both endured because Nicholas was so young and vulnerable."

The crowds on both sides were silent, listening intently. No longer focused on the group on the other side of the parking lot.

"I'm sharing this personal pain with everyone because I need you to understand. This morning Charlie was kidnapped. An enemy of my family took her—a Miami detective, a friend, my sister. We believe her abductor is a man we've nicknamed Mr. Tricky. He's military trained. He's proved to be a patient and deadly foe, and we believe he was hired by the Remirez cartel, run by Miguel Remirez. Miguel's brother Santiago died in an attack against our family less than twenty-four hours ago. Tech will be sending everyone pictures of both Mr. Tricky and Miguel Remirez."

My cell phone rang from my back pocket. I pulled the phone, reading the display: *unknown number.*

"Tech, I need a trace," I said as I sat on the hood and passed the megaphone to Grady.

Tech ran for his laptop as Genie rushed over, pulling hers from her flower-covered canvas bag. They both were ready by the fourth ring.

"Who is this," I answered.

"You know who this is," Miguel answered. "And you know what I want."

"Why are you calling?"

"I wanted to make sure my message was clear. I'd hate for there to be a misunderstanding. Stay out of my way, or I'll return your sister in pieces."

"I want proof of life. If I'm going to do as you ask, I want to know my sister is alive."

"Not an option."

"*If you want me to back off, you'll do it*! I want a picture! I want to see she's alive. If you don't send it in the next twenty minutes, I'll come after you so hard you won't have time to count the bodies dropping around you. Do you hear me, Miguel? I won't just hunt you—I'll kill everyone!"

Miguel hung up.

"Damn it," I said, slapping my palm on the hood of the SUV.

"Wasn't long enough to trace," Genie said. "All I can tell you is that he was calling from within the U.S."

"I did better than you, but I cheated," Tech said. "I started tracing from only Florida and California. He's still in California, probably at his estate there."

A man wearing a badge on his belt strolled over with his laptop. "If his phone is still on, we might be able to keep the trace going."

Genie and Tech both wore insulted expressions as they turned to look at him.

"Miguel would've turned the phone off, but thanks for the offer. Genie's FBI. She can give you the trace information if you want to double check."

The cop looked nervous. "Meant no offense," he said, offering his hand to Genie. "The name's Abe. I work with Charlie. Anything you need, let me know."

Genie shook it, but reluctantly.

Grady handed me the megaphone back, but before I turned it on, Mickey stepped out of the crowd. His features were dark and stormy. "Now what? Are you backing down?"

Not bothering with the megaphone, I yelled back, turning in circles as I did to answer his question for everyone to hear. *Let me be clear—this is war.* Miguel Remirez ordered the kidnapping of my sister. *My sister.* A cop in this city. A friend to many. A protector to many." I turned to point at Mickey, welcoming the rage filling me. "When my son was kidnapped, I had no choice but to wait. To hunt my enemies quietly. This. Is. Not. That." I turned again, looking at the crowd. "We fight. And we burn our enemies to the ground."

A roar of cheers on the not-so-law-abiding side erupted.

I raised a hand to quiet them. "Charlie's a survivor. She can take the pain. But she can't fight back unless given a chance. And the only way we can ensure she has that chance is if we go on the offensive. Every time they're forced to move her to a new location, she has a chance to escape. Our mission is to find her—to save her. But if we can't do that, then at the very least, we'll give her a chance to save herself. Because if given the opportunity, I believe she'll win."

"You can't do it by breaking the law, though," Quille yelled. "That makes us the bad guys, not the good guys."

I shook my head. "Today, we are gathered for one aligned mission—save Charlie. How we get there will require the efforts of both sides of this parking lot. Maybe the police or FBI will find her first. Maybe not," I said, grinning over at Mickey and Phillip. "I honestly don't give a damn which side finds her. Just find her. Turn this city upside down."

"Kelsey—" Tech called out. "A picture just came in on your phone." He turned his laptop around and showed me the picture.

Charlie was bound to a chair in some type of concrete or block framed building. I focused first on her surroundings: commercial building, unfinished, big space. Then I focused on her expression. *Defiant. Angry.*

As I expected, she was sending me a message. *She was ready. She was alert. She was in fight mode.*

"She's in a commercial building of some kind," I called out to everyone. "Likely the building is abandoned because we've found no real estate owned by Miguel in Florida. And she *is* in Florida still."

"How do you know?" Uncle Hank asked.

"I demanded a photo immediately because if she was being transported out of state or out of the country, then Miguel wouldn't have been able to reach his men on a plane or boat to get this picture."

"She's here," Ford said, nodding. "That's good news."

"Yeah, she's here," I said, staring past the parking lot at the buildings in the distance. "She's still in our backyard somewhere." I turned to the law enforcement side. "Search buildings in your assigned neighborhoods. Refresh the BOLOs for Mr. Tricky." I turned to the other side. "Get the word out. I want every drug dealer, prostitute, homeless person, and otherwise criminally inclined person in Miami watching for sightings of Charlie. Any tips will be rewarded generously. And if anyone spots her or Mr. Tricky—call me. We'll have an army ready."

"You mean law enforcement, right?" Quille asked.

"No, I don't," I answered.

Chuckles from the criminal side sounded behind me.

When everyone pulled their phones at the same time, I knew Tech had sent the pictures. I climbed down from the SUV. Everyone shuffled into their familiar clusters, cops by precincts and criminals by their bosses, before dispersing in different directions.

Mickey, Phillip, Papa Bianchi, Maggie, Kierson, Ryan, Spence, Baker, Garth, and Evie walked over to us, gathering to hear if I had anything else to say.

"We'll move some of the family out of the mansion," Phillip said. "The judge signed the papers for guardianship for Sophia and the children. You can continue working from there."

"I appreciate it, but I can't spare the manpower for security. If you can carve out some rooms for us to sleep on the third floor, we'll be able to come and go as needed. And if your guys can unload the luggage from the back of my SUV and take that back to the mansion, I'd appreciate it."

"Done," Papa Bianchi said. "Now, other business. Cartel man must die."

"I didn't hear that," Kierson grumbled, rubbing a hand over his forehead.

I ignored Kierson and answered Papa Bianchi. "If we kill Miguel, whoever is holding Charlie will shoot her. They'll no longer have a reason to keep her alive."

Mickey crossed his arms over his chest, staring coldly down at me. "What's the plan if we can't find her?"

"We'll find her," Spence said, sounding more determined than I felt.

"Damn straight," Cooper said. "There's no other option."

"He's right," Kierson said. "Charlie can't survive long term captivity. She's tough. A fighter. But if this goes on too long, she'll crack. It's her one and only weakness."

"Agreed," I said, nodding. "That's why we attack hard and fast. Mickey, this is your city. I need everyone you've got looking for her. How long would it take for you to position scouts throughout the city?"

Mickey watched me as he thought about it. "Give me thirty minutes. I'll also talk to Chills and have his men spread the word with the prostitutes in his neighborhood."

"I'll have my men pair up with Mickey's," Phillip said.

"Good. Grady, I need you to get Tech and Genie back to the mansion. I need the command center up and running. And call your brother Mitch. Have him pick up Nana and keep her safe until the dust settles."

Grady nodded before walking away.

"Maggie and Kierson, work Miguel's background and bridge the communication gap with Miami PD. They're not likely to share information with me. And reach out to other agencies to gather any intel they have." I turned to Cooper and Ryan. "I need you both for something a bit…"

"Illegal?" Maggie finished for me chuckling.

"Maybe," I said, smirking at her as I rounded the corner of the SUV toward the driver's door.

By the time I was behind the wheel, Ryan was in the front passenger seat, and Cooper, Spence, and Beast were in the back.

"I'm not sure this is a take your dog to work type of day," I said to Spence as I made a tight turn to circle around some police cruisers in the parking lot.

"You've got two unmarked cars that just pulled out behind you," Ryan said.

"I see them," I said, turning to the left on the first road.

"Beast knows Charlie's scent. If we get close to her, he'll help find her."

"Fair enough," I said, turning through an alley and then making a sharp right into another alley with barely enough room to drive through. As I passed a dumpster, I stopped.

Cooper jumped out and rolled the dumpster into the middle, blocking the unmarked car behind us. When he jumped back in, I took off, turning into traffic. I made another loop to the right before making a left, and was now traveling in the opposite direction.

"I think you lost them," Ryan said. "But make a few more evasive moves. They could be tag teaming the surveillance."

I continued a few more turns before I focused on my destination. My phone rang and Ryan hit the button on the stereo display to answer.

"I'm on speaker," I answered.

"So are we," Lisa said. "We have a team ready to pick up the family at the airport when they arrive. What else do you need?"

"Is Donovan there?"

"We're all here," Donovan said. "The family, the clubs, men and women from Aces... What can we do?"

"When I talked to Bridget his morning, they were jumping on a plane to California as soon as they loaded the family on the jet to fly to Michigan."

"That lines up with what I know. Jackson took an early flight out to meet them in Vegas."

"I need you to get word to them. Tell them plans have changed."

"You need them to turn around and fly south?"

"No. I need them to call me before they leave Vegas. They'll need *special* supplies. I have a contact in the area that can get them what they need."

"I'll get the message to them. What else?"

"I need a team in Mexico, surveilling the compound. It's only a matter of time before Miguel decides to rabbit south of the border."

"Hey, Donovan," Ryan called out. "Axel and Ripper are already in the vicinity. Get word to them. They'll handle it."

"All right, good. What's the plan here?"

"The plan is that you and the rest of the team lockdown security and protect the family. Protect my son. Because in thirty minutes, I'm declaring war on the cartel."

"Sunshine," Hattie said over the speaker. "What do you want us to tell the kids?"

"The truth. Tell them the truth."

"Can Nicholas handle the truth?" Lisa asked. "He's close with Charlie."

"He'll be scared. He'll act out. But we can't hide this from them. They're too smart. They'll figure it out on their own and it's better they hear it from family."

"What can the clubs do?" James asked.

"Gather friends of the family: Dallas, Dave, Steve, and their families need to be moved to the clubhouse. Doc too, actually."

"Are you sure that's necessary?" James asked.

"I'm going to burn Miguel's world down, James. I can't have anyone standing out in the open when the cartel returns fire. That includes both clubs. Go on lockdown. Keep your members and their families safe."

"For how long?" Renato asked.

"Until Miguel is dead."

"When will that be?"

"When I'm ready." I turned left, checking my mirrors for a tail.

"Still clear," Cooper said from the back seat.

"Lisa, call my brother Jeff. It's not likely the cartel will go after them, but at least warn them."

"I will, but wouldn't it be safer for Charlie if you didn't declare war?" Lisa asked.

"Maybe. But the longer Charlie's held captive, the weaker she'll get. I need to strike hard and fast to give her a chance. I know her. I know what she'd want me to do."

"You got this baby girl," Pops said. "We'll take care of the rest of the family, just bring Charlie home to us."

"That's the plan," I said as Ryan reached over and disconnected the call.

"Special supplies?" Cooper asked from the back seat. "This supplier you mentioned, are we referring to Gregory?"

Gregory was one of Cooper's mates from the military. He'd visited once when I lived in Texas and it just so happened Cooper was out on a security job. Gregory and I bonded over him teaching me explosives. I didn't learn enough to feel comfortable handling them, but I had a lot of fun. By the time Cooper came home, we'd blown huge holes in the field and were passed out drunk in Adirondack chairs in the driveway.

"Damn, Bones is so lucky," Ryan complained. "Why does he always get to have all the fun?"

I pulled up along the curb, a half block from the dentist office.

"At some point, are you going to tell us the big-picture plan?" Spence asked.

"Today, we send Miguel a message. See if it spooks whoever is holding Charlie. Maybe we'll get lucky and they move her and one of Chills or Mickey's guys spots her being moved. Maybe she gets a chance to fight back," I said, smiling to myself. "Basically, we're setting off a warning of sorts."

"And tomorrow?" Cooper asked.

"That's where I need help. We need teams in Mexico, California, Georgia, and Texas. When I say attack, we hit the cartel with everything we've got. We take his businesses, we take his family, we take his money. We strip him down until he has nothing left. We blow up his world."

"Like Jonathan?" Cooper asked.

"No. We literally *blow up* everything in Miguel's world. His compound, his California beach house, his businesses. It's going to be loud and scary, but we'll do it smart. No one dies. Not yet."

"Miguel will retaliate," Cooper said in a low voice. "He'll hurt Charlie."

I closed my eyes, breathing in and out at a slow steady pace. "I know."

"*And you're okay with that?*" Spence yelled from the back seat. "You're going to just let them carve her into pieces?"

I remained silent, not answering as I opened my eyes and focused on the dentist office down the block.

"Would this be a good time to share that Miguel's compound in Mexico is wired with explosives?" Cooper asked.

I turned in my seat, looking back at him.

Cooper held his hands up. "Wasn't my idea. I can't take the credit. Ryan arranged it. I have to admit, though, I'm a little stoked to watch the compound go boom."

"To be fair, Jackson helped," Ryan said. "As did my buddies Ripper and Axel who have the remote detonator tucked away. With Miguel and his family in California, it was easy to sneak in and out unnoticed. Only a handful of guards were roaming the grounds and a few housekeepers inside."

Cooper reached forward and fist bumped Ryan.

"When was this?" I asked. "And why didn't anyone tell me?"

"It was after our first run-in with the cartel, when Charlie warned us that she didn't think it was over," Cooper said. "We all thought it was a good idea to prepare for the *just-in-case* scenario."

I pondered their actions. "And Charlie knew? She knew you had countermeasures in place?"

Ryan shrugged. "She's a cop. She knew we did something, but we didn't share the details."

"We're on the right track then," I said, nodding to myself. "She knows we're ready to retaliate—*sooner rather than later*. She'll be ready."

"*Ready for what*? *To be carved up*?" Spence asked.

I looked at Spence in the back seat, growing frustrated, but didn't say anything.

"You don't know Charlie," Ryan said. "You think you do, but you don't."

Cooper placed a hand on Spence's shoulder. "She's been through some shit. Bad childhood shit. She's tough, but... captivity?" He shook his head. "She won't survive it."

"If she loses hope, it's game over," I said. "She'll mentally check out. And if that happens, we'll lose her for good."

"It's only been a few hours," Spence said. "We have time yet to find her."

"No, we don't," I said, turning back to face forward, looking out the windshield. "I've been here before, Spence. I've had someone I love taken from me. If we wait, she could be shipped to California or Texas or Mexico. Hell, they could export her out of the country and sell her to slave traders."

"It's now or never," Ryan said.

"It's Charlie's only chance," Cooper agreed.

I checked the time on the clock. "We should wait another ten minutes. Give Mickey and Chills time to get their scouts into position. While we wait, Cooper, tell me what you got out of Colby Brown."

"Not much. There's a drug pipeline that makes a stop in Atlanta before splitting off across the country. They use a warehouse on the southern edge of town. I didn't have time to scout the location. When they realize Colby's missing, they'll probably switch locations."

"Did you get the warehouse address to Tech?"

"Yeah, but last I knew he hadn't had time to run a search on it. I'll text him and remind him we need it ASAP."

"Anything else?"

"Besides Colby confirming what we already knew? No. He spilled that Miguel was obsessed with Evie, but when she ran away, he issued orders to find her and bring her back. Colby suspects he'll kill her. In Miguel's eyes, she betrayed him."

"Have Tech do the real estate check, then turn the address over to the Feds. Let them run with that one. Maybe they'll get lucky and shut the operation down before Miguel realizes Colby's missing."

"As you wish, my lady," Cooper answered.

I glanced back and confirmed he was still grinning as he texted.

Chapter Twenty-Seven

KELSEY
Friday, 2:45 p.m.

I waited, observing the flow of people down the block, until I could no longer stomach sitting idle. When I finally slid out of the SUV, so did everyone else.

"Spence, you're our getaway driver," I said, handing him the keys. "Keep Beast with you."

"Getaway driver for what?" Spence asked.

"The dentist office down the block is involved with sex trafficking," Ryan answered, pointing in that direction. "We've had eyes on the building for weeks now."

Cooper followed me to the back of the SUV. "They're tied to the cartel who took Charlie."

"Which means it's the perfect place to send a warning to Miguel Remirez." I opened the back hatch on the SUV and triggered the release for hidden floor storage. The compartment had been retrofitted for my special toys.

"Merry Christmas," Ryan said, reaching past me to grab two smoke canisters.

I pulled out several flash bangs and pull-tab flares. "I'll take the front door. Ryan and Cooper, come in through the second-floor window. Bridget disabled the security alarm on the window last week."

"You're going in through the front door?" Cooper asked. "You realize what we are about to do is a crime, right?"

I grinned over at Cooper. "I wasn't joking when I announced to a hundred law enforcement officers that I was about to commit crimes. It's only a matter of time before they're forced to arrest me."

"Why give them a reason though?" Spence asked.

Ryan answered Spence while clipping two flashbangs to his belt. "Not what she's saying. She's saying she'll be facing multiple crimes by the time this is over either way. But her objective is to make sure the cartel knows she's coming for them, thus entering through the front."

"You can't help if you're behind bars, though," Spence said.

"It won't be an issue," I said as I checked the clip on my gun. "At least not until Charlie's back."

Cooper nodded toward the building. "Is our visit a quick hello, or are we stopping to ask questions?"

"A little bit of both. We have three possible suspects inside. The plan is to let everyone else run for their lives, then see what the three remaining have to say. We might need to take one of them with us when we leave."

"Not much room in the SUV," Ryan said. "Should we order another car?"

"No. We'll make it work." I looked back at Spence. "Are you in or out? Because if you ditch us and take our ride, there will be hell to pay."

"I'm in."

"Do we need earpieces?" Cooper asked me.

"No. If this turns bad, scatter and evade. We'll regroup at Mickey's gym."

We all piled back inside the SUV. Spence drove us down the block, pulling alongside the curb near the back alley. Cooper, Ryan, and I exited the vehicle. The boys darted through the alley while I waited to give them a thirty-second lead.

As I started down the sidewalk, I said aloud, "This is for you, Charlie." I walked around the corner and pulled open the glass door of the dentist office.

The receptionist looked up. "Good afternoon. Can I help—" her mouth dropped open as she realized I was carrying my Glock in one hand and a flashbang in the other. She likely didn't recognize the flashbang for what it was, but it clearly scared her.

A man and a woman were sitting several feet apart in the patients waiting area. I looked at them, nodding to the door behind me. They rushed past and out the door. I turned back to the receptionist and raised my gun in her direction. "Women have been disappearing from this dentist office, suspected of being shipped off into sex slavery. You know anything about that?"

Her hands were raised into the air. "No. I swear," she said flinching away as I pointed the gun at her. "I've only worked here for two weeks. I was hired when they reopened after the fire. Their previous receptionist quit."

"Fine. Get out. But keep your mouth shut and don't call the cops," I paused to look at the name plate, "Jennifer."

She glanced at the name plate, then back at me, nodding her understanding. Grabbing her purse, she stumbled toward the door, forgetting she was wearing a headset that was still connected to the desk phone. The phone flew off the desk as her head was jerked back. She flung the headset off as she stumbled the last few feet out the door.

I looked up at the camera and waved before moving down the hall.

In the first room, I threatened and dismissed the patient, allowing her to leave but encouraging the hygienist with my gun to move down the hall and into the dentist's private office.

Cooper and Ryan led two more employees into the office. The dentist was already in his office when we arrived.

"You said three suspects, but we have four people," Ryan said.

"I can count," I said, rolling my eyes. "Thanks."

Two women and two men, including the dentist, cowered in front of us, kneeling on the floor not because they were ordered to, but because the threat of our guns naturally directed them into that position.

"You," I said, moving my gun to the forehead of the woman I knew Tech had already cleared. "Leave. But if you call the cops, I'll hunt you down."

She nodded and mumbled incoherently through her tears as she scurried from the room.

"As much as I'd like to spend time chatting with each of you," I said as I made eye contact with them, "I have a busy schedule today. Instead, we'll do it this way." I placed the end of my gun barrel in the center of the forehead of one of our prisoners.

Ryan and Cooper raised their guns to the other two.

"We're going to count to three," Cooper said.

"And if we reach three before one of you starts talking..." Ryan said.

"You die," Cooper finished.

"No, no, please," the woman cried, trembling.

Her pleading didn't faze me. "Which one of you is involved in the kidnapping of the women?"

"*One...*" Ryan said, drawing the word out, sounding deadly.

"*It's him. It's Patrick*," the woman said, nodding to the man on her left.

"*Fuck, Ashley! Really?* You're just as much to blame for this shit as I am."

"What the hell is going on?" the dentist asked.

I looked at the dentist, waving my gun toward the door. "Get out. And find somewhere else to work." As the dentist scurried, I nodded to Ryan and Cooper. "Load these two in the SUV. I'll need a few minutes to leave a message for Miguel. If I don't make it out before you hear sirens, then leave without me."

They each grabbed one of the suspects and hauled them to their feet.

I exited the room, following the back hall to the staircase leading to the storage room upstairs. I ran up the stairs. The room was filled with large four-drawer filing cabinets. Pulling a stack of files from one of the cabinets, I tossed them on the floor.

Then I activated a flare, dropping it on top of the papers.

Running back downstairs, I dropped another flare in the hallway after I checked the employee bathroom to ensure everyone got out. Making my way to the front of the building, I dropped a third flair on the stack of papers on the receptionist's desk.

As I exited the building, I pulled the pins on two smoke bombs, tossing them into the waiting room. Then I tossed in two flashbangs, without pulling the pins.

When the police and fire department arrived and forced the door open, the level of smoke would cause them to retreat until they could assess the fire. If I was lucky, that would be around the same time the flashbangs would explode, causing them to retreat and observe even longer. I needed the dentist office to burn to the ground. And without gasoline or another flammable, the only way to ensure that happened was by delaying the fire department from getting close enough to put the fire out.

Turning to jog down the entrance steps, I watched as Ryan ran past me covering his ears. I covered mine seconds before flashbangs from the back corner of the building went off. Any witnesses still in the area would duck for cover.

I ran behind him. The back hatch of the SUV was open. He jumped into the cargo area, and I followed him, both of us balling up in the small space.

Ryan pulled down the door hatch. "Go!" Ryan yelled, and the SUV tore off down the street.

I looked back at the dentist office as we drove away. Black smoke billowed out of the building, chugging skyward. I looked back at Ryan as I tucked my legs and leaned against the side panel of the interior.

Ryan was grinning at me. "What's next?"

I smiled back at him as I held my hand out, palm up. "I need a burner."

Ryan rummaged around in the bag he was sitting on top of, pulling out two burners from the side pocket. I checked the contact list on my regular phone, then after entering the number, called Mickey on the burner.

"Got something?" Mickey asked, knowing somehow it was me.

"I picked up a few passengers. I need a place to question them."

"Gym." Mickey hung up.

"Head to Mickey's gym!" I called toward the front to Spence.

"*Mickey? Mickey McNabe?*" our female prisoner squealed. "*This is all your fault!*" she yelled at her partner. "*I told you we needed to run!* I told you after Kendra disappeared that we were in over our heads."

"Shut the fuck up," the man said.

Beast, sitting next to the man and facing him on the back seat, growled in the man's ear, snapping his teeth.

The man leaned away.

"Did you hear them?" the woman continued. *"They're taking us to Mickey! He's gonna kill us."*

I looked at Ryan, who was still smiling.

"I'm not gonna tell yah again, Ashley—*shut the fuck up*! You don't want to know what the cartel does to rats. It's not pretty."

"Better than whatever Mickey McNabe will do to me!" Ashley yelled back. "I'll tell you everything," Ashley said, leaning toward Cooper who was in the front passenger seat holding a gun on them. "They have a warehouse on Cascade. On the south end. Not sure of the address, but it's a two-story building with foggy windows. That's where we drop off the girls. That's where they are."

I picked up my phone and called Uncle Hank.

"You okay?" Uncle Hank asked when he answered his phone.

"There's a warehouse on Cascade. South side. Two story with foggy windows. Get a team together and raid it."

"Is that where Charlie is?" Uncle Hank asked.

"I'm not sure. I only know that's where they take the girls when they snatch them from the dentist office."

"All right," Uncle Hank said. "You want uniforms to enter or our Italian friends?"

"Send in the blue line. We'll keep working the other side of the tracks with the less honorable side of society."

Uncle Hank snorted as he disconnected.

"You hear that?" Ryan asked, nodding toward the woman.

"No. What did I miss?" The woman hostage was still rambling to Cooper about their operations.

"They schedule the kidnapped victims for end of day appointments. Then Ashley here," Ryan shoved the back of Ashley's head, "is nice enough to offer the girls a lift after her boyfriend Patrick puts them into a drug-induced stupor."

"That's why the sting didn't work," I said. "It was a mid-morning appointment."

Ryan nodded as he shifted a leg within the tight quarters of the cargo area, stretching his foot to the other side of me. "But it also explains why they scheduled a follow-up appointment for Charlie for next week. A late afternoon appointment. They took the bait after all. The timing was just off."

I ran a hand through my hair. "Interesting, but I can't focus on the trafficking case right now. I need to stay focused on Charlie."

"You think she'll be at the warehouse?"

"It depends. If Mr. Tricky still has her, then no. He's too smart to keep her at the same location. But if his job ended at delivery," I shrugged, "maybe."

"What's the plan for these two?" Ryan asked.

"We leave them with Mickey. He can relay any details he bleeds out of them."

"You sure you're okay with that?" Ryan asked, no longer smiling.

"I'm okay with anything that leads us to Charlie. Is that a problem for you?"

"I got no problem," Ryan said, holding his hands up. "Just checking where your head's at."

"My head is exactly where it needs to be. I'll deal with my conscience another day."

We pulled into the parking lot of the gym and Spence drove past the main entrance and around the corner of the building to the back entrance. Mickey, Phillip, and several of their guards were standing there waiting.

Spence popped the back hatch, letting Ryan and me out.

Mickey and Phillip walked over to talk to me as the guards escorted our passengers through the back door of the gym.

"Heard a raid is getting ready to breach a building," Mickey said. "Surprised you're not with them."

"I'm heading over there now. But it was faster to give the search to the boys and girls with badges. Besides, I doubt Charlie's there."

"Could lead to someone who knows where she is, though," Phillip said. "Will the police share the information with you?"

"Not intentionally, but between Mickey and the FBI, we'll hear what we need to know."

Mickey glanced over his shoulder to the back door. "And them?"

"They're all yours," I said. "Relay any information back to Tech or Grady."

"I've had three addresses sent to me," Mickey said, handing me a piece of paper. "Suspicious activity reported at all three, but no idea what that entails. Could be nothing."

"We'll check them out." I looked over at Cooper, handing him the addresses before looking back at Mickey. "Did Benny the Barber ever stick his head out of his hidey hole?"

"Not yet. The rat squad pulled their team this morning, so I put two of my guys on watching the building. Why?"

"Benny knew about the job to kidnap Charlie. He might even know Mr. Tricky's identity. I'm jonesing for a little chat."

"I'll tell my guys to amplify their search."

"You do that. But Benny's mine. Don't forget that."

Mickey stared back, not committing either way.

"Let's roll," Cooper said, opening the back door of the SUV for me. "Let's get to the warehouse."

I started to climb into the vehicle but stopped, looking back at Phillip and Mickey. I nodded to the warehouse. "Thanks for helping. I know neither of you signed up for this."

"Sometimes we do the right thing," Phillip said, tilting his head as he smirked.

"And sometimes we help because statewide manhunts disrupt our other business interests," Mickey said.

I shook my head. "Always a pleasure, Mickey." I slid into the SUV.

Chapter Twenty-Eight

KELSEY
Friday, 3:02 p.m.

Beast was no longer snapping his teeth. He was stretched across the seat between Cooper and me with his head on my lap as I scratched the fur between his front paws. He was loving it. Cooper, on the other hand, was not appreciating the boy parts and hind legs flopping around on his side of the back seat.

I couldn't help smiling. No wonder Charlie liked having Beast as a partner. He looked vicious, but behind his muscular frame and weaponized teeth, he was all marshmallow.

"I can't get any closer," Spence said, pulling alongside a curb.

I looked over and watched the chaos on the other side of the parking lot. Two SWAT vans, at least thirty cop cars, and four ambulances were parked near the side of a two-story building. Emergency lights flashed from every direction.

I leaned forward, watching the cops escorting people from the main doors. Some were in cuffs. Others were shuffled over to the ambulances.

I climbed out of the SUV but stood close to Spence's rolled down window as I phoned Uncle Hank.

"She's not here," Uncle Hank answered.

"Anything of interest inside?"

"Like the old walk-in freezers occupied by missing women? Or the map on the wall?" Uncle Hank asked in a low voice.

"What map?"

"I sent pictures to Tech. It was an ordinary map of southwest Florida, but with locations marked by pins. One of which was dead center over the block of the dentist office."

"I appreciate you sending it to Tech." I glanced around. "I'm going to attempt getting closer to some of the women, so you might want to distance yourself from me. Wouldn't be good for your career."

"I hear ya. In the eyes of brass, you're radioactive right now. After your announcement this morning that you'd be partnering with Miami's most wanted, we've been ordered to keep our mouths shut when you're nearby. The commander wasn't too happy to hear you'd turned rogue."

"And you?"

"I don't care who you recruit. Whatever it takes to get our girl back is fine with me." He must've covered the phone with his hand while he spoke to someone because all I could hear was muffled voices for a minute, but then his voice came back clear again. "I have to go, but keep your head down."

"You too." I hung up and turned to the boys. "We're not staying. I'll try to question a couple of the women and then we'll bolt."

"We'll park down the block," Spence said. "Call us when you're ready for us to pick you up."

I jerked my head in a nod before walking away, toward the far corner where two of the ambulances were. As I approached, I recognized the medic from this morning at Charlie's apartment.

He nodded as I approached. "She's not here."

"I heard. Any gossip I can use?"

"Not that I've heard. This is Macy," the paramedic said, nodding to his patient. "She's one of the victims they pulled out of the building."

"Hi, Macy," I said, sitting beside her on the bumper of the ambulance. "Mind if I ask you a few questions?"

"What kind of questions?" Macy asked wearily.

"For starters, did you get abducted by a woman at the dentist office?"

"No, but Kia was," Macy said, seeming comfortable with my question. "Kia's the woman over there." She pointed across the lot to the heart of the investigation. I wouldn't be able to talk to Kia any time soon.

"Where did they get you?"

"A john. One minute I was taking off my shorts, and the next I was knocked out cold. Woke up here."

This new tidbit of information surprised me. She was the first girl who I'd heard was taken directly from the street. "What neighborhood were you working?"

"Down by the docks off Cape Street and Eleventh. Not my normal stomping ground but I heard you could make good money down there, so thought I'd give it a whirl."

"Were you working alone?"

She nodded, taking the ice pack the medic offered her and placing it on the back of her head.

"What day did they take you?"

"Weren't no *they* until I got here. But it was Tuesday. He took me Tuesday."

"The man who abducted you, what did he look like?"

"Big. Muscles. I was kind of excited to get someone as good looking as him. The usual guys paying for my services are from the less attractive crowd."

"Blond? Dark hair?" I asked, trying to keep her focused on her abduction.

"Dark hair. No beard, but had some scruff. You know, like hadn't shaved in a day or two. Nice clothes. Black jeans and a dark shirt."

I flipped through the pictures on my phone. Finding the one I wanted, I showed her the image of Mr. Tricky from the Outer Layer when he was caught on the security feed. "This him?"

"Yeah, that's him. That's him all right."

Her confirmation was intriguing, but I couldn't put the pieces together. I pulled a business card and handed it to her. "This number goes to my partner. We're a private security firm working a related kidnapping case. Call us if you think of anything else."

"And don't mention this conversation to the cops," the paramedic said to Macy, winking at her. "She's sort of gone rogue on them." He nodded toward me. "She's looking for her sister, Detective Harrison."

"Charlie Harrison?" Macy asked, standing as a streak of surprise crossed her face. "Oh, shit, no. I don't believe it. They snatched *Charlie*?"

"Earlier today, yes. They grabbed her inside her apartment. Did you hear anyone mention her name?"

"No, but shit makes more sense now. The guys holding us were spooked about something. Kept arguing about whether they should take off and leave us there. Something about they didn't sign up for a war with the Miami PD."

"Well, whether they signed up for it or not, that's exactly what they're getting. You stay safe, Macy," I said, placing a hand on her shoulder.

"Hey, lady," Macy said as I started to walk away. "Find Charlie. I know she's a cop and all, but she's one of the good ones. You know what I mean?"

"I know exactly what you mean," I said before walking around the corner of the ambulance.

I was skirting between two ambulances to question the next victim, but when I stepped around the corner I came face to face with Quille, Charlie's boss.

"You're interfering with an active investigation," Quille said, hands on hips.

"So?" I said, defiantly.

He smirked. "You get anything useful?"

"Not sure." We both looked back toward Macy. "She wasn't snatched at the dentist office like I expected. Make sure each woman is questioned for where they were abducted from. Could be important."

"We'll try, but some of them aren't likely to talk to cops," Quille said as he looked around. "If Charlie was here, she'd get them talking. She was good like that."

"Have Chambers give it a try. He's got that casual blue-collar look. If that doesn't work, get me their names and addresses and I'll follow-up when not so many uniforms are around."

Quille nodded. "Heard the dentist office caught fire." He shook his head. "Such a shame."

"Yeah. Breaks my heart," I said with a straight face.

"Any luck on your end finding Charlie?"

"We have a few addresses to check out, but nothing all that promising." My mind drifted back to Macy's abduction. Why would Mr. Tricky abduct? It didn't make sense.

"Hello," Quille said, waving a hand in front of me. "You were saying?"

"I need to go," I said before turning abruptly and running across the parking lot. I pulled my phone as I ran, calling Cooper. *Come get me. Now!*"

~*~*~

"Explain what we're doing here," Spence said.

"I told you. We're looking around," I answered from the passenger seat. I continued watching the business district pedestrian and vehicle traffic from where we were parked down the street.

"But why?" Ryan asked. "Why *here*?"

"Yeah," Cooper said, leaning forward. "I know you're doing your speed-thinking thing, but until we learn to read your mind, you'll need to actually vocalize a few words for us mere mortals."

"It's just a hunch," I said.

"Great," Ryan said. "We like your hunches. But what is it?"

"I think Mr. Tricky is either staying around here or has Charlie stashed nearby."

"Why do you think that?" Spence asked.

"One of the victims said Mr. Tricky *himself* abducted her from this neighborhood last Tuesday."

"That makes no sense," Cooper said. "Everything we know about him points toward him being a mercenary for hire. Why would he dabble in the sex trafficking trade?"

"Exactly," Ryan said, snapping his fingers. "He wouldn't bother with a street corner hooker unless she saw something he didn't want anyone to see."

"Why not just shoot her?" Spence asked.

We all looked at Spence.

"No, that's not what *I'd* do! I'm just saying why didn't *he* shoot her? He's already proved his moral bar is set pretty low."

"Maybe he thought shooting her would draw too much attention," I said.

"More likely it was a two-fer," Ryan said.

"A what?" I asked.

"A two-fer. The girl disappears and he pockets some cash."

"That's messed up," I said looking back at Ryan.

Ryan shrugged one shoulder. "Selling her was probably more efficient than finding a place in Florida to stash the body."

"So he either sold her for the cash or sold her to get rid of her, either way sucks," Cooper said, looking at the buildings ahead of us.

"I'll research the real estate on the block," Spence said, reaching for his laptop bag near my feet.

"You'll have more room if you don't have a steering wheel in the way," I said, opening my door to get out.

"No need," Spence said. "I'm used to working out of my truck." He clipped the back of his laptop with some doohickey to the steering wheel, turning it into a desk.

Cooper leaned forward again. "Ryan and I are going to scout the neighborhood. We'll meet back here in thirty."

"What should I do?" I asked them.

"Nothing," Cooper said. "Don't do anything. Just sit still. If Mr. Tricky is around here somewhere, we don't want him seeing you."

"Well, that's no fun," I mumbled to myself as Cooper and Ryan exited the SUV. I turned to look at Spence but he was already busy on his laptop.

I sighed.

Beast stuck his snout in my ear, snuffling. I smiled as I raised my hand to pet his big head.

Chapter Twenty-Nine

KELSEY
Friday, 3:47 p.m.

Bored with waiting for Cooper and Ryan to return, I decided to call Tech and check in.

"The all mighty and knowing Genie at your service," Genie said, answering Tech's phone on speaker. "How can we assist?"

"First, how many cops are within hearing distance," I asked.

"You realize Genie is law enforcement, too, right?" Kierson called out.

"Sure. But you guys are different."

"You mean you've trained us to pretend we didn't hear half the shit you say?" Maggie asked in the background.

"Something like that."

"Ford's here," Tech said. "You've got Ford, our friendly Feds, and Grady listening."

"Ford? He's a homicide detective, right?"

"And a friend," a man's voice answered. "Never gave a shit when Charlie used her criminal contacts to solve cases, and sure as hell don't care you're using them now to solve hers. I'm here to help, not to get in the way."

"Maggie?" I asked.

"Yeah, I believe him," Maggie answered. "I wouldn't announce you're planning to murder someone or anything like that, but on the grand scale of moral codes, I'd rate Ford much more flexible at bending the rules than Kierson, so you're good."

"All right then. Tech, I have a few addresses that were passed to me." I read off the addresses.

"Got it. I'm running the first one. Genie's running the second one."

"Skip the second address," Ford said. "It's a brothel, but low end. Charlie knows the owner. No way Madame Cora was involved. Charlie's sort of her friend."

"Does this Madame Cora know you? Can you go question her?" Maggie asked.

"I don't need to. You texted everyone on Charlie's contact list. Madame Cora was at the meeting at Charlie's apartment, and she gave her girls the day off to look for Charlie."

"A pimp giving her sex workers the day off?" I asked.

"Cora's not a pimp. She shares a cut of the profits with the girls and provides them food, housing, and even health insurance. She's a former prostitute. She runs a clean house, no drugs, no violence."

"How sweet of her. But how do you know she's not involved?"

"Kelsey, quit testing Ford's loyalty," Maggie said. "Charlie trusted him. She said he was a good cop."

"Fine."

"The first address is an abandoned building," Tech said. "According to the real estate listing, it would be a tear down if someone was stupid enough to buy it. But for our purposes, it could be something."

"I'll take it," Grady said. "I'm bored anyway."

"Okay, but don't go alone. Take a few guys with you, even if you have to tap into Phillip's guards."

"You want me to run an op with mobsters?" Grady asked.

"I'm short on manpower."

"I'll go with him," Maggie said. "I'll leave my badge at the mansion."

"I didn't hear that," Kierson said.

Genie giggled. "Third address just turned up something interesting."

Cooper and Ryan returned to the SUV, sliding into the back seat with Beast between them.

"How interesting?" I asked.

"It's a commercial building on the west side of Miami. According to the city's records, it was foreclosed on about six months ago."

"And?"

"The picture your Uncle Hank sent us, of the map the bad guys had on the wall where the girls were being held, showed pins marking several locations. One of those pins sits over the area where this building is located. The map wasn't detailed enough to give an exact location, but I find the coincidence suspicious," Genie said.

"Nice," I said, tapped Spence on the arm and pointed to the keys in the ignition. "We'll head that way."

Spence pulled ahead and then whipped a U-turn, taking us back toward the main road.

"Maggie and Grady already took off," Tech said. "You want me to call them and have them meet you there?"

"No. I'll call Mickey for an assist if needed." I pointed for Spence to make a left at the upcoming intersection.

"I can help," Kierson called out.

"This won't be one of those legal entries, Kierson. But thanks for the offer. Any word on the warehouse in Georgia that Cooper gave you?"

"DEA assigned a team to scout. They should be there in a few hours. I warned them that the clock was ticking before the drug network pulled up stakes, but didn't share that it was because Cooper kidnapped one of the drug bosses."

"It was more like a citizen's arrest," I said. "We just haven't turned him over to the police yet."

"Uh, huh," Kierson mumbled.

Genie giggled again. "Anything else?"

"Not yet. Keep digging on those addresses, though. Spence has also started working background on some businesses near the docks. I'll have him reach out if he needs help."

"Got it. Stay safe."

"I'll do my best. Hey, Tech, any word from the family?" I asked as I pointed for Spence to take the next right turn.

"All safe behind the perimeter of headquarters. Kids aren't taking the news well. You'll want to reach out when you can."

"I'll try to carve out time later. Now's not a good time. I don't think it will help Nick seeing me this angry at the world."

"Maybe. Or maybe that's exactly what he needs to see. He knows what you're capable of when you're pissed off."

Tech disconnected before I could say anything else. Which was just as well, because I didn't know how to respond. I rattled off the address to Spence and he nodded, seeming to know where he was going.

"What are we walking into?" Ryan asked.

"Don't know. One of the addresses Mickey turned over matches a pinned spot from the map where the abducted girls were held. I suspect there's at least a handful of nefarious fellows with guns there."

"Sweet," Ryan said, fist bumping with Cooper.

I rolled my eyes. I couldn't get Tech's words out of my head though, so I called Nicholas.

"Mom!" Nicholas answered on the first ring. "Did you find Aunt Charlie?"

"Switch to video. I need to see for myself that you're safe," I said, pushing the icon to switch my phone to a video call.

Nicholas' face appeared on my screen. His eyes were red, his face flushed. "Did you find her?"

"Not yet. But I will."

"Mom! You have to find her!" His phone display was lowered as he paced. He was angry. The phone moved around then Nicholas' face reappeared next to Whiskey's. Whiskey had Nick on one knee and Sara on the other. Sara's face was buried into Whiskey's shoulder. Whiskey held the phone, so I could talk to them.

"Kids, I'll find Aunt Charlie. I won't stop until I do."

"It will be too late. You'll take too long. She'll disappear like I did."

"No, Nick. This isn't the same. It's not the same at all."

"Yes, it is!"

I closed my eyes, taking a deep breath. When I reopened them, Nicholas was watching me closely on the video. "When Nola took you, I knew the only way to get you back was to be patient. To dog her every move. Hunt her. I knew she wouldn't hurt you unless I pissed her off, so I had to be careful."

Nicholas settled as he listened. Sara lifted her head to see the phone, listening too.

"But Charlie's not a little boy, powerless to her abductors. It's different. We need them running scared so Charlie has a chance to escape. Either I'll save her, or I'll give her a chance to save herself."

"They'll hurt her."

"Yes. And then we'll hurt them." I swiped a hand across my cheek, clearing a path of tears. "Nick, you know Aunt Charlie. You know she'd want me to go to war. You know she'd rather die than be held against her will."

The tears streaming down the kids' faces were a mirror image of my own. I felt Cooper's hand squeeze my shoulder.

Nicholas looked down, quiet. After a few long moments, he looked up again. The pained look was replaced with anger again. "If Aunt Charlie dies, I'll hate you forever." He jumped off Whiskey's lap and walked out of frame. Whiskey turned his head to watch him leave.

"Aunt Kelsey?" Sara asked.

"Yes, little bug," I answered.

"He doesn't mean it," Sara said. "He's scared."

"I know." I nodded, swallowing my tears as they trailed down the back of my throat. "Can I count on you to keep an eye on him?"

Sara nodded before sliding off Whiskey's lap and walking away.

"Whiskey..."

"We've got them, Kel. You do your thing; we'll do our part."

I nodded, not being able to speak, before disconnecting the call.

Ryan handed me my shoulder bag from the back seat. I took it, digging out a pack of tissues. After mopping up my face, I turned in my seat to look back at Cooper and Ryan. Beast was sitting proudly between them, tongue dripping sweat as he panted.

"Did either of you spot anything of interest down near the docks?"

"Nada," Ryan said. "Too busy. Too many businesses. I think it's a dead end."

"Or bad timing," Cooper said.

"That's what I observed," I agreed. "Macy was working at night, looking for johns. Most of the businesses I saw are eight to five establishments. My guess is this area is deserted after dark."

"Making it the perfect place to come and go. Too busy during the day to notice someone who doesn't fit in, but isolated enough at night to sneak people in and out."

"Which makes the timing interesting," I said, looking at Cooper. "If Mr. Tricky snagged Charlie mid-morning and his nest is in that busy business district we just left—"

"Then Charlie's not there yet," Ryan finished for me. "He'd have to wait until after business hours to move her to wherever he's set up his nest."

"Or knocked out in the back of a van, waiting to be moved," Cooper said.

"How the hell can you guys talk like she's just another case?" Spence said. "Damn. This is Charlie!"

"Yes, it is," I said. "Which is exactly why we're processing the clues like a case. Charlie's counting on us to keep our focus. Spinning out won't help her."

"You don't even sound like you care, though. You talk about her dying or being tortured like it happens every day. Like it's nothing new."

"Man, you need to shut it," Cooper warned.

"Fuck you," Spence said. "Maybe you don't give a damn, but I do. I give a shit about Charlie. I seem to be the only one."

"You are so fucking lucky you're driving right now," Ryan said in a threatening voice.

Spence, fists clasping the steering wheel, jerked the SUV to the shoulder, slamming on the brakes. *"There! That better?"*

I sat wide-eyed as I watched Spence throw his door open and Ryan did the same. Cooper climbed over the center council to take the driver's seat as Spence lunged at Ryan.

Ryan ducked and pivoted before jamming a fist into Spence's ribs so hard I saw spit fly from Spence's mouth. Beast started growling and snapping his teeth at the closed door.

I opened my door, stepped out far enough to reach the back door. "Ryan, get in the SUV!"

I opened the back door on the passenger side and Beast roared a growl as he launched out. I threw the door closed and hopped back into the front passenger seat.

Before Beast rounded the back of the vehicle, Ryan jumped into the back seat from the driver's side. His door closed as Cooper pulled away from the shoulder, leaving Beast and Spence behind.

"*Asshole!*" Ryan said, looking through the rear window.

"Was all that necessary?" I asked, waving a hand toward the road behind us. "He was on our side."

"Whether he knew your history or not, his tantrums were hurting you," Cooper said, reaching a hand out and rubbing my knee. "You've got enough shit to deal with without his shitty attitude piling on more."

I pulled the burner phone and called Mickey.

"Yeah," Mickey answered.

"One of the addresses is a possibility. The one on the west side."

"How many guys do you need?"

"Depends how trained they are. Two or three to cover the other exits should do it. We're currently down to a team of three. Spence was ejected from our team and left on the side of the interstate 95."

"Let me guess, he was shooting his mouth off?"

"Cooper and Ryan sort of had enough when Spence was saying that I was indifferent to the possibility of Charlie being tortured."

Mickey whistled. "Does he need a ride or an ambulance?"

"Just a ride."

"I'll take care of it. What are the chances the cops are near the address you're heading to?"

"I'm guessing they'll have unmarked cars in the neighborhood, but they don't know which building to target. We'll need to enter discreetly."

"Are you saying you'd rather we hide the AK-47s and Uzis?"

"Yeah," I said, laughing. "That would be a good idea. Anything new from our special guests?"

"Phillip's walking toward me as we speak. I'll inquire and update you at the new location."

He disconnected right as my regular phone started ringing. I set down the burner and answered my regular phone. "Kelsey."

"This address is a bust," Grady said on the other end. "It's a heroin den. Addicts everywhere, but nothing along the lines of what you're looking for."

"At least we can cross it off our list. And I have another job for you guys anyway. I need security cameras wired into the street lights near Cape Street and Eleventh. We think that's where Mr. Tricky lays his head at night. Tech will have the equipment needed, but the cameras have to be installed before dark."

"And where exactly do we acquire city worker uniforms and one of those trucks with a lift to work on street lights?"

I heard Trigger in the background, then Grady covered the mic on his phone as they talked.

A few mumbled comments later, Trigger's voice spoke over the phone, "Hey, boss. I'll take care of the cameras. No sweat."

"Call Katie or Bridget if you need help working out the details." We both hung up, and I tucked both phones inside my shoulder bag.

I glanced back at Ryan and saw he was on his phone, texting. "Saying hi to Tweedle?"

"No. Grady."

"Why are you texting Grady?"

"I want him to record Trigger during their assignment."

"You want Grady to document Trigger committing a crime?"

"That dude is crazier than Cooper. It's worth the risk to see what he does next."

Cooper chuckled, glancing over at me. "If Trigger gets caught, we can sell the video to raise money for his legal fees."

Chapter Thirty

CHARLIE
Friday, unknown time

My brain stumbled, trying to focus. *Something woke me. But what? And where am I? Why does my head hurt?* I braced an elbow on the floor, lifting my upper body. My head spun as a wave of nausea hit like a freight train. I closed my eyes, waiting for it to pass before reopening them again. I lifted my head to look around, but a hard slap hit me across the face before my eyes could focus.

I pushed against the floor with my bare feet, sliding my body away from my attacker. I continued scrambling backward until my retreat ended with my head knocking against a wall behind me. I looked up, forcing my eyes to focus, and found Mr. Tricky standing over me.

"Wake up, princess," Mr. Tricky said. "Time to play."

Pushing a hand against the floor, I straightened into a sitting position. "Well, that sounds ominous."

The wall behind me was odd shaped, and I glanced over my shoulder. It wasn't a wall, but a row of cabinets. *Odd.* I looked around, and though the lighting was dim, I was able to make out that I was in some sort of breakroom of sorts. A small tall-table and a few barstools were in the center near the far wall and a row of cabinets topped with a long counter were built along the back wall. A refrigerator in the corner. Seeing the refrigerator made me think of water, which made me realize my tongue was practically glued to the roof of my mouth.

I ignored the thirst and forced myself to think. To remember. This was the second location he'd taken me to. The first had been some type of industrial building with concrete block walls and damp, cool floors. If I wasn't positively certain we were still in Florida, I'd have guessed a basement of some sort. Wherever that location had been, it had been a short stay. After he forced me to hold a newspaper while he snapped a pic, he then zapped me again with his stun gun before injecting me with some cocktail of drugs.

"You disappoint me, Detective Harrison. After proving to be such a challenge to acquire, now that I have you, all you do is sleep."

"I'd be happy to return to my more challenging self, if you'd refrain from *drugging me*," I snapped sarcastically as I rubbed my temples. "What did you give me?"

"Just a little something to make you submissive."

I snorted. "Don't care how many drugs you give me; I'll never be submissive. *Unconscious*, yeah, that's a given. But *never* submissive."

"Hopefully your stay with me will be long enough to prove you wrong. Training you to be one of my pets would be entertaining."

The way he referenced making me his pet had my stomach rolling again. And despite the foggy brain and rolling stomach, I didn't miss his reference of *one of* his pets either. I was really hoping he was referring to a houseful of cats, not women.

"I've been tasked with sending a message to your cousin," Mr. Tricky said, moving to the countertop behind me. "Seems she's not behaving as planned."

I smiled, thinking of Kelsey, silently cheering her on. If I survived my captivity, it would be her doing. And if I didn't survive, my captor would die by her hands. Of that, I had no doubt. After all, she raised me. She's the closest thing to a mother I ever had. "Let me guess, Kelsey's not playing by the rules. She was never very good at following orders."

"I'm guessing it's genetic. You're not much of a rule follower either from what I hear. Tsk. Tsk. Internal Affairs doesn't seem to like you much."

"Well, if you're not pissing someone off, you're not living life right," I said, shrugging. "And speaking of living, any chance you're going to give me food or water anytime soon? Or is the mission to starve me until I die?"

"Probably best if your stomach is empty for this next part," Mr. Tricky said, reaching down and grabbing hold of my left wrist.

I struggled to pull my arm free, but in my weakened state, I was no match. Seeing the large knife, I knew what was coming and looked away.

Thwack!

Searing pain shot up my arm. I screamed out, but Mr. Tricky shoved a rag over my mouth so fast it likely sounded like someone turning on a TV, realizing the volume was dialed up to the highest level before muting the volume. I doubted anyone would recognize it as a distress mechanism built into humans when they're forced to endure severe pain.

My arm was dropped and I cradled my hand to my chest, refusing to look at the damage. I felt the warm wetness coating my shirt, knowing it was my blood.

"Now for the finish," Mr. Tricky said as I heard the click and whoosh of a torch of some kind.

I kept my eyes firmly closed as he grabbed my hand again. I passed out from the pain as my nostrils filled with the smell of my burning flesh.

Chapter Thirty-One

KELSEY
Friday, 4:43 p.m.

Cooper, Ryan, and I sat surveilling our surroundings. We'd parked next door to the building we were watching in the lot of an insurance agency. The neighborhood was a mix of residential and commercial, but the businesses were small. From where we sat, we could see the front portion of our target building and about half of the back. The building took up a single lot on the street side, then turned in an L-shape to a double lot in the back.

Unlike the insurance office, the building we were watching had no signage in front and its glass entrance door simply displayed the office hours. Near the center of the structure were two overhead bay doors for vehicles to pull inside. There was no telling how many people were in the building. And I identified three exits from this side of the building.

We'd also passed two unmarked police cars, so we knew we'd have to go in quick and quiet. I was glad I'd called Mickey for extra support.

"What are your spidey senses telling you?" Cooper asked me.

"They're telling me there's a reason for the blacked-out windows in the back of the building."

"A building this size would need at least four men guarding the interior," Ryan said, leaning forward between the seats.

"Worried we'll be out numbered?" Cooper asked Ryan.

Ryan fisted a hand and used the other to crack his knuckles. "More like hoping for it."

"The number of guards will depend on what they're guarding," I said. "This block is half residential. If they had cars coming and going at all hours, someone would notice."

"Doesn't that make it *more likely* that Mr. Tricky brought Charlie here?" Cooper asked. "Since no one would look twice during the day?"

"*Get down!*" Ryan called out.

Cooper and I didn't hesitate, sliding low in our seats with our knees against the dash as we hid.

"A black extended cab truck just exited one of the overhead doors," Ryan told us.

I peeked at Ryan between the seats, but he was watching something out his tinted back seat window.

"Can you see the driver?" I asked.

"No. Even the windshield is tinted black. It's turning left out of the drive. What do you want to do? Follow the truck?"

"Cooper follows. We search the building and catch up later." I opened my door and jumped out as Cooper turned the engine over. I walked around the front of the SUV and ducked alongside Ryan behind a delivery van. Cooper had already reversed out of the parking spot and was turning left to follow the truck.

"Now what?" Ryan asked.

I realized too late that Cooper had just driven off with my shoulder bag. Both phones were in the bag.

"Do you happen to have Mickey's number in your phone?"

"Nope. I can call Grady and get it."

"Shit." I looked over at the building. "It's almost five. This neighborhood is going to have a lot more traffic once people start coming home from work. We can't wait. It's now or never."

"You realize all your favorite toys just left with Wild Card, don't you?"

I looked toward the road where Cooper had driven away. "I sort of forgot, but there's too many cops in the neighborhood anyway. We need to do this with minimal noise."

"A challenge. I like it. But what's the plan if we have to start shooting?"

I started across the patch of grass between the buildings and the street, walking straight for the front door. "We make up a whopper of a story to tell the cops."

"Is this smart? Going in the front door?" Ryan asked, catching up to walk beside me.

"You got a better idea?"

Ryan looked around, then back at me as he sighed. "Nope. Not really."

I opened the glass door, walking in first. A receptionist looked up from the tablet she was reading and glanced briefly at me before locking in on Ryan. She took her time scanning his body from his head to his feet, going as far as leaning over her desk to see the tips of his boots.

"Excuse me," I said, holding my gun pointed in her direction.

She threw Ryan a wink and a smile before glancing at me. Her smile evaporated when she finally noticed my gun. She jerked backward, throwing her hands in the air.

"We don't keep no cash here," she said.

"Quiet," Ryan said, holding a finger to his lips. "You don't want to give her a reason to shoot. She's been itching to kill someone all day."

Her entire body trembled as she focused on me.

"You going to be good? Do as I say?"

She nodded rapidly.

"That a girl. Now strip."

"What?"

"Strip! And make it fast. We're in a hurry."

She started peeling off her clothes, tossing them my direction. When she was down to her bra and underwear, Ryan turned his back to her.

"Finish," I said. "No clothes."

"But—"

"*Now*!" I ordered firmly but kept my voice low.

She peeled off her underwear and bra, then tried to use her hands to cover herself.

I waved my gun toward the closet. "Get in the coat closet."

She rushed to the closet, jumping on top of a row of boxes along the interior and bending over to stay under the hanging rod. "Please don't hurt me," she said in a shaky voice.

"No one will hurt you as long as you stay quiet. Understand?"

She nodded rapidly again.

I closed the door on the closet as Ryan turned back around. He put his layers of muscles to use by sliding the heavy metal desk across the carpet and pinning it against the closet door.

I walked back to the entrance door, flipped the sign to closed, threw the deadbolt, and turned off the overhead fluorescent lights.

"Ready?" I asked Ryan as we walked down the short hall where a door stood center on the other side.

Ryan chuckled. "Why not. I'm kind of looking forward to seeing what you'll do next."

I opened the door and we both walked through. The room was empty. The space consisted of a long room, empty except for two cars and a van. Not a single piece of furniture, scrap of paper, or machine of any kind was present in the spacious room. On the far wall, where we already knew the building turned in an L-shape, were two metal doors without windows.

"Which one do you think we should try first?" Ryan asked.

I slid my gun into its holster which was clipped to my belt at the center of my back. "We'll have to split up," I said as I pulled my shirt down to cover the gun.

"That's not going to fly. Something happens to you on my watch, there will be a line of people taking turns kicking my ass."

"Doesn't matter. There's two of us," I pointed between us as I walked across the room, "and two doors." I pointed at the doors. "If your room is empty, then you can come join mine and vice versa. But if we stay together, it gives someone an opportunity to sneak up behind us."

"Fine. But scream if you're in danger."

I looked over at him with a scowl as we split off, me taking the left door, him taking the right. I was a little offended by the sexist assumption that I should scream.

Ryan smirked at me. "Okay, fine. Yell all manly or something if you're in danger."

I reached out for the door handle but waited until Ryan was in place. When he was ready to open his door, we gave each other the nod.

I opened my door and walked through as I looked around. A man stood near one of the blackened-out windows, talking on his phone with his back turned toward me. Three other men were playing cards at a table in the center of the room. A fifth man walked out of a bathroom zipping up his pants. He was the first to notice me.

"Well, hello, there," he said, gaining the attention of the card players who looked first at him then followed the direction of his stare until their eyes landed on me.

I kept walking toward the table with a flirty smile plastered on my face and keeping one ear on the guy with the phone in the corner who was now behind me. "I was wondering if you boys could help me. See my car—" I pointed toward the unseeable road, "—it's a piece of shit. And it died right in the middle of the road. Any way you gentlemen could help me push it out of the way."

"Uh," one of the card players said, looking behind me toward the back corner. "We'll have to ask the boss."

I turned my head toward the man on the phone and saw he was hanging up and his eyes were locked on me. He was angry. "How the hell did she get inside?"

"That nice lady up front said it was okay if I—"

"Shut the fuck up!" he yelled as he stormed over.

"Shawn," he said, pointing toward the front of the building. "Go make sure that idiot receptionist closed up for the night.

The guy named Shawn jogged past me.

"About my car..."

"Lady, you've got bigger fucking problems than your car. Anyone with you?"

"No, I—"

"Good," he said, grabbing my arm and dragging me across the room. "You and me, we're going to have a little chat." He threw open the bathroom door and shoved me inside, stepping in behind me.

As soon as the door closed, I kicked his right foot to the outside, throwing him off balance, then kicked his left knee from the inside outward, hearing it snap.

He started to yell, but I'd already pivoted to his side and his alert for help died as I bounced his forehead into the porcelain pedestal sink. He slumped to the floor.

I took his gun and phone, sliding the phone into my back pocket and tucking the gun into the front of my pants, pulling my shirt down to cover it. Walking out of the bathroom, I was careful not to let the others see their leader lying unconscious on the floor.

"That guy," I said, thumbing over my shoulder as I walked back toward the table. "He's so sweet. He said you all would help me with my car after all."

Three confused faces looked at me, then at the closed bathroom door. The guy closest to me started across the room to look for himself. I grabbed the folding chair, lifting it in the air and swinging it like a bat against the backside of his head.

The other two jumped upright, trying to move back from the table to pull their weapons. The one to my right had a chair smashed into his face. The one on the other side of the table managed to pull his weapon but failed to see Ryan sneak up behind him and put him in a sleeper hold.

"Guy who went up front?" I asked.

"What guy?" Ryan asked as he continued to choke his guy out.

"Shit," I said, jogging toward the door.

I flew through the door, hurrying toward the front office, but didn't notice the guy standing to my right until he lunged at me. I was no match for his two hundred plus pounds as he threw himself on top of me, both of us landing hard with me pinned under him. My arms were useless, pinned under his weight. I swung my one free leg upward, trying to bend at an impossible angle to latch it around his head, but missed.

Suddenly, the goon's weight lifted from my body and I looked up to see him floating above me, almost as if levitating. I rolled to the side, and as soon as I was clear, his body was slammed to the concrete floor. The guy doing the slamming looked like a sumo wrestler wearing a suit.

I looked to my side as Mickey held out a hand to help me from the floor.

"You good?" Mickey asked.

I watched Mickey's guard pick the goon up again, laughing as he slammed him a second time into the floor.

"What's in there?" Mickey said, nodding toward the front.

"A naked woman trapped in a closet."

There was a slight curve at the corner of Mickey's mouth. "And in there?" He nodded toward the back room.

I grinned. "Two unconscious men, a third without teeth, and not sure if the fourth is unconscious or dead. Ryan's been in a mood today."

I startled as the sumo guard dropped the goon to the floor again. "He's not quite right in the..." I tapped my temple, "Is he?"

"It's been a while since I've let him play," Mickey said, opening the door to the back room. "Best not to watch."

"Reminds me of when a dog catches a rodent and plays with it, throwing it up in the air and catching it with its teeth," I said, still watching Mickey's guard as Mickey shoved me into the other room.

"Hey, Kel," Ryan said, jogging over. "I think you should head outside."

I looked past Ryan and spotted Spence squatting just outside a doorway on the other side of the room. His fingers were webbed in his hair, his head hanging low, staring at the floor.

I looked back at Ryan. His eyes were a mixture of rage and pain. "What is it?" I asked.

The door behind me swung open and I pivoted, pulling my gun. Cooper stood behind me with his hands raised in the air. "Am I too late?" he asked with a playful grin. His smile fell when he saw Ryan. "What is it?"

"I was just telling Kelsey that I think it's best if she steps outside. Does no good to see what's back there."

"Is it her?" I asked as I shoved Ryan out of the way and started across the room.

"There's no body, but it's not pretty either," Ryan said, trying to hold me in place by the arm.

Cooper ran ahead of me, blocking my path. "Just give me a minute," he said, placing his hands on my shoulders. "You have every right to see but let me check it out first." His worried expression pleaded with me.

I couldn't speak, so I jerked my head in a quick nod. I stayed there, Ryan standing next to me, as Cooper walked toward the room. He stopped just outside the door, taking a deep breath before he stepped forward and looked inside.

With his hands on his hips, he exhaled, turning back to me. "He hurt her. There's a lot of blood, but if I had to guess, he chopped off a finger."

I closed my eyes, mentally preparing myself to see the place where my sister was tortured. I opened my eyes and walked to stand next to Cooper, looking inside.

The countertop was covered in a pool of blood, covering a chopping board. A large knife sat on the counter closer to the sink. The blood was still dripping onto the floor. Another small pool of blood was to the left on the floor.

I closed my eyes again, reining in my raw emotions. Tears and tantrums wouldn't help Charlie. I needed to stay focused. Keeping my eyes closed, I allowed myself to process the image of the room in my mind. The blood. The layout. *It's a crime scene, Kelsey*, I ordered myself, trying to catalogue facts. I opened my eyes, sweeping them slowly from one end of the room to the other side. When my eyes returned to the blood dripping off the countertop, I realized what my emotions were blocking my brain from processing. Rushing across the room, I reached out and placed my hand in the center of the pool of blood.

"What the f..." Spence said from behind me.

"It's still warm," I said, turning toward the door as blood dripped off my hand. "*It's still warm!*"

Cooper looked at my hand before walking over and touching the blood himself. "*Sonofabitch!*"

"No, Cooper. This is good. The building is air conditioned. It's cold in here." I waved my non-blood covered hand in the air. "If the blood is still warm, *then she was just here! She was here and—*" I realized what that meant. The black truck. The truck that Cooper had followed. If Cooper was here with me, then where was the black truck?

"I'm sorry, Kelsey. I'm so sorry. I lost the truck in traffic."

I felt the weight of his words hit me like a freight train. I'd counted on him and he'd failed me. Failed Charlie. He left the parking lot seconds after them. He could've saved her. "You lost her? You lost Charlie?"

"Kelsey..." Cooper shook his head, turning away. He paced twice before turning and punching a hole in the wall. "I lost her. I'm so sorry."

I charged him, shoving him against the wall before gripping the front of his shirt. "*She was in that truck!* She could *still* be in that truck! *How could you lose her?*"

When the realization that I was the one who chose to stay to search the building hit me, I gasped. If I had gone with Cooper, maybe she'd be safe. Maybe we could've saved her. It was me. It was my fault. "I didn't know," I said more to myself, trying to fight off the guilt flooding my system. "I thought she was here. I didn't know." I let Cooper guide me to the floor as a I gasped through my tears. "Cooper..." I whimpered, leaning my forehead against his chest.

"We'll find her," Cooper whispered, wrapping his arms around me. "We'll find her, Kelsey."

Chapter Thirty-Two

KELSEY
Friday, 5:37 p.m.

"We need to leave," Mickey said. "My guard says an unmarked police car has circled the block three times now."

I sighed, turning to face him.

"Are you going to be okay?" Mickey asked me.

"Okay? No. But I've got my shit together again. That's the best I can do right now."

"What's next?" he asked.

I thought about it. What was next? Genie had run the truck's license plate which came back as stolen. And every cop in the city was searching for it. "Did you get anything else out of the man and woman we dropped off earlier?"

"Nothing of interest. They only knew about the warehouse you had the cops search earlier. Oh, and that a guy named Bob with a Mexican accent was the person they called when they had a delivery. But they hadn't spoken to Bob in a few days."

"Crap," I said, running a hand through my hair. "I'm guessing *Bob* was actually Santiago. Unfortunately, Santiago took a header off my balcony last night and won't be talking to anyone."

Mickey remained silent but the corner of his lips ticked upward.

"What about Benny?" I asked. "Anything?"

"Not yet. I'll keep my guys sitting on the barbershop, though."

"I think I'll head down there. Take a look around for myself."

"What good will that do?"

"Charlie said that Benny inferred he was offered the job with her as a target, but he turned it down."

"And?"

"And... Benny might not have wanted the job, but he would've wanted to know who was working in his own backyard. Hell, he might've printed out a background on the guy. Maybe it's lying on his desk in his back office."

"Benny's not that stupid."

I lifted one shoulder in a shrug. "Even smart people make mistakes. Besides—" I said, walking out of the breakroom and down the hall. I could hear Mickey following behind me. "—no stone unturned and all."

"What about these guys?" Mickey said, nodding toward the half-beaten men we'd tied up in the center of the room.

"After we all leave, I'll call in law enforcement. They can pick them up."

"Might as well," Cooper said from just a few feet away, wiping his hands on a rag. "These idiots don't know anything."

"Still felt good to hit someone," Ryan said. "You want to give it a try? Let out some of that rage?"

I looked back at our prisoners—all bloodied and bruised. "I'm good. But if they weren't guarding Charlie, what were they guarding?"

Cooper looked at Ryan who looked back at him. Then they both turned and looked at Mickey's goons who shrugged. Cooper looked back at me. "We forgot to ask them. We were focused on information about Mr. Tricky and Charlie."

"Want me to find out?" Ryan asked.

I shook my head, walking over to the most alert prisoner. "What were you guarding?"

He looked at me, then Ryan. "Heroin."

"Where is it?" I asked.

He continued watching Ryan.

I kicked his leg, getting his attention. "Look at me when I'm talking to you, asshole. He's not the one you need to worry about right now. Where is it?"

"It's in the office. In the back. There's a fake vent in the wall."

I walked down the hall and turned into the office. An oversized air vent was along one wall. I squatted, looking past the grate between the holes. "Oh, shit. That's a lot of drugs."

Mickey squatted beside me, reaching out to yank the vent open with a handkerchief. "Must be at least thirty kilos."

"What's the street value?" Cooper asked.

"A lot," Mickey said, looking over his shoulder at Cooper. "Depends on how pure it is."

"If it's uncut, then they'll mix it with another product to expand the volume," I explained to

Cooper. "They could also mix it with other cocktails of drugs. Either way, we leave it. Let the cops grab it."

Mickey looked at me, not happy.

"I'm not going to let you walk out with thirty kilos of heroin. Just get that out of your pretty little head." I stood and took a step back.

Mickey stood, turning to face me. His eyes held their usual blackness as they watched me.

I pulled my phone and called Uncle Hank.

"Yeah?"

"Six men bow wrapped with thirty kilos of heroin in the back office. Get the address from Tech, then call the calvary before someone shows and frees the prisoners." I hung up the phone. "There," I said to Mickey. "You can either wait, hoping to grab the drugs before the unmarked cop car circles the block again or run like hell. Your choice."

Mickey wasn't happy, but he walked out. Cooper and I followed him down the hall. We all hurried to our vehicles, pulling out of the parking lot and onto the street. Cooper was making a right on the next street when we heard sirens coming.

~*~*~

Pulling up to the block where Benny's barbershop was located, I pointed for Cooper to park behind a silver sedan. I got out, walked over to the car, and leaned over to tap on the glass. The guy in the passenger side lowered his window.

"Yah?"

"You guys from Mickey's crew?"

"Yah."

"Seen Benny?"

"Nah."

"Any activity inside the barbershop?"

"Nah."

I looked at him, waiting for him to saying something meaningful, but he just stared back with a blank expression. "Nice talking to you."

"Yah." He raised his window.

"Anything?" Cooper asked when I returned to the SUV.

"Are you kidding? They're worse than Ryan on a stakeout."

"I talk when I've got something to say," Ryan said from the back seat. "Like what's the deal with the navy car parked half a block down?"

I followed his line of sight, spotting a navy four-door car parked facing us on the other side of the road but a half a block away. "Shit. That's an unmarked."

"We going to bail?" Cooper asked.

"No. Let's drive down the block and make a left, then we can make a wide circuit around and check out the back of the barbershop. I doubt there are cops at both the front and back. They're probably only here to keep an eye on Mickey's guys."

Cooper pulled away from the curb. Five minutes later, we made a slow pass behind the barbershop but didn't spot any cops. Cooper parked behind some retail office three doors down, and we walked back to Benny's.

"You got your lock pick gear?" Cooper asked me.

"Nope," I said, picking up a hefty rock and smashing it into the window.

I stepped back, letting Ryan reach in with a gloved hand and unlock the window before pushing it up. Most of the shops in this neighborhood had bars, preventing someone from getting in this way. Benny wasn't most people. No one was dumb enough to break into his barbershop. Well, no one who feared him at least. And don't get me wrong, Benny was no joke. I didn't want to know how many people he'd killed over the years. But with all the enemies I'd racked up over the years, what difference did one more make?

Ryan stood back as I placed a boot into Cooper's hand to be hefted up the few feet to the window. I threw a leg over the windowsill, *ducked and tucked*, and then drew my other leg inside. I walked through the office to the back door, unlocking it for them to enter.

"Don't you want gloves?" Cooper asked, offering me a pair.

"Why? Benny's not going to press charges. If he has a problem with us breaking in, he'll try to kill us, not file a police report. And since his eyesight went to shit he can't sniper shoot anymore. I'm not all that worried about it."

"Sucks getting old," Cooper said, chuckling.

They followed me into the office, each of us taking a section to search. I took the back bookshelf. I checked each book, one by one, opening them up. After flipping through them, I dropped them to the floor. In the first bookshelf, the last book on the second to lowest shelf, I found a key hidden inside a carved-out book. I pocketed the key, clearing the rest of the books from the shelf, before moving on to the next bookshelf. I was halfway through the next bookshelf, when I noticed the hidden switch.

"Cooper, roll the desk chair away from the desk."

Cooper had been searching the desk, but stood and pushed the rolling chair to the other side. I flipped the switch, jumping off to the side and ducking with an arm raised to protect my face. When nothing happened, I straightened, inspecting the bookcase.

"You ducked," Ryan said.

"What?"

"You ducked. You hit the switch, then ducked out of the way. What about us? You didn't even warn us."

"Sorry?" I cringed. "I didn't really think about Benny booby-trapping it until the second I hit the switch." I glanced at the panel which had only popped open a half inch. "And honestly, I'm wondering now if it's safe to pull open."

Cooper snorted. "Step into the hallway."

"You going to play eeny-meeny-miney-mo with what could be a trap set by Benny?"

"No. I'm going to let the bomb expert look while I hide behind you in the hallway." Cooper shoved me out of the room ahead of him.

"I don't know about this," I whispered to Cooper. "If there's anything behind the panel, it's unlikely to be worthy of risking our lives over."

"Clear," Ryan called out.

"Anything?" Cooper asked Ryan as he winked at me.

"Nice sawed-off shotgun," Ryan said, pointing. "Pressure release tab in the bottom corner. Pretty standard."

"Standard where?" I asked. "Where on earth is it standard to rig a short barrel shotgun inside a wall?"

Cooper threw an arm over my shoulder. "You're just jealous."

I knocked his arm off my shoulder and walked over and looked inside. The shotgun was pointing toward the window, between Ryan and me. "Can you remove it and unload it?"

"Not enough room. Looks like he welded it into the bracket it's held in. I cleared the trip wires, but I wouldn't stand in front of the other end of the barrel."

I lifted on my tip toes and leaned closer. The gun was indeed mounted permanently to the bracket, and the bracket bolted to a base board that lined the floor of the cubby. What I found interesting was the slight gap along the sides of the base board with the sidewalls. I reached up, placing my hand on the center of the barrel, and pushed upward. The base board lifted just a fraction.

"What are the odds he rigged something else under the gun to explode?" I asked Ryan.

"Not likely," he said, grabbing the barrel and lifting it up further. The base board popped up, and Ryan pulled on the barrel to slide it out of the cubby.

"Not likely," I said, glancing over at Ryan. "Meaning it was possible, yet you let me stand here with my face practically inside the bomb radius?"

Ryan smirked, setting the gun and mount on the desk to unload. "Payback for you flipping the release on the bookshelf with me standing directly in the line of fire."

"Okay," I said, nodding as I turned back to the cubby. "I deserved that."

Looking inside, my mood shifted. I pulled out one, then another, then another stack of cash. I turned, passing the stacks to Cooper, then reached back in the cubby and pulled out four more.

"These are hundreds," Cooper said. "And these are double stacked. That's twenty grand a bundle."

I handed him four more stacks, then reached in for more.

"Okay, that makes seven stacks. That's a hundred and forty."

I piled on four more stacks. Then reached in and grabbed the last two, adding them to the top of the pile built up in his hands and leaning against his chest.

"Two hundred and sixty? Holy, shit," Ryan said. "Anything else in there? Keys to a Ferrari? A Rolex?"

I pulled out a large manilla envelope from the cubby and looked inside. Passports. Driver's licenses. Birth Certificates. And a bag of some kind. Tugging the small bag made of fabric out of the envelope, I opened the string. Inside was a zip lock bag. I pulled the plastic bag out and my jaw dropped.

"Yowzer," Ryan said. "I suppose a bag of diamonds will do. I can live without the Ferrari."

"I'm good with the cash," Cooper said, shrugging.

"Well, at least we know Benny's still in Miami," I said, ignoring their comments. "No way would he have left all this behind if he planned on fleeing the country."

"Now what?" Cooper asked.

"Let's bag all this. We'll take it with us after we're done searching the rest of the place." I tucked the plastic bag of diamonds back inside the cloth bag, then stacked both the manilla envelope and diamonds on top of the pile Cooper was holding. He turned, walking toward the kitchenette across the hall, careful not to spill his loot.

I returned to the task of searching the rest of the books.

~*~*~

An hour later, we finished our search. Ryan ended up finding another hidden compartment in the kitchenette inside one of the cabinets. That one was also booby-trapped, but with some type of gas canister grenade. I didn't want to know what kind of gas Benny had filled the canister with. Ryan sealed it in a plastic container, surrounding it with paper towel so it wouldn't roll around and then went to the SUV to secure it in the back. Behind the canister was another hundred grand and two pistols.

I emptied a box of new white towels and loaded the shotgun and pistols, then sealed the box. Cooper carried it out to the SUV along with all the cash, fake documents, and diamonds. I locked the door behind him, returning to the office to take one last look around. I lifted a leg out the window, ducking to exit the way I came, when I spotted a small piece of paper stuck between the window's trim boards. I tugged on it, pulling it out. It was part of a newspaper, but it wasn't a big enough piece for me to see the paper's name or anything else that would identify it. I tucked it in my back pocket, then went to duck again, but stopped. With one leg outside, one inside, and hunched over, if Benny would've had a paper in his hand and exited the window, that's how the piece could've been got caught in the trim. But why would he go out the window?

I pulled myself back into the office, standing. I walked through the room and into the hall, inspecting the back door. Why didn't he exit through the door?

And that's when I saw it: a miniature sensor near the top of the door. I pulled my phone and called Mickey.

"Find Benny?" he asked.

"No. But there's a sensor on the back door. Did you do that?"

"I had Spence install it. I wanted to know if Benny decided to sneak in."

"Spence install anything else?"

"Another sensor on the front door. Why?"

"Just wanted to make sure I wasn't on a hidden camera when I committed a whole shitload of crimes."

"You're clear. He offered to add surveillance, but with my luck, my guards would've been the ones caught doing something illegal, so I declined."

"Perfect. Thanks."

"You still owe me for the drugs. I get we aren't on the same side of the law, but you could've looked the other way."

"And add to the addiction crisis in this country? No, I couldn't have looked the other way." I hung up, tucking the phone in my back pocket before returning to the window. I slipped one leg out and shifted my weight to lower myself. Ryan was waiting on the outside and lifted me down to the ground before closing the window.

"Where to now?" Ryan asked.

"The mansion. I need to check in with everyone."

Chapter Thirty-Three

KELSEY
Friday, 7:27 p.m.

By the time we arrived at the mansion, I was hot, frustrated, and tired. I'd started my day at two in the morning when I'd found Santiago sneaking around inside the house. Since then, I'd been pushing myself from one task to the next and rapidly running out of steam. I couldn't crash yet, though. Charlie was out there. She was counting on me.

Following the path around the house, I dipped my head in acknowledgment to the Bianchi family as I walked out to the tiki lounge. Behind Tech's makeshift desk, I sat in one of the rolling chairs and waited for both him and Genie to stop typing.

Ryan and Cooper had both entered through the front door, but exited a few minutes later through the back door, carrying plates of food. They joined us in the tiki lounge but sat on the lounge furniture, using the stands to set their food on.

Pimples, sitting on the lounge couch, lifted Cooper's plate to retrieve a newspaper under it. "Hey, Pimples," I said as I stood and walked over. "You got time to do me a favor."

"Anything. What'cha need?"

"I found this," I said, pulling out the piece of newspaper from my back pocket. "There's not much writing showing, but can you see if the printed part matches the bottom corner of any pages in your paper?"

"Sure thing," Pimples said as he took the scrap. "Where'd it come from?"

"Benny's barbershop. For some reason the paper was important enough for Benny to take with him when he left."

"Maybe he just wasn't done reading it," Jack said.

"Or had something wrapped up in the paper. Like a body part," Juan added.

"You're right. It's probably a waste of time."

"Most policework leads to nothing," Pimples said, flipping open the paper. "But that's the only way you get to the stuff that does mean something. Juan, go grab the papers from the recycle bin in the garage. I've got a couple days' worth here. If we don't find a match in the main paper, we'll go pick up some other publications."

Juan headed for the path along the mansion as Jack moved to sit in the center of the couch, closer to Pimples. "Give me half your paper. I'll help. I'm tired of sitting here with nothing to do."

"You need to eat," Cooper said, holding a plate out for me.

"I'm not hungry."

"I didn't ask if you were hungry. I said you need to eat."

"I'll eat later," I said, stepping around him to go back to the desk area.

He snagged his arm around my waist, whirling me around. Before I caught my balance, he jerked me backward, causing me to land, half lying, across his lap with my knees over the arm of the lounge chair.

"Damn it, Coo—"

A spoonful of food was shoved into my mouth as I struggled to get up. Forced to swallow part of it as I swatted at his hands, I turned my head so I didn't choke. As soon as I caught a gasp of air, another chunk of food was shoved in. Mad at being manhandled, I started swinging toward his head. He released his hold on me to block his face as he laughed. As I rolled off his lap, I reached over and grabbed Ryan's plate which was sitting on the other stand. I spun around, smashing the pile of food into Cooper's face. The paper plate, soggy from the food, folded to the shape of his head as I slid it upward and gave it a good rub.

He tackled me, pinning me to the ground and shoved more food in my face.

"*Okay! Uncle! Uncle!*" I yelled as I started to laugh. "What is it with you and food fights?"

"What is it with you not eating when you're stressed out?" Cooper said, laughing as he stood. "If you would've just eaten, then you wouldn't be wearing risotto and baked ziti right now." He held out a hand to help me up.

A noodle slid off my face. I caught it in my other hand, deciding to eat it. "I have to admit, the food tastes great," I said.

"Yeah," Ryan said. "It was great—until you took my plate and smashed my dinner on Wild Card's head!"

Three Italian women came rushing at me, wiping my face and arms before scooping up the food from the floor, then rushed away as Grandma Tannelli and Aunt Vianna shoved me into a chair with silverware in one hand, a glass of wine in the other. A plate full of food appeared on my lap. I looked over and Ryan had a new plate of food and was hunched over, eating. Cooper now sat in his chair again, with one hand holding silverware, the other a glass of wine and a plate of food on his lap.

"I could get used to this," he said, dropping his knife and spoon on the side table and using the fork to stab his food.

Grandma Tannelli was standing off to the side, scowling down at me, waiting for me to eat. The woman sort of scared me. I knew I could take in her a fight, but I got the distinct impression she was the type who didn't fight fair. I set the wine on the coffee table and forked a wad of food into my mouth.

"Found it," Jack said.

I looked over as I chewed, unable to speak yet.

"The matching paper," Jack said. "It was from last Wednesday. Is there something specific on this page we're looking for?"

I shrugged, still chewing.

"So... It could be anything in the paper?" Pimples asked.

I nodded, still chewing. I was pretty sure I was chewing a large wad of mozzarella, but it was the expensive kind. The kind that was cooked in big chunks, not shredded first.

"Let's each take a section," Juan said. "Watch the classifieds. Look for something that doesn't make sense. That's how they did it in the old days."

"That's how who did what?" Jack asked.

"That's how criminals passed messages."

"Says who?"

"I don't know. But all the crime movies and tv shows end up finding ads in the paper. Like for car service joints that went out of business fifty years ago or cross-breed dog ads that don't make any sense like a St. Bernard and one of those little miniature dogs."

I stopped chewing, grossed out by the mental image that popped into my head. I looked over at Ryan and Cooper, but they were looking down at their plates, laughing silently.

"Grandma Tannelli," Tech said, walking over. "Could I trouble you for another glass of chocolate milk?"

Grandma Tannelli took the empty glass and raced toward the mansion. As soon as her back was turned, Tech passed me a napkin. I took it and spit the unchewable wad of cheese into it.

"You should've cut it," Tech said, laughing.

"Or you can do this," Cooper said, taking a chunk of cheese and pulling it apart with his hands to create this three-foot stretch, before biting the middle that was sagging.

Genie giggled, walking over to sit next to me. "There's something wrong with you," she told Cooper.

"There's a lot more than just one thing wrong with him," I told her. "Where's Kierson and Maggie?"

"Kierson went to run interference for you at the building with the heroin. Something about your fingerprints in the blood?"

"Long story."

"About an hour later, Maggie called. They were done with whatever assignment you gave them and she was going to meet up with Kierson. I assume Grady is still with her."

"They could be a while," Ford said, walking across the patio. "That many drugs, a bloody room, and a handful of guys tied and beaten, equals a lot of paperwork. And by the way, Kierson told the DEA and the detective assigned from Miami PD that he didn't know where you were. I'd keep your head down."

"Planned on it. How'd you get through security?"

"Grandma Tannelli loves me," Ford said, turning to flash a bright smile as the battleaxe in question crossed the lounge, her expression morphing into one of pleasure as she smiled at Ford and passed Tech his milk.

"Such good boys," she said before patting Tech on the cheek.

"Yes," I said. "Such good boys." I spotted Mackenzie walking along the perimeter fence as she turned toward the dock, beyond where I could see her. I continued watching, and sure enough, she returned following the perimeter toward the front of the house. She was safe enough, with Bianchi guards scattered around the premises. But it was the way she was wandering, searching for something—*like a gap in security*—that had me crossing to follow her.

At the front of the house the guards ordered her away from the driveway. She pivoted in the other direction, following the path north of the garage, walking around it, then continuing down the north side of the mansion back toward the back yard.

"Might be easier if you just tell me why you want to leave," I called out to her.

Startled, she spun around. "Uh, I, uh, don't know what you mean. I'm just walking."

"I wasn't born yesterday, Mackenzie," I said, chuckling as I jogged to catch up with her. "It's okay. You're not in trouble. Let's chat."

"You're busy. You're looking for Charlie. That's more important."

"I've got time. Besides, Charlie would be pissed if I didn't make time for you in her absence." I waved her to follow me on the outside path, the furthest path from eavesdroppers, which led to the grassy area overlooking the ocean.

"Any luck finding Charlie?" Mackenzie asked as she looked out across the water.

I hesitated, considering how much to share. "What have you been told?"

"Not much." She released a long sigh. "I heard on the news she was kidnapped. I offered to go check some of the abandoned buildings we used to crash at, but Grandma Tannelli told me I was being silly."

"Your offer to help wasn't silly," I said, placing a hand on her shoulder. "It was generous and brave. Good on you. But the situation with Charlie is dangerous. She wouldn't want you to put yourself at risk."

Mackenzie seemed annoyed by my answer, but didn't say anything.

"I get it. The shit you've been through makes you feel older than the date stamped on your birth certificate. You had to grow up fast. But what about Liam? What happens to him if something bad happens to you? Think he'll be able to handle that right now on top of everything else?"

"No, but I'm not a kid anymore. And Grandma Tannelli and Aunt Vianna don't understand. They're planning something or keeping secrets. Every time I walk into a room, everyone stops talking."

I nodded. "And you're thinking what? It has to do with your stepdad?"

"You don't know him. He's scary. He's probably going to show up any minute with the police and take us. It's not safe now that he knows where we are."

"The secrets they're keeping aren't about your stepdad," I said, leading her by the shoulder away from the railing and back toward the mansion. "And before you rabbit, I think it's time your family started explaining a few things."

She walked beside me willingly as she lowered her voice with more complaints. "They also took my bag. You know, the one Charlie gave me. I can't find it."

"Well, that just won't do." More than a little annoyed, I led her through the kitchen glass doors, past the women speaking rapid Italian, and into the living room where Phillip and Papa Bianchi were. "We need to see the court filings and order signed by the judge," I told them.

Phillip looked at me, then Mackenzie, then at his father.

"Si," Papa Bianchi said, nodding his approval.

Phillip walked across the room and pulled some papers from an attaché. "Some of the papers have multiple names on them." He handed me the papers, glancing quickly at Mackenzie. He was referring to guardianship of her mother.

"She needs to know the truth. Where's Liam?"

"In the game room," Phillip said.

"I go," Papa Bianchi said, standing. "I keep eye on him. Teach him billiards."

I led Phillip and Mackenzie into the front den, closing the French doors behind us. We settled around a small sitting table. Before I could say anything though, someone knocked on the door.

Vianna peeked her head inside. "Everything okay?" She seemed suspicious of our private meeting.

"No, it's not. Please join us. I'm going to share information with Mackenzie. She has a right to know."

"I don't think Grandma Tannelli will like that. She ordered us not to," Vianna said, looking nervous as she entered and closed the doors behind her.

"I don't care. I don't answer to her. And let me explain something to the two of you." I looked at Vianna, then Phillip, giving them my serious expression. "If you want Mackenzie and Liam to stay here with the family, you need to start being honest with Mackenzie. She's been through a lot. The last thing she needs is secrets and uncertainty. If she fears they're not safe, she'll take off. She knows how to live on the street. She knows how to hide. If you want to keep her protected, your only option is to tell her the truth."

"Oh, honey," Vianna said, sitting next to Mackenzie and placing her hand on her shoulder. "We keep telling you everything is okay."

"I've heard that before," Mackenzie said, turning her face away from Vianna. Tears threatened to spill, and she blinked rapidly to hold them back.

"First, where's her bag?" I asked.

Vianna looked nervously from me to Mackenzie. "I moved it to the second floor. I unpacked it."

"And my money?" Mackenzie asked.

"I have it," Phillip said with a raised eyebrow. "Vianna gave it to me." He pulled out an overflowing envelope from inside his jacket pocket and slid it across the table. "I was going to have it deposited into an account in your name."

Mackenzie snatched the envelope, clutching it with both hands.

"Which is the opposite of what she needs it for," I said. "That's street cash. If she needs to run, the money will help keep her alive."

"But it's not safe to carry that much cash," Vianna said.

"It's safer than trying to find a way to earn money at her age," I said, trying to be vague enough not to embarrass Mackenzie. "The phone, cash, and clothes were given to the kids. They were told it was theirs, and if they wanted to leave, they were allowed to take it with them. They were not being held here against their will."

"You feel like a prisoner," Phillip said, nodding. "I get that. All the guards."

"There's been guards here since we arrived," Mackenzie said. "But before, if I wanted to leave the property, they said it was fine but asked to accompany me. To keep me safe, not keep me against my will."

"I'll talk to my men," Phillip said.

"And Mackenzie and Liam can continue sleeping on the third floor in the bunkroom," I said. "There's no reason to have their rooms moved."

"Okay," Vianna said, nodding.

I looked at Phillip. "Any update on our guest in the condo?"

"Vitals good. Still not awake yet. We just don't know if there's been any permanent damage. We'll be moving her tomorrow to the hospital."

"I think we should wait until we know," Vianna said, looking at me nervously again.

"No." I opened the file, flipping through the pages. "Mackenzie, these documents show that your stepfather's guardianship has been revoked. Your real father's family now has all legal say in your future. But the papers also have another name: Sophia Barrett."

"My mom? Why? She died," Mackenzie said, taking the papers I offered her as she scanned the court orders.

"The mother you knew might not be in this world anymore, but she didn't die. Your stepfather lied. There was a car accident, yes. That part was true. But she survived her injuries. She's been kept in a medically induced coma all this time. But Mackenzie," I said, placing a hand on her arm. "I know this is hard to hear, but she could be brain dead or severely mentally impaired. She might never be the woman who raised you."

"You're saying she's alive, but not really alive? I don't understand."

"We just don't know," Phillip said in a gentle voice. "We have doctors trying to reverse the coma, but so far she hasn't woken. She may never wake."

Mackenzie looked up at me with fresh tears flowing down her cheeks. "Can I see her?"

"No, honey," Vianna said, patting her hand.

"Please," Mackenzie pleaded. "I didn't get to say goodbye before. I need to see her."

I glanced at Phillip. "It's a reasonable request. Either you make it happen or I will."

Phillip looked at Mackenzie and nodded. "What about Liam?"

"No," Mackenzie said, shaking her head. "Not yet. I'll tell him, but not yet. I need to see Mom first."

"Very well," I said, standing. "Phillip, please provide Mackenzie a copy of all legal documents related to her and Liam's guardianship. Vianna, please make sure Mackenzie gets all of her belongings back." I started for the door, but Mackenzie called my name.

As I turned, she threw herself at me, wrapping her arms around me in a hug. "Thank you."

"You're welcome," I said, kissing the top of her head as I stroked her hair. "Be sure to tell Liam you're leaving for a little bit so he doesn't worry."

"I will." Mackenzie stepped back, wiping her tears away. "And he'll be happy to hear we can sleep in the bunkroom. He feels safe in there."

"Good. And next time..." I wagged a finger at her.

"I know, I know. Talk to you or one of my uncles before I do anything drastic."

"You got it." I kissed her forehead before turning toward the door, but I paused at the last minute.

"Phillip, Mackenzie offered to help search for Charlie and check some abandoned buildings she knows about but was told no. While I agree it's not safe for her to do so, maybe with your help she can identify them and someone else can search them?"

Phillip smirked, nodding at Mackenzie. "Good idea. I think we can arrange something that would keep Mackenzie safe and help at the same time."

"What going on in here?" Grandma Tannelli said storming into the room.

Before I could say anything, Phillip answered her in Italian with a sharp reply. She snapped back in more Italian. Then he clipped another short sentence reply.

She inhaled dramatically, then glared at me, before stomping out of the room.

"Is she going to poison my next meal?" I asked, looking toward the door.

"She won't kill you, but she's not above making you feel like you're about to die," Aunt Vianna said, giggling.

"Good to know."

CHAPTER THIRTY-FOUR

KELSEY
Friday, 8:07 p.m.

When I returned to the tiki lounge, I found more people had gathered. Kierson, Uncle Hank, and Quille spoke quietly near Genie's workstation. Grady, Ryan, and Cooper were clustered near Tech. Uncle Hank's poker buddies were huddled on a lounge sofa, still reading sections of the paper. Trigger was leaned over the coffee table, scarfing down a late dinner. Others were scattered around the back patio and tiki lounge, both law enforcement and lawbreakers.

"Let's compare notes," I called out, walking over to sit on the arm of a chair. "While most of us are here, let's go over everything and see where we're at."

Cooper walked over and tossed me a shirt. I looked down at the one I was wearing and laughed at the baked ziti smear. Since I was wearing a sports bra I pulled my shirt over my head, replacing it with the clean one.

"The other two addresses that Mickey gave you," Maggie said, starting the recap. "They were a bust. And despite Ford vouching for Madame Cora, Grady and Trigger did a search anyway. Nothing of interest popped."

"What about the locations pinned on the map where the girls were being held?" I asked.

"We can't determine an address on any of them," Quille said. "We've got units in each area, but until we can narrow it down, our hands are tied."

"I've been working on that," Genie said. "I think I've identified two of the pins. One is the residence of a known criminal, mostly assaults. The other is another foreclosed property."

"Where's the foreclosure?" I asked.

"It's being handled," Kierson said. "Miami PD is preparing to enter on the foreclosed property. A few Bianchi men are taking the ex-con's address."

I smirked at Kierson. "That had to have hurt. Assigning the mob to search an address?"

"What can I say?" Kierson said, shrugging. "It's for Charlie. You know I'd do anything for her."

Spence was sitting on the other side of the tiki lounge and didn't miss Kierson's expression. I was pretty sure Spence had figured out that Kierson was Charlie's ex.

"Okay. Let me know if anything turns up. What about the other pins?"

"There's only one more unidentified," Genie said. "It's in a sketchy neighborhood. Too many possible suspects."

The mounted screen was changed to show the area on the map where the pin was located. "That's Chills's stomping ground." I pulled my phone and called Chills.

"Nobody's spotted her, but we're still looking," Chills said when he answered.

"Good. But we have reason to believe the same crew who took Charlie has a property they're using for nefarious purposes in your neighborhood. Somewhere near the federal housing project."

"All kinds of nefarious around those parts. Can you narrow it down any?"

"Not really. Could be a stash house for women or drugs. The guards at the other location were big, stupid, carrying pistols, and Hispanic. And two of the properties we identified were abandoned foreclosures."

"There's plenty of foreclosures around the neighborhood, but not many Hispanics. Let me run it down." Chills hung up.

"Assigning a gangbanger to investigate," Quille said, chuckling. "Now I see the family resemblance between you and Charlie."

"It's more efficient. But it would help if you call units off the neighborhood. Give Chills and his gangsters some space."

"And then what?" Quille said. "Say they find the address. Do we just look the other way while they charge in and start shooting each other?"

"Do you really care? Personally, I've got no problem with criminals shooting criminals. Never have. I sort of think of it as they're doing law enforcement a favor."

"And if an innocent bystander gets killed?" Ford asked.

"Chills will call me if he finds the place and thinks they might be outmanned. If he feels it'll be easy enough to take down, he'll have a few guys play lookout, keeping civilians away."

I looked over, spotting Tasha in her lab coat stomping through the decorative grass as she made her way to the lounge.

"Tasha?" I called out. "Was there a body found I'm not aware of?"

"No," Tasha said while pushing her glasses up with her finger. She walked over, stopping within a few feet of me. "But I took a peek at the forensic evidence recovered from the building on Dolly Avenue."

Dolly avenue was the building where we'd found the heroin.

"We confirmed the blood was Charlie's," Tasha said.

"I don't have a report on that yet," Quille said, looking at his phone.

"Oh," Tasha said, blinking several times. "I must've forgotten to send it to you." She looked back at me and winked, handing me a folder. "We also confirmed your prints at the scene from where you touched the blood." She tilted her head sideways, studying me. "Why did you touch the blood?"

"It was still warm," I answered.

She thought a moment then nodded. "Makes perfect sense." She glanced back at Quille, then at me. "As soon as the official report is released, the detective assigned to the case is going to want to talk to you. Unfortunately, the administrator who handles distribution of such paperwork experienced a horrible case of diarrhea and had to go home. The report probably won't be released until tomorrow morning."

Maggie barked a laugh. Kierson looked skyward in disbelief. Quille groaned.

"Thank you, Tasha," I said as I laughed. "Anything interesting pop?"

"Traces of hydraulic fluid and clam shells."

"Clam shells?"

"It was a minor trace. The interesting aspect of it was that the clam shell dust was clean, absent of sand or oils."

"What does that mean?"

"It wasn't from a beach or restaurant. Likely it was tracked from somewhere with decorative clam shells."

"Like tourist shops?"

"Maybe. Or craft venues, a porch with a shell windchime, someone's home where a shell collection is stored." Tasha shrugged. "I could make a list of possibilities."

"That's okay," Grady said. "We get the picture."

"Anything else?" I asked Tasha.

She looked around, then sat on the coffee table, looking up at me. "Charlie's blood sample."

I straightened, nodding for her to continue as I locked down my emotions.

"There were trace amounts of a sedative. Ketamine. It was probably administered to her when she was taken this morning."

"So, it had worn off," I said, closing my eyes.

"Exactly."

"What does that mean?" Uncle Hank asked.

I inhaled a deep breath before answering. "It means she was conscious when she was injured. Whatever Mr. Tricky did to her, he waited until she was awake and alert."

"Son-of a..." Spence started to say but let his words trail off as he rubbed a hand against his forehead.

"Charlie's tough," Aunt Suzanne said, standing proudly with her shoulders pinned back. Her eyes were shiny from unshed tears. "She can take it. She doesn't back down from a fight, and she'd want the same from all of you. Just put it out of your minds." She looked around, staring at everyone. "You've got work to do. She's counting on all of you to help her."

"She's right," Cooper said. "Grady, did you get the camera installed down by Cape Street?"

Grady and Maggie both turned to grin at Trigger. Trigger looked up, flashed a grin at me, then went back to eating.

Ryan laughed. "Please tell me you got video of whatever stupid shit Trigger did."

"Sorry," Grady said, chuckling. "Didn't have time."

"These dumbasses stole a utility truck," Maggie said.

"I didn't hear that," Quille said.

Ford smiled, looking between Grady and Quille.

Maggie shook her head. "They only made it a few blocks before the police pulled the truck over."

"But Trigger had told me to stay out of sight," Grady said. "So, when we were pulled over, Trigger jumps out and starts running. The cops followed him, never noticing I was still in the truck. As soon as the coast was clear, I drove away. By the time we got to Cape Street, Trigger was already there, leaning against a light post, eating a mango."

"Excellent cab service in this city," Trigger said without looking up.

"So now you're wanted for two crimes in Miami?" I asked.

He shrugged, unconcerned.

"And the cameras?" Cooper asked.

"I've already got the feed running," Tech said. "I've been watching for the black truck or any other suspicious vehicles."

"What's our coverage?" I asked.

"The main road, both directions. We'll be able to see anyone driving in or out of the neighborhood for about a mile stretch."

"Good. But assign someone else to watch. We need you on research."

"I'll take a shift," Juan offered, shuffling toward Tech. "Can't find anything in that newspaper worthy of Benny's attention."

"Nothing?" I said, frowning.

"You knew it was a long shot," Juan said.

"I'm not ready to give up yet," Pimples said.

"Me either," Jack added. "Though I keep mentally listing all the other reasons Benny might've taken the paper with him."

"Like what?" I asked. "Convince me I'm wrong."

"Didn't say you were," Jack said.

"She means talk it out with her," Grady said. "What are the other reasons?"

"Well, could be he's a betting man. Had money on a game and hadn't checked the scores yet."

"I don't buy it," Uncle Hank said. "Being in the same room with Benny terrified the shit out of most men. I can't see a bookie brave enough to talk to him on the regular."

"And Benny was a saver, not a spender," Ryan said. "Serious gamblers don't typically have piles of cash squirrelled away."

"Benny could've wrapped a body part in the paper," Juan said from behind one of the monitors.

"He'd have used paper towel and a plastic bag," Cooper said. "Plenty of both in his barbershop breakroom."

"Car shopping?" Maggie said, playing along.

"Maybe," I admitted. "If he wanted to buy a car from a private seller. But then he'd have to drive himself to the location and if he bought a car, he'd then have two vehicles to transport."

"Benny's more than capable of stealing a car," Spence said, shaking his head. "No need to stick his head out in the open to buy one. He's a career criminal."

"Agreed," Ryan said.

"We'll I'm not finding anything in the classifieds," Jack said, tossing a section of the paper down.

"That didn't fit anyway," I said. "Benny doesn't have anyone to communicate with. He's a loner."

"How does he communicate with customers for hits?"

"Probably the dark web," Tech said.

"Agreed," Genie said. "He probably hires someone to middleman contracts, then has final say whether he accepts or not."

"Maybe he communicates with the middleman through the paper," Jack said. "But more likely this middleman just goes to the barbershop to talk in person."

"Are we wasting our time? Maybe," Pimples said, shrugging. "So what? It's better than sitting on our thumbs and worrying about Charlie."

Jack turned back to the paper, picking up the local community events section. The last section lying on the coffee table was the obituaries.

I stood as a plausible theory jumped out at me. "I need all law enforcement to leave."

"Excuse me?" Quille said.

"I believe you heard me just fine," I said, narrowing my eyes at Quille.

Kierson nodded for Quille to follow. "Let's head back to the station. Maggie and Genie can relay anything relevant back to us."

"They don't have to leave?" Ford asked, following.

"Kelsey's already corrupted them. They wouldn't recognize the line between legal and illegal anymore if it smacked them in the face."

Ford looked back, making eye contact with me. I shook my head.

"I better go, too," Uncle Hank said, kissing Aunt Suzanne's cheek. "I want to check in with some snitches anyway."

"Is there any more food?" Tasha asked, eying Trigger's near empty plate. "I haven't eaten today."

"Plenty," Aunt Suzanne said. "Let's go inside and fix you a plate."

As soon as they were out of hearing distance, I grabbed the obituaries. I laid one page in front of Jack and Pimples, handed another to Ryan, a third to Maggie. I took the last page, sitting beside Trigger. "Pair up. We're looking for an obituary. Look for someone who's likely to have a house here in Miami. Not a trailer or an apartment—but a house. And watch any mention of no living family or only out of the area family."

"Why?" Cooper asked, sliding his chair closer to Ryan's.

"Because," Grady said, grinning. "If Kelsey's theory is right, Benny is camped out in some dead person's house until it's safe to return to the barbershop."

"Damn," Pimples said. "That's not a bad idea. A lot safer than being spotted in a motel and a lot more comfortable than bunking down in an abandoned building."

"Probably still food in the refrigerator and cupboards too," Trigger said, leaning over the paper to start reading with me.

Several possibilities were eliminated either due to location of the house or no indication if relatives were close by.

"Got it," Ryan said, holding up the paper as he read. "Michael Streiner, age sixty-two, died at home Sunday night. Michael worked as a welder for Harbor Creek Manufacture in Wisconsin for twenty years before retiring and relocating to Florida last July. He is survived by his son, Michael Streiner Jr., an architect in New York. Funeral services will be held at the Evermore Living Funeral Home in Pardon, Wisconsin on Saturday, December 15th."

"Practically screams for someone to rob the place," Jack said as he stood.

"I agree. Any other contenders?" I asked.

"We've got one iffy one," Maggie said. "But it's not as obvious as Ryan's."

"I've got one possible too," Pimples said. "But I'm in the same boat. I'd pick Ryan's, too."

"Okay," I said. "Let's divide the list."

"Finders, keepers," Ryan said, holding up his page of the newspaper.

"Fair enough, but I'm going with you," I said. "Pick a third."

Ryan grinned at Trigger.

"Yes," Trigger said, clenching a fist and tucking it in like he caught an invisible football.

Cooper chuckled. "Spence and I can check out Jack's address."

"And I'll take Grady for mine," Maggie said.

"Yeah, no thanks," Grady said, taking the paper from her. "You might need an alibi if we do find Benny. His future isn't looking so bright. I'll call Mickey for backup."

"I'm not about to go back to sitting on my ass," Pimples said, standing. "Put us to work. That's why we're here."

"Yeah," Jack said.

"Pimples, you go with Grady," I said. "Jack, you're with Cooper and Spence." I looked around as everyone grouped up. "Do I have to explain what needs to happen if anyone finds Benny?"

The boys chuckled, but didn't say anything as they moved toward the front drive.

"I'll take that as a no," I said to myself.

I was grabbing my handbag as my phone rang. I answered it, seeing it was Chills. "What did you find?"

"Found the house, and the girls being kept against their will."

"And?" I asked, glancing at Trigger and Tech.

"That's about it. The guys holding them are low on the chain of command. They didn't have much to share other than the other building you already had raided."

"Okay, get the girls to one of Charlie's shelters. What about the men? They still alive?"

"Sort of," Chills said on a chuckle. "They could probably use some medical attention if you don't want us to finish them off."

"Text me the address, and I'll send the officials that way. I'll give you ten minutes to clear out of the neighborhood."

"Later," Chills said before disconnecting.

I tossed Tech my phone and he tossed me a burner before I started for the front of the house.

"I'm so jealous," Maggie said, pouting.

"Chin up, Mags," Trigger said as he walked past. "There's always next time."

Chapter Thirty-Five

KELSEY
Friday, 9:01 p.m.

"We got a live one," Trigger said, holding up the heat scanner to show me someone was sitting in a chair on the west side of the house.

"We might want to wait until after dark," Ryan said. "Not much coverage surrounding the house."

I stared at the house. "Every minute we wait is another minute that Mr. Tricky has Charlie."

"We can't rush it either," Ryan said. "Benny's a contract killer. We need every advantage we can get."

"Exit strategy," Trigger said, grinning at me.

He was reminding me of an op he'd pulled with Bridget in Kentucky. Bridget walked up to the front door and knocked. The guy hiding inside the apartment took off out the fire escape. Trigger was hiding behind the dumpster in the back alley and snagged him when he got to the bottom.

"But which way will he go?" I asked.

"Two streets to the south. The street there is busy enough to catch a cab or duck into a bar."

"It's too risky," I said. "Benny could easily evade us and we'd lose our chance."

"Either of you want to share what you're talking about?" Ryan asked.

"No need," Trigger said. "Kelsey killed my idea."

"It wasn't bad," I said. "But it needs another layer. Something to put Benny more in the frame of mind to flee for his life, so his defenses are down. Then we can snag him when he exits."

Trigger nodded to himself, thinking, then his head snapped up, staring out the window. A second later, he was bailing from the back seat of the SUV. "Give me ten minutes. Be ready to rush the back door."

"Text when you're ready," I said, not bothering to ask him about his plan.

"That's the brilliant part," Trigger said. "I won't need to text. Just be ready." He closed the door slowly so it didn't make a noise.

I watched in my rearview mirror as he jogged away from us.

"I love that guy," Ryan said, laughing.

"You don't even know what he's planning."

"Exactly. It makes working with him fun. Keeps you on your toes."

"We'll see. We better get moving."

"Where are we going?"

"We need to snag Benny fleeing the rear of the house."

"Right. Okay."

We both got out and made our way across the street before ducking between two houses and moving toward the place Benny was holed up in. When we were close to the back of the house, we tucked low next to an air conditioner. I checked my watch. It had only been two minutes. We had a few more minutes to wait.

Neither of us dared speak, not even in a whisper. If Benny heard us, at best, he'd disappear. At worst, he'd shoot us.

A few minutes later, I checked my watch again. Four minutes to go. I looked toward the street, hearing a loud vehicle. When I heard tires burning rubber against the pavement, I nudged Ryan to move with me closer to the back door with him on one side, me on the other, and our backs flat against the siding. The tires stopped squealing as what sounded like a very large engine vehicle approached at a fast pace. As the back door opened, the house itself seemed to lunge at us, knocking Ryan and me forward. Benny went flying past us, face first, off the back step and into the yard. Ryan recovered first, diving on top of Benny and pinning him down. I jumped up, grabbed my cuffs, and tossed them to Ryan.

Trigger ran around the corner of the house, blood streaming from his nose. "We should go," he said, nodding toward the road. "Someone might've called the cops."

Ryan was already hauling Benny to his feet. "You think?"

"It worked, didn't it?" Trigger said, all smiles.

"Did you break your nose?" I asked, grabbing Benny's other arm to help drag him across the yard toward the street.

Trigger stretched his t-shirt sleeve to wipe some of the blood from his face. "Didn't have time to disable the air bag. Fucker got me good."

"Shit," Ryan said, laughing when we crossed into the front yard. A canary yellow truck with black racing stripes and oversized tires was sticking out of the front of the house. Only the ass end of the truck was visible. The front half of the truck was covered under the crumbled house, with part of the roof lying vertically in the truck bed.

Ryan stopped to snap photos with his phone.

"How'd you get out?" I asked Trigger as he took Ryan's place on the other side of Benny.

"Kicked out the windshield, then fled through the kitchen window. Or at least, I think it was the kitchen. Hard to say for sure since all the rooms were sort of smashed together. Good thing Florida houses don't have basements."

Ryan jogged to catch up, taking Benny's right arm and giving me a break. Benny had yet to say anything. He kept his body slack, forcing us to haul his weight, as his eyes darted around.

"I'm telling you, man, we need to hurry. It's not only the cops I'm worried about. The dude who owned that truck," Trigger looked down the street, "big fucker. I mean, real big."

I ran the rest of the way down the street, opening the back door of the SUV before rounding the corner to climb behind the wheel. Ryan had the keys, so I couldn't start the engine.

The sound of a shot gun, followed by the shattering of the window on the back door I'd left open, caused me to drop over the center console, lying halfway across the passenger seat. I lifted my head to peek over the dash, seeing Trigger, Ryan, and Benny run toward the SUV.

"Start the engine!" Trigger yelled.

"Ryan has the keys!" I yelled back.

Another shot rang out, taking off the passenger side rearview mirror. The boys ducked behind the front grill. Without the keys, the best I could do was provide cover so I lowered my window and stuck my upper body out, twisting to sit on the door as I aimed over the hood of the SUV and fired several warning shots. The guy I was shooting at—an oversized redneck wearing a button-down plaid shirt with the sleeves ripped off—ducked behind a parked car.

The boys used the time to circle around to my side and slide into the back seat. I felt an arm wrap around my legs, holding me, as the engine started. The man with the shotgun jumped out, aiming to take another shot, but I was ready, firing several warning shots within a few feet of his toes. He retreated again to safety as the SUV started down the road at a good clip.

"Coming in," I warned whoever was driving as I dropped through the window, worming my way across Trigger's lap and over to the other side. I glanced in the back where Benny was half on the seat, half on the floor. Ryan was pulling the passenger door closed with one hand and holding a gun on Benny with the other.

"Well, hello, Benny," I said, grinning down at him.

Benny glared at me. "What the hell do you want, Harrison?"

"Don't play dumb. We both know what I want." I waved my gun at him. "Now strip."

"Go to hell."

Shifting my gun into my left hand, I leaned over the seat, placed the barrel over the center of his hand and fired.

The gunshot sounded like a cannon within the vehicle. Trigger swerved, startled by the noise, but corrected his driving. Ryan yelled something at me, but I had no idea what he was saying. The ringing in my ears drowned out all the noises around me except for Benny's scream.

Ryan clamped a hand over Benny's mouth, shaking his head at me. I shrugged. I was all done playing games. Better for Benny if he knew that now.

~*~*~

Through a series of hand signals, I directed Trigger to drive out of the city, and then had him crossing over the state from east to west. My ears were still ringing, making verbal conversation difficult.

After Benny had stopped screaming he followed orders, removing every stitch except his blue-striped boxers. His mangled hand had been wrapped with pressure gauze and with any luck, he wouldn't bleed out.

Just over an hour and half later, we arrived at our destination.

"You've finally cracked, haven't you?" Ryan asked as he leaned forward, looking out the windshield.

"What the hell is a bar doing out in the middle of the swamp?" Trigger asked.

A handful of pickups and SUVs lined the muddy lot in front of the rickety building. I recognized most of them, but not all.

"Wait here. Let me clear the place out," I said as I slid out of the SUV.

"I have to pee," Trigger said, opening his door.

"This is gator territory," I warned.

"I can wait," Trigger said, slamming his door closed.

I made my way across the spongey ground, then walked between two trucks toward the porch. Two steps at a time up the stairs and a few feet across the narrow porch, I took a breath before swinging the screen door open and walking inside.

One by one, the handful of patrons fell silent and turned to watch me.

"What do you need, darlin?" Carly asked from her usual position behind the bar.

There was no anger behind her voice. Just plain old, uncomplicated acceptance.

"I need your bar for a private meeting."

Carly didn't hesitate. She didn't even blink. "Everyone out!" she called out loud enough for everyone to hear.

Two men I didn't recognize hesitated, seeming confused. The rest started gathering their belongings and shuffling out the door, patting me on the shoulder or give me a respectful head nod as they passed.

"Order up," Tobias called from the kitchen.

"You old fool," Carly called back. "Put your hearing aid in. I just sent everyone packing!"

A minute later, Tobias rounded the hallway into the main room, stopping when he saw me standing there. "Bout time you come around for a visit." He took large steps hurriedly across the room to fold his arms around me. "Been worried about you."

"You don't hate me?" I whispered, hearing my voice crack.

"Hate you?" Carly said, walking over to stroke the back of her fingers across my face. "We got nothin' but love in our hearts for you darlin.'"

"But Eric…" I looked up, reining in my emotions. "I got him killed."

"Eric died because he was a brave, loyal soul. He lost his life trying to help a friend. He wouldn't want that same friend blaming herself for what happened."

"Amen," Tobias said, stepping back to have a good look at me. "You're too skinny. Let me cook you up something to stick to those bones of yours."

"Right now's not the best time. I need to use your place to have a little chat with a guy. Sorry to involve you two, but Miami doesn't exactly offer many options for a good ole fashioned interrogation."

"This about Charlie?" Carly asked. "We heard on the news she was kidnapped."

I nodded. "The guy I need to question is an assassin. He might look old and withered, but he's a sociopath. It's not going to be easy to break him, but he has information I need about the man who took Charlie."

"I got no problem with it," Carly said, glancing over at Tobias.

"I'm good. Let me just shuffle a few tables outta yer way," Tobias said.

I stepped outside, just beyond the door on the porch. Trigger had moved the SUV closer to the building in the now empty parking area. I waved the all clear and they dragged Benny inside.

Ryan gathered supplies from the back of the SUV which included a twenty-foot climbing rope. I took the rope, making a knot in one end and swinging that end over the ceiling's crossbeam, feeding the excess until it ended at the height I needed. Trigger hauled Benny to his feet, holding him in place, while I stood on a chair and tied his wrists.

Ryan anchored the other end to a long iron pipe, used as a footrest on the customer side of the bar, and cinched it tight. Benny now dangled in front of me, only the tips of his feet able to touch the ground. Pure evil glared at me, and I held that glare, staring back, unflinching.

Tobias returned and held out three items for me: a baseball bat, a fraying straw broom, and a large grill spatula for flipping burgers.

I took the bat but stared at Tobias. "What exactly am I supposed to do with the spatula? Spank him?"

Tobias rotated his wrist and slapped Benny—hard—across the face with the backside of the spatula. The slap was loud and applied with enough force to cause Benny's body to jiggle on the rope.

"I stand corrected," I said, laughing. I took the spatula, laying it on a nearby table. "You and Carly might want to disappear for a bit. This could get bloody."

"We'll be fine," Tobias said, waving off my concern. "I'll head to the kitchen and cook up some food. With any luck, you'll be done by the time dinner is ready."

Ryan dropped additional tools on the floor next to me. I looked at the supplies which now included a knife, bolt cutters, needle nose pliers, thick gloves, and a bottle of rubbing alcohol.

"Benny, I have to admit, I'm not looking forward to torturing you. Having been tortured myself, I can attest it's not a pleasant experience." I walked over to face him. "Save yourself some pain and tell us what we need to know. Tell us about the man who took Charlie."

Benny spat on the floor. "Got nothing to say."

"What if I were to tell you we found your cash and diamonds at the barbershop? That your little nest egg is empty?"

He continued glaring. "I've been in the business longer than you been alive. You think that was my only stash?"

"No, probably not." I paced a few feet, thinking. "So that's it? You're just going to tough it out?" I shook my head at him. "Why? Why protect this guy?"

"The only way to survive in this game is by keeping your damn mouth shut."

"But you won't survive, Benny," I told him. "You'll die protecting a man who means nothing to you."

"We both know you don't have what it takes to kill someone in cold blood."

"You're forgetting that I raised Charlie since she was a little girl. I fed her, clothed her, and held her when she cried. There's *nothing* I wouldn't do for her."

Benny snorted. "She was a lost cause long before she was taken."

I gripped the baseball bat in both hands and swung, hitting Benny in the thigh.

He screamed as he thrashed around on his rope.

I watched without emotion. And when he stopped screaming, I hit him again.

~*~*~

"I gotta admit," Trigger said from the barstool next to me, "beating answers out of someone isn't as much fun as I'd imagined it to be."

"Depends on the person," Ryan said from the barstool on the other side of Trigger. "Guy like Benny has a code. Makes it harder to get them talking. You take some meathead, though, and they'll sing after a few good punches. No such code."

Carly poured four shots to the rim. We each downed one.

I'd gone at Benny with everything I could think of that would injure him without killing him. I beat him, cut him, shocked him, burned him, and even doused cheap vodka on his wounds. He screamed a lot, but still didn't talk.

"He's gotta have a weakness," Carly said. "What about threating family or someone close to him?"

"Benny's a sociopath," I said, shaking my head. "The closest thing he had to a friend died a few weeks back. He doesn't have anyone else in his life as far as I know."

"And we already raided his stash at the barbershop," Ryan said. "So, bribing him won't work."

I heard the back door open and turned to look down the short hall. Lenny, a local marijuana smuggler and a somewhat friend, hobbled into the main room on his peg leg prosthetic, and wandered up to the bar.

Carly filled a beer mug, setting it on the bar for him.

Lenny looked around, nodded to me, raised an eyebrow at Benny then sat at the bar. "Quiet night," Lenny said before taking a drink.

"Thought I sent enough money for a real prosthetic," I said to Lenny, leaning over the bar to make eye contact.

"The peg leg is cooler, don't you think?" Lenny said, lifting his pant leg.

The upper part of the prosthetic looked standard. It was only the end closest to the floor which resembled a thick broom stick.

Carly rolled her eyes. "He thinks it makes him look like a pirate. He had a real prosthetic, but he decided to do the peg leg instead."

I laughed, sliding my shot glass to the other side of the bar.

"Do we have a problem here," Ryan asked me, nodding at Lenny.

I shook my head. "Lenny, we're trying to beat a few answers out of this guy, but not getting anywhere. Any suggestions?"

Lenny turned on his barstool, beer mug in hand, and studied Benny. "What kind of answers?"

"He has information about the man who kidnapped Charlie. We need that information."

"Charlie?" Lenny said with his eyebrows shooting skyward. "*Somebody took Charlie?*"

"Afraid so. Yesterday morning."

Lenny chugged a third of his beer before setting the mug on the bar. "Be right back." We watched him hobble down the short hall and out the door.

"This ain't gonna be good," Carly said, filling our shot glasses.

"Got a better idea?" I asked.

"Nope," Carly said before downing her shot.

"Me either." I downed mine.

I heard the back door open. I set my empty glass down as I looked over my shoulder.

A spike of fear hit me as I climbed on top of my barstool, then on top of the bar. Carly was right beside me in a flash, clutching my arm. Ryan and Trigger had stood, pulling their guns.

"What is that?" Ryan asked.

Lenny was carrying a large burlap bag as he hobbled toward Benny. Between the writhing movements inside the bag and the loud hissing, I was certain I knew its contents.

"You guys should get up here," I warned them.

Both Ryan and Trigger scrambled to the top of the bar.

"Tobias!" Carly called.

Tobias rounded the corner of the kitchen, saw Lenny's bag, then climbed up to join us on top of the bar.

"Ever seen a cottonmouth?" Lenny asked Benny.

Benny was eyeing the bag, swaying as he tried to climb the rope to distance himself from the bag.

"Mean snakes. And their bites? Hurt like hell. And they'll nail you a good three times before they've had enough. And in here," Lenny held up the bag, "well... I lost track of the exact number on account of I had a few beers earlier—might've even smoked a joint—but I reckon I got at least a dozen. It was a good day out in the swamp."

"No!" Benny yelled, his head swiveling toward me. "D.Z. That's the name of the guy who took Charlie. He's ex-marines. No one knows where he lives, but he's in the network. D.Z. That's his name."

"Those are initials—*not a name*," I said.

Benny bent his body away from the bag. "That's all I've got. That and he'll take jobs no one else wants. Kidnapping. Torture. High risk targets."

"Where's he from?" Ryan asked.

"Midwest, I think." Benny hollered as Lenny held the bag higher. "*I don't know*! D.Z. only came to Miami twice. He only accepts jobs on referral."

"How do we contact him?" Trigger asked.

"Only through referrals. You have to find someone he's worked for before."

I believed him. Every time Lenny shifted the bag, his face tensed with fear. He was telling the truth.

"Who killed Stuart Grenway—the rogue cop turned assassin?"

"What?" Benny asked, focusing on the burlap bag.

"Who killed Stuart Grenway? Was it you? Or was it this D.Z. guy?"

"Grenway killed Pauly." Benny for the first time turned his focus away from the bag of snakes, focusing on me. "I slit his throat and enjoyed watching him die."

"Why leave Grenway gift wrapped?" Ryan asked.

"Thought Charlie would get a kick out of it." When Lenny lifted the bag again, Benny squealed. Urine streamed from his boxers, puddling on the floor. "I'm answering your damn questions! Get those fuckers away from me!"

I too was ready for the bag of snakes to disappear. "Lenny, we're good."

"Glad I could help," Lenny said, grinning widely.

Lenny turned, but stumbled on his peg leg. Horrified, I screamed as Lenny dropped the bag.

Lenny jumped on one leg toward the back door but a snake latched onto his calf.

Benny thrashed wildly, attracting a half dozen snakes his direction. They launched upward and sunk their fangs into his flesh.

I pulled my gun, shooting three that were still on the floor. I took aim at the snake that bit Lenny, which was coiled up and preparing to strike again. I shot at it but missed the first time. The second shot blew the top of its head off.

I turned my aim toward Benny, but he was jerking around too much to shoot. I had to wait until one by one, each snake released and fell to the floor. Ryan and Trigger were also shooting, and soon the floor was peppered with snake parts and pieces.

"Fuck!" Ryan said.

"Tobias, get the med kit," Carly ordered as she climbed down from the bar. She dragged me down with her.

I was almost certain we'd killed all the snakes, but I kept my gun on a swivel as we moved toward Lenny.

Tobias cautiously met us in the center of the room, laying the kit on a nearby table and opening it. "We only have enough for one person," Tobias said, handing Carly a vial and needle. "Should I call an ambulance?"

"No," I said, turning toward Benny. "Give the medicine to Lenny."

"You bitch," Benny wheezed, hanging limply from the rope.

"Ryan, cut Benny down."

Ryan and Trigger worked together to lower Benny. I pointed to a chair by the wall and they helped drag him to it. Benny continued to wheeze, the reaction to the snakes' venom already setting in.

"Any last words," I asked him sincerely, squatting in front of him.

"Go to hell."

"If there was another dose, I'd give it to you. I mean it, Benny. But if you have any final wishes, I'd consider honoring them, depending on what they were, of course."

He glared at me, but finally nodded. "Make me a legend."

"I don't understand."

"No body. No one finds out about tonight."

"You want to be a ghost? Your end story untold?"

He nodded slightly—at least as much as his swollen neck would allow. "All I had was my reputation. Let it live."

I placed my hand on his shoulder, one of the few places where his skin wasn't ripped open. "You have my word."

"Kelsey," Benny wheezed.

"Yeah?" I said, leaning closer to him.

"She's not who you think she is," he said, his voice cutting in and out on hisses as he tried to inhale.

"Who?"

"Charlie..."

"What do you mean?"

His wheezing got worse as his throat and face rapidly swelled. I stayed with him as his airway cut off. He jerked around, gasping, then choking. He clutched his chest before his body slumped and stilled.

I stood, turning to see Trigger make a cross his heart.

Ryan stood over Carly's shoulder but his eyes flashed my way. He shrugged his indifference, showing no remorse over the death of Benny the Barber.

I wished I felt the same.

Chapter Thirty-Six

CHARLIE
Friday, Late

I could hear him in the other room. First it was just an occasional sound, a slight movement. Now it was louder. He was louder. He was angry.

I worked harder at loosening the duct tape at my wrists behind my back. If I could get at least one hand free, I'd at least have a fighting chance.

Hearing his heavy footsteps moving in my direction, I threw myself back to the concrete floor and stilled. As the door opened, I closed my eyes.

"You pretending?" Mr. Tricky asked, walking over to kick me in the shins.

I groaned, fluttered my eyelids, then settled again, giving the impression that the drugs still had me in a stupor.

I heard him walk away, the door closing and what sounded like a key in a deadbolt. I stayed perfectly still as I heard his footsteps further retreat into the building and another door close.

Sitting up, I worked frantically at the tape, forcing my wrists in opposite directions to stretch the material. The skin around my wrists burned from the chafing, but I ignored the pain. I refused to die in some damp, moldy building.

Feeling the tape roll on one side, tearing away from my skin, renewed my fever to be free. I started simultaneously shifting my feet back and forth in the same manner, hoping to free them too. I felt the tape around my wrists give and realized that while my hands were still bound, I was no longer attached to the vertical pipe behind me. I rolled to the side, away from the pipe. Lifting my knees to my chest, I moved side to side, maneuvering my hands under my butt as I curled into a ball. When I'd maneuvered them past and to my thighs, I shifted into a sitting position. I tucked my knees to my chest and moved my hands under my feet.

With my hands now in front of me, I set to work at chewing at the tape, pulling and biting, even spitting on the material as I worked to free myself.

Within minutes, one hand was freed. With the use of my hands, I quickly released my ankles, ignoring the sting from removing the tape too quickly. I didn't care about the pain. I only cared that he'd left. If I could find a way out of this room, I could escape.

I stood, bracing a hand against the wall to steady myself as the room appeared to shift sideways. The drugs Mr. Tricky had been feeding me were still wreaking havoc on my brain.

I looked around, but there wasn't much to see. The room had cinderblock walls, damp with sweat and mold. The floor was bare. I looked at the door which was showing signs of rust at the bottom, but not enough to weaken the metal. The lock I'd heard Mr. Tricky latch had a shiny security plate covering the inside. He'd obviously prepared the room in advance.

Turning to the back wall, two small windows offered a minimal amount of light into the room. Whether the illumination was from a street light or the moon, I wasn't sure. But the heavy iron bars told me escaping through the windows wasn't an option.

I moved to the door. The door opened into the room, leaving the hinges exposed to me. I used my fingers to pick at the vertical pins that held the hinges together, but I couldn't lift any of them high enough to apply the right amount of pressure.

I needed tools, but didn't have any. I didn't even have shoes or pants. Mr. Tricky had stripped me of everything except my underwear and t-shirt.

Wait, I thought, reaching my hands behind me to unhook my bra. I pulled one strap off my shoulder, stretching the band to shift my arm through. Then I dragged the other strap down my arm and held the bra in front of me. The wire. The support wire was all I needed.

I started chewing at the end of the bra, tearing at the material with my teeth. It took some time, but eventually I had one end exposed and was able to pull the thin strip of metal out. I tossed the bra to the floor and used the metal to wedge the top of a hinge upward. Once raised a half inch, I set to working on the other two hinges.

After lifting the third hinge, I placed the wire between my teeth and holding the door tight to its frame with one hand, jerked all three pins out of the hinges. I released the breath I'd been holding as the third hinge bounced on the floor where I'd dropped it. Taking the metal underwire from my teeth, I used it to shimmy between the door's hinge knuckle and the knuckle attached to the door frame. Once looped through the singular hole, I folded the metal and grasped both ends in my hands, tugging up and out with all the strength I had left.

The door popped free at the middle and bottom, but held in the top hinge. I tugged again, feeling the metal strip cut into my palms, before the thin piece of metal snapped in half. I dropped the pieces to the floor, bending to grab the lower section of the door itself, pulling with every ounce of strength I possessed. The last hinge separated, popping the door from its frame, and opening an angled gap large enough for me to squeeze through. I slid out, into the next room.

A quick glance around the room confirmed I was alone. I was in some type of office building. The glass front was protected by a steel gate, used by many storefronts to secure shops afterhours. It was unlikely I'd be able to exit through the front without tools. I turned toward the back, running on bare feet to the solid door. I leaned against the wall, listening to the other side. *Nothing*. I reached out, turning the handle on the door, and pulling the door open inch by inch. *Still quiet*.

I peeked into the room, careful to check each corner as I stepped through. I was surprised to see a large black truck parked inside a roomy storage area.

Running toward the truck, I opened the door, searching for keys. None. I reached up, pushing the emergency service button. *Nothing.* He must've disabled it so the truck couldn't be tracked.

I jumped out, leaning under the steering wheel, but was disappointed to find the wires had been pulled and cut into a mangled mess. It would take me hours to rewire.

"Son of a bitch," I muttered to myself as I turned away from the truck.

Not willing to waste any more time, I grabbed a wrench from a nearby workbench and moved to the overhead door, pushing the button. Shuffling back against the wall, I waited for Mr. Tricky to come charging forward.

When he didn't appear, I peeked out of the now erect door but didn't see anyone. I was in a shopping district of some sort, but based on the condition of the back alley, it wasn't one of the more popular ones. The alley appeared to serve as rear entrances to the building I was in and the one across the street. Wide enough for a bread truck, but too narrow for a semi.

I slipped out of the building, moving along the wall until I reached the end. Another narrow alley ran behind a long strip of buildings. Not willing to backtrack the other direction, I moved left, now jogging toward the end of the new alley.

Three buildings later, I stopped to peek around the next corner. It was a real street, but served as a dead-end loop into the shopping district. All the businesses were closed, most windows posted with For Sale signs.

I had two choices. I could find a place to hide and wait until morning, which was the smart choice. Or I could keep going.

I looked down at the wrench still gripped in my damaged hand. The one with the missing finger. The damage Mr. Tricky had inflicted was permanent, but if it got infected I could lose the whole hand. I looked further down at my feet. They were black from running barefoot, and my right foot was bleeding on the outside from something sharp I'd stepped on. Overall, though, I was energized by my freedom.

I decided to keep going.

Chapter Thirty-Seven

KELSEY
Saturday, 1:58 a.m.

"Kelsey," Grady's voice said from nearby. "Wake up. You're home."

"Home?" I asked, trying to pull my eyelids apart while my brain started waking.

"Not Michigan. Come on. Wake up," Grady said, pulling me into a sitting position.

My eyes blurred then focused on Grady as he was pulling me from the SUV. I looked around and realized we were back at the mansion. I must've fallen asleep.

"You're a mess. What the hell have you guys been doing?" Grady asked.

"Can't tell you," Ryan said to Grady as he handed me my gun and holster. "Kelsey made us swear to secrecy, which sucks. It's a good story."

"It's just not fair," Trigger said, grabbing my elbow to help maneuver me in my semi-conscious state toward the door. "Such a badass story. What a waste."

"Ms. Harrison!" one of the Bianchi men called out as he jogged toward us. "You had a package delivered earlier."

He handed me the small box. My hands wrapped around it as my knees weakened.

"When was this delivered?" Grady asked the guard.

"About an hour after Ms. Harrison left this evening. The messenger said it was for her eyes only."

"Damn it!" Grady said, taking the box from me. "Next time, let one of us know immediately."

I turned and walked away, entering the mansion. I didn't want to see it. I didn't want to know if it was a finger or an ear. I didn't want to see what body part had been delivered. It wouldn't help.

I stumbled toward the kitchen, surprised to find Grandma Tannelli still up. "Are you still planning on poisoning me?" I asked her as I slid onto a stool on the other side of the breakfast bar.

She studied me a long moment before turning toward the cupboard. "Not tonight. Maybe tomorrow." She filled a cup of coffee and set it in front of me.

"How did Mackenzie take seeing her mother?"

"Strong girl. Smart. She happy momma alive. If her momma dies, will be bad."

"If her mother dies, then at least this time she got to say goodbye."

"And if brain dead? Poor child. She grieve all over. She be sad."

"She was already sad. And it's more important that she trusts you. That she knows you are being honest with her."

"We see. Time will tell."

"Yes, you'll see. Time will prove my point." I looked toward the patio doors. "Anyone still awake and working?"

"Everyone is awake. They're looking for some man. Some D.Z., they say. Dumb name."

I slid off the stool, the warm cup cocooned in my palms as I shuffled out onto the patio, moving toward the tiki lounge.

"You look like roadkill," Maggie said, pausing from whatever she was typing on the laptop perched in her lap. "When was the last time you slept?"

"Just took a nap, actually," I said, sitting beside her on the lounge couch. "Where are we at?"

Maggie narrowed her eyes at me. "Ryan called us and gave us the information on Mr. Tricky's initials being D.Z. Wouldn't say how the information was acquired, though."

"And neither will I, so don't waste my time asking," I said.

"Fine. The FBI had a file on a D.Z., but no real name, no photo. The guy was nothing more than an occasional mention in the dark web. Always spoken about, but never online himself as far as we know."

Ryan nodded to me before speaking. "Both Mickey and Phillip are trying to get contact information for our mysterious D.Z. So far, no luck."

"Wild Card and I reached out to our military contacts. We asked for a list of names with D.Z. for initials," Grady said, sitting on the arm of a chair. "We asked everyone to forward our text message to their military contacts, creating a chain message of sorts."

"And it worked," Tech said, pointing to a screen. "We had twenty-two possible names sent to us, but only one guy meets the criteria."

I stood and walked over to the mounted screen, hanging just under the tiki canopy. *David Zimmer. Thirty-eight years old. Served two tours in marines. Legal residence in Chicago, Illinois.*

"Damn," I said, shocked that we'd finally found Mr. Tricky. "I can't believe you guys found him with nothing more than his initials."

"It helped that eighteen of the names returned to us were deceased," Grady said. "Two more were still serving overseas."

"Does David Zimmer have an electronic trail? Credit card usage that we can follow?" I asked.

"Nothing in the last week," Tech said. "We sent Quille the guy's photo and file. He updated the BOLO."

"The FBI is raiding his residence in Chicago first thing in the morning," Maggie said. "They have surveillance teams assigned to the front and back entrances until then."

"Why wait?"

"It's two in the morning," Kierson said. "The building is an expensive high rise with other, let's say, *affluent* residents, including the judge who signed the warrant."

"Anyone heard from Bridget?" I asked.

Tech smirked. "Bridget's pissed at Bones. He's being all bossy on the assignment you gave her. Kind of took over. But they got the job done and she, Jackson, and Bones stayed in Cali to wait for instructions."

"I also reached out to some buddies in Texas," Cooper said. "They took care of some prep work for me. They're ready when you are."

I looked at Grady, not wanting to ask, but needing to know. "How bad was the package?" I asked, referring to the one waiting for me when I'd arrived back at the mansion.

Grady looked at Cooper, but Cooper looked away.

"A finger," Ryan answered for them both. "Her pinkie. Just above the first knuckle."

I nodded, ignoring the nausea that rolled over my body. "Could've been worse," I said to myself. "Could've been worse."

Uncle Hank, sitting with Juan and Pimples near a row of monitors, cleared his throat. "We need to get Charlie back before you retaliate, Kelsey. They've proven they're willing to carve her up. We need to get her back before you do anything else."

"Maybe," Pimples said, not looking up from the monitors. "But so far, Kelsey's plan is working. Charlie's captor had to relocate her once already. And we know what vehicle he's driving. Come daylight, we might just get lucky. If we don't, then keeping the pressure on to give Charlie a chance to escape is our only move."

"Agreed," Maggie said, closing her laptop. "It also lets Charlie know we're searching for her. Gives her hope to survive. If we give her nothing else, let's give her that."

I reached over and placed my hand on top of Maggie's.

"So... What's the plan? Move forward or hold?" Cooper said.

"We hold for the night," I said, standing. "We need sleep. I can't think straight anymore. I'm not even sure what day it is."

"What about Miguel's other holdings?" Tech asked. "The Feds seized the assets for the trucking company, and we've got plans in place for his estate in California, the mill in Texas, and his compound in Mexico. But that leaves his condos, a small pharmaceutical company, a bakery, and his retail mall."

"The condo in Atlanta is covered," Cooper said. "When I was retrieving Colby Brown, enough blood and broken furniture was left behind to keep a forensic team busy for a week. One anonymous call to the police, and the condo will be locked down and unavailable to Miguel."

"I assume they'll find your blood at the scene, too?" Kierson asked.

Cooper shrugged. "I'm licensed for bounty hunting. I was only restraining a known fugitive to bring him to justice."

"He's alive then?" Maggie asked.

"Resting in comfort until the bruises and swelling heal a bit," Cooper answered with a sly grin.

Kierson sighed in relief, running a hand through his hair.

Cooper looked at me and winked. "You'd think after all this time, they'd have a little faith."

"Your nickname is Wild Card," Kierson grumbled. "Doesn't exactly imply you're the sanest of the group."

"Doesn't scream killer either," Ryan snapped. He walked over to the bank of monitors near the poker boys and pointed at one of the screens. "What's that?"

"What's what?" Pimples asked, sitting up straight. "I didn't see anything."

I got up and walked over, watching the screen over Juan's shoulder.

"That," Ryan said, pointing again.

A black blob of a shadow at the edge of the screen appeared, then ducked back into the shadows behind a bush.

"Animal, maybe?" Uncle Hank said.

Tech leaned past Pimples and adjusted the zoom. "Too big for an animal."

"Look," Pimples said, pointing toward the other side of the monitor. "Car coming."

The black blob stepped out again, this time moving toward the headlights.

"Oh, shit!" I yelled, running toward the front of the mansion. "It's Charlie!"

Chapter Thirty-Eight

CHARLIE
Saturday, hours before daylight

I'd followed the overgrown landscaping along the edge of the buildings, staying parallel with the main road. I'd traveled at least a half mile, and though I considered myself in great shape, the fatigue, blood loss from earlier, and lack of food and water were taking their toll. I wasn't sure how much longer I could keep going. In the distance I could hear vehicles, though. I had to be close to the edge of the dilapidated neighborhood, close to civilization.

I looked back again, over my shoulder. I kept getting the feeling I was being watched, but couldn't sense my watcher's location. Probably just frayed nerves. It had, after all, been a long day.

A gap in the landscaping forced me into the open once again as I hurried to the next clump of brush and hunkered down. When all remained silent, I continued forward. Something scurried across my bare foot, causing me to jump back into the open grassy area. That's when I saw it. The car headlights. I started moving toward them but they suddenly swerved. They were now barreling right toward me, launching over the curb.

"Fuck," I yelled to myself as I ran the other direction. I looked around as I ran, realizing my mistake. I'd entered one of the long, dead-end alleys. All the buildings were locked securely. My only hope was to reach the end and find somewhere to hide. The car swerved behind me, clipping my left leg and sending me spinning toward a storefront. I slammed into the security gate on the front of the building, bouncing back to the concrete walkway. I rolled, tucked my right leg under me and lunged forward in the other direction, back to the main road. My left leg gave out and I screamed as I fell back to the sidewalk.

"Stubborn bitch," Mr. Tricky said as he charged me, grabbing a handful of my hair before dragging me toward the car.

I punched, scratched, and fought with every ounce of remaining energy. Screaming at the top of my lungs, I hoped someone would hear me. Hoped they'd call for help. Hoped a police cruiser was close enough to lend aid.

Mr. Tricky controlled me by my hair as he worked to open the trunk.

Realizing I was still holding the wrench, I twisted sideways and swung downward. The wrench slammed into his kneecap.

Mr. Tricky howled as he jerked the wrench from my hands and tossed it across the alley. A blow to my face with his fist caused my vision to blur as I dropped to the ground on my right knee, feeling my body sway to the side.

After another blow to the face, everything went black.

CHAPTER THIRTY-NINE

KELSEY
Saturday, 2:07 a.m.

In the front driveway, Grady nudged me toward the rear door of the SUV as he slid into the driver's seat. Cooper opened the door, shoving me inside before sliding in behind me. Ryan took the front passenger seat, and as his door closed, Grady launched us in reverse. I was thrown forward until Cooper's arm stopped my forward momentum. I slammed backward into the seat as Grady launched forward to exit the mansion's drive, cutting the wheel for a fast turn. I was swaying toward the door on my side of the vehicle when Cooper's arm once again snagged me.

"What's the deal with the back window?" Cooper asked, sliding me to the center of the bench seat, away from the gaping hole, and securing my seatbelt.

"Shotgun," I answered as I gripped the lap belt to steady myself as Grady made another sharp turn.

"And the missing rearview mirror?" Grady asked.

"Same shotgun," Ryan answered.

"And all the blood in the back seat?" Cooper asked as he leaned forward to see additional blood stains on the floor.

Ryan looked over his shoulder at me. "Kelsey shot someone. But I can't tell you who."

Cooper looked at me, grinning. "You are *so* not getting your rental deposit back."

"This isn't one of the rentals. It's from the vehicles I keep in Florida. It has my special storage compartment."

"Sweet," Cooper said, turning in his seat and leaning over the back to open the floor compartment.

He tossed forward flak jackets. I handed two of them to Ryan. I put the third over my head and started cinching the straps. When Cooper flipped back into a sitting position, I handed him the last jacket. Ryan reached a hand into the back, holding out earpieces. Cooper and I each took one, placing them in our ears.

"Tech, you there," I asked after pushing the small button to turn the mic on.

"Here," Tech answered.

"I'm here, too," Genie said. "Tech sent Grandma Tannelli inside to wake me. Man, what a frightful experience."

"I can imagine. Was law enforcement notified?"

"Yes," Tech said. "I called Quille. He was rolling all units."

"And by all units," Genie said. "A whole two units are in the area. They have more on the way, but it will take a few minutes to lock down the perimeter."

"Did you get a make and model on the car?" Grady asked.

"Silver four-door Pontiac," Tech answered. "Older model, maybe late nineties."

"Wait a second," Genie said, interrupting. "Patrol spotted the car. They're in pursuit."

"Grady, step on it! Get us there!" I called out.

"I'm going twice the speed limit," Grady growled back.

"It's now a car chase. One silver Pontiac Grand Prix versus three cop cars. Everyone's heading North. Wait—" There was a long pause. "The Pontiac turned right, back into the business district."

"According to the map, it's a dead end," Tech said. "Grady, you're three blocks away. Turn left on Cambridge Place."

"I see the police cars up ahead," Grady said. "Are you sure there's no outlet?"

"I'm sure the car can't drive anywhere," Tech said. "Not sure if there's an escape route on foot."

"Take a left on the street before it!" I ordered Grady, checking to ensure I had my gun. "Genie—"

"Let the cops know you're coming in from the other side? Already on it," Genie said. "Kierson and Maggie are following your lead in the SUV behind you."

Grady cut the SUV to the left, one block ahead of the flashing lights. Cooper grabbed my arm as my upper body swung to the outside again.

"Team Pimples and Team Trigger, drive around the police and take the next street," Tech ordered. "We'll alert the authorities of your presence, too."

"Roger," Juan's voice confirmed over the mic.

"Wait, who's all in the other vehicles?" I asked.

"Kel," Trigger said. "It's all good. We got Uncle Hank and Spence with us, too."

I nodded, knowing he couldn't see me, but returning my focus to the end of the street which was fast approaching. In our headlights we spotted a sole figure running to the north. He was the right size and build to be Mr. Tricky, now known to be Daniel Zimmer.

Grady drove the SUV to the end of the street and slammed on the brakes. Everyone except me ran after the shadowy figure who disappeared around the next building.

If Mr. Tricky was running solo, that meant he'd ditched Charlie. I had to find her. I ran between the end of a building and a tall retaining wall toward the street the police had turned onto.

I heard someone behind me and glanced over my shoulder.

Maggie was running hard to catch up. "She'll be okay. We'll find her."

We rounded the corner together, Maggie flashing her badge as several uniformed officers aimed their guns at us. "FBI. Suspect fled north. Any sign of Detective Harrison?"

"No, ma'am," an officer said before he and his partner moved around us, running north. Two other officers stayed behind with the Pontiac.

I ran to the driver's door and looked inside, confirming the car was empty. Reaching inside, I released the trunk.

Maggie was already standing next to the trunk and pulled the lid upward. "*She's here*! *Get an ambulance!*"

"Maggie?" I asked, my feet frozen to the asphalt.

"She's alive. Strong heartbeat and breathing on her own. I think he knocked her out."

I stumbled forward, stepping around the back of the car and looking inside the trunk. Charlie was lying inside, her face swollen and discolored, her hand missing a pinky, her bare feet dirty and slashed by multiple tiny cuts, but I could see her lungs moving her chest back and forth.

I fell to my knees, reaching my hand inside the trunk to hold her hand as I cried.

Chapter Forty

KELSEY
Saturday, 5:02 a.m.

Phillip greeted us in the mansion driveway, opening the passenger door for me. "How's Charlie?" he asked.

"She's pretty banged up, but she'll live." I slid out of the SUV and turned toward the house. "Mostly bruises except for the missing pinkie. We thought she had a broken leg, but it was only a small fracture. The doctors say it should heal on its own with sufficient rest. It'll hurt like a bitch for a while, though."

"Is she awake yet?" Phillip asked.

"In and out. The plastic surgeon put her under anesthesia to work on her hand. And they gave her some morphine to help her rest."

"Will you be staying in Florida, then?"

"No. We're arranging transportation back to Michigan for late tonight. What about Sophia? How's she doing?"

"Great. She woke for a spell this morning and asked for Liam and Mackenzie. So far, no sign of any brain damage. With any luck, we'll be flying her and the kids home tomorrow."

"Wow," I said, stopping to look over at him. "That's incredible."

"It is. And we owe it all to you and Charlie."

"It was all Charlie. She's the one who found the kids and then investigated until she found Sophia. I was too focused on the sex trafficking case. I didn't see any of the rest of this coming."

Phillip nodded. "Mickey wanted me to ask if there was anything else you needed."

"Not right now, but I'll let you both know if something comes up. I have a few calls to make, then I'm going to shower and sleep, in that order. I have a team at the hospital guarding Charlie—in addition to the twenty or so cops and a few Feds. I'm reasonably sure she'll be safe for a few hours."

Phillip chuckled as he wandered off toward the private office. I walked through the living room, past the cackle of Italian women in the kitchen, and out the patio doors, crossing the patio to the tiki lounge.

"So? We staying or leaving?" Tech asked.

"We'll leave tonight. I need a burner to call Bridget," I said.

"Here." Tech handed me a phone and the running list of everyone else's burner phone numbers.

I typed in the number of Bridget's burner and hit the call button.

"How's Charlie?" Bridget asked as a means of answering.

"She's alive. Everything ready there?"

"Just waiting on you. Are you sure about this? Pissing Miguel off might backfire."

"I'm sure. Once you confirm the house is empty, you have a green light."

"What about Miguel's other businesses?" Bridget asked.

"Pass the word to Jackson and Cooper. Have them relay to the other teams that everyone has a green light. But make sure everyone knows that if there's any doubt that an innocent could get hurt, they are to abort."

"I'll pass along the message," Bridget said before hanging up.

I gripped the phone, turning back to Tech. "Did you get access to Miguel's accounts?"

"Yeah. I'm ready when you are."

"Do it. I want every dime wired to various charitable organizations across the country and in Mexico."

Tech smiled a vicious smile as he rolled across the concrete to another table. He started typing madly on a keyboard.

"Also, wait a few hours and then send the files we prepared to the media. I want boycotts at his other businesses, especially the mall, by lunchtime. His employees and customers need to know Miguel's affiliation to sex trafficking and narcotics smuggling. Just give the other teams time to hit his estates first."

"Will do," Tech said without slowing from his work behind his computer. "I got this. Go sleep."

I pulled the back panel off the burner phone, removing the sim card before dropping the rest of the phone to the ground and stomping on it. Then I walked to the grill on the back porch, dropped the sim card on the concrete, poured lighter fluid on it, and used the long-handled grill lighter to ignite it.

Pimples walked over, taking the lighter fluid from me. "I'll douse it again if it doesn't completely melt."

"Thanks," I said before turning and entering the mansion. I ignored everyone as I crossed the kitchen and living room and took the elevator to the third floor. I was bone tired.

Thirty minutes later, freshly showered, I lay in bed, imagining the destruction taking place across the country.

Bridget, Bones, and Jackson had installed enough explosives to level Miguel's California estate and send it sliding off the cliff into the ocean.

Cooper was handling the smaller explosions at the textile mill in Texas which would damage the main machinery and shut down operations.

The Feds had already stopped the drug pipeline and seized assets for the trucking company.

Jackson's friends in Mexico would destroy Miguel's compound across the border.

The Vegas condo had already been looted and vandalized to the point where not only was it no longer livable, but Miguel would be kicked out by the association that managed the buildings.

His drug research company had already suffered an attack last night by an animal rights activist group. After freeing the research animals, they set the lab on fire.

And with the media across the country reporting Miguel's long list of crimes and detailing his various American business interests, his employees were about to be educated on who they truly worked for—a man well known for his affiliation with sex trafficking and narcotics.

Most of the employees, especially at the retail mall, would quit their jobs. The average blue-collar American would riot against a man who'd kidnap women and children.

As I stared at the ceiling, I envisioned each piece of Miguel's world burning to the ground. His family stripped from him. His fat bank accounts emptied. The businesses he'd built from the ground up, abandoned and left to die. His homes turned to sawdust.

Life, as he knew it, was over.

Now I can sleep, I thought as I rolled over and closed my eyes.

~*~*~

I slept for seven hours, waking early afternoon. Feeling groggy, I showered, hoping the hot water would wake my brain cells. Wrapped in a towel, I walked into the bedroom, only to find Grady sitting on my bed.

"Sorry," Grady said, standing and looking away. "I just wanted to make sure you were okay."

I walked over to the dresser, opening the drawer, but my mind flashed back to Charlie's unconscious body in the trunk of Mr. Tricky's car. "Seeing Charlie in that trunk. Seeing her so helpless..."

Grady walked over and pulled me into a hug, holding me tight.

I let him. Instead of pulling away, I leaned into his warm embrace. I accepted his comfort, feeling safe, loved, and protected in his arms.

Time passed as he held me, but eventually I felt Grady shift positions, maneuvering our bodies so he could lean toward me. His lips met mine, demanding a response.

Kissing him back, I welcomed the feeling of passion over the feelings of anger, despair, and guilt. I welcomed the response of my body to the tingling sensation of pleasure.

Grady's hands stroked my back, over the towel as I raised my own hands to web my fingers into his hair. I arched my back, pressing my breasts into him as he deepened the kiss.

"Hey, Kel!" Cooper called out from somewhere on the third floor. "I just got back and wanted—" Cooper rounded the corner into the bedroom. "Oh, shit. Sorry." Cooper ducked his head and turned away.

I clutched the towel to my body, stepping away from Grady, but it was too late. Cooper was already gone.

"Damn it," I said, running one hand through my wet hair as I clutched the towel with the other.

"He'll be fine. I'll talk to him," Grady said, pulling me toward him.

I stepped away, turning my back to him. "Can you leave?"

"Kelsey, I—"

"No, Grady," I whispered, stopping him. "The answer is no." I turned and faced him, tears streaking down my face. "Kissing you was a mistake. It wasn't about you. It was about escaping all the shit that's happened. Kissing you had nothing to do with *us*." I waved a hand between us before looking back toward the door, wishing Cooper was still standing there. Once again, I'd hurt him. I couldn't seem to stop hurting him. Hurting both of them.

"We're good together," Grady said. "It feels right. Why deny it?"

"Back when we split up, when Sebrina was still in town, something happened." I took a moment, not sure how to explain. "Something between Cooper and me."

Grady must've read the guilt on my face. "You slept with him."

"No." I looked up, shaking my head. "That's just it. I didn't. I wanted to. I even tried to seduce him. But," I paused thinking of the moment, "Cooper led us into the bathroom. He maneuvered us into the shower. The water was ice cold." I smiled, remembering how shocking the cold water was. Like waking from a deep trance. "He did it on purpose. He wanted me to snap out of the moment."

Grady stared at me, waiting to understand.

"He knew, Grady. Cooper knew I was looking for an outlet for my emotions. He stopped me because he knew I was sad and confused. I was angry. And Cooper knew I was trying to escape all those feelings."

"Why are you telling me this?"

"Because it's the foundation of our entire relationship, Grady. Me escaping my past, seeking out sex with you. Seeking comfort and acceptance. From the first time we slept together after my kidnapping, I've used you to bury my feelings, to distract myself. And I needed that shelter. But I never chose you. I never chose anyone."

Grady's fists balled as his jaw locked in anger. He jerked the bottle of lotion from on top of the dresser and launched it across the room, hitting the glass in the French door, shattering it.

I didn't move, just watched his expression fill with rage before he stormed out of the room.

I keep hurting them, I thought sadly.

CHAPTER FORTY-ONE

CHARLIE
Saturday, 2:30 p.m.

I pushed the button to shift the hospital bed into a sitting position before dragging my throbbing leg up the bed with me and pulling the sheet up to cover my chest. The thin hospital gown I was wearing was inadequate coverage in front of my boss and coworkers. I also wanted to raise my hands to run my fingers through my hair, but every muscle in my body hurt.

I turned back to my visitors. "So, tell me. What did I miss while I was away?"

Quille snorted. "You make it sound like you took a vacation."

Ford grinned at Quille before answering me. "What you missed was the Miami PD turning this city upside down in your honor."

"Like it did much good," Quille said. "Most of the time, we were trying—*and failing*—to keep up with your cousin's investigation. She's insane, you know."

I smiled proudly. "Yeah, I know. She's like a pit bull: loyal, smart, and fiercely protective."

Quille scowled as he looked toward the window. "So far, Kelsey's wanted for questioning in a fire, an insane act of vandalism involving a truck driving through the front of a house, two shootouts—"

"That we know of," Ford added. "I wouldn't be surprised if more turned up."

Quille ran a frustrated hand over his balding head, "—and torturing a few heroin dealers."

"That's it?" I said, continuing to grin.

"I think that's plenty, but ATF also suspects she's behind the bombings of a cartel leader's estate in California, his estate in Mexico, and a manufacturing plant he owns in Texas."

"Interesting." I wasn't surprised Kelsey went on the offense with Miguel Santiago. It wasn't how I would've done it, but it had a nice flair to it. *Kelsey style*. "But I have no knowledge of any of the events you are referring to."

Quille snorted. "And if you come across any knowledge—keep it to yourself. Just because I'm rooting for her, doesn't mean that I wouldn't arrest her. You damn Harrison women are going to be the death of me."

I tried not to laugh as I turned my attention to Warren, the detective assigned to Mackenzie and Liam's missing persons' case. "And what brings you by?"

"Thought you'd like to know Sophia Barrett was not only alive, but she was kidnapped from a medical facility Friday morning. Turns out, Councilmember Barrett was keeping her drugged and held against her will. We arrested Mr. Barrett."

"The kids? Ever find them?"

Warren chuckled, shaking his head.

Quille rolled his eyes. "We know you had the kids. And they're safely tucked away in the temporary custody of their grandmother until Sophia is well enough to take care of them. And we also know it was you who kidnapped Sophia. You've still got a chunk of that plastic stuff stuck to the side of your face."

"Damn," I said, grinning at Quille while rubbing the side of my nose. "I thought the nurse got it all. Am I in trouble?"

"You're always in trouble," Ford said, grinning down at me. "But after Sophia's statement, we were able to document that you were protecting the kids from their stepfather and saving Sophia. And, by the way, that ridiculous security video of you fleeing the medical facility with half your fake face falling off—doesn't show enough of your real face to prove without a doubt that it was you."

"Again... I have no knowledge of the events you are referring to." I folded my hands together over my stomach, lacing my fingers together as I tried to suppress my laughter.

They shook their heads.

"What about your case?" I asked Ford, referring to Bernard Bacon.

"We closed the file. All the evidence points to Mr. Tricky, otherwise known as David Zimmer, who unfortunately hasn't been captured yet. If he's still in the country we'll find him, though. There's a statewide hunt for him."

"And I.A. wants to talk to you," Quille warned. "I told them you were on medical leave until the doctors cleared you."

"What do they want this time?" I asked. "Oh, wait, let me guess... They think I kidnapped myself?"

Quille shook his head. "No, but just as crazy. They want to talk to you about Benny the Barber. According to them, he's still missing. They want to know if you had anything to do with his disappearance."

"I didn't, but we both know they won't believe me." I pulled the paper-thin blanket upward to add another layer of protection from the cold air blowing out of the ceiling vent. "Benny will turn up eventually. As soon as he's confident Mr. Tricky is no longer in Florida, he'll relocate back to the barbershop and the cycle of him playing games with the police will continue."

"You think Mr. Tricky left Florida then?" Ford asked.

"Yeah, I do. He's been in the for-hire business a long time. He'll duck into one of his safe houses and ride out the storm."

"Then what?" Quille asked.

"Then he'll probably come looking for me."

"Why?" Quille asked. "From what I hear, Miguel Santiago hired him. And thanks to your cousin, Miguel's now on the brink of ruin. What's the point of Mr. Tricky coming after you again?"

"Pride."

"Shit," Ford said as his shoulders tensed. "Is he that crazy? He'd come after you just to save his hitman reputation?"

"If I were him, I would," I said, shrugging. "He's dogged. Mission oriented. His career is likely the only thing he has. He won't like having a failed mission hanging over his head."

"Then hopefully the Feds will catch him soon," Quille said. "In the meantime, you have guards posted at your door. Both with badges and without. You're safe here."

"And this giant of a guy," Warren said, holding his hand in the air near the seven-foot-high mark. "I don't know who he is, but he's huge."

"Awe," I said, feeling a sappy thrill of warmth. "Garth's here? He's in the hall?"

"If you mean the giant, yes," Ford said. "And he ordered us not to overstay our welcome, so we better get going. The guy scares me."

"I appreciate the visit. Do you mind asking Garth to come in as you leave? I'd like to talk to him."

Ford inclined his head in an affirmative.

Quille patted me awkwardly on the shoulder. "You take the time to heal, but not too long. We need you."

I nodded, but didn't say anything. Truth be told, I was pretty sure my days of wearing a badge were over. I think Quille knew it, too.

Ford waved goodbye and led the party out of the room.

A minute later, Garth popped his head inside the room. "You wanted to see me?"

"Come in. I wanted to ask about Evie. Is she still safely tucked away at the club?"

Garth nodded. "She's keeping busy overseeing the renovations for the sex rooms." Garth moved to the foot of the bed where he stood with his hands clasped in front of him in a sentry position. "You need anything?"

"I could use a stiff drink. What do you think my chances are?"

Garth's eyes flickered to the morphine machine that had only been detached from my arm a few hours ago. "Might want to wait until the rest of the morphine clears your system."

"Then I'll settle for something more realistic. Can you track down all my vehicles and have them moved to the parking garage at the club? Most of them should be at the mansion."

"You don't want them relocated to your apartment building?"

"No. Bridget meant well with the remodeling of my apartment, but it has too many blind spots now. No way will I risk someone getting the jump on me in my own home again. I'll find somewhere else to live."

"Will you need a room at the club until you find a place? Or will you be staying at the mansion?"

"She'll be flying back to Michigan this evening," Kelsey answered for me as she waltzed across the room, tossing her bag into a visitor's chair. She looked at me and pointed. "No arguing either. You need to be protected while you heal."

"I'm perfectly capable of taking care of myself," I said.

"You scared the hell out of me, Kid. You had the whole family worried. Please, don't argue. And your nephew is never going to believe you're okay until he sees you with his own eyes."

I looked at Garth, but he stood emotionless, waiting loyally to hear my answer. I looked back at Kelsey. "Fine. I'll fly back and stay two weeks in Michigan. But that's all."

Garth dipped his head before stepping away from the bed. "I'll make sure your vehicles are collected and ask Evie to prepare one of the rooms for you to use just in case you need it." He took another step back before leaving.

My phone dinged and I picked it up from the stand. I'd mostly been ignoring all the texts and voicemails. I'd already received three messages from Spence, but the truth was, I wasn't all that into calling him back. I liked him. He was hot and smart, and best of all, he had a cool dog. But we'd just met a few weeks ago and after everything that had happened, I wasn't sure I wanted him around until I was done processing it all.

The new text message wasn't from Spence, though. It was from Mickey McNabe. It read: *Heard you lived. Hope you liked your get-well gift.*

I typed a response: *Alive and well. And loved the present.*

I looked over at the present he was referring to. An antique Samurai sword in a wooden case with a glass top. I had no idea what possessed him to buy it, or even if he bought it legally, but I loved it. It was unique and dangerous, just like him.

I turned back to Kelsey. "Find Miguel yet?"

"Not yet, but we will. He's practically broke with nowhere to live. It's only a matter of time before he contacts his insurance company to start the claims process."

"And then what?" I asked, already knowing the answer.

"And then we have him arrested. And if we don't have enough evidence to arrest him in the U.S., he'll be shipped back to Mexico. His wife has already filed for divorce and we have a security team protecting her and the kids. Since she's American, she's not subject to his exile. And she's this close," Kelsey held her thumb and finger an inch apart, "to filing a criminal statement against Miguel. Maggie's working her over pretty good."

"And you think prison is the answer? You don't think Miguel could still get to us from behind bars? Hire another hitman to come after us? Come after Nicholas or Sara?"

"I think Miguel's power is on low battery and his threat level has been significantly reduced. Even if he tried to rebuild, there's been so much media about him, I don't think he'd be able to hire enough employees to keep a business afloat."

"It's not enough," I said.

"It will have to be. Besides," Kelsey said, placing a hand on top of my damaged one. "The pain will fade. The anger. I know it's hard, but it does get better."

"This?" I said, holding up my hand where Mr. Tricky had cut off my pinky. "I don't care about this. Hell, they even make some cool prosthetic fingers these days. I'm thinking of getting the silver one with diamonds embedded. Make it look like a piece of jewelry."

"Then why are you so angry?" Kelsey asked.

"I'm angry because Miguel came after us. I'm angry because he's a threat against our family. I'm angry because once again, you're *letting him off the hook.*"

"I don't think prison is letting him off the hook. And if he gets shipped home, we've already heard the Mexican authorities plan on arresting him as soon as he crosses their border."

"It's not enough," I said again, turning to look toward the window.

I heard Kelsey sigh and after a long moment, I heard the hospital room door open and close. I looked back to confirm I was alone.

Chapter Forty-Two

KELSEY
11 Days later, Tuesday, 7:07 a.m.

"Where is everyone?" I asked Hattie as I entered the kitchen and filled a cup of coffee.

"Oh, here and there," Hattie said, putting a pan of muffins in the oven. "Alex and the girls planned a day of shopping, and before you ask," she raised a hand to cut me off from saying anything, "yes, they took guards with them."

"And the kids?"

"With Pops at Headquarters. They're playing in the yard with Jager, running off some of that pre-Christmas energy. I swear, Christmas can't come soon enough. They're nearly bursting with excitement."

"Two more days, right?" I asked only half certain I had the day of the week right.

"Yes," Hattie said, giggling. "Are you done shopping?"

I sighed, leaning against the counter, cupping my coffee with both hands. "I have two more gifts to buy, but I'm stumped."

"Whose gifts?"

"Cooper and Grady's."

"Ahh," Hattie said, smirking. "I guess shopping for your ex-husband and ex-boyfriend could be challenging."

I raised an eyebrow. "Challenging? It's a land mine. And, honestly, I expected both of them to be gone by now. I didn't think they'd stay for Christmas. So I put off thinking about it, and now I'm screwed."

"It's no surprise they're still here. Both Mr. Tricky and Miguel Remirez are still a threat," Hattie said.

"Exactly," I said, throwing my hands up. "They're staying close to protect the family, but *hello—it's that awkward holiday season.*"

Hattie giggled again, leading me by the arm over to the dining room table. "What about tickets for a cruise or a beach getaway?"

I snorted. "Yeah, nothing says give me distance like a plane ticket."

"You're right. That might be too obvious."

We both sat, thinking.

"Clothes?" Hattie asked.

I raised an eyebrow.

"Right. Too impersonal. Same goes for gift cards. And neither of them wears jewelry," Hattie continued, thinking aloud. "What about electronics? A tablet or something?"

"I don't know anything about tablets. Can you personalize them?"

Hattie looked at me with a blank face, blinking. "Well to tell you the truth, I have no idea. Maybe we should ask Tech. Or Sara. We could ask her."

"Ask me what?" Sara asked, skipping into the kitchen through the garage door.

"Sorry," Whiskey said, following her inside. "Didn't mean to interrupt."

"It's all good," I said, waving off his concern. "Sara, can tablets be personalized? Like set up different for different people?"

"Sure. I have games on mine. Nicholas has his filled with books. Why?"

"Hattie suggested I get Grady and Cooper tablets, but I'd want different things put on them. Like on Grady's, he'd appreciate stuff having to do with work. Like being able to read his emails and check the assignment schedules without needing his laptop. But on Cooper's, maybe music and games, or even funny videos."

"Sure," Sara said. "I can help you load them with different things, but we'd have to go to the store to buy them. There's not enough time to order them online."

"I've got Anne adding them to her list," Whiskey said, texting from his phone. "She'll pick them up and charge your card."

"Perfect," I said, high fiving Hattie. "Christmas, here we come."

Hattie giggled. "If only your love life were that simple."

Whiskey handed me a bag. "Anne's still sorting the boxes that were shipped from Florida to Michigan. She came across this and wanted me to give it to you."

I opened the bag, startled by its contents. It took me a moment to remember we'd raided Benny's stash of money and diamonds from the barbershop. "Well, shit."

"Most people are happy to find a bag of money and jewels, sunshine," Hattie said, peering into the bag.

"It's blood money."

"Oh," Hattie said, leaning away. "In that case, what are you going to do with it?"

"I already paid Mickey and anyone else who helped find Charlie, so I guess I'll donate it."

Whiskey took the bag. "Any charity in particular?"

"I found it in Miami, so makes sense to donate it to the women and children center that Charlie sponsors there."

"I'll get the address from Charlie and see that it's shipped anonymously," Whiskey said before turning toward the door.

"Whiskey?" I called out.

"Yeah?"

"You're not going to, *uhh*, *borrow* any of the diamonds for a gift to Anne, are you?"

He laughed but didn't answer as he walked out.

Chapter Forty-Three

CHARLIE
Tuesday, 8:30 a.m.

I felt him again. Watching me. I knew he was out there, but he wasn't close enough for me to sense his location. He could shoot me, I supposed, but I didn't get the feeling I was being watched through a scope. Besides, if killing me quickly was all he wanted, he'd have finished the job yesterday when I felt him watching. No, he wanted me close.

I continued jogging, but slowed my pace. Not only was I trying to get a better sense of his location, but my leg was protesting the mile long run. The doctor had warned me to take it easy, but I wasn't about to sit on my ass for four months. It hadn't even been two full weeks yet, and I was already feeling a little stir-crazy. Besides, the fracture was barely visible on the x-rays, appearing like a small scratch. I'd survived worse.

As I approached the end of the jogging path, I felt the distance grow between me and my watcher. He was keeping his distance from the houses, which was good for the sake of the family's safety. If he continued to lurk in the area, I'd have two options. I could relocate back to Miami, hoping he'd follow. Or two, the option I was rooting for, I'd find where he was hiding and surprise him.

As the woods cleared, I slowed to a walk to follow the dead-end road back to Kelsey's house. To my right and left, crews were finishing the exterior siding on the new houses.

"Hey, Charlie," one of the men called out, waving to me.

I waved back but didn't stop. The crews seemed friendly enough, but my mind was focused on Mr. Tricky. Last night, I'd searched the under-construction homes, hoping Mr. Tricky was bunking down at night in one of them. No such luck. I also had all the no-tell motels within three counties covered by slipping cash to the hotel clerks. If he checked into any of them, I'd get a phone call.

The local police were keeping close tabs on the bigger hotels, but Mr. Tricky would never stay at one of them. Too many eyes tracking his movements. No, he'd want someplace isolated. No witnesses. Like he'd chosen in Miami. Either a dilapidated area or a commercial block where he could come and go without anyone paying much attention.

He'd pick privacy over comfort. Somewhere he could kill me without anyone hearing my screams.

Passing Lisa's house, I slipped between the houses and crossed the grass into the back yard, careful not to slip on the snowy bank as I made my way down the short hill to the walkout basement. As I entered the basement gym, the warmth from the furnace poured over me and I kicked off my now wet shoes and stripped my winter coat, tossing both in the corner. I'd take them upstairs later. Right now, I needed to get back to work hunting Mr. Tricky before he succeeded in finishing his mission: Killing me.

~*~*~

I smiled to myself as I left the old war room in the basement. After three hours of scouting online maps, I'd found a possible hiding location for Mr. Tricky. I wouldn't know for sure until tonight, but I was okay with waiting.

On the north side of downtown were several abandoned factories. Kelsey had used one of them last November as a location to meet Miguel for their so-called truce. The area was perfect for Mr. Tricky, but most of the buildings were not suitable for sleeping.

Except one.

One building had once upon a time been used for apartments. The two-story structure had a partially caved in roof and multiple smashed windows, but I suspected it still had a few rooms on the first floor in good enough shape to drop a rollout mattress and sleep for a few nights.

I'd spent the last hour studying the building from online satellite photos. Behind the apartment building was a crop of trees, and on the other side of those trees was a small, unkept park. The location had a lot to offer a man on the run who needed to be able to escape in multiple directions.

Yes, I thought as I climbed the stairs. *It's the perfect location for someone like Mr. Tricky.*

I rounded the corner at the top, expecting a room full of people, but both the kitchen and living room were empty. I heard Kelsey laughing down the hall and followed the sound to her bedroom doorway. Sara was sitting on Kelsey's lap on the bed, and Kelsey was laughing at something Sara was doing on the tablet she held.

"Playing a game?" I asked, entering the room but stopping to lean against the wall.

"Sara is," Kelsey answered. "We were loading games on Cooper's Christmas present, but she decided to add herself as a player to one of them. She's in the process of leaving a high score for him to beat."

"Nothing like a little healthy competition for Christmas. He'll love it."

Sara giggled. "That's what I said!"

Kelsey rolled her eyes. "You need something? Or are you bored?"

"If you don't mind, I'm going to take a soak in your tub. It's bigger than the one upstairs."

"Sure," Kelsey said as a worry line appeared on her forehead. "Is your leg hurting? If it is, I still have that prescription of pain killers if you need them."

I shook my head. "My leg didn't like this morning's jog is all. The pain is manageable."

She nodded but still looked worried. "What were you working on in the basement?"

"Just catching up on some emails. I had a lot of business communications to clear." I pushed off from the wall and started for the bathroom. "I forwarded you the third-quarter financial statements for KNC Enterprises. Sorry they were late."

"Charlie?" Kelsey said, causing me to stop and look back at her. "Is everything okay?"

I thought about the possibility of finding Mr. Tricky's hidey hole. "It will be," I answered, before stepping into the bathroom and closing the door.

CHAPTER FORTY-FOUR

KELSEY
Tuesday, 4:45 p.m.

Finished with the tablets, I drove across the street to Headquarters, intending to check in with Tech on the two open cases I was still working. When I parked, I spotted Grady coming around the corner of the building with two duffle bags in hand. He tossed both into the passenger side of his truck, before walking around the back of the truck toward the driver's side.

I walked toward him, calling out his name loud enough for him to hear. "Are you leaving?"

"Yup," Grady answered, stopping to talk, but not looking directly at me. "I took an assignment in Nevada. Donovan's short on men with it being the holidays."

"I bought you a Christmas present. Just give me a minute." I walked back to my SUV and returned a minute later with the wrapped box, handing it to him.

"I don't have a present for you," Grady admitted. "I wanted to buy you something, but... The way things have been, I didn't know..." Grady stopped talking, running a frustrated hand through his hair.

"I get it. I couldn't figure out what the appropriate gift for you was either. And it's not much. Just something I thought you'd like. And Sara helped. Go ahead. Open it."

Grady tugged the end of the package open, pulling the box out of the wrapping. "A tablet?"

"Sara connected the tablet to your work email and linked the files for Silver Aces to an icon on the screen. You can access almost anything for work."

"This is great. I won't have to take the laptop everywhere." Grady looked up at me. "Thanks. I mean it."

"I'm glad you like it. I know it's not much, but I wanted you to have something. There are also a few books on there."

He nodded as he opened his truck door, placing the tablet inside. "This will come in handy when I'm out on assignments."

I believed him, but I could tell his mind was on something else.

"Can I ask you something?" Grady asked.

I refrained from groaning, but barely. "Will it lead to another fight?"

"Probably." Grady looked across the lot to where Jackson and Reggie were carrying wrapped boxes out of headquarters and loading them into one of the SUVs. "But I need to know."

I slipped my hands in my back pockets to keep my fingers warm. I'd worn a winter coat but hadn't put on gloves. "Go ahead. Ask what you need to ask."

Grady's neck and shoulder muscles tensed as he looked the other way, toward the road. "In that vision of yours, the one where you're sitting on your porch with everyone... Where's Wild Card? Is he with you?"

"I don't know," I lied. "And it doesn't matter. The point was that you and I don't want the same future. It's not about Cooper."

"You sure about that? Because I think you have more of this future shit figured out than what you're admitting."

"Grady, I never meant to hurt you. I never meant for this *thing*—" I motioned to the two of us, "—between us to go this far."

"But you knew, didn't you? You knew you'd never love me the way I loved you. You knew we'd never be together."

Anger snapped inside me. I was tired of all the blame landing on my shoulders. "You knew it too! You knew I kept avoiding conversations about marriage and kids. You knew I didn't want to talk about getting our own house. You knew every time I escaped for an out-of-state job that I was fleeing because you were crowding me. You were pushing a future at me I didn't want."

I watched him as his anger simmered. His jaw set, fists clenched.

"*You. Knew*. You saw this coming." I ran a hand through my hair. "I *hate* my part in this mess. Hate that I let my son get close to you. That *I* got this close to you. But the fact is you were in my life because I needed someone to lean on. I needed someone to hold me when I didn't feel strong enough to stand alone."

"*But why me*?!" Grady snapped. "Why didn't you call on Cooper?"

I watched him, wondering if telling him the truth would help him find closure or just cause more pain.

"Son of a bitch," Grady said as he realized the reason. His skin visibly paled as he wiped a hand across his face. "I should've seen this. You were *running*." He looked like he was going to be sick as he leaned against his truck. "You were running from your feelings *for him*. You were afraid he wouldn't love you when he found out all your secrets. Found out about your childhood."

"It's always been him," I whispered. "He stole my heart years ago, but I didn't think I could trust him with the rest of the truth."

"*He handed you divorce papers and then walked out. And yet it's him you still want*?!" Grady yelled. "*Why?*"

"When Cooper gave me those papers, he was giving me a choice. He was offering me an out, and I took it. I thought if he knew the truth about me, he wouldn't love me, so I decided to use the divorce papers and miscarriage as an excuse to run. And I kept running until he found me. But I realized too late that no matter what I said or did or what awful things he discovered about me—Cooper's feelings would never waver. During all the chaos, he was always where I needed him to be, supporting me. Even when I was in a relationship with Bones, and then later with you, Cooper continued to stand by me. And during all of it, he's never asked me for anything in return."

"*I've been here*! I've been here the whole damn time," Grady growled. "I'm the one who held you when you cried. The one who stood by you."

"*For you, Grady*! Yes, you were here—*but it was all for you*! You needed to be my hero. The man to win the heart of the damsel in distress. But Cooper was here for *me*. He was whatever I needed him to be. Whether that was a friend, a protector, a co-parent to my son—it didn't matter. Whatever I needed, whether I asked or not, he was there. Even as he suffered watching me with someone else, he did it because the only thing he wanted was my happiness." I ran both my hands into my hair, dragging the mass behind me. "Grady, I crossed the damn country to escape Cooper's love. And doing so felt like I'd lost a piece of my soul, but I thought I needed to escape. Because the truth is, if Cooper rejected me after learning my secrets, it would've broken me. It would've hurt me worse than a thousand cuts."

Grady's face fell as he listened.

"Years ago, when I met Cooper, I'd lost my son. I was out of control trying to find him. I was angry and scared and exhausted. Cooper saw all those emotions, but instead of demanding answers, he guided me away from the edge, focusing me on horses, shooting practice—anything he could think of to help me get my feet back on solid ground. I fell in love with the man who accepted me without needing to know about my past. I should've known he'd never blame me or judge me."

"So that's it. He's the one."

"I don't want to hurt you, but I also don't want to keep living this way. I want more, Grady. I want it all."

"Just not with me."

"Just not with you," I whispered. "I'm sorry."

"Don't be," Grady said as he jerked his truck door open. "At least now I know the truth." He swung himself into his truck and slammed the door shut.

I moved off to the side as he squealed his tires to drive out of the lot, turning left on the highway, toward the interstate.

"Goodbye, Grady," I whispered.

I heard someone walking my way and turned to look. Jackson and Reggie.

"That looked intense," Reggie said, inspecting my face for tears, but not finding any. "You okay?"

"Yeah," I said, nodding. "But I'm not sure he is."

"We couldn't help but overhear bits and pieces," Jackson said, glancing at Reggie before glancing at me again. "Maybe you should share some of that insight with Cooper before he leaves?"

"Leaves? Where's he going?"

"He picked up an assignment for Aces. He's in the apartments, packing a travel bag."

I didn't say anything, just started walking along the side of Headquarters to the apartments that were in the back of the property.

"Room twelve," Reggie called out.

I raised a thumb in the air, but still didn't say anything. I crossed the backyard and my stomach started wobbling. I felt nauseous thinking about what I'd say.

Then I realized. This was Cooper. It didn't matter what I said. It didn't matter what I did. The only thing that mattered was the truth. *I loved him.*

The doorway loomed ahead as I started running toward it. I flung the door open, turned to the right and ran up the stairs to the second floor. Jogging down the hall, I threw open the door to room twelve, startling Cooper who stood five feet away packing his bag.

Cooper laughed with a hand on his chest. "You scared me. Some security guard I make, right?"

I stared at him, the words I'd come here to say refusing to come out.

His smile faded as he studied my face. "What's wrong?" He walked over and cupped my face, staring into my eyes for answers.

I couldn't get the words out, so I did the only thing I could think to do—I kissed him. *Really* kissed him.

In a nano second, he was kissing me back as he kicked the door closed behind me. His hands met my waist and stroked up the side of my ribs. He turned us, walking me backward as his tongue warred with mine, sparking a fury of passion. I couldn't breathe. I couldn't think. I could only feel my body heat against his.

He reached behind me, tossing his bag to the floor before pinning me against the mattress—his body pressed tight against mine. Our hands stroked. With layers of clothes between us, I still found myself riled up as our bodies moved against each other, causing friction.

I was edging toward a blissful release when Cooper rolled off me abruptly, throwing his back against the mattress. He panted heavily as he closed his eyes and reached his hand out to grasp mine.

I rolled over, straddling him as I sat above him.

"Kel, I can't do this," Cooper said, opening his eyes. "This isn't what I want. This will only cause more pain."

Yesterday his words would've broken me, but not today. "I know, Cooper," I said, laying a finger over his lips. "You can't be my emotional escape. You can't be merely a fling to me. I know."

He moved his fingers to my wrist, lifting my finger from his lips. "It's not that I don't want you. Damn, you can feel how much I want you, Kelsey. I've always wanted you."

"I know," I said, leaning over to gently kiss him. "You need to hear something, Cooper. You need to listen because what I'm about to say scares the hell out of me."

He raised his hand to the side of my neck, using his thumb to stroke my skin. "You can tell me anything, Kel. Don't be scared."

I struggled, trying to tell him I loved him. Trying to tell him that I saw us having a future together.

Trying to explain why my heart pounded against my chest and my eyes threatened to flood the room. Instead, I said, "I don't want a divorce."

He smiled warmly up at me, shifting his hand to the back of my neck to pull me closer. "I know."

I frowned. "Oh, yeah? And just what do you know?"

"You have a team of lawyers scattered across the country. If you wanted a divorce, I'd have been served papers by now."

"Got me all figured out, huh?"

"Not even close," Cooper said, laughing. "But just because you don't want a divorce, I'm not foolish enough to think you want to play husband and wife again either."

"You're right. But I'd be interested in something somewhere between marriage and dating."

His eyes narrowed as he watched me. "And Grady?"

"I told him the truth," I whispered.

This time he pulled me close enough that I could feel his breath on my face. "What truth?"

I placed a hand on his face, smiling at him. "That I love you. That I've always loved you. That you are my future."

Cooper sat up, pushing me gently back into a sitting position with him. He held both sides of my face as he stared into my eyes. "Tell me this isn't a dream. Tell me that this is really happening."

"I'd rather show you," I said, pulling his t-shirt over his head.

Before my lips met his, he'd pulled my long sleeve t-shirt over my head. My skin felt like it would melt against the heat of his chest as he captured my lips in his. He devoured me with his hands as he rocked my body against him.

My own hands roamed his familiar, hard body and in doing so, we began tearing at each other's clothes in a mad frenzy. When we were both naked, he rolled me to my back, staring down at me with such love that I felt like I would break. He continued to watch me as if memorizing every reaction as he slowly entered me.

Cooper knew how to work my body, and within minutes he had me climaxing. He held on, waiting out my release before building me back up for another. Being with him felt so wonderful, so right. I was overwhelmed by the feeling of him, of being with him. I looked up through watery eyes. "I love you."

He lifted me, straddling me over him as he sat on his heels. "Show me," he said before his mouth met mine again.

And I did. I showed him with more passion than I thought one could possess without bursting.

And when we were both spent, he rolled us so his back was against the mattress and I was lying limp and satisfied next to him.

"Best fucking Christmas ever," Cooper panted, staring up at the ceiling as he stroked my hair.

I laughed, tipping my head back to look at him. "Which? Me having sex with you? Or me telling you I love you?"

"Neither," Cooper said, rolling on top of me again. "You stopped running from this thing, this relationship. That's my present." He smacked a kiss on my lips, then rolled himself off me and off the bed. "I'm going to miss my plane, though. We'll have to finish this later."

"*You're leaving*? Now?" I asked, sitting up.

I felt overly exposed so I snagged his discarded t-shirt and pulled it over my head.

"I promised Donovan I'd take a job. He's short staffed."

"But what about us? What about what just happened?"

Cooper pulled a clean shirt on, then leaned over and pulled me upright, snaring me in his arms. "What about us? Are you changing your mind already?"

"I just thought we'd talk. Sort this out?"

"Sort what? What's to sort? You live in Michigan with your family, and you'll be in Texas next month. Then you'll be back in Michigan, until you take a trip down to Florida to visit Charlie. Then back to Michigan, until it's time to go to Texas again."

"Sounds about right," I said, a grin forming. "And where will *you* be?"

"I'll be where you are, except when I'm working or when you get annoyed with me, then I'll leave. But you know me." He kissed me gently before pulling back just enough to stare into my eyes. "Kelsey, I will always come back to you. I don't know how to stay away. You're part of me."

"I do know you," I said, playfully biting the tip of his chin. "But doesn't it bother you? Spending so much time away from your ranch?"

"The ranch hasn't felt like home since the day you left Texas. I go where you go, until you decide otherwise. Deal?"

I puzzled over what he'd said. Was it what I wanted? Did I want him wandering in and out of my life, or did I want something more permanent? "I'm not sure."

Cooper laughed, smacking his lips against mine again before turning to grab his bag. "I get that."

"I'm glad one of us does."

"You just broke up with Grady. You love him, too. It will take time. Besides, I think it's best if we keep our change of status a secret from the kids for a while. I don't want Nick hurt if you change your mind." Cooper tossed me my bra and underwear. "You staying here or walking out with me?"

I dressed in a hurry, checked my hair in the mirror, then walked out with him. "What about Christmas? And New Year's? How long will you be gone?"

Cooper threw an arm over my shoulder and laughed as we walked down the hall. "Like I'd miss Christmas. I'm only covering security for some pop star at a concert tonight in Chicago. I'll be back before you're even awake tomorrow."

I stopped walking, turning to look at him.

"What?"

I whacked him in the gut. *"You could've told me it was only an overnight job!"*

"And miss the panicked look on your face?" Cooper grinned down at me as he leaned in and kissed me.

Chapter Forty-Five

KELSEY
Wednesday, 3:03 a.m.

Vehicles coming and going down our street in the middle of the night had become common with all the security shifts, so I hadn't paid much attention when I heard one of the vehicles in the driveway start. Nor had I looked to see who it was when I heard the vehicle pull out. But when I got a text from Tyler asking where Charlie was going this late at night with my personal SUV, alarm bells started ringing in my head.

I dressed in the dark, not bothering to turn on the light or answer Tyler's text. As I snapped my holster onto my jeans, I mentally prepared for the unknown.

Charlie had been acting strange all day. Like she had a secret and was intentionally avoiding being in the same room with me so I wouldn't figure out what it was. And I'd tried. Several times I'd followed her to another room or tried to corner her. But she was the queen of evasive.

Walking down the hall I was surprised to see Cooper dropping his bag on the dining room table.

"What on earth are you doing up?" he asked.

"Got a text. Need to go figure out what game Charlie's up to."

"I just saw her leave," he said, thumbing toward the door over his shoulder. "Want me to call her?"

"Nope. I want you to get out your phone so we can track her."

As Cooper pulled out his phone Tyler and Trigger entered the house through the garage door.

"Charlie's tracker says she's here," Cooper said. "Her phone must be upstairs. What's going on?"

"Tyler, can you track my SUV?" I asked.

"I can't, but Tech can," Tyler said, pulling out his own phone. "I'll stay here and watch the house."

"I'm not sure what we're doing, but I'm in," Trigger said, seeming excited.

"Get your guns, boys. I have a bad feeling," I said as I moved toward the garage.

~*~*~

We regrouped in front of the house, opting to take Trigger's pickup since it was the last vehicle parked in the driveway. The truck didn't have a back seat, so I found myself wedged between them with my legs hung over Cooper's knee as I sat somewhat sideways.

"Don't I pay you enough to buy a real size truck?" I asked Trigger, trying to turn my body at a more comfortable angle.

"There's nothing wrong with this truck. I've had it since high school."

"It shows," Cooper said, watching his phone for the text messages Tech was already sending as he tried to narrow Charlie's location. "There's more rust on the outside than metal."

"Careful now," Trigger said, patting the dash like it was his pet. "Sally's sensitive. Unless you want to see us stranded on the side of the road, you should be nice to her."

"Sally?" I said, rolling my eyes in the dark cab. "And you should've mentioned her proclivity to strand people before we left the house. This truck is older than you are."

"She's been good to me, overall. And I was saving for a new truck, but then decided maybe I'd buy a house instead."

"Buy a new truck," I said, wiggling again to shift away from the seatbelt buckle which was poking me in the ass. "I'll build you a house."

"For reals? You'd build me a house?"

"Next year, but yeah." I gave up adjusting to get comfortable and sighed. "I still own all that land across the street next to Headquarters. Originally, I was going to build a motel over there, but the idea has lost appeal. I think Charlie got it right when she bought the mansion. We have all this money, but we've been so busy making more that we forgot to enjoy it. It got me thinking about building a dozen or so two-bedroom houses and creating a small residential neighborhood across the street for the guards and friends of the family."

"Wait," Cooper said, looking up from his phone. "What about your idea of building a pool house with a bar next to Headquarters? I liked that idea."

"There's plenty of acreage for the pool-house bar *and* twenty or so small houses, but I'm no longer interested in building anything that requires any level of supervision. In fact, I've tasked Herman Stykes to start selling off the companies we own. Charlie and I spend way too much time and energy managing things we care nothing about."

"Stykes..." Cooper said. "Is he the crazy lawyer from Pittsburgh who likes things *just so*?" Cooper made air quotes.

"That's the one."

"Let's stay on topic here," Trigger said. "Is this a for sure thing? Or is this like the motel idea you had but abandoned later? Because I don't want to blow my savings on a truck, then find out I don't have a place to live."

I looked over at him and could make out his grin in the light as we passed a street light. "You're not fooling me. Just last month I paid you a bonus on that job in Kentucky which was enough to buy *three* trucks."

"My momma always told me to save for a rainy day. You wouldn't want me to defy my momma, would you?"

"One of these days, I'm going to fly out and meet your momma. I've gotta meet the woman who raised someone as crazy as you."

"And in other news," Cooper said, showing me his phone display. "Tech says Charlie parked your SUV next to an old city park five blocks north of the center of downtown."

I took his phone, read Tech's text message, then switched to google maps, entering the address. From there, I expanded the screen and the map to see the area. "Shit."

"What?" Cooper asked, looking over my shoulder.

"I think Charlie's hunting Mr. Tricky."

"What makes you think this is about Daniel Zimmer?" Trigger asked.

"It's his kind of neighborhood," Cooper answered. "Isolated and mostly abandoned. No prying eyes. Multiple escape routes."

"Trigger, change of plans. When you hit downtown, pull over and park."

"What are you thinking?" Cooper asked, texting Tech back.

"I'm thinking you jog to the park and I'll move to the center. If he's in that area of the abandoned buildings, one of us will be on both sides to cut him off from escaping."

"What about Charlie? Where will she be?"

"Knowing her, I suspect she's searching the abandoned buildings."

"That's not good. If she manages to find the right building, she'll be facing him on turf he's already scouted."

"Exactly. Which is why you need to hustle to get to the park because Trigger's going to draw them out for us."

"And how am I going to do that?" Trigger asked as he pulled over to the left side of the one-way street that led through the center of downtown."

"You're going to crash your truck," I said as Cooper and I slid out.

"*What?*" Trigger yelled. "Crash Sally? Are you insane?"

I turned back to look at Trigger. "I need both Charlie and Mr. Tricky focused on flashing lights on main street. My guess is he's inside one of the buildings two blocks east and four blocks north. Call headquarters and have more security sent this way to secure the perimeter, then wait ten minutes for us to get in place before crashing your truck into one of the street lights. And make it a good one. We need the attention of the police and fire department so their sirens draw Mr. Tricky out in the open."

"And buckle up," Cooper said, chuckling. "Wouldn't want you to get ticketed for driving without your seatbelt."

Cooper shut the door and grabbed my arm, steering me toward the first block. We jogged at a good clip for three blocks before I turned to the east and he kept heading north. I jogged close to the building, hoping the shadow would conceal my movements. The street lights continued to get further and further apart as I moved toward my destination.

I slowed, approaching the second block, stopping completely at the corner of the building. I flinched, hearing a loud crash to the south. Even though I'd told Trigger to crash his truck, I hadn't anticipated it being that loud. I also didn't expect the secondary crashing noise, which startled me again.

I was suddenly torn between going to Trigger to confirm he was okay or slipping around the corner of the building and heading north as planned. After thirty seconds of contemplating, I sent a small prayer up for Trigger as I slipped around the corner, hugging tight to the building. I moved north to the end of the building and stepped back into an alley, looking around and listening for any nearby sounds. Other than a scurrying creature deep in the alley and the sound of sirens in the distance, the area seemed deserted.

I slipped out again and edged along the face of the building to the next alley, repeating the steps of scouting the area before advancing two more buildings, then yet another two.

I was now in the center of the area I suspected Mr. Tricky and Charlie to be in. Four blocks to the south, red and blue lights accompanied the sound of sirens. I suspected every emergency vehicle within city limits had been dispatched by the sound of the sirens and my worry for Trigger's well-being increased.

Deciding to trust Trigger hadn't hurt himself, I held my position, leaning just far enough around the corner and staying low to scout the area. Two minutes later, I spotted movement up half a block and on the other side of the desolate street. A large form silently moved with skill across a patch of grass and stopped next to a building to look toward the commotion at the end of the street. Based on the person's size, I suspected it was Mr. Tricky. The question was, where was Charlie?

I didn't have long to contemplate before a noise further to the north had the darkened figure turning in the other direction. I didn't dare move, knowing I was close enough that doing so could attract attention. The dark form, barely within my range of vision, did the unexpected and stepped out into the open.

Shit, I thought, wondering what the hell was going on. I leaned out slowly to see further up the street, and when I did, what I saw scared the shit out of me. *Charlie*.

She walked gracefully into the street, stopping in the center to set her gun down on the asphalt.

What the hell is she doing? I thought. I looked back at Mr. Tricky and was further shocked that he mirrored her actions, setting his gun down before walking to the center of the street. He stood waiting for her next move.

I blinked a whole three times, conscious of everything as I gripped my gun, readying myself to jump out and aim at Mr. Tricky. But before I could advance, Charlie started running. Running down the center of the street—directly toward Mr. Tricky.

No, no, no, I thought, slipping out of the alley and following the shadow of the building to get closer.

Chapter Forty-Six

CHARLIE
Wednesday, 3:37 a.m.

Now or never, I thought to myself as I set my gun on the glass riddled street. I kept my eyes locked on Mr. Tricky, challenging him to a show of strength. I was gambling he'd welcome the invite. The alternative was that he'd grown bored over the last few days and was ready to put a bullet in my head.

But my gamble paid off when he set his gun on the sidewalk before moving casually to the center of the street, directly in front of me. He stood straight—confident of his abilities—with a stream of flashing police lights several blocks behind him, accenting his outline.

I waited, studying him as he did the same to me.

In many ways we were equals. Dark. Violent. Loners. We honored our own code and recognized it within each other. That's how I knew he wanted to kill me with his bare hands. He needed to feel my death. He needed to earn it.

I recognized that feeling because I felt it as well. He needed to die, but a bullet was too quick. Too impersonal. I wanted him to know when he left this earth it was because of me. I needed to defeat him to move on with my life. I'd rather die fighting than live my life scared of shadows. That was my childhood.

Fear. Guilt. As an adult, I'd grown past those crippling feelings. I refused to go back to that life.

Taking a deep breath, I narrowed my eyes and focused on Mr. Tricky, charging ahead in his direction. He watched me approach and when the distance was half what it had been, he launched forward to meet me.

One of us was about to die.

~*~*~

KELSEY

I ran to the center of the street, closing the distance, but I knew I wouldn't get there in time. I could shoot Mr. Tricky, but his back was turned to me, and to my knowledge his only weapon was now sitting on the sidewalk. I couldn't shoot an unarmed man. Not even him.

And even if I had it inside me to take such an action, I couldn't chance hitting Charlie. She was too close.

~*~*~

CHARLIE

Three feet away from each other, I let go of all thoughts, all my fears, every emotion. I focused on the distance, his movements, spotting the subtle shift of him turning his right leg outward to execute a left-foot kick.

I dove low, grabbing his thigh as he kicked out, and swung myself under his leg before popping up beside him with his body half turned away from me. Before he could pivot, I planted a solid kick to the inside of his right knee, the one that was bearing his full weight. I both felt and heard a bone crack as he stumbled forward on his other leg.

I stepped back, giving him space as I raised my hands in front of me and turned my body to the side, balancing my weight in a fighter's stance. I wanted this. I wanted more than a quick death. I was determined to break him one bone at a time.

"You're going to pay for that, bitch," Mr. Tricky snarled, turning to face me as he favored his weight on his left leg. "I'm going to rip you to pieces."

"Come and get me, asshole," I said as we both held our arms in front of us in defensive stances.

His eyes flickered to something behind me, but I didn't dare take my eyes off him. I watched him hesitate, then pivot to dart toward one of the buildings along the street. I glanced behind me, spotting Kelsey running toward us.

"Son-of-a-bitch," I grumbled, taking off toward Mr. Tricky before he got away.

His knee was slowing him down and I caught up with him in the alley. Swinging low to pick up a discarded beer bottle, I continued running as I threw it at his good leg. He went down on his bad knee but bounced upright again as he turned to fight me. I didn't stop my momentum fast enough and he caught me off guard, throwing an elbow to the side of my head before spinning me around to use as a shield. I looked up to see Kelsey entering the alley with her gun aimed our way.

Anger radiated through me at the thought of her shooting him. The thought of her interfering. This was my fight.

I curled my body upward, using my hands on his forearm as a pullup bar before throwing my legs down and arching my back, kicking hard at both his knees. As he stumbled, his grip on me loosened and I tucked under his arm to the side.

Not willing to give Kelsey a chance to shoot, I jumped on his back. I locked one arm under his head with my elbow pointed toward his chest and with my hand flat against his face. I reached my other hand to his opposite shoulder and twisted it around to grab his jaw.

"*Charlie, don't!*" Kelsey yelled.

I forced my arms in opposite directions, closing my eyes to savor the moment his neck snapped. His lifeless body slumped forward, and I pushed off to stand.

Mr. Tricky landed on the asphalt with his knees under him and one shoulder and his forehead propped against the filthy asphalt, propped up ass first. His days of harming people were finally over.

~*~*~

KELSEY

I heard the snap of his neck, but it wasn't what shocked me. What threw me, had me stepping backward in surprise, was the look on Charlie's face.

Joy? Gratification? I couldn't place the exact emotion.

I stood staring at a stranger. She looked like Charlie. She moved like Charlie. But it couldn't be her. Charlie would never kill someone in cold blood. She'd never stand over the body and... Smile? No, she wasn't smiling. But something. Something unnatural. Something dark. Like she enjoyed it.

"Charlie," I whispered, partially to her and partially to myself. I needed her to look at me. I needed her to snap out of whatever trance she was in that had her looking gleeful about killing someone with her bare hands.

"I'm sorry you had to see that," Charlie said, slowly looking up at me. "I kept telling you, but you wouldn't listen. I'm no longer that kid. That little girl. The one you need to protect."

"But you're not this. This isn't you. This person... This person who takes joy in killing someone."

"Two girls. Both with shitty parents. But when paired together, they became unstoppable." Charlie took a slow step toward me. "One grew up strong, surrounded by her new family, raising a child. The other grew to be just as strong, but the world around her was darker. Her beliefs shifted. She saw her enemies for what they were, vermin that needed to be eradicated."

"*You are not this person!*" I yelled, pointing at Mr. Tricky's dead body. "*You are not a cold-blooded murderer.*"

"You're wrong. I'm not you, Kelsey. I won't let *men like him* keep torturing and killing innocent people. I'll kill each one of them with my bare hands if I have to, but I won't let them hurt anyone else."

"There are other ways! You're a fucking cop, Charlie! You swore to uphold the law!"

"*At what cost?* Huh? My nephew was kidnapped by men like him. You were tortured by men like him. Your family has been hunted by assassins, mobsters, biker gangs, and every other freakshow criminal. *How can you still believe in the system*? It's not protecting you. It's not protecting your family. You keep locking them up, but they keep coming after everyone again. *When will enough be enough for you?*"

"The day I turn into this," I waved my hand at her and the dead body, "I'll take my own life." My stomach rolled and I stumbled over to the wall, placing my palm against the brick as I vomited.

I heard feet pounding against the pavement behind me but knew it was Cooper.

A minute later, I felt his hand on my back as another round of bile lurched forward. I heaved until there was nothing left. Cooper stood behind me holding my hair with one hand and rubbing my back with the other.

I barely noticed Cooper though as Charlie walked over to us.

"I need to get my gun before those cops come patrolling this way," she said calmly. "Do you guys need a ride back to the house?"

I spat the lingering taste of vomit onto the asphalt before speaking to her. "Why? Why did you do it?"

"You know why," she said as she started to walk past me.

I grabbed her arm, wheeling her around. Before I could stop myself, I slapped her.

Charlie stepped back, pulling her arm free and lifting a hand to her face. She stared at me in surprise.

Cooper moved to stand between us, holding a hand out in each direction to keep us distanced.

Charlie's eyes narrowed in anger before she turned and started to walk away again.

"You're not welcome at the house!" I called out.

She stopped but didn't turn around. She just stood there.

"I can't have you around Nicholas and Sara. Not like this. Not if this is the person you're choosing to be."

"Kel, you don't mean that," Cooper said, placing a hand on my shoulder.

"She killed him, Cooper. She killed him with her bare hands and enjoyed doing it." I looked up to see his reaction, but he didn't seem surprised. I knocked his hand off my shoulder and took a step back. "You knew... You knew she was dangerous. You knew she'd lost control."

"I didn't know she'd go this far. I swear it, Kel. I knew she operated differently than you, but she's your sister. I didn't expect this. I would've told you."

I turned and walked in the opposite direction. I walked past Mr. Tricky's corpse and out the other side of the alley. And I kept walking.

I knew the men of Aces were out there somewhere, sitting on the perimeter. If I kept walking, eventually they'd find me. Until then, I needed to be alone. I needed to process what I'd witnessed. What it meant.

Chapter Forty-Seven

KELSEY
Christmas Day, 4:37 p.m.

The day started before sunrise with Nicolas and Cooper jumping on my bed yelling: *It's Christmas.* I'd opened one eye, glad to see Cooper had dressed sometime before Nicholas charged into the room. After wrapping myself in my robe, we'd drifted to the dining room where everyone gathered to eat an early breakfast of pancakes and sausage while opening stocking stuffers.

After sufficiently layering the dining room with dirty dishes and scraps of wrapping paper, we all moved down the hall to the family room to open presents. The entire process took weeks to prepare but was over in less than an hour.

The kids, including Carl, were most excited about Cooper's over the top gifts. He'd bought them each an all-terrain go cart. Luckily, there was a speed control setting that required a password to be changed, which Cooper promised he'd already set to the lowest level. Pops must've been aware of the presents because he bought them crash helmets and other safety gear.

Anne wasn't upset by Sara's new go cart. She was still in shock over Whiskey's one knee proposal with a black velvet box and the resulting antique diamond and silver ring she now stared at on her finger. I wasn't sure how she could be so surprised, but good for her.

Hattie and Pops seemed excited by the Alaskan cruise I'd booked them on, and Cooper loved his tablet. It had taken him two hours, but he'd finally beaten Sara's high score on the game she'd loaded.

As for me, I loved all my gifts, but my thoughts kept drifting back to Charlie. It was the first time we'd spent Christmas apart. I wondered where she was. If she was with friends or hiding in her apartment alone.

As upset as I was with her, I could never hate her. No matter what she did. And even though the memory of her killing Mr. Tricky caused my stomach to roll, I regretted sending her away. I needed to protect Nicholas from Charlie's dark side, but that didn't mean she'd be cut from our lives completely.

I drifted down the hall and into the atrium off my bedroom. The kids were outside with Jackson, Cooper, and Pops, once again taking their go carts for a spin. While they were busy, I intended to relax in my quiet area. Maybe even sneak in a nap.

"Knock, knock," Donovan said from my bedroom doorway, before walking toward me. "I've got a late Christmas present for you."

I sat on one couch as he sat on the one across from me. "Funny. I don't see a present. Besides, you guys got me that sidecar for my motorcycle. Thanks again. I love it."

"Yeah, that was all Lisa. You can stop pretending you like it. I told her your bike was for speed, not running errands."

I giggled. "Yeah, it's not going on my bike. Cooper suggested I buy a second bike to attach the sidecar to, then I don't have to worry about hurting Lisa's feelings."

"I should've thought of that. Instead, I kept suggesting she send it back and get you a zip line kit instead. She was being stubborn, though."

I raised an eyebrow. "So... The zip line kit Bones got me was your idea?"

"Figured you'd like it no matter who it came from," Donovan said, shrugging. "Was I right?"

"Yeah, you were. I can't wait to install it on the second floor at Headquarters."

"Indoors?" Donovan asked, laughing.

"Why not? It would be fun to end the day at work by zipping down to the gym floor. Whiskey said it wasn't an issue to anchor it because of the steel support beams."

"As long as I get to try it right after you, I'm all for it."

"Deal. Was the zip line what you wanted to talk about?"

"Nope. Even better: *Information*. I've got news about Miguel and Sebrina."

I sat forward, waiting impatiently. "Get on with it then. Did you find them?"

"A friend from the DEA just called. Their bodies were found near the Remirez compound. Looks like there was some type of confrontation and they shot each other."

"Shot each other?"

Donovan raised his hands in an I-don't-know gesture. "They both had guns next to them and they both had bullet wounds."

I could envision a scenario where Miguel was about to shoot Sebrina, deeming her no longer worthy of breathing, and in that same scenario, Sebrina reacting quickly to turn against Miguel. The problem was the timing. It was too conveniently close to Mr. Tricky's death. Like *someone* was cleaning up loose ends.

I pulled my phone and texted Cooper: *Track Charlie for me.*

I waited almost five minutes until a response was returned.

Cooper's text read: *She's in San Antonio, Texas. What's she doing in Texas?*

I didn't answer him. My guess was she wasn't in Texas. It was more likely that she left her phone at a hotel in Texas while she snuck into Mexico to kill Miguel and Sebrina.

Son-of-a-bitch. She really is out of control.

My stomach rolled again and I raced for the bathroom, knowing I wouldn't be able to keep the bile down.

"Please, don't tell me you're pregnant," Donovan said, following me into the bathroom and holding my hair. "Lisa would be ecstatic, but the situation between Grady and Cooper is complicated enough without playing the *who's the daddy* game."

I spit before leaning back on my ankles and unrolling a few squares of toilet paper to wipe my mouth. "I'm not pregnant. Just surprised by the news of Sebrina and Miguel."

"I thought you'd be happy. Isn't one of your rules to never worry about bad guys killing other bad guys?"

I didn't tell him that I suspected the killer was Charlie. That she had both the means to pull it off and the disposition.

"I'm going to go lie down. I'm not feeling well."

"Do you need anything? Medicine? Tea?" Donovan asked, offering me a hand up.

"Just to brush my teeth and take a nap, both I can handle on my own. If you wouldn't mind keeping an eye on Carl so he doesn't bypass the safety controls on the go carts, I'd appreciate it."

Donovan agreed before slipping out of my suite. Next both Hattie and Pops came to check on me, but soon left.

I lay in bed, thinking of Charlie and where I'd gone wrong raising her. Had she always been this way? Had I missed seeing the signs? Was it somehow my fault?

After nearly an hour of worrying and wondering, I rolled over to my side, contemplating getting out of bed and rejoining the family when Cooper walked in wearing his devilish grin.

Before I could ask what he was up to, he pulled a paintball gun from behind his back—*and shot me.*

He darted back out the bedroom door, laughing all the way down the hall. I held a hand to my stinging shoulder as I looked around me. The wall, the bed, along with my expensive sheets, and my body were covered with neon purple paint.

"*Cooper! You're a dead man!*" I yelled, launching out of the bed and toward the hall.

"*You gotta catch me first!*" he yelled back while laughing.

CHAPTER FORTY-EIGHT

KELSEY
Early January, Texas

I stood on Cooper's front porch with one boot on and the other dangling from my hand as I stared at the greeting card. I'd opened it on my way out the door, but when I saw who it was from, I stopped to give it my full attention.

The card was simple enough—*Merry Christmas and Happy New Year, from Charlie.* But the newspaper clipping she'd tucked inside caused a chill to race down my spine.

The article was in Spanish, likely a paper from Mexico. And though I'd only recently started to learn the language, I could make out enough words to piece together the content. It was the news story of Miguel Remirez and an unnamed American female who were found dead of gunshot wounds.

"I was right. She hunted them down and killed them," I said to myself, trying to process.

"Who hunted who down?" Cooper asked, walking up the stairs.

I couldn't answer, my mind warring with my emotions, so I handed him the clipping and the card.

He read the article before looking at Charlie's signature on the card. When he was done, he stared past the drive to the pasture beyond, not saying anything for a long time. When he finally spoke, it was in a low voice, speaking slowly. "I know this is hard, but I've seen this before. War veterans who left the service. No longer having the same value associated with human life." He placed a hand on my shoulder. "Hell, I live in Texas. The gun toting state." He tucked the card and clipping in his back pocket and then guided me over to the porch chair, pointing toward my boot.

I sat, leaning over with my mind in a fog as I slid the second boot over my foot. Afterward, I placed my elbows on my knees and bent to run my hands through my hair. "This isn't her. This isn't who she is."

"It's not who you thought she was," Cooper said, sitting in the other chair. "But I think this is who she's been for a while now. I saw the signs when we were in Florida. And that was before she'd been kidnapped and had her finger cut off."

"What signs?"

"Little things, mostly. Like when she chopped the tips of a wife-beater's fingers off. And things I heard at her precinct that I.A. was investigating. People disappearing. Pimps and drug dealers." He shrugged, but I could tell by his expression he wasn't as indifferent about all this as he pretended to be. "I know you have this internal code. A code that tells you when someone should live or die. And whenever possible, you choose to have the bad guys arrested. But not everyone's moral code runs the same."

"She hunted them down. She murdered them. And what scares the hell out of me is, I think she enjoys it. I think she likes killing."

"She's not diabolical. She still knows the difference between the good guys and bad guys."

"Are you sure?" I stood, walking over to the edge of the porch to look across the field. "The way she smiled when she killed Mr. Tricky..." I said, letting my words trail off. "Cooper, she scared me."

"She scared you because you never saw that side of her before. Before that night, you only saw the scared girl you'd raised. The girl who had followed your lead and shared your values. But she's not that girl anymore. And more importantly, she hasn't been that girl for a very long time."

"Then who is she now? A murderer? An assassin?"

I heard him move closer before I felt his arms wrap around my waist. "She's human."

I crossed my arms over my waist so my hands rested on top of his. "I don't want this for her. I don't want her life to be so dark. I don't want her to be haunted by the blood on her hands."

"This is who she is—*right now*. It doesn't mean she'll always feel this way. But, Kel, think about the last few years. When Nicholas was taken, Charlie watched the sister she loved more than her own life, emotionally ripped to pieces. She lost her nephew. She lost you. She lost the only two people who mattered to her. It changed her. Hardened her. The pain, the anger, it builds up when you don't have someone to help you through it."

"I know that, but—"

"No," Cooper said, whirling me around to face him. "You don't, Kel. You can't know because you are a different person than Charlie. People are drawn to you, to your passion. You've never been alone even when you tried to be. You're surrounded by people who love and support you wherever you go." He moved my hair away off my shoulder, running a strand between his fingers. "Charlie's not like you in that way. She doesn't make friends as easily because she doesn't trust people. She doesn't let them get close enough to see the real her. When you left Miami, she lost the only person she truly trusted."

"She had friends in Miami. She had Baker and Garth. She had Uncle Hank and Aunt Suzanne. And she had her friends from work."

Cooper rolled his eyes. "Baker? He's about as warm as an icepack. And Garth is loyal, but not someone you pour your heart out to. And the others... Well, they love her, and she loves them, but do you really think Charlie can confide her dark secrets with any of them?" He tipped his head at me, a slight challenging smirk on his face.

I crossed my arms over my chest. "You're wrong. She's never been alone. She's always had me. Even when I moved away, she always knew how to contact me."

"But it was safer for Nicholas if she didn't reach out. So instead, she bottled her anger until it started seeping out."

I sighed. "I need to help her." I bit my lower lip as I looked up at him.

"That's just it; you can't." He used his thumb to free my lip. "This is something she needs to work out for herself. And in the long haul, she might decide to continue down this path." Cooper cupped my face in his callused palm. "And whatever she decides, you need to find a way to accept her. And plenty of guys at Aces have no issue with eradicating the bad guys either. Pedophiles, rapists, serial killers. Everyone has their own moral code when it comes to dealing with the ugliest of criminals. Everyone must decide for themselves what lines they'll cross. Even you. Your code might be seen by some as over the line, too."

"I don't kill in cold blood."

"I know. But the way Benny died? The bodies that dropped when you escaped Nola? The shootout at the store when the biker gang came after Anne and Sara? Handing Pasco on a silver platter to Mickey in prison, knowing what he'd do to him?" Cooper shrugged, feigning indifference to the list of questionable decisions I'd made. "You have your own set of rules, but that line is different for everyone."

"Shit," I said, feeling the weight of his words and leaning my forehead against the crook in his shoulder. "I'm a bad guy, too."

Cooper laughed, smacking a kiss on the top of my head. "I hope not. I've done a helluva lot worse than you."

I took a step back, breaking our circle. "So that's it? I do *nothing*?"

"I didn't say that. The worst thing you can do is make her feel her opinions don't matter. Instead, find a way to let her know you still love her, even if you don't agree with her choices. It's important she knows you're still part of her life."

"I do love her," I said, confused. "She knows that."

"Does she? Now that she's let you see her true self, does she know? Or did you distance yourself from her because you didn't approve of her actions?"

I *had* distanced myself from her. I'd worried about the rest of the family being around someone as dangerous as she was. I'd worried about how I felt about her attitude toward death. "I'll fix it. I'll call her and invite her to Texas."

"Good," Cooper said, leaning over to kiss my forehead before stepping away. "But right now, sounds like we've got company."

As he walked down the porch, I looked toward the road and watched several trucks and SUVs travel in a line down the long driveway and park in the grass, one after another. Everyone climbed out of vehicles, carrying various bags of food, coolers, and folding chairs.

Cooper walked over and carried an oversized cooler for Pops. Hattie giggled at something he said before she walked my way, followed by Anne, Katie, Lisa, and Alex—who was wearing a ten-gallon cowboy hat and pink cowboy boots.

I watched as Nicholas chased after Sara, and his dog Jager chased after both of them. Jackson and Bones started the grill on the other side of the house. Donovan bounced Abigail in his arms as he chatted with Tyler.

I looked to my left as Hattie looped her arm through mine. "It's a beautiful day, sunshine."

I smiled but before I could answer, Tech called out my name as he crossed the driveway from the barn to the house. He must've been working in the War Room on the second floor of the barn. He stopped in the yard, looking up at me. "I've got a lead on that murder case in Arizona."

"Tell me about it after lunch," I said. "Let's not spoil the day. Take a break from work. You deserve it."

"Don't mind if I do," Tech said, pulling a beer from a cooler.

I'm home, I thought as I watched everyone. They all laughed and seemed to carry on without a worry in the world. This was exactly what I'd envisioned my future to be—*someday*.

But not yet. Not fulltime at least. I wasn't ready for retirement. My mind already sparked with curiosity back to the murder case, wondering what the lead was that Tech had unearthed. The reality was, I enjoyed solving crimes. Helping people. I wasn't ready to give that up yet.

I looked over at Hattie, patting her arm with my hand. "You're right, Hattie. It *is* a beautiful day." I leaned my head on her shoulder. "It's the perfect day."

I thought of Grady and my heart ached at the pain I'd caused him. I wished he was here. I wished he could see this moment with everyone gathered so he'd understand.

I looked over and watched Cooper play with the kids. He'd allowed Nicholas to lasso him but the lasso was loose and fell downward to around his thighs. Sara ran over, jumping over the slack in the rope, Jager chasing after her.

Cooper was watching Sara when Nicholas jerked hard on the rope. It cinched around Cooper's knees, pulling his legs out from under him. Cooper went down, hard, on his backside. Everyone paused for a moment, waiting to see if he was hurt, but his quick laughter was joined by everyone else as he tried to untangle himself.

Nicholas cheered for his own victory.

"I made the right choice," I said to myself as I smiled.

"What was that, sunshine?" Hattie asked.

I lifted my head to smile at her. "Nothing. I'm just happy."

Pops chuckled from behind us. "About damn time."

Thank you for joining me on this journey with Kelsey and her many cohorts. If I've done my job right as a writer, you won't soon forget this crazy cast of characters. My ultimate hope is they'll live on within your imaginations for a good long time.

Special thanks to the following superstars for their part in getting this book across the finish line:

Judy G. and Kathie Z. - The amazing beta readers who call me out on big bloopers.

Sheryl Lee with BooksGoSocial – My proofreading guru. I'm so lucky I found you!

BOOKS BY KAYLIE

KELSEY'S BURDEN SERIES
LAYERED LIES

PAST HAUNTS

FRIENDS AND FOES

BLOOD AND TEARS

LOVE AND RAGE

DAY AND NIGHT

HEARTS AND ACES

HUNT AND PREY

HEROES AND HELLFIRE

STANDALONE NOVELS
SLIGHTLY OFF-BALANCE

DIAMOND'S EDGE

More books in progress, so stay in touch via my website:

www.BooksByKaylie.com

Printed by Amazon Italia Logistica S.r.l.
Torrazza Piemonte (TO), Italy